Contact details for the author can be found on

www.the realtomfield.com

On Twitter @therealtomfield

Facebook: The Real Tom Field

For my mum, Mary Anne Ryan,

My hero and my inspiration.

Volume One – Part One

The

Newsmaker

The Palais Royal Musée du Louvre never failed to impress him. He had spent many hours here over the past few days, delicately studying every inch, yet somehow he was always pleasantly surprised by how beautiful it was. To the voice on the phone, the station was of particular significance as it gave direct access to the Louvre museum. This meant there was a constant stream of people entering and exiting the busy station.

The voice on the phone had demanded that it be here.
And total destruction was imperative.

As well as the constant stream of Parisian commuters, there were the tourists; innocent men, women and children from all walks of life, each one desperate to soak up a part of the Parisian culture, to feel like a part of something.
As much as he hated to do so he had to admit, it was a most impressive station. Underfoot it had a deep, shiny floor and on the wall, display cases full of carefully copied artifacts, modeled on the classical heroes of Ancient Greece and Rome. All of this was, to him, symbolic of the Western World; extravagance, waste and overindulgence.
His mind drifted back to earlier this morning. Everything had been so simple. Nobody had noticed the discarded electric wheelchair, or the olive skinned Metro employee in the filthy, brown overalls, who had wheeled the dirty-red device onto the carriage and then slipped away into nothingness.

Whilst perception is everything, people only notice what they're told to notice; an unattended suitcase or lone bag on a train - even someone dressed too warmly for that day's weather. People had become so over vigilant that they had become blind to everything else. The news constantly spat out instructions to be alert, look for anything out of the ordinary, and report anyone behaving suspiciously. They reminded him of sheep and it was only a matter of time before the wolf would get them.

He watched as a young couple excitedly skipped out of the station hand in hand, lost in their love and the romance of Paris. They stopped for a moment, and after the man had whispered something in the woman's ear, she shrieked and kissed him passionately on the lips. It was a captivating moment and he briefly felt himself being caught up in it.

He reluctantly averted his eyes from the couple at the sound of the pretty, blonde waitress's voice, "Anything else Sir?" she asked, followed by the most beautiful smile, before turning to attend to another table. She liked him, he could tell. Usually he'd have taken the time to flirt, an act that would result in him sleeping with her. It always did.

He checked his watch. It was 8:54am. He drained the last of his coffee from the cup and a perverse smile played on his lips as he left a generous tip for the pretty young girl, making sure she had seen him place it on the table. She smiled her beautiful smile in acknowledgment. He took pleasure knowing she would soon be outside to collect it, yet might never have the opportunity to spend it. The thrill of having control over her destiny and indeed her death, outweighed his desire to keep her alive as his reward for a job well done.

He quickly moved from the café and up the metro stairs and into a recess out of harm's way, but still with a good view of the carnage which was soon to unfold. He checked his watch again, and counted down the seconds.

5...4...3...2...1...

A satisfied grin quickly spread its way across his face. It was 8:55am, and the explosion had gone off exactly as planned. He covered his face with a scarf so as not to be identified at a later date on CCTV, and joined the crowds of people screaming as they ran away from the source of the explosion, reveling in the destruction and despair which he had caused.

Now for London and New York.

ONE

Ryan Ward sat on a bench in St James' Square drinking his Starbucks coffee in the joy of the glorious July evening warmth, looking at the elegant Victorian buildings that circled the small square shrouded in trees. He always found architecture far more interesting than people. Their longevity and beauty was nothing short of impressive, but what really appealed to him was the fact that, architectural moments of madness aside, buildings were consistent and what you saw was what you got. In his line of work, people were rarely what you saw. He had learned that lesson the hard way.

He gazed across the small, neatly tendered lawn that was the centrepiece of the square, and was amazed that the grass was so green in spite of the mini heat wave that had engulfed London for the past two weeks. He loved the seclusion of the square. It was the only place he could feel alone in a city that never slept.

To passers-by, Ward generally went unnoticed. He was an unassuming man in his early thirties and anyone who did happen to glance at him would be forgiven for assuming that he was employed in IT or banking. Based on a glance, he had a sense of professionalism but harmlessness about him, which seemed to put ordinary people at ease. To them, there was no way that he could pose a threat. But they would be wrong. To the many who had heard of him, and to the select few who knew him, he was the most efficient and intelligent assassin that both the U.K and American governments possessed.

He was a ghost, and that was just how he liked it.

Despite his ordinary appearance, if you looked hard enough there were tell-tale signs which hinted that there was more to him than met the eye. Most notably it was his eyes which set him apart from others. They were a deep, dark brown, and the horror that they had seen was firmly imprinted on his retinas, and despite his haunted stare they gave nothing away. No fear, no confusion, no emotion, just a hint that there were secrets. Dark secrets.

His short brown hair was always neat, styled with wax to hold it in place. He had a slightly rounded chin, with a strong jawline, and eyebrows that were soft and perfectly positioned above his eyes, which made him seem approachable, particularly to women. He could appear to be of average height and unnoticeable when wanting to fade into the background, or seven feet tall when standing over a man with his Glock cocked and ready to fire.

But today, as he sat on the bench in the square, he wasn't working for either government. He was working for those that couldn't defend themselves.

Eloisa Hammond was Irish by birth and every inch the Celtic queen with her porcelain skin, emerald green eyes and thick, dark hair, which flowed down to her waist. But beauty aside, she was not a woman to be messed with. She was tough, stubborn and never shied from confrontation, possessing a steely determination which was more in tune with his own than any woman he had ever met, or was ever likely to meet. She was the only woman he had ever come close to trusting. In his line of work, trust left you open to vulnerability, but Eloisa had proven time and time again that she would never betray his confidence. She had been privy to his deepest, darkest secrets and yet never once had she come close to uttering them to another soul.

She was a UNICEF Executive based in their New York headquarters, and despite her Irish heritage, she felt more American after living in New York for ten years. She was officially an Administration Executive, but in reality, her role was to feed droplets of information to Ward of any wrongdoing against children, which the Executive Committee of the United Nations Economic and Social Council were powerless to act upon, due to the political impact it would have.

The governments of the U.K. and U.S. could never officially sanction murder.

Last week she had given him the name of an Estonian man, Urmus Misker, who was trafficking children as young as ten into Europe with the promise of a better life. In reality, Misker was grooming them for a life driven by fear which would invariably end in prostitution and drug addiction. All of these children were managed by cells of fellow Estonians, who handed over their obligatory twenty percent of profit to Misker at the end of every month.

Ward had done his homework and established that Misker lived in an obscenely expensive Mews house in affluent Mayfair, in the heart of London. He had used his unique contacts to arrange a meeting on the promise of taking no fewer than 60 girls a month for distribution throughout the UK. Unsurprisingly, this proposition was readily embraced by Misker who was eager to set up a meeting. Once the date had been confirmed, Ward had carried out covert surveillance to obtain a definitive description of Misker and his trusted Lieutenant, Otto Kukk, a former Estonian Special Forces commander.

The meeting had been arranged by a contact of Ward's called Charlie 'Dunno' Dunman. The nickname had been born out of typical East-End wit – Charlie knew everything about the criminal underworld. Clear instructions had been sent via a third party that Ward would be sitting on a particular green bench in the square at 10:30pm, drinking a coffee from his right hand, with his left arm stretched out along the back of the bench, to show that no weapons were at hand.

Staring out at the immaculate lawn, transfixed by the greenery of it, his mind wandered again to the impressive structures which surrounded the park. Directly in front of him, and only two hundred yards away, was a row of buildings that housed the affluent and those who held prominent positions in London.

Today, these buildings also housed a ghost - one whose reputation was even more legendary than his own. This 'ghost' was known to him only as 'The Optician', the nickname that he had acquired because quite simply, no one could ever see him but he saw everything. They had never met, yet Ward considered him to be one of his only true friends. He was also the only man of whom he was truly afraid.

He had first worked with The Optician four years ago in Syria during an operation to eliminate a highly sophisticated terrorist cell. Ward had simply been told that the best sniper in the world would be assisting him, and that they would never meet face to face. Their only communication would be conducted via cell phone. During the mission, a solid friendship had been born, based mainly on the fact that they were both keen supporters of the New York Mets. They still regularly spoke on the phone to discuss the latest game or, as was becoming more and more common of late, the poor form of the team.

He was never too sure how to take The Optician's claim that he would eliminate the Mets coach if results did not pick up, as he had been witness to his work countless times, and had seen his accuracy from over a thousand yards away. Ward had no doubt that a packed baseball Stadium full of witnesses would not cause The Optician any problems; no one would ever see him.

From their first contact, he had promised The Optician that he would never seek to identify him. He largely kept his word, however the temptation burning away inside him had led him to begin to piece together The Optician's background.

He refrained from seeking his name, but he had deduced that he must have been in the military - a Navy SEAL or DELTA Force without a doubt. He had a thick Brooklyn accent, and his admiration of certain ex Mets players all being of a particular generation, led him to deduce that he was also in his early thirties, but due to the youthful verve and energy of him, he could equally be younger.

He felt the hairs stand up on the back of his neck and turned his head sharply. His highly heightened senses told him that Misker and Kukk were within thirty feet of him, and approaching from directly behind him. He prepared himself for contact. Ten seconds later, he felt a hand grip his left arm in a vice like grip. Another hand brushed across the front of his body looking for hidden weapons or wires.

Kukk was a giant of a man, standing at about six-six by his estimation, and he had a neck the size of a tree trunk. His shaved head also told him that Kukk was tough; a thick, deep scar ran across his forehead. On closer inspection, he noticed that it broke in the middle. Perhaps they were two separate scars, or caused by an instrument that broke when it made impact with his hard looking forehead, he thought to himself. Kukk squeezed even harder on his shoulder to get a reaction. He had seen this from men wanting to be tough guys a hundred times, and never felt any shame in playing along with it. He feigned fright and intimidation, so that Kukk believed he had control. After all, it wouldn't hurt. So he hunched his shoulders and let out a loud "Ouch!" and then added, "Your hands are hurting me."

The humour for his own benefit and totally missed by Kukk.

Kukk looked beyond Ward's left shoulder and nodded; this was the cue for Misker to come and sit down on the bench to his left, while Kukk took up position behind him, keeping a tight, almost painful grip on his right shoulder. He pushed down on his shoulder with excess pressure, keeping him firmly in his seat.

"I do apologise for Otto, Mr. Lane. He takes my protection very seriously. One has to be very careful in our line of work." Misker's accent was heavily Eastern European, but Ward could tell that he deliberately tried to sound as well-spoken as he could to appear more menacing, compensating for a childhood spent living in poverty no doubt. It reminded him of the old characters in the James Bond films that used to fascinate him as a young boy. He resisted the urge to roll his eyes; any false move, no matter how insignificant could betray his cover. He forced himself to remain in character.

"Yes I agree Mr. Misker," he said with a slight quiver in his voice, deliberately playing along for equal effect.

"So, Mr. Lane, you want sixty of my finest product every month?" Misker asked.

"Initially, yes, and if the quality is as good as you claim, I will take more."

"I am interested to verify, and also for my own peace of mind, that you are not with the police. Tell me, Mr. Lane, how are you planning to distribute such a high number of products?"

Ward knew this question was coming, it always did. The key was to have the answer prepared.

"It's simple, really," he replied bluntly, adding a non-patronising smile so as not to humiliate Misker, "There are fifty cities in England, and I have contacts in each of them who run different parts of my organisation for me. Keeping things simple is how I have made my money, Mr. Misker. I never get too greedy. One girl in each city and eleven throughout London makes sixty. Additionally, if the police raid one of my establishments they are not going to think too much about finding one girl, but seven or eight in one place from one Eastern European country leads to Serious Crime Squad involvement. With their resources, that would invariably lead them to me. If I were greedy, I would have started at one hundred."

"But you are planning on expanding your operation at a later date, yes?" Misker asked.

"Most definitely, but I have a question. How young can you get the girls?"

11

Misker and Kukk looked at each other and smiled smugly. This was a sale that they could never be beaten on. Misker always had the youngest, freshest and prettiest on the market.

"How young do you want, Mr. Lane? I am sure you appreciate that the younger the child, the more risk is involved for my associates. This drives the price up. If you want girls under ten, I want double."

"Ten thousand pounds per child? That is a steep price, even for the highest quality," Ward exclaimed.

"These are high quality units, Mr. Lane. Untraceable and prepared ready for use," Misker replied, his smug grin never faltering.

"What do I do if I am unhappy with the children you supply, Mr. Misker? I mean, how do I know that you are going to deliver what I pay for?"

He felt the grip tighten on his right shoulder. Kukk clearly didn't like his boss being questioned, and he felt Kukk's nails begin to dig into his skin. If he hadn't been taught to tolerate pain this would hurt, he thought to himself.

"A business relationship is about trust, Mr. Lane. If you are unhappy with the merchandise that I provide you can return them and I will replace free of charge. This I will offer as a commitment to our relationship but only for our first deal."

"And what will happen to them if they are returned?"

"What I do with them is not your concern, Mr. Lane. Questions like that make me suspicious," Misker said, looking Ward up and down as he spoke.

Kukk moved his hand around to the back of Ward's neck and squeezed even harder. He sighed with irritation at the thought of putting up with this charade much longer.

Kukk took the sigh as an exhalation of pain, which he believed, was confirmed when the Starbucks cup in Ward's hand dropped to the floor. Unknown to him however, the cup had not dropped through pain or shock. The cup was the signal The Optician had requested. Within one second of the cup hitting the floor, Kukks grip had released and he was falling back onto the grass. A 7.62 millimetre bullet had hit

Kukk right in the centre of his forehead and passed through the back of his skull. The blood and brain matter exploding from the back of his head had been kept to a minimum, but a small portion had found its way onto the back of Ward's head and the right side of Misker's face.

He turned to Misker, no longer the confident businessman of ten seconds before. The colour had drained from his face from the shock, and his eyes were darting left and right, in an attempt to find the source of the gunshot that had killed his henchman. He looked every inch the rat that he was.

"You won't see him," Ward said bluntly.

"Who are you?" Misker stammered, now the thickness of his Estonian replacing the poorly-imitated English accent he had spoken with previously. His eyes were wide, reminding Ward of a deer which had been caught in the headlights.

"If you want money I have plenty!"

"I don't want money, Mr. Misker; I have more money than I will ever need," he replied. It was always the same. Each and every time a rat was caught in a trap, it thought that money would buy its life.

"What I want – no, what the children want - Mr. Misker," Ward stated, correcting himself, "Is simple retribution. In a minute, a bullet is going to force its way through your face, scrambling your brains and blowing them out of the back of your head. In a minute, you will cease to exist. Tell me, are you afraid?"

Misker immediately started retching. He was afraid. Ward had looked into the eyes of many condemned men before and knew better than most what real fear looked like. Because he despised what Misker was, he took great pleasure from watching the reality of the situation dawn on him. He always did.

"Please, you don't have to do this! I can get you whatever you want. You don't want money? I have diamonds. Take what you want! You can have it all!" Tears streamed down his face, leaving dark lines on his skin. "Just don't kill me!"

Coldly, Ward turned to face Misker, unable to hide the contempt from his face. He'd had enough of the snivelling idiot now, "What I want is to rid the world of scum like you. You abuse innocent children for your sick pleasure and profit. You talk about them as 'products, units and merchandise'. You are going to die for your sins, and it is no more than you deserve," he said, staring coldly into Misker's eyes as he spoke.

Raising himself up off the bench, Ward was transformed. Misker looked up at him and cowered in fright. The ordinary, non-threatening man he had been sat beside moments before was gone and in his place stood a giant. He appeared to be at least seven feet tall, and Misker felt his eyes burn right through him.

Ward pulled out his silenced Glock from the waistband at the back of his jeans. Misker was frozen with fear, unable to move. He just sat there, mouth open, trying to decipher the message Ward's eyes were engraving onto his soul. Without any grand gesture or parting words, he took two steps back and shot Misker in the face. The bullet tore through the flesh, bone and skin, and obliterated his head. His lifeless body slumped forward and slid down the bench and onto the floor.

Looking over Misker's shoulder, he saw a black transit van pull up and three men step out in Metropolitan police uniforms. His phone rang. It was The Optician.

"I see the clean-up crew have arrived. Are we done?" he asked.

"It looks that way, wouldn't you say?" Ward replied, "Don't tell me; you're getting bored?"

The Optician let out a laugh before replying.

"Not as bored as you looked last week when we were playing the Yankees, dear friend. I was sitting three rows behind you, and you looked on the verge of suicide."

Ward looked down at Kukk on the floor and noted that the bullet had entered his head exactly in the gap between the two scars on his forehead, joining them together. He smiled, turned to face The Optician's general hiding place and, before the question could leave his lips, The Optician answered it.

"I couldn't help it. It just didn't seem right for there to be a gap."

With that, the line went dead.

Ward shook his head and walked away down Charles 11 Street. As he approached the junction, he removed his cell phone from his pocket, pulled up Eloisa's contact details and typed two words into the handset. "It's done," they read. He pressed send, tucked it back into his pocket and turned onto Regent Street, melting into the throng of tourists littering the streets with their novelty shopping bags and enormous cameras.

TWO

In Washington D.C. news of the devastation in Paris had reached the ears of Paul J. McNair, and he had spent the past 30 minutes trying to figure out what the hell he was going to do. The usual suspects had been surprisingly quiet on the issue, which didn't help, none of them claiming the responsibility for what would, by their standards, be a huge victory. He sighed. At fifty-one years old, he wielded more power in the U.S. and U.K. than the Directors of both the CIA and MI6 combined, but his age was beginning to catch up with him. You wouldn't think it to look at him, he was in excellent shape, carried little body fat, and his greying hair still had enough sandy colour in it to make estimating his exact age difficult. His face was stern, yet open and trusting. He always wore the same suits, plain, dark blue with a crisp white shirt and yellow tie. He had always considered yellow to be a neutral colour which inspired trust. It was as far removed from the deep blues and reds worn by politicians in the Senate, who always seemed to have trouble gaining confidence from anyone. They were politicians that he had never trusted and never would. He had spent a lifetime taking care of the off-limit issues which troubled governments on both sides of the Atlantic. It was he who made the tough decisions and cleaned up the messes that the politicians weren't willing to risk their political futures over. Of course, this didn't prevent them taking the credit when it went right. Since he was thirty-four years old he had been the most valued security advisor of five Presidents and five Prime Ministers, although he had never met a single one of them face to face. Deniability was had by all in every sense.

He was revered, and looked upon with caution by those who had managed to make senior level in the security services, and all of the directors, in all agencies, were made fully aware of the fact that they were simply there to support him in any way that he deemed fit. His office was sparse, furnished with only a large mahogany desk, two telephones and a computer screen linked to both the CIA and MI6 mainframes. He had complete access, and was the only person on Earth with the codes to access the most sensitive information held by both. There were two large lamps, one in each corner of his office behind his desk, and no other furniture. He had no other chair but the one he sat on. He had no desire to let anyone get comfortable in his office. Like a pupil in front of a Headmaster, the dishonest ones always reverted to child-like traits and shuffled their feet and had no idea what to do with their hands when lying to him, the honest ones stood still. He had been an exceptional asset to the CIA under the Reagan regime and was fast-tracked for promotion to director level. This was a tactical move, as much to keep him quiet, as to utilise his analytical talents and ruthless decision making skills. After all, he was dangerous.

His problem was simple.

The bomb that had been detonated earlier that morning in Paris, killing 189 people so far was unfortunate, but something for the French to deal with.

It was his problem because he had found out two hours ago that London and New York were the next targets. A CIA operative in Iraq had come by this information when torturing a suicide bomber whose device had failed to go off. He even provided the name of the bomber, Asif Fulken, a name known to the security services as a former member of the Freedom From the West splinter group, or FFW, as the group had become commonly known. No intelligence had been gathered on Fulken, and recorded in his file, for fourteen months following his exile from the group due to his weakness for Western vices.

The FFW had not yet claimed responsibility, meaning that Fulken was acting alone. McNair was extremely alarmed by this. Fulken had been one of the most extreme and violent members of the FFW, and with no guidance restricting his behaviour he was a loose cannon. He thought over his options carefully; however, there was only one answer he reached, no matter what angle he took.

He needed Ryan Ward to find Fulken.

Over the past fifteen years, he had built up a core group of lethal, highly trained and supremely intelligent assassins that did what he ordered without question or fear. Known as the 'Deniables', the group was born out of an attempt to rectify a shambles of a covert operation in Afghanistan which had led to multiple deaths and senate questions being raised. The most elite MI6 and CIA operatives had been summoned in order to fix the situation before either Britain or the Americans could receive any political backlash.

He had always felt that his greatest achievement was keeping them all apart so they would never meet, although he wasn't naïve enough to believe that they hadn't at least established some semblance of who the others were. After all they were the best. He always kept the balance right, Five

18

Americans and Five British. That would ensure that both governments would equally move heaven and earth to keep things moving smoothly, and provide unlimited financial support without hesitation. He always inwardly smiled when he heard the general perception that the British and Americans, while the closest of allies, kept secrets from each other. That was as far from the truth as it was possible to be. They were sisters, they were family in every sense of the word, and he was both the mother and father who held the family together.

To his operatives, he was simply known as Centrepoint.

Ryan Ward was the best, in every way. His sheer effectiveness in the field meant that he was happy to overlook Ward's inability to follow the simple command of providing progress reports to him on a regular basis, something he would not tolerate from any other operative. Everything was about winning or losing to Ward and that, in his eyes, was what set him apart. Ward was so hell bent on winning that he would carry through any task to the bitter end, even if it was likely to end in his own demise. He couldn't say the same for the other operatives on his team, except perhaps, for The Optician. The fact that Ward had acquired seven million dollars and kept it for himself after destroying a diamond dynasty that sponsored terrorism in South Africa was even ignored. Ward had hidden the money expertly, but not expertly enough to prevent McNair from following the trail and locating the bank account which held the balance. Unluckily for Ward, nothing took place without McNair knowing about it, but fortunately for Ward, he didn't care.

Whether or not Ward would be mobilised wasn't the issue; the issue was whether to have him in New York or London. Ward was unique. Although he was born British, he was equally American. In any situation, if Ward was asked to choose which country to defend first, he wouldn't be able to. He knew that Ward would die with as much pride for the Stars and Stripes as the Union Jack. He decided the best thing to do was call him and get his opinion on the matter. Even though it was almost eleven pm and the streets outside were empty.

Ward was woken up by his cell phone vibrating. He checked the screen for the caller ID. It was Centrepoint. He swiped to answer.

"What's the problem?" he asked, without a hint of tiredness in his voice despite just being woken up.

"You've heard the news from Paris I take it?"

"Yes. Has anyone come forward?"

"No, but they don't need to," Centrepoint declared, "We know who did it."

"Who?"

"A man called Asif Fulken. We thought we'd lost him fourteen months ago, but he's very much back on the radar. It looks like he's alone. I don't need to tell you how serious this is."

"How do you lose someone? And maybe you should call The Optician? He's ready to go, and could do with a distraction from playing dot-to-dot," Ward replied.

He ignored this comment, knowing full well what had occurred earlier that day. He had got used to the fact that Ward used The Optician a number of times for non-directed operations but to keep him onside, he allowed it.

"Simple. When he was banished from the FFW, we no longer considered him a threat. Security got a bit lax, I'll admit that, but we had no way of knowing he would end up carrying out something such as this."

"Every time," Ward sighed, rolling his eyes simultaneously.

"Specifically meaning?"

"Not important," Ward remarked dismissively, but then he couldn't resist adding, "But you seriously need to sort out your recruiting criteria, because you're dropping the ball over there. Maybe stop hiring kids straight out of college."

"That isn't the problem. Our intelligence suggests that the next targets are London and New York. We're not sure which will be hit first. All we know is that it's not a matter of if, it's when. The wheels are already in motion."

Centrepoint then paused before asking the next question, "Any thoughts?"

"Geographically, London would be the logical choice. It makes no sense that he would fly to the States only to return to England. He's just been in Paris, and without the FFW backing him up, it's unlikely he's got much support to be able to move around freely. Plus, too much transatlantic travel will increase his chances of being picked up on CCTV at the airports. He will be aware that we are looking for him," Ward then paused, clearly deep in thought. "Saying that, security wise Europe is now on high alert. He knows that, so it would be safer to travel to the States."

"Your best guess?"

"If I was him, I would try and double bluff us. As a former member of FFW he will know how our analysts think and assume that we expect him to go straight to the States. Naturally, he would then concentrate on London."

"You don't think he would know that we are waiting for him to hit London and therefore hit New York?"

"No, I don't. If he is acting without the FFW's support, he's brazen, almost arrogant. I don't think he will care if we are expecting him or not. It's a challenge," Ward said emphatically.

"OK. I want you in London. Meanwhile, I will put the appropriate people in place in New York. Let me know who or what you need."

"What have you learned from Paris so far?"

"Not many specifics but we have a lot of footage available. I've contacted UKBC News and they will be expecting you at 8:00am to view the footage they have at their headquarters in North London. They had a news team in Paris running a story on the Louvre. Filming began two hours prior to the explosion, so they stuck around to catch all of the mayhem unfolding. We have accessed all of their data and have it here as well, but talk to the reporters and the camera crew and see if they noticed anything else. Your contact there is Martin Walker, their chief news editor," Centrepoint replied.

"OK, I want you to arrange for Lawson to collect me at seven sharp. Provide us with a list of people who would be likely to shelter Fulken, and we will see what we can get from them."

"It's already done. Check your secure e-mail. I don't need to tell you how tight we are for time on this one. There's no margin for error."

"Understood," Ward said.

"I want updates every hour, on the hour. I need to know where we are with it at all times. Find out everything you can about this guy."

Ward didn't detect the usual assertion in Centrepoint's voice; instead, he picked up on a small hint of desperation coming through from the other end of the phone.

"Why are we on this one? Why not the usual counter terrorism teams? There is total justification in eliminating this guy when he gets caught, so why call us in?" he asked.

"Just do your job Ryan," Centrepoint replied, before hanging up the phone.

"OK," he replied as the dial tone rang in his ear.

He threw back the covers and pulled his body out of bed, and went to the kitchen. He grabbed the carton of orange juice from the fridge, ripped open a quarter inch hole and poured half of the contents into his mouth. After a quick check of the news headlines on the TV, he got down on the floor and began his morning routine; five hundred sit-ups, five hundred press-ups followed by the same number of squat thrusts, until exhaustion set in, all the while trying to decide his next move.

THREE

Mike Lawson arrived driving a silver BMW five series. In the States, most government cars were generally black Ford sedans, but in the UK they tended to drive a much better class of car. Ward had always thought of this as ironic, because the roads in the UK, particularly London, were so congested with traffic, that a car rarely exceeded twenty miles per hour.

He had always liked Lawson. He had worked with him a number of times in the UK, and he was one of only a handful of MI6 agents that he could actually say he trusted. Lawson was an intimidating guy to look at. He had excelled in the SAS for seven years, and having read his service file, he knew that Lawson was probably equally as efficient, analytical and apt at taking out the bad guys as he was, if not better. Lawson was in his mid-thirties, stood about six feet four and was muscular to the point where he just stopped short of looking like a bodybuilder. He was also probably the most handsome man that Ward had ever seen, with light brown hair showing no hint of grey, and piercing blue eyes that people couldn't help but get lost in. He knew that Lawson was no longer committed to pushing his body to its physical limit to retain his fitness, and had always wondered how he managed to remain so toned - Lawson had always responded to any questions on the matter by attributing his physique to lots of sex. He had no doubt that when Lawson said lots of sex kept him in shape, that he was telling the truth.

What he admired most about Lawson was the speed at which he worked. Many times when he had been out in the field, he had contacted him for information, contacts or help, and the response was always five times quicker than anyone else could provide.

Lawson, on the other hand, never knew what to make of Ward, or Smith, as he initially called him. Before his first contact with Ward had taken place, he had been instructed by his superiors never to ask his name or speak a word about any conversations or information that they shared. He had simply been told to address him as 'Smith'. Lawson, however, knew that this man he worked so well with was really the mystical Ryan Ward, although they had never discussed it and Ward had never confirmed it.

Despite never being open about his real identity, what Lawson did know about Ward was that he would never betray him, and would do his utmost to protect him in the most extreme of circumstances. He knew that Ward had killed at least eleven people when they had worked together over the years in the U.K., but Ward had always made sure that Lawson never actually witnessed an assassination. Deniability was everything.

"Good morning. How are things?" Lawson asked without turning to look at Ward.

"Good thanks. You've been fully briefed, I presume?" he asked.

"Yes. We have an 8:00am appointment with a sexy news reporter from UKBC News."

Ward ignored the comment, as he had learned to do very early on in their relationship.

"The file for this Fulken guy is on the back seat," Lawson continued.

He reached behind him and patted the back seat until his hand found the manila file, picking it up and opening it to scan through its contents. There was little in there that he had not read in the e-mail Centrepoint had sent him, the only useful content being the seven high-quality photographs of Fulken that the security services had managed to get their hands on. To his surprise, Fulken looked average – attractive even. He was of average height; had no distinguishing features, and he would pass by most people unrecognised. This was very worrying indeed. No wonder he had managed to keep hidden for such a long period of time. However, he now had a clear picture of his target ingrained in his mind and he was coming for him.

"I want us to pay a quick visit to someone on the way," he said quickly. "You know who Kareem Abdur-Raufe is?"

"He's a radical preacher in Stratford. We also know he is involved in prostitution and protection rackets, So much for purity of mind," Lawson replied.

"Take a left up here, it's quicker," Ward said.

The morning traffic through London was slowing down to walking pace already. Lawson swerved into the bus lane and ignored the looks of disgust and the incessant beeping of car horns, which sounded their displeasure at his inability to obey the rush hour traffic protocols.

Abdur-Raufe lived in a beautiful Georgian house with a short, gravel drive, which was close enough to the main road to impose itself on the rest of the street. He clearly wanted people to know he was above all others. The hypocrisy that he displayed by living in splendour, while preaching to others that possessions are not as important as faith, was never mentioned by those who knew him for fear of reprisals. As Ward had seen countless times over the past eight years, fear is what makes the world go around.

"How do you want to play it?" Lawson asked, turning off the ignition.

"Let's just see how it plays out."

They stepped out of the car and walked up to a solid, black front door. Ward noted that there were no windows on either side of the door, but there were CCTV cameras. Before they could knock, the door was opened by a young guy in his early twenties. He scanned him from head to toe, concluding that he must be from Afghanistan given his style of dress.

"We need to see Mr Abdur-Raufe urgently," Lawson said as the guy stared into his eyes, transfixed.

"Why, sir?"

"Because if I don't talk to him within the next two minutes the full resources of the British government are going to obliterate his crappy little empire," Lawson growled, giving him a hard, cold stare.

They both pushed past him into the hallway, while he just stood there, unable to do anything about these two men who, he thought, would break his neck if he attempted to question them.

"Quickly little man, my patience is wearing thin," Lawson said.

Frightened, the guy scurried off through a large set of mahogany double doors to the right.

Ward took the opportunity to look around the hallway. The floor was immaculately clean, the black and white ceramic tiles resembling a giant chess board. Exotic, brilliant green plants towered above them in all four corners, the smallest of which was at least six feet tall. There was also one on either side of the grand staircase, which was wide at the bottom, curving into a shorter width after five steps. Aside from the colourful foliage, the only other items that caught his eye were the two antique, tapestried chairs which sat to the side of the mahogany doors. Without a doubt, these were sentry posts .

His thoughts were interrupted by the guy returning with an announcement.

"He will see you now," he stated sombrely, and beckoned them both towards him.

"He'll have his men in there with him," Lawson whispered.

"Don't worry; you're here. I'd back you against ten of his men every time," Ward replied without looking at him.

As it was, there were only six men in the main room with Abdur-Raufe. A quick scan of them all confirmed to Ward that the two sitting closely to the left of Abdur-Raufe would be the only ones likely to put up a fight, although they both looked more like brawlers than fighters, with their broken noses and feint scars. The nearest one to Abdur-Raufe was rotating an eighteen-inch piece of wood, carved to look like a miniature baseball bat, between the thumb and forefinger of his left hand, glaring at them with a look of pure hatred. The one next to him was wearing a black scarf wrapped around his head, like a headband, which seemed odd as he had very short hair.

The other four presented no threat at all, as Lawson weighed more than all of them combined, and the chances of them having firearms in the house within reaching distance were minimal. This line of work was a lot easier in the UK than the US due to the availability of guns.

Abdur-Raufe was sitting in a large, burgundy leather chair adorned with gaudy golden handles that curved downwards at the end. His legs were crossed and his hands were draped over each handle. He was in his late fifties, completely grey and had a long, unkempt beard that retained what Ward assumed were the last few black hairs on his body.

"He reminds me of ZZ Top," Lawson said.

The two guys next to Abdur-Raufe bared their teeth at the indiscretion of the comment, and Ward was reminded why he liked Lawson so much.

"What do you want?" Abdur-Raufe demanded in an authoritative tone.

Without replying, Ward moved forward and stopped just two feet short of Abdur-Raufe. As he did so, the guy with the miniature baseball bat stood up and put his hand firmly against Ward's chest. Before anyone in the room could adjust to the situation, Ward brought up his right fist with lightning speed and punched the guy full force in the throat, causing him to jerk backwards, before doubling over whilst gasping for air. He dropped the bat and collapsed forward onto the floor in a heap. Ward scooped the bat up.

The guy wearing the headband jumped to his feet and Ward jabbed the bat hard into his right eye. No backswing. No warning, just a simple jab. Fighting a blind man is easy.

As the guy started flailing his left arm in Ward's general direction, he took a large backhanded swing of the bat and slammed it into the guy's right temple, just below the rim of his headband, and it smashed into his skull with a sickening crunch. He hit the floor like someone had removed the bones from within his body and he had nothing left to support his body weight.

The guy, who had been holding the bat initially, was still on his knees, his left hand supporting his weight flat on the floor, and his right hand gripping his throat, so Ward raised the bat two feet and brought it down hard against the back of his skull. He lost consciousness before his face smashed hard into the floor.

He had no need to look behind him. He knew that Lawson would have his back. As it was, the other four guys stood still, frozen in fear, as much over the sheer size of Lawson and the gun that he was holding in his hand, as to what they had just witnessed.

"You've killed them!" Abdur-Raufe screamed, jumping quickly from his seat, pointing his arm in the direction of his two guys, "You've killed them!"

Ward stepped towards him and pushed him back into his chair with such force that he wasn't entirely convinced he hadn't dislocated the elderly man's shoulder.

"And you are two minutes away from being killed yourself unless you tell me what I want to hear," Ward threatened in a quiet, calm voice.

"Salif, call Mohammed. You can't do this, we have rights, we are protected, and my solicitor will destroy you," Abdur-Raufe screamed to one of the guys near Lawson.

Ward stood towering over Abdur-Raufe and looked down at him with contempt.

"You have no rights while I'm here. I'm everything people like you fear. I'm not governed by rules and having to think about your human rights. I don't exist. The beauty of being me is

28

that I can't be found, and no one will look for me once I've killed you," he said calmly.

"I will tell you nothing. I am of no use to you, so you may as well kill me," Abdur-Raufe said defiantly.

He turned towards Lawson and nodded in the direction of the four guys cowering next to him, wide-eyed and clearly terrified.

"Take them out of the room. Secure them somewhere. I will be two minutes," he ordered.

Lawson pointed his gun at them and herded them towards the mahogany doors. Without speaking or looking into Lawson's eyes, they shuffled out of the room with Lawson behind them pointing his gun at their backs. The doors closed with the crisp, loud sound of the locking mechanism falling into place.

Ward looked at Abdur-Raufe and smiled, and then he put his hand into the back of his waistband and pulled out his Glock, and then pulled out the suppressor from his jacket pocket. He maintained eye contact while he screwed the two components together slowly, ensuring the threads met in perfect tandem. One last firm twist and the silencer was in place.

"What are you doing?" Abdur-Raufe cried with panic.

"I'm going to kill you. No point in talking to you. You have already told me that you won't tell me anything and I have an appointment in twenty five minutes so I may as well save myself some time."

"What do you want to know? I can help, please don't kill me," Abdur-Raufe begged, "I have children, I have wives. Please tell me what you want?"

"I know everything you do. I know that you are guilty of using religion as a mask for your own greed. I know you manipulate young men into carrying out your criminal activities to accumulate money for your crusades, when really it is for your own personal greed. I know that you import drugs from Afghanistan and that you frighten men into handing their daughters over to you for prostitution. So killing you will mean nothing to me. However, I'm a fair man, so I will give you a sporting chance. I will ask you some questions; you will answer truthfully. Do you understand the consequences if you lie to me?" he asked in a soft, calm tone.

"Yes I do. I promise I won't lie."

Ward knew he wouldn't lie.

"Have you been contacted by Asif Fulken?"

"Yes," Abdur-Raufe replied.

"What did he want?"

"He wanted a secure place to hide. I told him that I couldn't provide that."

"Why?"

"My life has taken me in a different direction."

"Did you know he was going to bomb Paris?"

"No. I assumed that the FFW were after him and he was seeking a place to hide from them," Abdur-Raufe replied nervously.

"Why would he hide from them?"

Abdur-Raufe suddenly appeared to relax.

"What?" Ward demanded.

"You don't know, do you?"

Ward raised the Glock and pointed it at Abdur-Raufe's head. He started to talk.

"Our cause is one that demands loyalty and devotion against the devil that is the West, against the greed that the West represents. Yes I am guilty of choosing the wrong path too, but I have not turned against my leaders," Abdur-Raufe declared.

"How has he turned? I'm running late for my appointment," he reminded him.

"Asif has taken all of his training, his skills and his craft and left a big void in FFW that they are finding hard to fill."

"So they are pissed off with him and want him back?" Ward asked.

"No," Abdur-Raufe replied, "They are after him because he is selling his skills to the highest bidder. Asif is a mercenary now, with no faith or loyalty. The West is now his market. He works for the highest bidder."

"Are you telling me that the bomb he planted in Paris was not related to your cause?"

"Yes I am," Abdur-Raufe smugly replied.

"Do you know where he is now?"

"No I do not."

"Then I have no further questions or use for you," Ward said. And with that, he straightened his arm and pulled the trigger and shot Abdur-Raufe in the chest. He then put one bullet in the back of the head of the two guys who were still unconscious on the floor, even though he was pretty sure that the bat guy was already dead. Always best to be sure.

"Any use?" Lawson asked, as Ward joined him in the hall.

"Yes. You need to get a clean-up crew here quickly. And what are the chances of these four keeping quiet?" he enquired.

"They won't say anything or ever come back here again, I guarantee it."

Ward didn't ask why, even though he could see that Lawson was desperate to tell him.

"We're running late," he said.

FOUR

Asif Fulken was patiently waiting for the call in his hotel room in Argyle Street, London. The voice said he would call at 08:00am.

He was late.

The hotel was nothing spectacular. It was middle range at best, popular with tourists and couples who were having a night out in London to explore the wide range of restaurants or see a West End show at one of the many theatres. He had chosen the hotel three weeks ago and booked it for three nights, but he hoped that he would only need it for one.

He was fully aware that he was the most wanted man in Europe right now. If nothing else, the security services were efficient, but hiding from them was easy compared to hiding from his former family, the FFW. He was now sporting bleached blonde hair, and had two diamond studs fixed into his right ear. Changing his appearance had been one of the first things he did after leaving Paris. His passport, which was genuine, and brought from a drug addict in Barcelona, would not warrant a second glance. He was now Miguel Ramos, thirty two year old student from the Basque region. And if he didn't come back to his hotel, no one would think too much of a single Spanish student failing to return for the remainder of his stay after sampling the single nightlife in London.

He looked in the mirror and scowled. He hated this cheap new look, and it took all his strength to remind himself that it was only temporary and was crucial for this phase of the operation. After Paris, where everything had been so simple, he knew the British were more vigilant and that the volume of CCTV cameras in London made it impossible to walk the length of any one street without being recorded. He had got a real sense of satisfaction from the bomb he had disguised in the wheelchair, and he was sure that if he wanted to, he could use that tactic again.

The positive thing was that the British security forces would be monitoring the city with additional resources, which meant fewer specialist people, and more officers hauled in for compulsory overtime to work the streets, and those that didn't want to be there were never as vigilant.

He turned away from the mirror and smiled to himself about how simple, yet profitable, his plans were. He was being paid two million dollars for an outlay that was no more than a few thousand Euros, for the activation switch, fuse, battery and other necessary wiring. He had collected the one hundred pounds of explosives from a derelict farmhouse in Dover at no cost to himself. The extended FFW family were still more than willing to assist him upon request. He had planned it to perfection. He had built the bomb to perfection too, installed it into a suitcase and added some further sulphur based powders to increase the initial flash as instructed.

He never planned how he was going to plant a bomb before he had carried out extensive reconnaissance of the target because too many things change, and deviation from a set plan normally ends in disaster. He preferred to take a live look, and he believed that simplicity was always the key to a successful bombing. The American movies always made it so complicated and complications lead to mistakes.

As he looked out of his hotel window, he knew that this plan was suited perfectly for London. He would call a black taxi company and request that they collect two suitcases from his hotel and transport it to his chosen destination, where his partner would be waiting to be taken to the airport for a vacation. A bonus would be payable to the taxi driver, but he had to be at the collection point at nine thirty am exactly as his partner would be finishing a meeting, which left only a small window of opportunity to make it to the airport. Clear instructions that the taxi could not be late were passed over and he agreed to hand over fifty pounds deposit to the driver for the airport journey when the suitcases were collected. He himself was the man's partner who was staying overnight in a hotel, and he was unable to meet him himself as he had to head to Manchester to catch a different flight. A tracker was placed inside the suitcase so that he could monitor its location, and when the bomb was where he wanted it to be, he would detonate it by cell phone. He now had nothing to do but watch the clock.

Then his cell phone rang.

"Hello?"

A clear, well-educated voice which sounded like the person who it belonged to had experienced a privileged upbringing asked, "Are you ready?"

"Yes. Everything is in place. Have you deposited the next two million dollars?"

"Everything is in order. Are you clear on the timing? It has to be at exactly 09:30am this morning in the location that we agreed."

"Yes I am and don't worry, everything will be exactly as you requested or at least within five metres. But just so you know it's not too late to change location to the other sites I suggested. It will increase the death toll."

"You measure the results in numbers. You are so short sighted, Asif. There is more to be gained from this than suffering," the voice replied, irritation reverberating through the phone.

"It's your money, do what you want," Fulken replied nonchalantly, "But the last part, in New York, you promised me creative freedom. That still stands I hope?"

"Yes it does. The location is all that matters to me and the timing. After that, you can do what you see fit and aim for as high a number as you desire."

"And my bonus, the four million dollars?"

"Just do what you're told and you will get everything we agreed. Now tell me again, just for my peace of mind, exactly what time and where?" the voice asked.

"Time: 9:30am; Location: Front entrance of Westminster Abbey."

"I will contact you again when you are in New York on the third number I gave you. No mistakes."

And with that, the line went dead.

Fulken smiled to himself. There were people walking the street right now who were not going to make it home tonight. He thought back to the pretty waitress in Paris and wondered if any more women like her would perish. He then felt a need for sex wash over his body and promised himself that he would find a woman to quench his appetite when he had finished in New York.

FIVE

Ryan Ward had been recruited by MI6 straight from University eight years ago when he had been at Oxford studying Law. The initial interest from them had centred on his unusually high IQ. Ward regularly scored around the 175 mark which made him smarter than Albert Einstein, but not as smart as Leonardo Da Vinci - if you believed that the intelligence quotient accurately identified how smart a man was. Ward himself had never put any emphasis or importance on the IQ figures he achieved. He had always thought that if he had to choose someone to live and move in his world, and to be able to think and act logically and calmly under pressure, the choice between Da Vinci with his alleged IQ of 220 and Muhammad Ali with an IQ of 78 was a no brainer, unless there was a plan to draw someone to death. Then, he would be prepared to reconsider.

MI6 are master manipulators. They convinced Ward that he was earmarked to work as an analyst in their Headquarters on the Albert Embankment in Vauxhall, a south western part of Central London, on the bank of the River Thames. He soon learned that this was never the intention, before realising that he was being trained to kill.

Their headquarters were relatively new, and were based in a building that Ward absolutely despised for its ugliness. As the building was laid out over numerous layers, and there were 60 separate roof areas, and this had always made him think that the architect who had designed the building, Terry Farrell, added a roof every time he struggled for inspiration.

He spent virtually all of his time at headquarters, locked in a dark room way below street level. Hidden beneath the streets of London was where the majority of the sensitive work was carried out. This had a dual purpose: it made the people who worked there feel important, and it limited the security threat to the information which was squirreled away down there. This had suited him initially, because he was able to spend three hours a day in the state-of-the-art gym packed with enough equipment to fill a football pitch.

Their extensive background checks on him prior to his recruitment had shown them that he had all the designated characteristics to become an undercover operative.

There is a misconception about the spy world; that all operatives run around with guns, James Bond style, saving the world. In truth, most of the work is done following the electronic footprints of people by analysts who would not know how to load a magazine into a gun let alone shoot one. Of all those who work within the National Security Services, no more than three in five thousand have actually fired a gun in anger.

When an individual is identified as being one of the three in five thousand, a small persuasion team is formed to make sure that the desired candidates are recruited. This tactic is not used solely by MI6; all Security Services recruit from their most prestigious universities in this manner. It was established by Ward's recruitment team at MI6 that not only was he very smart, but he was physically fit and a team player. He played Soccer for England Universities, and he had an edge to him. This edge was demonstrated when he had almost been expelled from Oxford for beating three fellow students with such ferocity that, two of them missed their finals due to extensive convalescence.

High spirits had gotten out of hand at the end of term and three members of the rugby team had thought a demonstration of strength against Oxford's star soccer player was in order. They knocked on Ward's door at 3am and when he opened the door; they burst in, armed with duct tape and a plan to kidnap him and post a video of him on the universities social media website declaring that rugby players were far superior to their feeble soccer playing counterparts.
It backfired.
He fought back with such ferocity, that two of the victims would not make a formal statement to the police, for fear of reprisal. Ward, to his credit, admitted the assault and told the police that his only thought was to hit out until no one could come back at him. This argument lost some of its validity when it was established that he had stamped no fewer than four times on the heads of each of his victims. At this point, there were serious doubts about his future at Oxford, his future working in law, and the likelihood that he would escape criminal charges and subsequently jail.
The assault on the rugby players was all that MI6 needed to make their move. They had already been watching him closely, and the incident confirmed his suitability to them beyond doubt. They intervened, made all potential police charges vanish and convinced the disciplinary panel at Oxford that no record of the incident should ever be filed. In return, all he had to do was agree to work as an analyst for MI6. It was an offer that he gratefully accepted.

When a person joins MI6 or the CIA, like any job, they start with the basics. He spent his first three months at Vauxhall learning how information was collected and managed. How key words in search engines and text messages were immediately flagged up, and he was amazed to discover just how much of the data that people send is monitored, and the sheer volume that is sifted through on a daily basis. He learnt how easy it was to listen in on people's telephone calls, access cell phones and read their online messages. He enjoyed this.

His recruitment team noted with satisfaction how inquisitive he was and how his intense appetite for learning grew, and after three months they considered him ready for the next phase of his development.

To test his ability to remain controlled and composed when faced with the most horrendous situations, he was allocated his own case to investigate. It was a case that had been progressed to an extent by MI5, the sister agency of MI6, which is specific to protecting the UK and its citizens at home, but they had hit a brick wall. It involved a paedophile ring in Birmingham that was abusing children as young as three and using the dark web to distribute pornographic material showing the abuse.

He embraced this challenge with such commitment and sense of duty that he was working eighteen hours a day, seven days a week, and by using his new found skills in tracing digital footprints, within three weeks he had identified the two ringleaders of the group and every paedophile who had shared the material.

He presented his findings to his recruitment team and was surprised to be faced with the question of what he thought an appropriate punishment would be. He stated that he felt there was no place on earth for those kinds of people, but the courts would no doubt take the correct action.

Two weeks later, he was informed that the ringleaders of the gang could not be prosecuted, due to a technicality, and breaches of their human rights, in the way the data evidence against them was collected, and now their hotshot lawyer was countersuing the Government for defamation of character.

This was Ward's introduction to the politically correct madness that had engulfed Society on both sides of the Atlantic. He suffered a crisis of faith and confidence in what the Agency stood for, and decided that he wanted no part of it.

He submitted his resignation and was told that assault charges could still be brought against him for up to seven years for the incident at Oxford, and his resignation was being declined. He was then asked again what he felt an appropriate punishment for the paedophile ringleaders would be. Again, he simply stated that there was no place on earth for people like that and someone would administer the appropriate justice.

Six months later, after he had finished his intense firearm training, the two ringleaders were found dead in an apparent double suicide, and eight members of a paedophile ring had been killed, the police assuming by the father of one of the victims, but they weren't digging too deeply to find the culprit. After that, according to the records of MI6, Ryan Ward the analyst never existed. Ryan Ward, the assassin, the killing machine, the deniable quantity that no one was responsible for, had been well and truly born.

SIX

The headquarters of UKBC News was a giant building; it reminded Ward of a giant greenhouse. There was no character to it at all, the entire façade composed of thick, fifteen-foot high glass panels.

"I think we are here," he said to Lawson, pointing to the gaudy twenty-foot high 'UKBC NEWS' lettering stuck on top of the building like a cake topper. This raised a smile from Lawson as he pulled to a stop in front of a checkpoint. Ward looked into the tiny booth and took note of the overweight guard standing by an x-ray machine holding a clipboard in his hand. Next to him, a frustrated young woman tapped her foot impatiently as her handbag was scanned through multiple times. Lawson groaned at the sight of this. There was nothing worse than dealing with a rent-a-cop carrying an over-inflated sense of self-importance, gleaned from the fact that his uniform loosely resembled that of a real police officer. Eventually, the guard was satisfied that the handbag did not contain any contraband, and allowed her to enter, and then approached Lawson's side of the car. He rapped on the window.

"Good morning Sir, your details please."

Lawson looked at the guard quizzically.

"We have an appointment with Martin Walker. My name is Lawson."

"And what is your meeting about, Sir?"

"That's of no concern to you; just raise the barrier so we can park."

The guard scanned down the paper on his clipboard and then said, "Well, according to my records you are late by twenty five minutes, so unless you give me a good reason I am going to have to advise you to make another appointment."

Lawson immediately stepped out of the car, much to the guard's surprise. All sense of superiority vanished as soon as he caught sight of the giant of a man unravelling before his very eyes. By the time Lawson was standing upright, the guards' mouth was wide open, and he was too stunned to flinch as Lawson leaned in to within six inches of his face.

"Listen, fat stuff," Lawson spat, "I'm having a bad enough morning without some donut-guzzling moron telling me I can't get to my meeting. Now raise the barrier before I punch a bullet-sized hole through your stupid head."

The guard looked up at Lawson with real fear in his eyes and then the most bizarre thing happened.

"Back off and put your hands on the car!" he screamed.

Lawson sighed, Ward burst out laughing and the guard imitated a strange Sugar Ray Leonard shuffle before raising his hands into the sparring position. At this point two other guards appeared from behind a small attendants' hut. They looked more senior and certainly more sensible.

"Problem Gilbert?" one of them asked

"Nothing I can't handle, Sir." Gilbert replied, still holding his hands up.

Lawson frowned and took the more senior looking of the two aside.

"I'm here to see Martin Walker, yes we are late, and no, I won't disclose what it is about," he said before putting his hand inside his jacket pocket and pulling out his warrant card.

The senior guy studied at it and apologised, before barking orders at Gilbert.

"I can't apologise enough for the confusion sir. Gilbert, raise the barrier now. Drive through, park to the left and let Reception know you are here. It's just through the double doors," he said, pointing to the large double doors marked 'Entrance'.

Lawson climbed back into the car and the barrier was raised.

"The guy wasn't scared of you at all. Maybe you are losing your edge," Ward teased.

"He was deranged. Anyway, what was that shuffle thing all about?" Lawson asked, "He must be one of those care in the community employees that big companies have to employ."

With the car parked, they walked through the main entrance doors into the reception area. Lawson signed in to the visitor's log book, taking care to flirt with the pretty young receptionist as he did so. As usual, Ward ignored it and waited until Martin Walker's PA eventually arrived to inform them that Walker would be with them momentarily. Three minutes later, Walker appeared, walking down the stairs into the foyer and approaching them with an outstretched hand. Walker was in his late forties and in good shape, despite being a little wiry as a result of too many late nights at the office downing cups of coffee, as opposed to following a strict exercise regime. What little hair he had left was shaved neatly into a number two cut all over.

"Martin Walker," he announced in a very clear, concise and well-educated voice that didn't quite match his appearance. He eagerly shook Lawson's hand first, as Lawson had, by habit, positioned himself so that he would be the first to make contact.

"Mike Lawson," he replied, shaking his hand firmly, "This is Andy Chennell," he added, pointing towards Ward.

Lawson always picked different names for Ward, and in all the time that they had worked together, he had never used the same name twice. It hadn't crossed Ward's mind to ask him whose names they were, although this time he couldn't help but wonder who Andy Chennell was. Martin Walker looked at Lawson and handed him a business card. He then looked at Ward and clearly assumed he was too unimportant to need one.

"Come upstairs please gentlemen, the team are all ready for you. Can I interest you in a beverage at all?" Walker asked politely.

They both shook their heads and followed Walker up the stairs into an open plan office. It was occupied by at least seventy people, all either tapping away at their keyboards or walking across the floor frantically with bits of paper in their hands. At least two thirds of the people were women, and Lawson couldn't help but smile at several of the more attractive ones as he made his way past. It was an impressive working environment.

Walker led them through the bull-pen and into a closed room at the far end. There were four people already in situ one side of a large oak table drinking coffee. There were three men and one very attractive woman, who Ward knew without introduction would be the news reporter.

"Right everyone; this is Mike Lawson and Andy Chennell. They are with MI6 and as discussed earlier, they will be working with you today," Walker stated with an air of self-importance.

"Introduce yourselves one at a time," he continued, his hand gesture signalling that it was their opportunity to speak. He then glanced down at his watch and frowned, clearly late for another appointment.

Ward studied the man closely, and concluded very quickly that he didn't like him. He was jittery, nervous and disinterested in what they had to say. He hadn't even attempted to hide that fact from either of them.

"Excuse me everyone, as much as I'd love to stay and chat I must dash. I have a busy office to run and I'm down four of my best people," he said looking at those settled around the table. He then turned to Ward and shrugged his shoulders before adding, "Nigel will answer all you need to know and he knows probably more than me anyway." And with that, he turned and left the room, giving all the occupants one of the most forced smiles it was possible to produce.

"Hi guys, I'm Nigel Reid. I'm the producer at UKBC," the guy sitting at the far left of the table said.

Ward thought he seemed rather mouse-like, a thought further cemented by the fact that he couldn't keep a slight tremor out of his voice as he spoke. He was thin, dressed in a checked blue shirt, had patchy stubble around his face and greasy hair that looked as though it hadn't been washed for weeks. He was the kind of guy most people have worked with before; the one who runs around all day and never gets on top of his work. Ward and Lawson both nodded a greeting back in tandem.

"Good morning gentlemen," the attractive young woman said, holding her gaze for much longer on Lawson's eyes than was necessary, "I'm Abbi Beglin, UKBC News correspondent. I have worked for the company for six years and have travelled extensively throughout the world. I majored in....."

"That's probably enough for now Abbi," Reid cut in before she could finish, "They don't require your resume."

"One other thing, I'm single and looking," she said, brushing her hair to one side and throwing Lawson a stunning smile that he promptly returned. She had long blond hair, perfectly formed features and beautiful blue eyes. She was definitely attractive, her look certainly impressed him, and she clearly only had eyes for Lawson.

"Thanks, Miss Beglin, but we are here to work," Ward said brusquely, turning to Lawson and firing him a warning gaze. He then turned to Beglin and stared her down to ensure she had understood that Lawson wasn't the subject in hand. She lowered her eyes, tucked her hair behind her ear, and fiddled with the papers on her desk. She looked suitably warned.

"I'm Gary Parker, cameraman," the second guy uttered loudly; far louder than was necessary over the awkward silence which had fallen over all those in the small conference room.

Ward liked this guy instantly. He looked fit, in his early thirties and had short, ginger hair falling just shy of his strong shoulders. He was the only one in the room that had an honest look about him. Ward and Lawson both smiled their acknowledgment before taking seats at the table.

45

Next to him was the final unknown entity in the room; a tall, thin man with long hair and a thick beard that covered his whole face.

"I'm Gary Lewis," he said in a helpful tone, "I'm the sound man," he added, just as Reid clapped his hands together to turn the attention on himself.

"Right everyone; we have two hours of footage prior to the explosion. Gentlemen, would you like to see it from the start?" Reid asked, turning to Ward and Lawson.

"No," Ward replied, "We have people looking at it now. Just show me the moment that the bomb went off."

Reid picked up a remote control from the table and pointed it at the offensively large flat screen TV that filled the wall to their left. The screen crackled into life. The image was of Beglin applying her make up as the camera rolled with the Louvre standing magnificently in the background. A time stamp was positioned in the bottom right hand corner of the frame, reading 06:56. Reid quickly forwarded the footage to 08:54am.

"Any moment now gentlemen," he declared.

Ward looked at the screen as Abbi Beglin detailed the impending exhibitions due to take place at the Louvre. He could make out the entrance to the Metro station positioned behind her. He focussed fully on the entrance, drowning out the sound of her voice. Eventually, the sound returned to his ears as a loud 'boom' echoed through the speakers. On the screen, Beglin's shoulders hunched and her neck retracted into her body as the blast ripped out into the Paris streets. Immediately, the camera by-passed her and focussed on the Metro entrance. There was smoke billowing out of the entrance as people tore out of it. Some were screaming, others were crying, and a few were silent with shock.

The camera bounced up and down as Gary Parker ran to get closer to the action. More and more people were filing out of the station. When the clock in the bottom right hand corner hit 08:56, the first people to suffer injury came pouring out. One woman, carrying a young child in her arms, collapsed onto the floor cradling her child against her cheek. A small red speck on the child's shirt rapidly increased in size until the material was sodden and the blood was pooling onto the floor. An elderly man in a suit had obviously just been out of range of the blast and had scald marks to his white shirt.

A young woman staggered out with blood pouring from her forehead. It wasn't the blast that maimed or killed people; it was the flying objects and shrapnel.

They sat in silence and watched for a further six minutes as the injured were helped out and the emergency services poured in. Everyone sat there in silence. Lawson was the first to break it.

"That's enough, turn it off will you? There's nothing to be gained from watching these poor people suffer."

Reid used the remote to pause the footage on the image of an unconscious middle-aged man being carried out by two women, his stomach torn to shreds by the shrapnel. One of the women was doing her best to keep his intestines from falling onto the pavement, but it was clear she was fighting a losing battle as they spilled out of the parts of the cavity her hands were too small to keep closed. Their faces were contorted in anguish. Ward studied the image closely. The girls couldn't have been any older than twenty, and their close resemblance to the casualty told him that they were his daughters. After what seemed like an eternity, Reid turned off the tv, thinking better of leaving the image on the screen for the entirety of the meeting.

"Did you notice anything or anyone suspicious prior to the blast?" Lawson asked.

"Not really," Reid remembered. "We tend to concentrate on the quality of work that we are producing and only on what the viewer sees."

Lawson looked at Gary Parker, the cameraman, before firing a question at him.

"Why did you run towards the blast while everyone else was running away?"

"It's my job. I had eight months in Afghanistan filming; I guess I'm kind of used to it. I know there's sometimes a second blast, but I didn't think anything of it," Parker replied.

"Did any of you at any time see something that was out of place?" Lawson asked them all collectively.

"No," Abbi Beglin said, "I think my reaction of surprise and fear shows that," she added, twirling her hair at Lawson as she spoke. Ward cleared his throat loudly, and she quickly stopped and stared at her lap.

Lawson turned to Gary Lewis, the soundman, who answered before the question could even leave his lips.

"Definitely not," he stated with authority.

"Any sounds that you might not have picked up at the time but have noticed since you reviewed the footage?" Lawson asked.

"No. Like everyone has said there was nothing. I've been over it at least six times to see if I can hear anything but there is nothing."

"Is there anything that any of you can tell us that might help us find out who did this?" Lawson asked them collectively. His experience told him that someone must have seen something.

"There was nothing out of place," Nigel Reid said. "I've produced thousands of news reports all over the world and I have a sense for when things aren't right. Up until the moment of the explosion, there was nothing wrong at all."

Ward had not spoken since saying that they were there to work. He closed his eyes as Reid's words "Nothing wrong at all," played over and over in his ears. There was something very, very wrong that made no sense at all. It made every single hair on his body stand on end. It was clear that no one in the room apart from him had noticed it. Not even Lawson, who was usually the first to jump on anything out of the ordinary. The problem was that they had been in the room for just over ten minutes, and he knew that everyone in the room was telling the truth.

He was snapped out of his thoughts by the office door swinging open and a young woman, dressed in a smart black suit, ran in, looking like she had run a marathon. She looked at Nigel Reid and, with eyes wide open and little breath in her lungs, delivered the news,

"There has been another explosion, two minutes ago."

Lawson looked at Ward with worry etched into his face.

"Where?" Reid asked with urgency in his voice.

"Outside Westminster Abbey," she replied.

"What the hell are you doing still sitting here?! Get going. NOW!" Reid barked at the other three

"Sir, we already have a team there," the breathless young woman said, "They were interviewing the Secretary of State for Culture, Media and Sport about the public funding required for the essential repairs to the Abbey."

"Was it a live feed?" Reid asked.

"No," she replied, "But they will be able to upload it as soon as we want it from the van."

Reid looked at Ward and Lawson apologetically and said,

"I'm sorry gentlemen, but I have to go. See yourselves out."

With that, the four UKBC employees left the room and Ward and Lawson were left alone to process what they had just been told.

"Not good," Lawson said.

"Let's go," Ward ordered, "We're going straight to Westminster; I want to look at something."

SEVEN

Asif Fulken watched as the police and fire department vehicles sped past, their sirens shattering the early morning calm that was London before the throngs of people hit the street. He counted nine police cars and fourteen fire trucks in just three short minutes. He knew that due to the way the British valued their heritage and their iconic buildings, the authorities would be more worried about damage to their landmarks than any deaths their people might suffer. He still felt disappointed and cheated about the location of the bomb but consoled himself with the fact that another two million dollars had been earned. Two million for the Paris bombing, Two million for London and a further Two million for New York, plus the Four million dollar bonus, and he would be ten million dollars richer just for doing something that showed those elders at the FFW just how devastating losing him was. Definitely as great a loss as the land or power losses they had suffered throughout the region. It had been as simple as he had thought it was going to be.

The cab driver had arrived exactly at the time requested, 09:15, and he had two cases waiting with him. Both large suitcases of Burberry design. He had filled one with clothes and weights, and the other with his one hundred pound masterpiece. It was a very heavy case. Manageable to lift by someone like him, but not without making it obvious that he was struggling with an excessive weight, and more importantly, it needed to be handled with care. So he made sure, he was waiting at the bottom of the steps to the hotel in Argyle Street with the suitcase that contained the bomb when the cab driver arrived. He watched the driver park and open the trunk. He was a short, stout man in his fifties with a completely bald head and thick arms that were covered in awful looking, worn tattoos. He knew that this man was probably in the forces years ago; looking at the tattoos he was displaying, and so his death would be another bonus

"Taxi for Mr Ramos," the driver said

"That's me," Fulken said in a deliberately camp way adding an over exaggerated Spanish ring to his English words.

"Just the one case is it Guv?" the driver asked.

"There is another up there in the foyer mister, the same pattern as this one, but it's a little heavy for me, so could you get it please, and I'll put this one in," he asked, pointing to the entrance of the hotel. Fulken had placed the other suitcase inside at the far side of the hotel foyer, to buy him a few more seconds.

"No worries Chief," the driver said, and started to head up the stairs to the hotel entrance.

He lifted the case with both hands and moved slowly across to the cab, checking that the driver was out of sight before using all of his strength to lift the suitcase up onto his knees and position it against the car fender, before using his knees and hands to slide the suitcase in flat, and then finally clicking the receiver switch on the handle, which was disguised as a lock. By the time the driver came out of the hotel struggling with the other suitcase, he was standing five feet away from the vehicle lighting a cigarette.

"What the bloody hell have you got in here?" the driver asked, by now looking very red in the face.

"My boyfriend loves his shoes and outfits," Fulken replied in his camp tone. This was enough to put an end to the conversation between the two of them.

51

He checked his watch and saw that it was now nine eighteen am. He had three minutes to waste

"So, my partner has hardly any time to spare and you will be collecting him outside Westminster Abbey at exactly nine thirty as agreed yes?" Fulken asked.

"Yes Guv," the driver replied.

"I will give you a bonus of fifty pounds to get him to the airport on time too."

The driver's eyes lit up. A massive cab fare to the airport and a fifty pound bonus, and that was without any tip the guy he collected might give him. A great morning's work.

Fulken took his time getting his wallet out, pulled out three twenty pounds and one ten pound note and then approached the driver,

"I have put another twenty pounds in there for your added discretion," he said, deliberately looking coy, "My friend has a partner, a woman actually, and she wouldn't be very pleased if she knew he was going off with me for a few days when he is meant to be on a business trip, and she will be at his meeting with him, so the extra twenty is to ensure that you do not get there before nine thirty and be hanging around, because she might be loitering. Is that OK?" Fulken asked.

"Whatever tickles your fancy Guv," the driver said, "Each to their own, I say. Don't worry I will pull up at nine thirty on the nose and if I see a woman going loopy, I will drive off!"

"Thank you, so kind," Fulken responded. He glanced at his watch. It was nine twenty one. "Off you go, don't want to be late," he added.

"Will do Guv," the driver replied.

He watched the driver pull away and thought to himself, what a fool, so simple, so trusting. He deserves all he gets.

He walked away from the hotel and turned the corner twenty yards away. He approached the coffee shop that he had made a note of when he had arrived at the hotel yesterday, walked in and ordered a latte. The latte was in front of him in less than two minutes and after he had paid, he walked outside to the tables and chairs that were lined up on the street and sat down. What a glorious sunny day he thought to himself. He checked his watch, it moved to nine twenty-nine am and he dialled the receiver number, the screen of his phone converted to a road map, and he could see a red dot slowly approaching the opposite side of the road to Westminster Abbey, exactly where he needed it to be, and just as the flashing dot pulled to a stop directly opposite the grand old building, his watch struck nine thirty, and with the most spiteful of ironies, he entered the code to set off the bomb. Zero-nine-one-one.

He sat drinking his coffee calmly. He savoured the noise of the sirens and noted that literally everyone walking past had their ears to a cell phone and were talking in hurried tones and looking around frantically. People were coming out of the shops around him looking over towards the direction of Westminster Abbey, even though it was impossible to see anything due to the height of the surrounding buildings. He finished his coffee and headed on foot, slowly, towards Kings Cross Station which was just over half a mile away. When he got to within sight of the station, he headed into a barber's shop and asked the young girl working there for a number one crew cut all over and to be quick as he had a train to catch. He left the barbers ten minutes later and walked into the station. He had purchased his ticket to Liverpool yesterday morning and showed it to the ticket inspector who was manning the platform gate. By 10:22 he was sitting on the train as it pulled out of Kings Cross for the two and a half hour journey to Liverpool. So simple he said to himself again. So, so simple.

Ward and Lawson arrived at Westminster Abbey around the time that Asif Fulken's train was pulling out of London. The area was already sealed off and there were armed police, the Army and fire-fighters everywhere. Lawson pulled up to a row of bollards which were set out across the road directly opposite the Abbey, and they climbed out of the car. He walked up to the bollards and showed his warrant card to the officers securing the scene and he and Ward were promptly waved through. Lawson walked up to a guy that he obviously recognised; an MI5 operative Ward assumed, and asked him for an update.

"Thankfully it looks like only thirty people were killed," the guy said to Lawson, "And most of them were Japanese tourists," he added almost in relief.

"Who is securing the area?" Lawson asked.

"Bomb disposal."

"There is nothing else here," Ward said.

"We will determine that" the guy said aggressively. But Ward wasn't listening or looking at the damage, he was looking around behind him.

"What are you looking for?" Lawson asked him

"Confirmation."

He looked at the colleague of Lawson's who had clearly taken an instant dislike to him. "The bomb," Ward said, "It went off out here not in the Abbey?"

"Yes. A cab pulled up and boom!! It must have been a suicide bomber. The people who took the blast were tourists who had just stepped off of a bus on an organised tour," the guy replied.

"Number of injured?" Lawson enquired.

"Another thirty. The ones who died shielded the blast in effect because they were standing in a big group waiting for their tour guide," the guy replied.

Lawson nodded. He looked at Ward who had his back to him again, looking in the opposite direction,

"Are you still looking for confirmation?" he asked Ward.

"No. I have it. You need to make a phone call. Tell Charlie that we will meet him at 2:00pm in The White Horse," Ward said, "Then take me back to UKBC in Haringey and get one of your team to make sure that any footage that they took here this morning is available and waiting for us to watch. I have to make a phone call."

He moved about twenty feet away from Lawson, took out his cell phone and noted six missed calls, all from Centrepoint, but he could wait. He dialled Eloisa's number and it went straight to her voice mailbox. He simply said, "Eloisa, I'm coming home," and hung up.

EIGHT

Lawson tore through the traffic, jumping red lights and driving along Bus Lanes. Any traffic violations would be wiped out later. Right now there was a bomber on the loose. Nothing else mattered. They arrived at UKBC News and without question; Gilbert raised the barrier and waved them through. Ward assumed he had been reprimanded about his over-vigilance by his boss. They didn't bother reporting in at the reception desk and they walked straight up the stairs to the open plan newsroom. The scene inside was chaotic. It looked similar to the situation room in the White House. Ward had been privy to being in there once as a consultant for the extraction of a team of Navy Seals, after a rescue mission had gone wrong in Russia. There were people running everywhere, talking on phones, little team briefs taking place with groups of eight or fewer all huddled around one main speaker. Everyone ignored them and stayed focused on the events that were unfolding in front of them. On the large screens, a newsreader was talking about the explosion and flicking between live pictures of events outside of Westminster Abbey and footage of the Metro blast in Paris, while a 'Breaking News' scroll ran across the bottom of the screen declaring there had been an explosion at Westminster Abbey.

"Find Walker," Ward said to Lawson and watched as he walked over to the first attractive woman he saw, noting that he walked past at least three more senior looking males on the way through to her. He watched her smiling, running her fingers through her hair and then playfully smacking Lawson on the arm. 'Jesus', he thought to himself, does he ever let up? Lawson came back a few minutes later and said, "Walker is in a senior meeting room on the third floor. Apparently the big boss is here and he wants a handle on this thing."

"Who's the big boss?"

"Lord Ashurt-Stevens."

"Where are they?"

"In a secure meeting room on the third floor, which is strictly out of bounds."

At that moment, the whole room went quiet, like a scene from an old western movie when the man with no name walks into a bar. Every person in the room apart from Ward and Lawson looked up at the giant screen. They instinctively followed the lead of everyone else when they heard the musical introduction for the news programme. A stern looking newsreader started relaying the information about the explosion and the deaths of the Japanese tourists and then Abbi Beglin appeared on the screen, clearly somewhere inside the building, informing the viewing public that, "The news editors have been assisting MI6 in the search for the Paris bombers prior to this morning's events and we believe that they knew this scene of devastation, this scene of destruction was a possibility," she proclaimed.

"How can they be that stupid? There is an unwritten rule that they all abide by. They know the panic that will cause," Lawson said as he put his hands behind his head and exhaled long and hard.

"Ring your bosses and get your end of it sorted. It's best I do this alone," Ward said.

"Do what?" Lawson asked, and then watched Ward walk over to the elevator and press the 'Up' button.

Lawson then understood.

He stepped out of the lift on the third floor and immediately located the secure conference room. There were two guys standing outside a closed door. One in his thirties and the other greying a little and in his early forties; they were both fit-looking and muscular. Not your average security guards he thought. Bodyguards, close protection and probably ex forces, but not enough to deter him in the slightest. He approached the door and they adjusted their positions so they were filling up the doorway.

"This area is out of bounds, Sir, please return to a lower floor," the older of the two said.

"I need to go in there now," Ward said calmly.

"As I said, Sir, this area is out of bounds so please return to a lower floor", he repeated, this time trying to sound assertive and threatening.

"And as I said, I need to go in there now."

The younger guy moved a step forward and said,

"Last warning, please leave this floor."

Ward had never been one for posturing, he just saw that as wasting time, so he took three steps forward and stopped about two feet away and raised his hands in an open palm gesture as if he was about to try and reason with them and then with lightning speed, he brought his right foot forward with all of its force and kicked the guy between the legs. He immediately doubled over and fell to the floor on his knees. Before the other guy could react, he swung a left hook full onto his nose, and as it connected he could hear the bone break and the guy's head shot back and smashed hard against the oak panelled doors. The guy slumped to the floor holding his nose. He had no need or desire to inflict more pain upon them. He respected anyone who had been in the forces, and he was aware that they were probably only employed for the fact they looked the part rather than their capabilities, and on a pretty poor salary too, so he decided against further strikes instantly. The doors opened sharply and a tall, thin man in an expensive looking suit looked at him and then at the two guys on the floor,

"Mr Lawson or Mr Chennell?" he enquired.

Ward didn't respond.

"Fair enough, I understand your need for secrecy and so no name is needed," the guy said, "I'm Lord William Ashurst-Stevens. Pleased to meet you," he added, holding out his hand.

Ward ignored the invitation to shake his hand,

"Where is Walker?" he demanded

"Walker has gone home to rest; it will be a long night."

Behind Ashurst-Stevens were three men seated at a table, all over sixty and all looking totally unfazed by the commotion they had just heard.

Ashurst-Stevens saw Ward looking at them and said,

"My legal advisors, the best that money can buy."

And they probably were the best.

"How can we help you? You have our full resources at your disposal."

Since he had left MI6 and became one of the 'Deniables', the most rewarding part for him was that he didn't need to conform to rules, and certainly didn't take legal threats seriously. He knew that he could shoot all three of them there and then and it would never be his problem to sort out. It would be down to Centrepoint, but at this moment in time, he needed to confirm something, so he played along.

"I'm so sorry about your men, Sir. No hard feelings?" he said, looking at the lawyers for effect.

"Of course not. You men do a sterling job and you are under a lot of pressure right now, so we will forget it ever happened. Agreed gentlemen?" he replied, looking at the lawyers. They all nodded in agreement.

"I would like to look at the footage ten minutes before and ten minutes after the explosion in Westminster if I can?" he asked politely.

"Of course, I'll get Walker to run through it with you now," Ashurst-Stevens replied.

"I thought Walker had gone home?"

Ashurst Stevens smiled and just said,

"He must be refreshed already. Let me accompany you downstairs."

They headed into the corridor and walked towards the elevator.

"I want to know. Why would you say that about MI6 and cause panic?" Ward asked.

"That was Walkers idea I'm afraid. As soon as I knew about it I stopped it, hence my legal team being here with me. I know the rules; I will smooth this over and put it down to misinformation. Walker is a good man and a great editor, but he had visions of a Pulitzer Prize, I think. He will be reprimanded accordingly," Ashurst-Stevens replied.

"OK," Ward said. "Just put it right."

They stepped into the elevator and Ashurst-Stevens pressed the 'One' button. They never spoke again and when the doors opened on the news floor they stepped out and every single person in the room gazed over towards them both.

"Mr Walker is over there in the meeting room. He would have been briefed about assisting you in every way by now. Any problems, here is my card with my direct number. Please keep in touch," Ashurst-Stevens said.

"I have one question?"

"Ask away?" Ashurst-Stevens replied.

"What's on the second floor?"

"Our financial, advertising and marketing departments," Ashurst-Stevens replied, "Why?"

"I just wondered why it seems the busiest floor in the building," he replied as he turned his back on Ashurst-Stevens and walked over towards Walkers office, leaving Ashurst-Stevens to ponder what he had meant by his question. He walked straight into the meeting room without knocking and saw Walker sitting alone at the large table. He looked terrified.

"I'm sorry, it was a bad error of judgement," Walker said immediately, "We will correct it in the bulletins from three onwards," he added.

"Show me the footage for ten minutes before and ten minutes after the explosion at the Abbey," Ward demanded.

Walker turned on the giant TV again and played the footage. In the ten minutes prior to the explosion, the Secretary for Culture, Media and Sport was talking about the need to invest public money in the world famous Abbey, whilst it stood behind him like a towering symbol, carved perfectly out of centuries old stone. The camera then zoomed close up to the Abbey and showed the cracks in the stonework, while the reporter's voice-over explained the structural defects that had been discovered. The camera then went back to the Secretary who continued to say that the welfare cuts the Government were imposing were on a separate agenda, when behind him, a black cab pulled into view, stopped, and exploded with a deafening noise and bright white flash.

Ward stood up. "I need to be able to get hold of you at all times."

"There is still another ten minutes of footage," Walker said.

"You have a direct dial number?"

Walker handed Ward his business card.

"I don't understand, I thought you wanted to see all of the footage?"

Ward turned and walked out of the room and eventually found Lawson talking to Abbi Beglin in the building's reception area.

"Let's go," he said.

As Lawson turned to follow him, Beglin shouted after him, "Make sure to ring me tonight Mike."

"Did you confirm whatever it was you needed to confirm?" Lawson asked.

"Yes I did. I know what's happening. And I have an idea how to stop Fulken."

"Want to share?" Lawson asked.

"No," Ward replied, "Trust me on this Mike; you don't want to get involved. I need to go home to New York to check some things first."

"Charlie is expecting us in twenty minutes," Lawson said.

"Then we had best be quick."

NINE

Charlie 'Dunno' Dunman always held court in the East End of London in a place called Stepney, and he conducted his business from a pub called The White Horse. It was a rundown building that looked totally neglected from the outside with the paint peeling off of its grey walls. It looked out over Stepney Green Park and never had any customers apart from those who did not know the area and wandered in there by mistake, before being promptly told to leave. The account books showed a steady and profitable flow of customers, but this was simply to make it look like a functioning business. Inside, the floors were bare, and the boards had not seen any varnish for over twenty years. Just inside the entrance, there were two tables either side of the doors, which would always seat Charlie's trusted lieutenants, four to a table, and another group of men seated four tables behind, either side, forming a pathway to the bar. To the left of the bar there were toilets and a fruit machine, and to the right, three booths. The booths were divided by old pine screens and the chairs were covered in the worn burgundy material that old English pubs always used, tucked under battered tables that were as solid as they were worn. The left hand booth seated Charlie's four most trusted men, his killers, and to the right his accountants and solicitors, three of each. He called this booth his 'Think Tank'. Charlie always liked to double check things, and then check again. The centre booth was where Charlie sat, always alone, and when he needed to discuss something with someone, he would shout their name and they would be sitting next to him by the time the last syllables of their names faded. It was a place where people who knew Charlie never wanted to be summoned, because it generally meant it was unlikely they would return home. Lawson had introduced Ward to Charlie when he was chasing a group of mercenaries, who were operating across Europe for an American investment company. Charlie had not only found out the names of the mercenaries but where they were heading next and all within twenty-four hours. From that day, Ward had asked for Charlie's help on numerous occasions; the last time being a week ago, when he needed a meeting arranged with Urmus Misker, the child trafficker.

Charlie's real name was Charles Dunman. He used the surname 'Dunno' because the British loved their irony. Charlie knew everything that happened in the criminal world throughout the British Isles. And always a long time before the security agencies did. Charlie didn't like dealing with standard police, hence the standard reply of "Dunno" when they questioned him. The truth was; Charlie knew everything. He knew for sure who Ward really was and he liked him a great deal. He admired the fact that he didn't play by the politically correct rules that governed the world nowadays. He also liked how he had an old fashioned view that bad guys were OK if they kept their own house in order; which meant the old, women and children were never harmed or intimidated. Not like these modern day criminals who had no morals. Charlie was in his late-fifties and still looked frightening. He was just over six foot and had a solid neck which supported a head that was shaved bald and a face that looked like it had survived a thousand back street brawls. Which it had.

But Charlie was a smart man; highly intelligent and intuitive. He was also the king of an empire that spread throughout Britain and was worth well over two hundred million pounds. The police and security services left Charlie to his own devices and in return, he did what was right. In the late nineties the police across England were hunting a murderer and rapist known as 'The travelling Ripper', a man who had killed fifteen women across the country and left no clues to his identity. The police were getting nowhere. The Metropolitan police top brass asked Charlie to help with the search in return for effectively leaving him to his own dealings, unchallenged. Within three days 'The Travelling Ripper' was caught and the police revelled in the glory of how efficient and smart they were. In truth, Charlie had got the information regarding the drivers from every haulier in the country by means of theft, intimidation and what he felt he was owed, and his 'Think Tank' identified who it was by simply establishing delivery routes, dates and times. Charlie had helped the security services out many times since.

Ward and Lawson walked up to the doors of the pub and stepped in. Charlie's lieutenants stood up and then sat down immediately when they registered who it was. They walked through the pathway of tables and up to Charlie's booth.

"Alright Gents?" Charlie asked in a thick cockney accent, standard speak for any real East End gangster. "How are you Mikey? Still shagging anything that moves?"

"Of course I am Charlie. You still robbing old ladies?" Lawson replied.

Charlie laughed and gestured for both of them to sit down. He looked at Ward,

"I found the cab company who delivered it and know how it went down. I assume that is why you are here?"

"Partly," Ward replied.

Charlie raised an eyebrow and looked at him. Another thing he liked about Ward was that he was never predictable like the rest of them. Lawson raised an eyebrow at the same time. "The other part?" Charlie asked.

"Lets' do the cab first," Ward said.

"Simple really. A geezer phones up A to B Cabs in Hyde Park, says he wants a cab to the airport, so they jump at the chance of a big fare. They pick him up down in Argyle Street and the geezer spins him a line that the cases are for someone else who needs collecting from the Abbey," Charlie replied

"No one at the cab company would find that odd?" Ward asked.

"Odd? Don't be naive, who do you think does most of the drug transporting throughout London? Picking up packages and delivering them is normal. The supplier is not in the cab, the cab company are just doing their job and deny all knowledge of what they are carrying, after all, it's normal practice and the police are left scratching their arses as usual." Charlie said with a snort.

"No information on who made the call I guess?"

"Afraid not. It was a disposable mobile. I've already checked."

"Time of call?"

"Yesterday evening."

Ward looked at Charlie and smiled,

"I have a question to ask you Charlie. You have a pen and paper?" he asked.

Charlie called over the booth to where his think tank was sitting and a small piece of paper and a pen was in font of Ward within three seconds. He wrote something on the paper and folded it, and then slid it across to Charlie who picked up the paper and read the question, and then without pausing, he wrote something underneath, folded it up and slid it back to Ward, who without reading the answer, picked it up and put it in his pocket.

Lawson looked at Ward.

"Don't tell me, it is best I don't know?"

Ward just nodded.

"Thanks Charlie," he said and stood up to leave.

"By the way," Charlie said, "Misker seems to have disappeared," and he gave Ward a big smile followed by a wink.

"Where now?" Lawson asked.

"Take me home," he replied, "I've got to make a call to Washington."

TEN

Centrepoint's frustration with Ward's inability to keep him informed of his movements was under control because he knew where he was. He had ordered Lawson's bosses to keep him informed of his movements at all times. Both Lawson's phone and car had trackers on them. Ward never shared information as he worked a mission, but he could normally work out his progress by the resources he asked for, but that was it. There was nothing in writing, no records, just a straightforward summary. He would then make a personal record of events, in a code that only he understood in his private legers, and secure them in a bank safe in Washington. There was enough information in the ledgers to bring down the Governments of the UK and the U.S, and if the truth of their operations was ever known, it would probably result in the international community alienating both Governments for a long time. He had instructed missions to be carried out by his team of 'Deniables' in every member Country of the European Union, every country in the Middle East, the African nations, every country in the Americas as well as Russia, Korea and China and therefore, his political sway was most impressive.

"Can I ask you something?" Lawson said.

"Of course you can," Ward replied.

"What did you ask Charlie?"

Ward paused for a second and then said,

"Mike, I want you to know that you are one of the few people that I trust in the world. The fact that we always work together isn't luck, I request you, and only you, every time, without fail. I won't work with anyone but you in the UK because I don't think there is anyone as good as you or as capable of watching my back as you are," he said, and saw Lawson visibly grow in the driver's seat.

He felt pleased that he had told him of the high regard that he held him in.

"But I don't not tell you things because I am untrusting or because it is some ego thing, I don't tell you things to protect you," he added.

"Protect me how? I've called a clean-up crew this morning, I know how many people you have killed and I know that you keep me away from certain conversations like at UKBC so what else is there to protect me from?"

"Have you ever actually seen me kill anyone? Maybe they were dead when I got there?"

"You know what I mean," Lawson replied.

"My point is that I'm not accountable to anyone, if some of the stuff we do ever got out, they aren't ever going to risk dragging me out in front of a Parliamentary or Senate committee. They will just make me disappear. But you will have to answer questions and they will hang you out to dry," Ward said.

"I just sometimes feel that you don't trust me, that's all."

Ward pondered this for thirty seconds and then said,

"You really feel like that, after all the times we have worked together and covered each other?"

"Yes I do."

"OK. You can ask me one question and one only. I'll answer truthfully."

Lawson was quiet for a few minutes and then said, "Really! You know that I am desperate to know what you asked Charlie and what he replied, don't you?"

"That's two questions, I said one."

"And I want to know if you are who I have always thought you are," Lawson said.

Ward did not respond.

Twenty minutes later they arrived at Wards house and Lawson had still not asked the question that had been offered to him.

"Well?" Ward asked.

"OK. What did Charlie write on the piece of paper that you gave him?"

"Money."

Lawson looked confused and then dejected.

"Don't suppose I can change my question?" he asked with a smile.

"I'm going back to the States tomorrow morning, but be available because I need you here to work this side of the pond," Ward said as he opened the BMW door and stepped onto his gravelled drive.

"Will do," Lawson said, followed by a barely audible "See you soon Ryan Ward."

Ward showered and changed and then ate a brief meal. He turned on UKBC News to see the latest updates; Abbi Beglin was now reporting live from outside Westminster Abbey and he wondered how long it would be before she slept with Lawson. There was no further mention about working with MI6 but no retraction of the fact either. The report switched back to the studio and there was a 'Terrorism Expert' making all kinds of ludicrous suggestions. Where did they dig these 'Experts' up from, he thought to himself. The guy was clearly a text book 'Expert' who wouldn't last five minutes in the field. He knew that this 'Expert' was a million miles away from establishing what was actually happening.

But he knew.

He knew exactly what was happening, he just didn't know why or through whom yet. He picked up his cell phone and called Washington.

"About time," Centrepoint said as he answered.

"Sorry, I've been busy," Ward replied.

"Progress?"

"Some."

"Tell me where we are?"

"I need you to get me home to New York first thing in the morning."

"You think he has finished in London? That didn't seem like much of a devastation bombing," Centrepoint stated.

"I don't think it was meant to be, New York is meant to be the big one."

"You are basing that on what?"

"Angles."

"Angles, as in an approach angle?"

"Sort of."

"Where do you think Fulken is now?"

"He won't be in the States for at least three days. He will go somewhere like Canada or Brazil first and then work his way in from there," Ward replied.

"Border control are on high alert, our people have an e-description of about five variations of what he could look like, we might get lucky and catch him before he goes underground in New York," Centrepoint said hopefully.

"That's if he is planning to hit New York and doesn't change it."

"You think that is likely to happen?"

"Not if I don't put too much pressure on the people I think are behind it and alert them that we are onto them."

"Who is behind it?" Centrepoint asked.

"And also Fulken won't want to change it. He will revel in the kudos of achieving his aim. He's arrogant and that will be his downfall," he said, ignoring Centrepoint's question.

"We are on high alert. This can't go wrong. We have to work out where and when he is planning to hit and make sure we stop it. We can't have any terrorist succeeding on our own soil," Centrepoint said.

"He won't."

"What makes you so confident of that?"

"Because the people behind this are going to tell me everything we need to stop him," Ward said calmly.

"Who is behind it?" Centrepoint asked for the second time.

"I don't know yet but I know where to look" he replied.

"Then get looking quickly."

"I need some money placed into the access account."

"How much?" Centrepoint asked

"A few hundred thousand dollars"

"Why?"

"To buy some information," Ward said

"Expensive information."

"You get what you pay for."

"It will be in their account within the next ten minutes," Centrepoint said.

"OK. Get the jet ready and text me the details."

"The jet is not available, you'll have to travel like a normal person," Centrepoint said, almost sounding pleased.

"Great, more time wasted," Ward said sarcastically, "Make sure Gilligan meets me at JFK when my flight lands and that he is assigned to me for however long this takes," he added and then he hung up the phone.

He then called Eloisa.

"Hello?" she said. Just the sound of her voice saying one simple word made him feel happy.

"Hey. It's me. I'll be home tomorrow. Are you free?" he asked.

"I will make myself free, your place or mine?"

"Either. I've missed you."

"Likewise Ryan. Are you taking care of yourself?" she asked.

"Yes I am."

"I mean really taking care of yourself?" she said with genuine concern.

"I always do Eloisa. You know that."

She seemed quiet, almost distracted.

"Are you happy?" she asked.

"I'm fine," he replied.

But he wasn't happy. Every time he spoke to her he just wished that they could lead a normal life.

"No you aren't. I can tell by your voice. What is it?"

"Do you ever get tired? Tired of all of the bad things we know and our commitment that we have a duty to put them right?"

"We do what we do. No one even knows we do it, but so many more people sleep soundly in their beds at night directly because of what we do so no, I never get tired of doing that for them," she said, trying her best to reassure him.

"It's just that…….." he tailed off.

"What? Tell me?"

"Do you ever want more? I love you and hopefully you love me, but we spend so much time running around saving the rest of the world that we come a long way down the list in terms of our priorities."

"What do you want?" Eloisa asked.

"Normality would be good. I would like to go to work and not have to feel sick to the stomach with anger and sadness about the things that I see people do. I would like to come home to you every night and play fight and eat takeout."

"Sounds good to me. We will have time for that Ryan. It won't always be like this."

"I know. I just had a bad day today, lots of nasty things."

"Anything you need my help with?" she asked

"Anything you need my help with?" Ward countered.

"The only thing I'm starting to resent is the people at work for the droplets they keep feeding me, knowing that I feed them to you. I feel like I'm using you and they me," she said.

"Don't ever say that again or think like that," he said, "We do what we do for the children, not for the suits you work with. That is what makes me sleep well at night, knowing that I am keeping those children from further harm," he said firmly.

"That came out wrong," she said.

"Eloisa, nothing you say is ever wrong. You share, you offload and I listen. It's how we work. Why we are so perfect for each other. We accept that at this moment in time our fight is for others, not for us, but inside, we both know that it won't always be like this. Our life will begin, away from all of this bad stuff, but at the moment, we are still the strongest to lead our respective fights and we both do it better than anybody," he said with clear belief in his voice.

"I love you Ryan. Hurry home."

She sounded happy again.

"I'll be there tomorrow. I can't wait to see you. I'll be at the apartment by lunchtime, will you be available?"

"Try keeping me away," she replied, "See you then."

"Bye," he said. Then the line went dead.

He threw the cell phone onto the sofa and got up to make a cup of coffee. He promised himself as he stood in the kitchen, arms resting on the worktop watching the kettle boil, that one day; life would be just plain and simple. One day things would be normal.

ELEVEN

The message Ward received about the flight home had
arrived just twenty minutes after his conversation had ended
with Centrepoint. He was to catch the four thirty am flight to
JFK from Heathrow airport, an MI6 car would collect him at
three thirty and as usual, he would skip around passport
control and go straight into the business class lounge, where
his relevant boarding passes would be waiting for him. At the
other end the same thing would happen, but in reverse. Off
the plane, into the business class lounge and a CIA escort
would guide him past the passport controls.

He had two homes in the States. Both homes were bought
with the money that he took from the South African diamond
mining family; one in New York and one in Santa Monica. It
made him feel like he belonged in America. Having one home
in England made him feel that he was never too far away
from walking into his own place of sanctuary. Due to the vast
size of the States, just having one place and being three
thousand miles away from home in the same country, never
sat right with him. His apartment in New York was where he
felt more at home than anywhere else. It was in Washington
Street, a neighbourhood in Brooklyn. More specifically, it was
in an area that the locals had affectionately named DUMBO.
It was a place that had provided the backdrop to a number of

iconic movies; 'Once Upon a Time in America' being one of them. His apartment building was built from red brick, discoloured through years of industrial grime, but still retained a grace through its own simplicity, He lived in a sixth storey apartment in the building and when he walked out into the street, a glance to the left gave him the iconic view of the Manhattan Bridge and across the East River the skyscrapers of New York. DUMBO stood for 'Down Under the Manhattan Bridge Overpass'. It was an affluent area now, a long way from its questionable past, yet it still retained rawness and an edge. It also afforded him all of the anonymity that he craved and needed to be able to operate effectively.

He was to be met at the airport by Sean Gilligan his CIA contact and support. Ward trusted Gilligan as much as he did Lawson and for the same reasons. He knew he always had his back.
The main difference between Gilligan and Lawson, or rather the main difference between MI6 and the CIA was that Gilligan had less sense of fair play. The British still held on to their old beliefs of giving opponents a fair, fighting chance, whereas their American cousins were much more clinical and lethal and didn't worry so much about rules. This same ethos was reflected in the way their politics operated. Political corruption in the UK was on a very small scale compared to the U.S. and Ward always believed that this summed up the difference between what he felt were his two countries of origin. He always thought that the Americans got it right. After all, the President of the U.S. was always considered the most powerful man on the planet.

Gilligan was a descendant of Irish and African American great-grandparents who had settled in America and built a life and family. He was strong looking; he had a shaved head, sparkling hazel brown eyes, and a constant half grin on his face that made him look like he always wanted to have fun; in spite of his six foot three frame that looked more like it was built to carry wheelbarrows and bricks. He stayed true to his heritage and was proud of the fact that he was of Irish descent. Something he had in common with Ward as well. Ward's own mother was Irish. Due to the nature of his work he kept her identity well-hidden and he always called her from a payphone.

He and Gilligan were cut from the same cloth, Gilligan just never knew it. America and Britain might have been Ward's homes, but his heart also belonged to Ireland too. As the plane began its descent into JFK; he pictured Gilligan waiting for him in business class and just knew that the first thing he would see was his smile.

As it was, Gilligan was waiting for him as soon as he stepped off of the plane. As he walked out of the door onto the jet bridge he saw a beaming smile.

"Good flight?" Gilligan asked.

"Must have been, I slept most of it," he replied as they started to walk into the main building, "Have they briefed you?"

"They have told me that you are aware of an impending attack on our soil and that we have a green light to do whatever it takes to stop it," Gilligan replied.

"And that sits OK with you? It's completely off the books this one. Your job is to clean the mess up after me, cover my ass and do what you see fit with no rules."

"About time, I'm sick of you being the only one who's allowed to have fun," Gilligan said, his smile working overtime.

"I want to go home for a bit and freshen up. Then you can pick me up when I call, and I'll tell you what I need, and we can take it from there. This will be a round the clock job. You OK with that?" Ward asked.

"Sure, it's only my sons third birthday tomorrow, no big deal to the wife," Gilligan said, putting his fingers to his head in the shape of a gun and pulling the trigger.

"I'm sure he won't mind when you save the day and get yet another commendation due to all the work I do. How many have you had now after working with me, five? Not bad for a glorified driver," Ward said with a smile.

"But a very good driver none the less," Gilligan retorted. "So where are we?"

"I'll run through it later, I need to see someone first. Home please driver," he said with a limp backhanded wave of his right hand.

The journey from JFK to DUMBO took just forty minutes, which was good for just over eighteen miles. He stepped out of Gilligan's sedan and said, "I'll call when I am ready."

"Yes master", Gilligan replied, "I am honoured to be in your presence," he said before pulling away and offering the middle finger of his left hand as a parting gift.

Ward put in the entrance code to get into his building and got into the elevator to the sixth floor. As soon he stepped out of the elevator onto the clean, beige carpet in the apartment block hallway, he instantly felt like he was home. He opened his door, walked in and his heart jumped as soon as he stepped into the open plan living area, as he saw Eloisa making coffee in the kitchen. She looked up and smiled. He looked at her for a long thirty seconds, neither of them speaking and said,

"Can I tell you something?"

"Of course," she replied.

"I sometimes get completely lost in what I am doing and never think of anything but winning. But when I set eyes on you, I feel an overwhelming sense of missing you. Is it odd that I miss you more when I am with you than when we are apart?" he asked.

"That all depends why you miss me. I'm a woman Ryan, I like to hear what you miss about me as much as the next woman," she replied, widening her eyes in mock surprise, "So why don't you tell me?"

"How much time do you have?"

"No more than three minutes because I am late as it is. I will be here straight after work this evening, so depending upon what you tell me now, how tonight goes is down to you."

He loved that about her. She knew how to play him. No falling at his feet or big hugging scenes when he walked through the door, her strength and control excited him.

"So you'd better make it good," she said. "Go!"

"I look at you and I see the most beautiful woman in the world. From your long dark hair to your beautiful green eyes, I see perfection. I love your little button nose and your perfect smile. But that pales into insignificance when I list the things that make me feel extremely privileged to have you in my life," he said, as he moved closer to her and stared intently into her eyes.

"Such as?" she asked, with a fun, quizzical look shining in her eyes.

"You are extremely bright, caring, kind, determined, loyal, strong, gracious, eloquent, sweet........"

"OK Ryan, I'm blushing."

She moved forward and held his head in her hands and looked deep into his eyes.

"I love you," she said, "You are my soul mate."

Then she kissed him slowly and with a tenderness that only two people who feel they belong with each other can feel. He felt himself getting instantly aroused. She sensed this and said, "But I have to go, I'm running really late," and pulled away.

He felt a wave of dejection run through his body and then she added,

"Plus, as much as I want you more than anything in the world right now; I know that if I make you wait, tonight will be all about me as you will be so eager to impress."

She picked up her bag, grabbed her coffee in her flask and walked up to the door. As she opened the door to leave she said,

"God, I want you so much. You really are the best kisser in the world."

And with that, she was gone.

She knew how to play him.

There was definitely no doubt about that whatsoever.

He had one call to make before he jumped into the shower.

He took out his cell phone and dialled the number.

"Hello Ryan," a female voice answered.

"I need your help, like immediately," he said. "Is Tackler with you?"

"Of course he is," the voice replied.

"I need you both for the next few days. Can you drop everything else, it's important?"

"This sounds urgent?"

"Yes Nicole-Louise. It's very urgent."

"Then you had best come on over. The Old Man has already said we need to be here around the clock for you."

"See you in an hour," he said and then he hung up the phone.

TWELVE

An hour later, Ward was ringing the intercom of Nicole-Louise and Tackler's building on Park Avenue in Lennox Hill. "Come on up," a gruff, barely awake voice said. He walked in and climbed one flight of stairs to the first floor and knocked on the door of apartment fourteen. The door was opened by a guy in his early thirties, who was wearing navy blue towel shorts which came down to his knees, and a white, grubby tee shirt which had a picture of a front page of the New York times stating, 'Sid Vicious is Dead!'. The guy was no more than five feet seven and could only have weighed a maximum of one hundred and forty pounds.

"Hello Tackler," Ward said.

"Hello," he replied, "Come in."

Nicole-Louise and Tackler knew everything that there was to know about Ward because they were the ones who had made his electronic footprint disappear. It would not be an exaggeration to say that they were among the top five computer hackers in the world. They found everything eventually. Ward had paid them two hundred thousand dollars of Centrepoint's money to move the seventeen million that he took from the South Africans, making sure ten could not be traced and only seven would be discovered. The incredible irony was that two months later, Centrepoint had paid them another two hundred thousand to find the seven million he believed Ward had taken. The three of them would always laugh at this.

"Oh look, it's our lack of sleep for the next few days," a woman said as he walked into the living area.

"Hello Nicole-Louise," he said with a smile.

"No time for pleasantries," she said, ignoring his smile. Nicole-Louise was tall, had long, light brown hair and alert, blue eyes. And the fact that she was always so cool under pressure and dressed so casually was what Ward loved about her the most.

She and Tackler made an odd couple. They didn't seem to fit. She was outgoing, strong, confident and vibrant and he never said much. He told Ward once that he hated people in general but liked him a lot. He always took this as a real compliment until Nicole-Louise told him one day that he only mentioned that to him because he made him feel uneasy, and he was petrified that one day he would kill him. The compliment lost its weighting that day.

Nicole-Louise studied him to gauge how worried he was. She always did this and somehow, she was always able to measure by his demeanour how serious a situation was. She was the only person who could do this with him.

"Well?" she demanded rather than asked.

"I want you to search for everything possible on someone. I want you to hack into everywhere and find something, anything, that doesn't look right. I want you to hack into the FBI and CIA systems and get me every bit of information on all FFW sympathisers, where they are, and who would be most likely to want to help someone. I want you to try and find a bomber who is coming to New York any day now."

"What kind of bomb?" Tackler asked.

"A big bomb. You know what happened in Paris and London over the past few days I take it?" he asked.

They both nodded at the same time.

"It will be bigger than that, much bigger. So right now, the three of us are the best chance of stopping it."

"No pressure then," Nicole-Louise said.

"Names?" Tackler asked.

"The bomber is Asif Fulken; start there and with the FFW list," he said.

Tackler scribbled Fulken's name down as Ward spoke.

"How long do you think we have? You said a few days?" Nicole-Louise asked.

"He won't be here yet. If we find him before he gets here then we will stop it happening. You two chase him from here and I'll chase him from the ground. I need that FFW list urgently."

"We will have it in an hour and will e-mail it to your phone," Tackler said.

"Do we know where the bomb will go off?" Nicole-Louise asked.

"No, but I think we will stop it," he replied.

"What makes you so sure of that?" Nicole-Louise asked, still studying him intensely.

"Because I already know who the people behind the bombings are."

THIRTEEN

Outside in the street, he called Gilligan.

"I'm on Park Avenue, come and get me, driver."

"You are at Nicole-Louise's and Tacklers?" Gilligan asked.

"I was."

"I'll be there in thirty," Gilligan replied.

Ward hung up.

He kept playing over and over in his head what he had seen on the footage that UKBC News had showed him, and while he admitted to himself that they were subtle moments in the grand scheme of things, he also knew that they were the defining moments in stopping the New York bomb. Gilligan turned up after twenty five minutes and pulled into the kerb driving the standard black Sudan and he climbed into the car.

"Sorry I'm early," Gilligan said, flashing his big smile.

Gilligan was a big guy in every sense of the word, and not just because he was six foot three and must have weighed pushing two hundred and eighty pounds. He was in his early forties and a lot of his muscle had lost its granite like feel, but it still retained enough definition to send out a signal that said, 'Don't mess with me'.

He had been brought up on the tough streets of Harlem and Ward knew that he would get the right feel for everything that was happening in New York. His facial features always made Ward smile; he was the spitting image of the former boxer Marvin Haggler. He was a brawler too, and he often wondered if they had been adopted when young and were both unaware of each other's connection to each other. It was a point he had raised with him a number of times, and a point always met with contempt by Gilligan.

"So, what do you know about the FFW funders and supporters here in New York?" he asked.

"As much as anyone but the Kingpins tend to move around so they aren't always in one fixed place," Gilligan said.

"So how would we go about finding the Kingpins? Like today?" he inquired.

"Easy. Everyone who comes to New York descends on Times Square. Like everywhere else in the world, there are all sorts of terrorist groups watching who comes in and who is new on the block. It isn't just us who monitor the visitors. The FFW eyes down there belong to a guy called Bassam Khadil. He's a bit of a punk, pretty harmless if I'm honest. He just plays at being a terrorist. All he really does for them is act as a phone boy, communicating information for the real important guys to establish who is who and why," Gilligan said with the tenacity that he had grown to rely on from him.

"Then we should go and pay him a visit," Ward instructed.

They drove the couple of miles to Times Square and pulled into a side road just off of West 46th Street, close to the Church of Scientology of New York. Gilligan stepped out of the car without saying anything and Ward followed until he stopped at the rear entrance of a building. The walls of the building were thick with grime, only broken up by the occasional piece of graffiti, which demonstrated that the street artist who signed it, 'Paynt-Tuch', was more talented in his artwork than he was with his grammar. There was a cold looking grey door made of thin steel; secure to the passing eye, but likely not impregnable. Gilligan approached it and said, "OK I'll do the talking to start with? Your limey accent probably won't get us invited in."

"Go for it but be vague. Ask them what they have heard about an impending event happening soon. Let's play a little dumb, see what they give us before we turn the screw."

"OK," Gilligan replied.

"One more thing," Ward added, "How many guys are likely to be in there and is this likely to turn nasty? I'd hate for you to get hurt."

"I'm pretty sure I can cope but if I get scared I'll give you the nod," Gilligan said, flashing his smile.

'God, I swear you and Marvin Haggler were separated at birth," he said, his face showing no sign of a smile.

Gilligan knocked on the door and the door rocked. 'Definitely not impregnable' Ward thought to himself. A short Middle Eastern guy opened the door, probably from Iraq, he concluded.

"What do you want?" the guy asked in very poor, broken English.

"I want to see Bassam Khadil," Gilligan said with authority.

"He not here, I not see him, I never heard of him," the little guy comically replied, and he went to close the door. Gilligan put his foot in the crack of the door and his shoulder against it. The guy was not going to be able to close it.

"Don't waste my time, this is important," Gilligan said as he pushed through the door and stepped past the little guy.

"You stop there. You not scare me Mr. Marvin Haggler, there will be trouble," he protested with a less than convincing threat, which Ward found impossible not to be amused by. Gilligan turned and delivered a right hook into the little guys stomach that lifted his feet of the ground about six inches, knocking the wind clean out of him before he fell to his knees, doubled over, desperately trying to get air into his lungs.

"Go Marvin!" Ward said, a comment Gilligan chose to ignore. They walked along a small corridor, across a worn brown and orange carpet, towards a brown door, which had paint peeling off and without breaking stride; Gilligan turned the handle and walked in.

Inside the room there were five guys; all similar in size and stature to the guy who had opened the front door. The room was clearly the kitchen, judging by the filthy yellow lino floor, and it contained a sink, dirty looking refrigerator, a stool and two cupboards on the walls that were open and housed such items as tea, biscuits, sugar and various items of food that Ward did not recognise. Four of the guys were sitting around a grubby looking table in the centre of the room, talking and drinking from ornate Turkish coffee cups. The other guy was sitting on a stool, glued to a laptop he had on the side counter. The four at the table looked up startled and the guy on the laptop closed the lid to hide whatever it was he was viewing on the screen. Instinctively, the four guys sitting down put their hands flat on the table to show they were offering no threat and holding no weapons. Ward noted that this was something they were used to and that surprise visits by various arms of the security service were something that they knew how to respond to.

"I want to talk to you," Gilligan said to the guy sitting at the head of the table. The hierarchy of command working even this low down the chain, the head of the table being the place to be, and so this must be Bassam Khadil, Ward thought to himself.

"What do you want?" Khadil replied.

"I want to know who is new in town," Gilligan said.

"Well there is a new pimp on 7th and a great new show at the Marquis theatre," Khadil flippantly replied.

"Very funny," Gilligan said, "I need to know what's happening. We have wind that something is going down and you are the eyes and the guy who knows the most, so we need your help."

Gilligan was smart. His deliberate massaging of Khadil's ego had him thinking he was important straight away. Ward noticed that it was plainly clear from Khadil's reaction that he had no idea what Gilligan was talking about. Guys that low down the food chain are never trusted with important information, but that wasn't what they were there for.

"No matter what I know, I would never share with you. I am a warrior fighting a holy war and what is going to happen will be part of our cause," Khadil declared, looking at the other three guys around the table to demonstrate how important he was, and that he could be trusted with the secrets of the elders. All three of them looked back at him in awe.

Ward walked over towards the guy with the laptop. The guy immediately held it close to his chest, wrapping his arms around it to protect it, almost with the intensity that a mother protects a new-born.

"Listen Khadil," Gilligan continued, "We know you are a big player, so what can you tell me?"

"The end is coming, the west will fall," he declared in a totally unconvincing tone.

Ward stepped towards the guy with the laptop. The guy held it even tighter. He leant forward and without speaking, tried taking it from him. As he pulled the laptop towards him, the guy's vice-like grip meant that he came towards him too. Without warning, he jerked his head forward eight inches and smashed his forehead into the bridge of the guy's nose. The guy released his grip on the laptop immediately. One of the men at the table went to stand up in a half-hearted attempt to look tough, but Gilligan put his right hand on the his shoulder and the force of Gilligan's hand pushing down sent a clear enough indicator that he would be fighting a lost cause, and so he promptly re-assumed his sitting position. As the guy fell to the floor clutching his nose, Ward opened the laptop and hit the return button so that the screen came back to life. He studied the screen for no more than two seconds and then closed it again. He put the laptop back on the counter and turned towards the table, slapping the guy on the back of the head as he moved towards the group sitting down. He stopped next to the guy sitting to the right of Khadil and said, "You don't know anything, do you?" looking straight into Khadil's eyes.

Khadil was momentarily confused by Ward's accent. The realisation that something big was happening crept over his face.

"Here's what you will do," Ward said, "You will tell me the name and address of the person that you relay your information to. If you don't, my friend here will beat it out of you, so we get it anyway."

"I can't. I can't betray my brothers," Khadil replied in a quivering tone.

Before he had finished his sentence, Ward smashed his left elbow into the side of the face of the guy sitting next to Khadil.

It caught the guy square on the jaw with a sickening crack, which echoed around the room as the blow landed. The guy let out a high-pitched scream and rolled to the left and fell off of the chair and onto the floor, right next to Khadil's feet.

"Who do you report to?" he calmly asked Khadil again.

"Hassan Al Holami," Khadil replied without hesitation.

"How do you contact him?"

"By cell phone," Khadil stuttered.

"What does he tell you to specifically look for?"

"Anyone who doesn't look like a tourist, any potential homeless kids who could be persuaded to join our cause, any police activity that seems out of place. And I also notify him of the arrival of any brothers that have arranged to come here."

"Where do I find Al Holami?"

"I really can't tell you that, there will be reprisals."

Ward kicked the guy on the floor who was still whimpering, clutching his jaw.

"Where do I find Al Holami?" he asked again, "He will never know you told me."

"He's in Bowery on East 3rd street, apartment block 153, number 4, ground floor, opposite the marble cemetery," Khadil conceded.

"Good. If he knows we are coming, I will come back and kill you all. Is that clear?" Ward asked calmly.

"Yes. Just do not mention you spoke to me," Khadil begged.

"I won't."

He nodded towards Gilligan and they both walked out of the kitchen. As they opened the door the guy who Gilligan had punched in the stomach was still on the floor, just about catching his breath. They walked past without comment or a second glance.

"You sure the FFW have a handle on any of this?" Gilligan asked.

"It's a dilemma for them. They know Asif Fulken is coming, but they also want him dead for running away from the brotherhood. They would not be able to actively assist him but they would willingly hide him. If the bomb did go off, they would welcome the destruction it would cause, but after that he would still be hunted. I think they will be prepared to give him a safe house and maybe the equipment he needs, but he will still effectively be on his own."

"You think we will stop this?"

"Yes I do," Ward replied, "I know the bomber, roughly who is behind it and roughly when it will happen."

"How do you know all of this stuff when everyone else is in the dark?"

Ward ignored the question.

"One last thing, what was the guy on the laptop looking at to warrant you giving him a slap?" Gilligan asked as they climbed into the car.

"He was watching pornography."

FOURTEEN

Asif Fulken had gotten to New York with no problems whatsoever. The train journey to Liverpool had been the riskiest part of the journey and that went without incident. The ferry across to Dublin had been uncomfortable, simply because he preferred his feet to be on solid ground at all times, and it was a constant battle to stop himself throwing up, a task not helped by the constant smell of vomit that engulfed every toilet on board. The seven and a half hour flight from Dublin had been the most pleasant part of his escape from London. It gave him time to reflect on how smoothly his plan was going, and how he was always one step ahead of the inferior people who hunted him. He had no doubt that by now, the CIA would know he was behind the bombings in Paris and London, and knowing this gave him a sense of power. He thought how hundreds of men were looking for him and how they would never find him. He was too alert, too on his game, and too smart. The leaders of the FFW were his main concern. They did not want anyone acting outside of their control, but he believed with complete conviction, that once the mission was complete and the leaders could take the credit; then he would be forgiven and left to live his life in peace.

He had entered New York at Newark instead of JFK, using an American passport that he had stolen from a tourist in Paris. An Afghan who had a U.S. passport, acquired when he had sought, and been granted, asylum in the States. He always used the same technique to get passports, and only ever used live passports, never fake ones. Passports that weren't genuine were relatively easy to detect and with the introduction of scanners and CCTV at major airports it was harder and harder to fool the watchers. His technique was tuned to perfection. He would cruise the gay bars of local tourist spots in cities and look for the closest match that he could get to himself physically and facially. The men who frequented these bars would normally be travellers who had a desire to experience the local gay scene, and they would nearly always be travelling alone. He would then look for the appropriate nationality, which fitted in with where he wanted to travel to. This could be time consuming and on some occasions, it had taken up to four nights to find the right guy, but he would always wait until he got it right. Thoroughness would lead to fewer mistakes being made, and fewer mistakes would lead to less chance of discovery.

He would then spend the evening complimenting the guy and plying him with drinks before leaving the bar for a night of passion and excitement at the guy's hotel. Once there, he would find the passport and at the appropriate time, steal it. He would then say he was overcome with the urge to party again and drag the guy out for even more drinks and fun and then after the night had ended, suggest a romantic walk, before killing the guy in a secluded spot. With no I.D or clues as to who the guy was, it would generally take a couple of weeks to identify his victim and by that time, he would be long gone. And all of these murders would be put down to robbery and the naivety of a traveller abroad. Later, he would alter his appearance in the appropriate way. Passport pictures last for ten years. He had never understood why they were not updated every year. People change dramatically in ten years. He had been pleased to note that the passport he was using, in the name of Shah Daud Sultanzoy, only had three more years before it expired. The thing people change most over ten years is hair. It can thin, it can be longer, shorter or it can be lost and styles change dramatically. That's why Fulken had gone to the barbers near Kings Cross and got a number one cut all over. Sure, he looked slightly different to his passport picture but the customs people would just see a change of hairstyle and put it down to that. People will always see only what other people want them to see. As predicted, he went through customs without a hitch, even receiving a "Welcome home, Mr. Sultanzoy," from the Customs Officer who studied the passport that he had presented, a little longer than necessary and then, due to the politically correct madness of westerners, felt the need to welcome him home so as not to cause offence. The politicians, the do-gooders and the liberal people who swarm the media made everything a hundred times easier and Fulken loved them for that.

He walked out of the airport and went straight to the cab rank. He picked the first cab he came to and climbed in. The driver was a Mexican guy in his mid-fifties and he looked like he was coming to the end of his shift. He was the kind of guy who wouldn't notice or remember much.

"Bowery," he said to the driver.

"Anywhere specific in Bowery?"

"I'll tell you when we get there," he replied.

"Been anywhere nice?" the driver asked.

"I don't want to be rude, but I'm tired, so just take me home," he replied, adding a yawn at the end of the sentence for extra effect.

When they reached the corner of East 1st Street, he said, "Here will do."

The driver pulled into the kerb and said, "That will be seventy seven bucks," an amount that he found offensive but made no comment on. He handed the driver eighty five dollars, a smaller or larger amount would stick in the driver's memory.

He walked up Bowery until he reached the end of East 3rd Street, and he slowly took in all the surroundings. The buildings weren't as high as in other parts of New York. Most of them were only about six or seven floors high. There was lots of red brick and grey stone buildings and they seemed to blend in well together. A few trees lined the street, adding colour to it, and the occasional person sat on the steps of their apartments watching the world go by, but not scanning or expecting anyone. He walked up East 3rd Street and on the opposite side of the road, walked past number 153 to get a feel for the property and to see if anything looked out of place. The apartment that he was heading to was above a row of shops that housed a video store, a launderette and a grocery store. To the right of the building was a church and the front of the apartment block was partially hidden by trees. A good location he thought to himself. He slowly walked all the way up to the end of the street and stopped in Walmart to buy a disposable cell phone. He put in the sim card he had been given and turned it on, and was pleased to see that the battery was three quarters charged. He then slowly walked back again to apartment 153 and stopped about forty feet short, on the opposite side of the street, and dialled the number that he had kept in his miniature pocket book hidden in the inside of his jacket lining. There was no answer. Something that didn't cause too much of a panic, but made him wonder if the number was no longer as reliable as he was led to believe it was. He dialled the second number he had. Again, no answer.

Now he started to become a little concerned. This was an unusual turn of events as the brothers were always reliable. Had something gone wrong? Was him coming to New York a mistake? Was trusting them a foolish thing to do, knowing he had fallen foul to the FFW leaders? All of these thoughts rushed through his head at once. For the first time since this started in Paris he felt less than completely positive that he would achieve his goal. This unnerved him for a few seconds but he breathed in and reminded himself that he was Asif

Fulken and he did not lose. He waited ten minutes and dialled the first number again. This time someone answered.

"Hello?" the voice said.

"I am in need of a brother," he said.

"You have arrived safely?" the voice asked.

"Yes my brother. You have a safe haven for me?"

"Not here. You need to move away, head towards Greenwich Village and I will contact you on this number when it is safe," the voice said with urgency.

"A problem?" he asked with equal urgency.

"Some men are on their way, my men in Times Square told me they were hit this morning by a team of fifteen and they forced my whereabouts out of them by torturing them with electrical charges. They are coming to see me, but we will fight to the death and protect your quest," the voice said, "Now go, it isn't safe."

"You are a good friend Hassan," Fulken said and hung up the phone.

He turned and walked slowly away, concealing himself within the trees and passers-by. As he neared the end of East 3rd Street, he did not notice the standard black Sudan driving on the opposite side of the road, slowly checking the area and the surroundings. And the two men in the car, Ward and Gilligan, did not notice Asif Fulken either.

FIFTEEN

"Drive past a couple of times first, let's see if anything looks out of place," Ward said to Gilligan.

They drove up East 3rd Street and then slowly back again. Everything looked normal.153 was an unassuming building, a row of shops underneath and a row of trees which offered just a little concealment.

"What do you know about this Al Holami?" Ward asked.

"He's a pretty clean guy; on the radar but not flashing brightly. He doesn't preach publicly or act as a spokesman for the community; he's actually considered pretty low risk."

Ward despaired at this. He knew that the tactic being used was to have cells of clerics and supporters who publicly proclaimed hate for the west and flagged themselves up as high risk targets so they drained resources. This allowed the real puppet masters more room to operate.

"And this is what the analysts have concluded, is it?" he responded with contempt.

"You know as well as I do, buddy, the brains live in a different world to us."

They drove on and parked about one hundred yards further up from Al Holami's apartment.

"How is this going to go down?" Gilligan asked.

"The same way as at Khadil's place. We'll be vague, like we know something is going to happen but we don't know by who or what. We should be able to gauge by his reaction if he knows anything," Ward replied.

"You want me to do the talking?"

"Go for it, Marvin."

They got out of the car and Ward said,

"You cross the street and approach the building from the other side of the road."

Gilligan crossed the street. They walked just a little slower than normal down the sidewalk, Ward had his hand in his jacket pocket, wrapped around his Glock.

Always prepared.

When he reached the entrance to the apartment, Gilligan crossed the street. The door had a buzzer entry system numbered one through to thirty, and they looked at each other.

"Pick a number between one and six but not four," Ward said.

"One," Gilligan proclaimed.

"God you are lazy," he replied. He pressed the buzzer for number five. A female voice answered.

"Hello?" she sounded young and barely awake.

"I'm really sorry to bother you but I have lost my keys, any chance you could buzz me in?" Ward asked in his clearest accent.

"Are you British?" she asked.

Ward smiled.

The Americans love a British accent and they instinctively trust the person the voice belongs to.

"Yes I am. Only been in the apartment about a week and I'm losing everything already," he replied, trying to sound as bumbling as he could.

"Hold on, I'll come and let you in," she excitedly said. The intercom went silent.

"You never know," said Gilligan, "She might be a looker."

They waited about twenty seconds and the door opened.

She was a looker.

She was a pretty girl in her early twenties, wearing a Jets top and blue shorts. She had jet black hair and had the tailored beauty that only American girls have. She looked Ward up and down, taking no notice of Gilligan whatsoever.

"So, you know anyone in New York?" she asked. As much as Ward wanted to get into the building immediately and off the street, he didn't want to arouse suspicion.

"Only my work colleagues," he innocently replied.

"How about me and you…………" before she could finish her sentence there was a crack and a boom, her back arched and she lurched forward, a spray of blood following her. A second crack filled the air and a bullet smashed into the doorframe, to Ward's left. Gilligan sprung up the steps to the right of the door and pulled the girl out of the doorway by the scruff of her Jets shirt and checked for a pulse.

"She's dead," he shouted.

Ward put his arm around the side of the door and fired three shots in the direction of the staircase. This gave him enough time to sprint into the hallway and take shelter behind the wall under the first flight of stairs. He could hear two sets of feet running up the stairs and shouted to Gilligan, "Clear." Gilligan stepped into the hallway and edged towards the bottom of the stairs with his gun pointing up after the footsteps as he moved.

"Let's go," Ward said, and took the lead, sprinting up the stairs. They reached the first floor without further incident. As they got to the foot of the stairs leading to the second floor, Ward caught a glimpse of a leg disappearing. He cautiously moved forward with Gilligan two steps behind him, with his back to him, and when they got halfway up the flight of stairs he heard a door swing open and the boom of a gun being fired. As he turned he saw Gilligan holding his gun horizontally, and a dead guy with half of his head missing lying on the floor to apartment number nine.

"I've got your back, go," Gilligan said.

Ward took three steps and then he stopped dead. The sunlight was breaking in through the hallway windows and he could see the clear outline of two shadows stretching down onto the stairway wall and carpet. He counted to three and exploded up eight steps and fired without seeing the targets. One shot straight, one slightly to the left. Two direct hits. Both guys fell to the floor, and Ward climbed to the top of the stairs. The guy he had hit with the first shot was still alive, clutching his stomach, the other guy stone cold dead with a large hole in his chest.

"Where's Al Holami?" he asked. The guy said something in Arabic that Ward couldn't decipher and so he asked again, "Is Al Holami here?"

The guy said something else that he couldn't understand and so Ward raised his gun and shot the guy in the head.

"He might have been useful," Gilligan said.

"He can't creep up behind us and shoot us if he is dead," he replied without even looking at Gilligan. He continued to climb the steps slowly. They reached the top of the stairs and the only place left to go was out onto the roof through the emergency escape door. The door was ajar.

"They want us out there so we are sitting ducks," Gilligan said.

"So let's give them a target then. Find out where they are," and with that, Ward burst through the door, sprinted twenty feet forward with lightning speed, and dived behind a skylight which was raised about two feet. He heard the distinct sound of two different guns being fired, the bullet whistling through the air as he hit the ground. He now knew that there were two shooters there. He also knew that one would have to be waiting for Gilligan to appear and that meant only one of them would be focusing on him. He changed his magazine, even though he had nine bullets left. Always prepared.

He heard a shot fire and concluded that Gilligan was on his game and was showing the other shooter enough to warrant a shot but more importantly, to give enough away so that he could work out how to take him down. He didn't need to worry about the other guy. He knew with utmost certainty that Gilligan would take his opponent out. Keeping his body flat to the floor, he looked out from the left of his cover and saw nothing but flat roof. He pulled himself in, adjusted his body and looked out to the right. There was an outhouse there. A wooden shed, probably used only for storage, he thought. As he was gauging the distance and likelihood of the guy being there, he saw an arm appear from the right hand side of the shed and then some hair. He pulled back out of sight before the guys eyes had come out from his cover. He needed Gilligan to make his move now. He didn't fancy playing hide and seek for the next half an hour. Sure enough, almost as if he was reading his mind, there was an explosion of four shots and then Gilligan shouted, "You want me to take yours as well as you are taking so much time?" Ward put his head around to the side of the skylight and saw no movement from behind the shed.

"You want to kill him or shall I?" he shouted.

"Please. No shooting. I'm coming out," a voice from behind the shed shouted.

"Throw your weapon out, punk," Gilligan screamed. A handgun was tossed about six feet to the front of the shed. The guy walked out, arms raised high above his head.

"Please, don't shoot!" he pleaded as Gilligan started to walk towards him.

"Stop!" Ward shouted. Gilligan stopped immediately, "He might be wearing a bomb," he continued.

Gilligan instinctively took three steps back.

"Go and pat him down," he said.

"Why don't you go and pat him down?" Gilligan replied.

"Because I'm more important than you."

"I'm not wearing a bomb Mister, I promise," the guy shouted.

"Shut up," Ward ordered.

"Go and pat him down anyway," he nodded to Gilligan.

"You go and pat him down!" Gilligan replied

"I told you, I'm more important than you, just get it over with."

"I'm not wearing a bomb, look!" the guy pleaded and lowered his hands.

"Stop," Ward shouted, "One inch lower and I will blow your head apart," he added.

"How can you be more important than me?" Gilligan asked
"I just am," he replied.

"Well I disagree with that. You don't even exist. They give
you anonymity so you can run around killing whoever you
want so there is no come back on anyone. I am a top
Government Agent, decorated in fact, so that makes me more
important than you."

The guy was now visibly traumatised by the revelation about
Ward and eyed him up and down in sheer panic.

"Fine," Ward said, "I'll just shoot him in the head and then
search for a bomb after. He won't tell us anything anyway,
these warriors never do," he said as he walked towards the
guy with his gun pointing at his head.

"I will, I will tell you anything you need to know. I have
information, please, I know where Al Holami is," he pleaded.

He reached him and punched him hard in the stomach, a
right handed uppercut catching him unawares and the guy
doubled over.

"He's not wearing a bomb," he shouted to Gilligan. He
grabbed hold of the guy's jacket and pulled him along the
floor to the edge of the building. The guy screamed as Ward
let go of him.

"Where is he?" he demanded.

"Greenwich Village," the guy replied.

"Where?"

I don't know exactly."

"Not good enough," Ward said and lifted his Glock.

"I know it's close to Washington Square Park."

"You are lying."

"I'm not, I swear, it's somewhere on West 8th Street."

"No good, that means nothing, too vague. You are lying to me.
Stand up, look me in the eyes and I will know if you are
lying," he challenged the guy.

He pulled himself up to his feet and stood upright, about a
foot away from him. He was a small guy, about five foot five
and he had to crane his neck to make eye contact with him.

"Now, where is Al Holami?" he asked, slowly and clearly.

"I told you, in Greenwich Village."

"Where in Greenwich Village?"

"On West 8th Street, the building behind the recording studios."

Ward studied his eyes for a moment. He knew when a man was lying. He knew what fear looked like and he could see that this guy saw a seven foot giant looking down at him. He knew that he had told him all he knew. There was no more to tell. So he shoved him hard in the chest and the guy fell back, his legs catching the low roof wall and he went over the edge of the building with a deafening scream. The thud as he travelled the six floors and hit the ground could be heard from the roof. He walked to the edge of the building and looked down. He had landed head first on the sidewalk, a fact he deduced by virtue of his brains spreading out everywhere, and the few people who were on the street were screaming and already on their cell phones calling for help.

"Was that really necessary?" Gilligan asked.

"They killed that girl and tried killing us. I'd say it was totally necessary," he replied.

"Couldn't you just have shot him?" Gilligan enquired.

Ward ignored the question.

"I'd better make a call and get this cleaned up," Gilligan said with a sigh.

"I have to go home for a few hours anyway," he said. "You can drop me off, come back, clear this up and collect me about four."

"Anything else you wish to add?" Gilligan asked sarcastically.

"Yes," replied Ward, "I think it's safe to say that they know something."

SIXTEEN

"I'll see you at four. I'm back down to Bowery to sort out your mess and then I'll be back to pick you up," Gilligan said as he pulled over close to Ward's apartment.

"Find out what you can about this place in Greenwich. Find the studio and see what information your people have relating to it. Nicole-Louise and Tackler have probably got further than the whole of the CIA combined, so call them first," Ward said as he got out of the car.

He walked into his apartment building, and when he opened the door to his apartment, he stopped dead in his tracks when he saw Eloisa. She looked stunning in a white blouse and black pencil skirt.

"That smells nice," he said as he took off his jacket and threw it onto a chair before stepping through to the kitchen area and kissing her passionately; long and hard.

"God I've missed you," he said.

"And I you," she replied as she pulled away and smiled.

He looked at her for a brief moment. She was flawless. Her beautiful, thick, long shiny hair, her light skin with a hint of bronze, her green eyes that made him feel like he wanted to stare into them and lose himself in them for hours. Every part of her was perfect.

He took her hand and led her slowly through to the bedroom, stopping at the end of the bed and kissing her lightly on the lips. Standing behind her, he moved her hair to one side and began to kiss her neck gently, and she instinctively closed her eyes and tilted her head back to expose more of her neck for him to explore. As he kissed her neck her breathing became more and more heavy, almost reaching a gasp. Her hands reached out for his and they joined together in perfect unison. "You taste incredible," he said

"Please, don't stop," she begged.

He let go of her right hand and moved his to her front. As he continued to softly kiss her neck, he started to unbutton her blouse, the first button to open being the one between her perfect, pert breasts. He continued down to her navel until the last button separated and her blouse fell open.

He turned her around and kissed her lightly on the lips once more as he took her blouse off of her shoulders and let it fall to the floor.

She pulled at his tee-shirt and lifted it over his head and threw it onto the floor. She dug her fingernails into his chest while he removed her bra, feeling his incredibly toned body not move at all under the strain of her grasp. As they continued to kiss each other, now with more intensity and their tongue's entwining, they pulled at each other's lower clothing and within one minute, they were completely naked. He pushed her on the bed with force, and she responded to this by completely submitting to him and they got lost in each other for the next two hours. When they had finished, Eloisa was exhausted. Ward was a long way from being spent but she said,

"I have to go back to work for a meeting, we can't do it again." He looked dejected, "Not just once?"

"No. We will have plenty of time later," she replied, "What were Misker's last words?" she asked, referring to the Estonian that Ward had eliminated in St James' Park.

"He begged me not to kill him. He was petrified."

103

"What are you doing in New York?" she asked.

"There's a bomber on the loose and he's heading here."

"Is he here already?"

"I don't think so."

"Will you stop it from going off?" she enquired.

"Yes I will," he stated.

"Then I have nothing to worry about. I know you will win. You always do."

He gave her a reassuring look.

"Let's make love again," she said.

They showered together and made love under the warm spray. Within 10 minutes of leaving the shower, she looked as immaculate as she did when he first walked through the door a few hours ago.

"Don't you wish that we could spend more time together?" he asked her.

"Of course I do, but we both have a calling that we can't ignore. When I have bad days and feel lonely, when you are running around God knows where, I remind myself of the good that we are doing. I remind myself that hundreds of children are sleeping safely in their beds at night through our direct actions," she replied, with a smile that filled him with warmth.

"I just sometimes think that there has to be more. We always meet briefly, sometimes I feel that what we have is casual and has no meaning to it at all," he said.

"Of course it has meaning. I trust you more than I trust anyone in the world. I share my darkest secrets with you and you do bad things to bad people on my behalf. How many other people in a relationship have that between them?" she asked.

"None I guess. Do you think we will ever be normal?"

"Yes I do. We will have that in the future but for now, our time together is precious. When I am with you I feel so much love for you and I see my whole future in your hands. When I leave, I feel sad for a little while but crave the next opportunity to spend time with you and that makes me love you and miss you even more. That's when I realise how lucky we are, how what we have is so special and that without a doubt, we are going to be together forever."

He looked at her and smiled. Eloisa was the only person on earth who could put exactly what he felt into words because she felt the same. He felt safe, important and complete when he was in her company.

"Thank you," he said.

"What for?"

"Just for being you."

Sometimes, he thought, in the right moment, saying thank you, was all that needed to be said.

The moment was broken by his cell phone ringing.

"Great timing," he answered

"Are you by a TV?" Centrepoint asked.

"Yes. What's wrong?"

"Turn it on. Channel 301."

He turned on his TV and selected channel 301. It was USBC News, the American arm of the Lord Ashurst- Stevens media empire. The scroll across the bottom read;

'BREAKING NEWS....... BOMBER TARGETING NEW YORK – SECURITY FORCES CHASING SUSPECT BUT HAVE NO LEADS'

"Is that for real?" he asked.

"The bulletin should come on soon. It's on a five minute loop," Centrepoint replied.

"How can this be allowed to happen? Look at the panic it will cause."

"Unfortunately we can't control the news. Freedom of speech comes before all else," Centrepoint said with an air of sarcasm.

"Chasing suspect but have no leads," Ward repeated, quoting the second part of the scroll, "How incompetent does that make us sound?"

"Well technically, they are right aren't they? We have our suspect but we have no leads. We don't even know if Fulken is in New York yet do we?"

105

"Not for sure but I believe that he is close and will be here any day now. No positive ID's from the border people I take it?" Ward asked in hope more than expectation.

"Nothing at all."

"Have you contacted any high level people at UKBC or USBC News to get that taken off?"

"I'm working on it. Here comes the loop, watch it."

He lowered the phone and watched the news report.

Abbi Beglin appeared on the screen and proceeded to explain how the security services on both sides of the Atlantic have been working with her and her news crew to try and establish who was behind the Paris and London bombings. She explained that they had worked closely with members of MI6 and that there were no leads or clues to go on, but they were sure that the bombers next target was New York.

So much so, that the focus of their investigation had now moved stateside. Ward had heard enough and turned the TV off. He brought the phone back to his ear.

"I need you to make me an appointment with their top people over here," he demanded of Centrepoint.

"Then I'll make you an appointment with the chief news editor again, Martin Walker. He is there in New York for the Annual News Television Awards taking place in three days' time," he replied, "Where exactly are we on this Ryan?"

"Just make me the appointment and let me know when he will see me."

Ward hung up the phone.

"Is everything alright?" Eloisa asked.

"Just people interfering, making things more problematic as usual," he replied. "Don't you worry about it, you go and save your world and I'll save mine," he added with a smile.

Eloisa came to him and kissed him softly, and then said, "Let me know as soon as you are done and we can spend some proper time together. I love you," and with that she turned away and walked out of the door. She was gone again.

He picked up his cell phone and called London.

"Hello?" Lawson's familiar voice said.

"Have you seen the news?" he asked

"Yes, an hour ago."

"Did you know that was coming?"

"What do you mean?" Lawson asked.

"Well I would put a thousand dollars on the fact that you have slept with Abbi Beglin by now," the line went quiet, "So did she mention it?"

"Not a word. I was as surprised as you were."

"Can you use your charm and get everything you can out of her. I need to know who told her how this story was going to run."

"OK. I'm seeing her shortly when she leaves the office at ten," Lawson confirmed.

Ward looked at his watch. It was three thirty, making it eight thirty in London.

"That means you have an hour and a half to do some other things for me then."

"Shoot."

"Find out all you can on Martin Walker the Chief News Editor. I mean everything. Family, education, school friends; I want you to dig so deep that you find what he use to dream about when he was six months old," Ward said.

"I'm on it. I'll get my best two people on it. They will find anything that is there to be found," Lawson replied.

"Thanks. And squeeze Beglin for all she is worth," he said and then hung up the phone.

Everything was now taking shape in his mind and the picture was becoming clearer to him. But this was going much deeper than he initially thought. At the moment, he was raising more questions than finding answers. Why would the broadcasters break protocol and reveal that an impending incident was coming to New York? And why would a rogue FFW bomber be so brazen in what he was doing?

He picked out the note that Charlie Dunno had written on and looked at the one word on it. He couldn't link the word to what was happening, but he knew deep down that Charlie was probably right. He always was. The silence in the apartment was broken by the ringing of his cell phone.

"Your chariot awaits sir," Gilligan said

Ward checked his watch. "You are two minutes early," he said and hung up.

SEVENTEEN

Asif Fulken was in Greenwich Village, trying to blend in. Blending in is not easy to do when you have no particular place to go or no specific thing to do. He didn't want to be close to places where a large number of people were, this invariably led to a greater police presence; so he found himself in a place called The Four Faced Liar, just off of West 4th Street. An apt name for him he thought. It was a casual bar; the kind of place where students go to discuss poetry and talk about the text book politics they believe in. He had stumbled across the bar when walking down the street. From the outside, it looked like a normal shop front. It looked more likely to sell furniture than alcohol. Inside, there was a long bar on the right hand side, with a number of worn, wooden bar stools running along the front that had clearly seen better days. Seats for the hardened drinkers he thought. Behind the bar, the whole wall was stocked heavily with bottle upon bottle of alcohol. He ordered a soda and went and sat on a table in the corner of the bar, placing the copy of the New York Times that he had purchased an hour ago on the table and started to read. No point in pretending to read when you have a newspaper in front of you he thought; regardless of the fact that he had no interest in the newspapers content. The western media, it truly was an evil thing.

He placed his cell phone on the table and waited patiently for the call from Al Holami. He wasn't concerned about there being a problem, the security people were always getting close, but as far as he was concerned, their misguided tolerance always stopped them from pushing too hard. Sure they had a few people who were of similar warrior status to his people, but they were few and far between. Take away their weapons, their jets and their bombs and they were weak. In psychological combat, they would always lose. All of these thoughts were running through his head, and he was starting to feel invincible once more.

His cell phone rang.

"Yes?" he answered.

"Are you in New York safely?" the very well-spoken English voice said.

"Of course I am."

"You have caused quite a stir."

"Wasn't that the intention?" he asked.

"Now they know it is you behind it they are panicking," the voice said.

"And so they should. It won't read well if I get caught," he proclaimed.

"For me or you?" the voice asked.

"Everyone involved."

"There is nothing that comes back to me I hope? You know the consequences if there is?"

"Are you getting worried?" Fulken asked.

"Should I be getting worried?"

"My friend, I am teasing you," he replied, "There is nothing that can trace any part you might have played in this. You have my word."

"I'm to take the word of a terrorist on good faith? It may well be that you are at the top of the tree in your game, but there are some equally competent people chasing you, so I have been informed."

"What people?" he asked.

"Well, according to my people, men at the top in their fields, the very best," the voice said.

"Well, I will kill them too," Fulken proclaimed.

"Are you putting the wheels in motion?"

"I have a minor problem at the moment which will be resolved shortly."

"Do I need to be concerned?"

"No. Just the big bears sniffing around. It is to be expected," he said reassuringly.

"Are they getting close?"

"No. They are working through a list of potential contractors. They are simply trying to squeeze everyone that would be likely to help me and hoping to get lucky."

"And will they get lucky?"

"No they will not."

"Why not?"

"Because no one but you and me know what is happening."

"And you are confident that it will stay that way?" the well-spoken voice asked.

"One hundred per cent," Fulken replied in a tone of voice that reassured the listener completely.

"How long will it take you to prepare and to be ready to present the quote?"

"No more than twelve hours once I have everything that I need."

"With regards to the equipment that you need, do you have it?" the voice asked

"I will do once my friends have provided shelter. They are very resourceful," Fulken said with confidence, "And my creative freedom on this project will please you no end."

"I'm concerned that you underestimate those chasing you."

"Don't be concerned. All that matters to you is that you meet your payment agreements. I'm not the kind of business partner you want to disappoint," Fulken said threateningly.

"I will provide twenty four hours' notice before anything happens. You know that, yes?" the voice asked.

"Yes. As with the other two deals, you will know exactly where we are with this at all times," he replied.
"Good. I will be in touch soon."
The line went dead.

He sat at the table feeling very confident. He continued reading his paper for a further five minutes and his phone rang again.
"Yes?"
"My brother, it is me. Sorry for the delay," Al Holami said.
"Is everything fixed?" he asked.
"Yes. We had to sacrifice five of our brothers to escape but they died as martyrs," Al Holami proclaimed.
Fulken rolled his eyes. This man was clearly no warrior or a man in tune with being involved in a big operation. His references on the phone to martyrs would be picked up by anyone scanning the airwaves and lead to problems. He made the decision that when this was done, he would kill Al Holami for his incompetence.
"My brother," he said, "Refrain from using certain words on the phone. Speak like a businessman."
"I am so sorry to offend you. You are right. Please forgive me," Al Holami replied nervously.
"You have a nice place prepared for me?"
"Yes. The place is on West 8th Street. There is a recording studio there called Chiming Recordings. Next door is the safe house, apartment block 50, number 22 on the fifth floor."
"Good," Fulken replied.
"That is your safe place and I have staff in there waiting for you and they will source and acquire whatever you need to make your stay with us successful," Al Holami said, with a tone of voice that showed he was clearly pleased with himself for embracing the game and talking like a businessman.
"You have done well my brother. I shall see you there in thirty minutes. I need to finish reading my newspaper first," he said and then hung up.

I am definitely going to kill that fool, Fulken thought to himself. But for now, I will tolerate him, and probably his people too. I cannot leave any lose ends. The voice may not be able to get to me but he and his people know where all of my family are.

He thought back to the first contact that they made with him fourteen months ago when they gave him an opportunity to escape his captors, an opportunity that he took with both hands. The day after they had set him free, they had shown him the pictures of his family; the family that he had hidden so well, who he truly believed were untraceable, going about their normal everyday business. He had agreed to their plan, and with the money that he was being paid, he could move them all to a new country to start again. All in all, he concluded, all of this had worked out very well. One part left to complete and he would be free of them forever. Then they could never bother him again.

EIGHTEEN

Ward and Gilligan drove to Nicole-Louise's and Tacklers in silence. Ward sensed that there was something bothering Gilligan.

"What's wrong?" he asked.

"Nothing's wrong. Why do you think there is?" Gilligan replied.

"Because we've been in the car for ten minutes and you haven't made one wisecrack yet."

"OK," Gilligan said, "When we were in the building on East 3rd Street, and I took that guy down as we were walking up the stairs, I was thinking what if I hadn't of been walking backwards?"

"But you were walking backwards," he replied.

"I would have been a sitting duck," Gilligan continued, "And my two boys would have no daddy coming home tonight."

"Wouldn't happen," he said dismissively, "People like us don't survive through luck."

"Luck is just luck," Gilligan replied with a sigh.

Ward paused for a few moments and then spoke,

"We get by on instinct. You instinctively walked backwards, in a split second you had assessed the situation, carried out a mental risk assessment, and got in the right position. You didn't think about that. You just did it. You always will," he said.

"You're right, I know you are. Just with it being my boy's birthday tomorrow, it kinda gets you thinking about things like that."

Ward could see how much being a family man and a father meant to Gilligan. At that moment he envied him more than anyone else in the world. He had it all. He also gave a thought to Gilligan's kids waiting for their giant of a father to come home, all excited. He imagined Gilligan picking his boys up, one in each arm, and them laughing. It made him feel a little guilty for telling Gilligan that for the next few days, his life belonged to him.

"Here's what we will do. We have a lot of people to see today but we will be done by 10pm. Tomorrow, have the morning with your boy on his birthday and we can go hunting the bad guys after that. I'll meet you at twelve wherever I am."

Gilligan's face lit up. It warmed Ward,

"You sure? Honestly, you don't mind?" Gilligan asked.

"Yes I'm sure. And anyway, I'll probably get further without you," he replied with a smile.

"Thanks. I mean it."

"No worries, Marvin."

They arrived at Nicole Louise's' apartment fifteen minutes later. Tackler answered the door.

"Hey. Come in," he said.

Ward and Gilligan walked in.

Nicole-Louise was sitting at her workstation.

"Do you have anything for me?" Ward asked.

"Yes we do," she said. "This studio that you wanted us to look into and the surrounding buildings brought up something interesting," she replied.

"Such as?"

"Pretty much the whole block is owned by a guy called Sameh Ismail. He's a former Afghan national who came here under direct supervision of the CIA and then became a U.S. citizen and totally legit businessman just six months later. There is no reference about him in any CIA databases anywhere," she said in her efficient tone.

Ward looked at Gilligan, "He must have a handler. Can you find out who?" he asked him.

"I have a few friends who work in off the record operations, I'll see what I can do," he said as he walked to the side of the room and took out his cell phone.

"That's not all," Nicole-Louise continued, "It seems from the really, really hidden stuff that I found, that he used to be on one of the agencies most wanted lists."

"Why?" Ward asked.

"I can't find that information anywhere."

"What do you have on Al Holami?"

"A lot," she replied, "And that's the problem. We didn't even have to try too hard to find it. We have been doing this long enough to know when information is hidden not to be found and when it is put there to be found."

"So you think that Al Holami is a simple patsy? That Sameh Ismail is the real threat and Al Holami is a simple runner?"

"Yes I do," she replied.

"So can you build me up a picture of Ismail and get me an address for him?" Ward asked.

"We can do anything. It will just take time."

"Time is something we don't have."

"That's odd," Gilligan said from the other side of the room. They all looked at him.

"What?" Ward asked.

"According to my source, and he's very reliable, Sameh Ismail is dead. He died fourteen months ago."

"That can't be right. His bank accounts, his business and all of his bills are live and being used, even today," Tackler shouted, looking over his shoulder.

"Used for what?" Ward asked him.

"Hang on, I'll go back and look," Tackler said, as he spun around and got to work on his computer.

"Where are you with the list of potential bomb makers and likely suppliers of explosives in the New York area?" he asked Nicole-Louise.

"There are three likely people. Two bomb makers, one supplier," she said as she hunted around for a piece of paper.

"Here it is." she said after ten seconds of searching, "The two bomb makers are Ahmad Saleem who lives in Hell's Kitchen on West 46th Street, and Ali Yassin who lives in Midtown East on East 55th Street. The supplier is Osama Ayad who is in Kips Bay on East 29th Street. Their addresses are written down here," she said as she handed Ward the piece of paper, "I have pictures of Saleem and Yassin but nothing yet on Ayad. I will e-mail it as soon as I have it," she added, passing him two crystal clear printed sheets with the two men's pictures on it.

"So," Ward said, "Al Holami isn't the support here, Sameh Ismail is but he is dead so he can't be the one and the CIA have no record of him?"

"Sounds about right," Nicole-Louise replied.

"That's not quite a dead end," Tackler interrupted, "The last three large transactions on his bank account were cash withdrawals made at local banks. The last withdrawal being for thirty thousand dollars."

"When?" Ward asked.

"This morning," Tackler replied.

"Where?"

"Kips Bay."

"I need to make a call," Ward said and left the room.

He called Centrepoint.

"I wondered when you would bother calling in," he answered.

"What do you know about Sameh Ismail?" Ward asked.

"What do you want to know?"

"Is he dead?"

"No," Centrepoint replied.

"But he is protected, right?"

"For good reason, yes."

"Which is?" Ward enquired.

"Not something you need to know. But he's not helping Fulken that's for sure," Centrepoint stated.

"How can you be so sure?"

"Because Sameh Ismail is Asif Fulken."

"Explain the whole thing to me clearly," Ward demanded.

"It's pretty simple. The CIA got him on board two years ago. His intel led to the capture of at least six live cells that were operating in both America and the U.K," Centrepoint replied.

"And in return we gave him?"

"Full immunity from any prosecution, a passport and citizenship, and businesses to the tune of half a million dollars."

"So how did he turn half a million dollars into a business that owns about six properties?" Ward asked.

"There is some confusion there, or rather a lack of specifics. He got the right people running them for him I guess," The Old Man replied, sounding decidedly disinterested.

"That's it?" said Ward, "You gave him all of that and then just walked away?"

"It's never that simple, you know that"

"Then what happened. Who lost him?"

"He disappeared, fourteen months ago. Just one day he was there, the next day he wasn't," Centrepoint conceded.

"That's it, just like that, and that never set alarm bells off?"

"Of course it did. His handler couldn't find him. A guy called Gill Whymark."

"But then he was just erased from the records and everyone hoped he wouldn't come back? But now he has, and all of the big boys in Washington are in a panic?" Ward said.

"That's about it," he replied.

"So now I know why they called us in. If it goes wrong, it's nothing to do with them?"

"That's about it," he repeated.

Ward hung up the phone and walked back into the room where the others were waiting for him.

"Everything OK?" Gilligan asked, noticing the frown on Ward's face.

"Sort of," he replied. He then spent a few minutes repeating the conversation that he had just had with Centrepoint to them all.

"Christ," said Gilligan, "That's really bad for the agency."

"We at least have a better starting point than we did before," Nicole-Louise said without turning around.

118

"How so?" asked Ward.

"We have the cash withdrawal dates and we can hack into the bank security cameras and see who takes it out. We can also steal all the money that belongs to Sameh Ismail so he has no resources," she said.

"Hack into the bank and find out who withdrew it but leave the money in the accounts for now because we don't want to let him know we are on it," Ward replied.

"I still can't believe that all of this is down to our own people," Gilligan said yet again.

"What's done is done," Ward said, "What we have to do now is move forward and resolve it in the way we know best,

We can point fingers and criticise people after," he added.

"This is getting difficult. Even if we know that Fulken is actually Ismail and find the guys who are supporting him, we still have no idea who is behind it," Gilligan said.

"I think what we now know has made all the difference in finding the people behind it too," Ward replied.

"How so?" Gilligan asked with raised eyebrows.

"With regards to piecing it all together," he said, "Our job just got a whole lot easier."

"How is that exactly?" Gilligan asked.

Ward ignored the question.

"The closest place to us on this list is in Midtown East so we should visit that first. This guy Ali Yassin," Ward said looking at Nicole-Louise, "What do we know about him?"

"He is an Iraqi national who has been here for twelve years. He owns an electrical shop down on East 55th Street and according to the information; the CIA had him detained at Guantanamo Bay four years ago, for two months, when a plot to blow up Madison Square Gardens was foiled," she said with her usual efficiency.

"They had nothing on him?"

"No. They held him for so long because his place had traces of explosives all over it but they found no equipment that could put a bomb together and he just pleaded innocence. After the intervention of his lawyers, they had to let him go."

"But he is high on our list of potentials?" Gilligan interrupted.

"Yes, he was third on the list," Nicole-Louise replied.

"The other two?" he asked.

"Both dead. Ironically they blew themselves up when building bombs, so you can move him up to the top spot," she replied without a hint of sarcasm.

"Can you hack into the satellite feed now and see what is happening?" Ward asked.

"Of course I can," she tapped her keyboard for a minute and said, "Here it is."

All three of them walked over to her and crowded behind her, looking at the screen.

Just off of 2nd Avenue and adjacent to a synagogue on East 55th Street, a little red dot was flashing. The area looked busy but not overly. The roads were clear. It was hard to get a defined look at the people on the street from the imagery in front of them but nothing looked out of place or suspicious. They all watched what was happening for a few minutes in silence.

"Let's go," Ward said to Gilligan.

NINETEEN

On the drive to Midtown East, Ward's phone rang. It was Centrepoint.

"Yes?" he answered.

"I have set an appointment for you with Martin Walker at 8.30pm tonight," The Old Man said.

"Where?"

"USBC have offices on 6th Avenue. He will be expecting you."

Ward hung up the phone.

"Problem?" Gilligan asked.

"We have an appointment with a guy at USBC on 6th Avenue," Ward said.

Gilligan nodded.

"That works out well for us, we won't be far away, and by the time we have cut across from Midtown East and seen him we will be done for the day," he added.

Gilligan nodded again.

They continued the drive and Ward studied the photo of Ali Yassin that Nicole-Louise had given him with an intensity that unnerved Gilligan, and he got the feeling that Ward was psyching himself up for the kill, like his eyes were fixed on Yassin's, but he said nothing. They reached 2nd Avenue and parked the car.

"What number?" Gilligan asked.

"310," Ward replied.

Gilligan crossed the road without prompting and walked opposite Ward at a steady pace.

They reached number 310. It was a twelve story building built out of brown brick. It was a newish building and the bottom floor housed a few shops; 'Eclectic Electrics' being the one to the far right, and the one they were interested in.

Ward walked past and stopped just past the Conservative Synagogue. Gilligan crossed the road and joined him.

"How do you want to play this one?" he asked.

"I want to start putting real pressure on them," Ward replied, "I think time is running out."

"I'll follow your lead then, Chief," Gilligan said, gesturing with his hand for Ward to lead the way.

They walked back towards the shop and entered.

The inside was typical of an electrical shop. The shelves were laid out in neat symmetry, like looking down on blocks of buildings with a satellite. They were all stacked neatly and everything was in a logical order. Plug fittings through to cables, light switches through to lights, and there were small signs defining each area such as Lighting, Bathroom and Commercial.

The floor was covered with a clean, grey carpet that made the place look cared for.

There were three employees in the shop. They all looked like Iraqi nationals as Ward expected. People were inclined to support their own when setting up business in a new country, and they were all looking very busy, picking items up and re-positioning them on the shelves.

There were two customers in the shop, both construction workers by the look of it, one being served by three other guys behind the counter, and the other looking at refrigerator elements, completely confused, judging by the way that he was scratching his head and rubbing his chin.

All of the guys behind the counter looked like they didn't belong there. They were all big, each over six feet and muscular looking, a fact emphasised by the cut off, red tee shirts emblazoned with 'Eclectic Electrics' that they wore.

Judging by the way the guy in the middle seemed to be holding a more prominent position, with the two other guys giving him at least three feet of space on either side, he was the main man and they were the lieutenants. But none of the people in the shop were Ali Yassin.

Ward approached the counter just as the first contractor finished paying for his goods and left the shop. The guy in the middle eyed him suspiciously. Ward held eye contact with him.

"Hello, Sir, how can I help?" the guy to the right of the main man asked in clear English.

"I'm looking for some specialist equipment," Ward replied.

As soon as the two lieutenants picked up on his British accent, and after taking a long look at Gilligan, their body language completely changed. They all seemed to breath in, arch their shoulders back, and attempt to show him how big they were.

The guy in the middle did not break eye contact with Ward

"We have lots of that here, Sir. What is it that you are specifically looking for?" the guy on the left asked.

"Great service guys," he said, "I can't remember the last time I walked into a shop and got hit with dual customer service like this."

"What do you want?" the guy in the middle asked Ward aggressively.

As he finished his sentence, Ward heard the shop doorbell ring which notified him that the other contractor had left the shop. Empty handed and still confused no doubt, Ward thought to himself.

Gilligan walked to the door, put the lock down and turned the shop sign to 'Closed'.

"What do you want?" the main man asked again, this time in an even more aggressive tone.

"I told you," Ward said, "I want some specialist equipment."

"Meaning?" he asked.

The guy to the right of him nodded to someone over Ward's left shoulder, and the three employees who were working on the shop floor all converged behind them and stood still,

123

hands passively down by their sides, but clearly with their weight on one foot, ready to pounce.

Ward heard Gilligan snort his contempt, and knew without turning around that he would be looking them up and down, sizing them up and that they would be hoping that this did not escalate into violence because from just looking back at Gilligan, they would know that they had no chance.

"Meaning that you are the go-to people for what I want, so you can provide me with what I need. Isn't that how customer service works?" Ward innocently asked.

"So what is it you want?" the guy in the middle said for the third time, still holding his aggressive tone.

"I want some equipment to make a bomb," he said, as nonchalantly as if he was asking for a 3 Amp fuse, "And after that, I want you to tell me where Ali Yassin is."

"We can't help you with either," the guy in the middle replied, "Please leave our shop," he added, raising his voice.

"It's not your shop, is it?"

"I am the manager and I don't want you here. We have rights, we are protected and we don't have to listen to your crap so get out now before we throw you out," the guy said, moving from behind the counter to the left.

The lieutenant who had been standing to the left of the main man leant under the counter and came out with a baseball bat; the other lieutenant leant under and picked up a cosh. Ward raised his eyebrows in a mock startled look. The main man then put a hand in his trouser pocket and pulled out a switchblade, making a grand gesture in extending the blade fully.

These were no more than simple followers, he thought. Reasonably adequate in a street fight but they would hold no sway with the elders and had no influence on the impending events.

But they would more than likely know where Ali Yassin would be at this moment in time.

Ward turned around and looked at the three guys that Gilligan was standing square onto and they all had a resigned look on their faces.

"Anyone else?" Gilligan said, aiming the question at all three of them rather than one specific person. None of them responded.

He turned back to the counter and looked at the leader, "You come into my country and talk about your rights. You think you are more important than our own people and you abuse our hospitality. You think you can ignore my requests?" he said in a completely calm and measured manner.

Confusion covered their faces. They were struggling to compute how a guy with a British accent was declaring America to be his own country. He always used this to his advantage.

"You stand there trying to intimidate me with bits of wood and a blade," he added. "How disappointing."

Without any additional words or grand gestures, he pulled out his silenced Glock from inside his waistband and shot the guy in the kneecap.

The scream of agony rang around the shop, even before the echo of the gunshot had faded away.

The other two guys, the faithful lieutenants, had a huge dilemma now.

Would they attack a guy holding a gun with bits of wood or face the humiliation of surrendering without a fight?

He knew the answer, and paid no attention to them at all.

The only guy who could help him was the guy rolling around the floor, clutching his right knee in agony.

"Was that necessary?" Gilligan asked.

Ward was unsure whether it was an attempt at humour or genuine concern. He chose the former and ignored it.

He looked at the two lieutenants who were frozen to the spot. "Do either of you know where Ali Yassin is?" he asked nonchalantly. They both shook their heads.

"Then I may as well kill you both now," he said, raising his Glock.

"Stop, please, I have his phone number," the guy with the cosh said.

"We already have that," Ward lied.

"Not his private number you don't," the guy pleaded.

"Write it down for my friend there," he said pointing towards Gilligan.

The three guys under Gilligan's care all nodded in unison towards the guy with the cosh, prompting him to do it, and do it quickly.

The guy wrote it down and handed it to Gilligan.

Ward looked at the guy who was holding the baseball bat and there was something in his eyes that told him that he had changed his mind and was going to back the option of making a stand. This feeling was confirmed by the way that the guy was shifting his weight onto his left leg.

Ward wasn't going to wait; he wasn't going to see how it played out. Taking unnecessary risks wasn't part of his DNA. He turned slightly, raised his Glock waist high and without a pause, shot him in the kneecap of the leg that was holding all of his weight.

The guy collapsed into a heap and let out a scream identical to that of his friend, who by this time, was hyperventilating with the sheer pain that the bullet had generated.

The last guy holding the cosh was now frozen in complete terror. Ward crouched down to the main man and bent in towards him.

"There are no rules and no protection for you in my world, so I am going to ask you questions and you will answer them. If I think you are lying to me I will put a bullet straight into your head, no second time of asking. Do you understand?" he calmly said.

The guy nodded through gritted teeth and short, desperate breaths.

He could tell by the look of fear in his eyes that he was not going to lie to him.

"Do you know Sameh Ismail?" he asked.

The main man nodded.

Ward knelt on his knee and the guy let out a sickening scream.

"Yes, I know who he is," he said quickly.

"Has he been here today?"

"No," the guy said.

"Do you know who Asif Fulken is?"

"They are one and the same," the guy replied.

"Is Ali Yassin making equipment available for him?"

There was the slightest of pauses and the guy said, "Yes."

"Do you know what Fulken has planned?"

"No."

"I need more," Ward demanded, as he started to lean on the guys' knee again.

"No, I swear I do not. But I know it is big. Ali has been cautious all week and saying that something very big is coming."

"Did they make the bomb here?" Ward asked with an air of conviction that said he already knew the answer, even though he had no idea.

The guys' pupils widened. This was his moment of truth, Ward could see that. The guy paused for a split second and he could almost see the conflict swirling around in his brain. But he knew he would answer.

Anyone who answered one question would always answer them all. It was just how it was.

"Not the complete bomb," he said, an air of defeat running through his voice.

"I need more."

Ward leaned forwards again.

"They made the timer and the switch."

"How will it be activated?" Ward asked.

"Through a cell phone."

"You said 'They' made the switch. Who are 'They'?"

"Ali and Ahmad Saleem," the guy said.

"Do they have the explosives?"

"No."

"Where will they get them?"

"From Osama Ayad. Then they will put everything together."

"Do you know Al Holami?"

"Yes."

"Where does he fit in?" Ward asked.

"I heard Ali talking to him. He is to provide shelter for someone important."

"Who is it?"

"I don't know," the guy replied.

He didn't know. Ward could see it in his eyes.

He raised his gun in line with the guy's head and looked him in the eyes, "Where is Ali Yassin now?" he asked.

"I don't know," the guy said, desperation running through his voice.

"Then you haven't told me anything I don't already know," Ward said.

"Wait!" the guy said in panic, "There is something I know."

"What?"

"Ali was saying something about meeting their guest tomorrow on West 8th Street."

"By the recording studio?" Ward asked.

"Yes! That's it. I swear," the guy replied.

Ward stood up, and looked at Gilligan,

"It seems Nicole-Louise and Tackler were very much on the ball," he said.

"Yes but what are we going to do with this mess?" Gilligan asked.

Ward thought for a few seconds.

They could take them all into custody as accessories but that would alert Ali Yassin that they were onto him, and if they just walked out then they would be on the phone to Yassin immediately.

"We should just kill them all now," Ward replied without a hint of a smile.

Gilligan looked at him and then looked even harder to see if there was a twinkle in his eye to show he was joking, but he saw nothing. This unnerved him.

The three guys who Gilligan was standing guard over looked at him, pleading with him to do something.

"You know someone who could babysit these guys in here until tomorrow?" Ward asked.

"I would need to make a call but I could have someone here in ten minutes. Our clean-up crew loves it when you are in town, overtime goes through the roof!" Gilligan replied.

"Make the call," Ward said,

He looked down at the main man on the floor,

"If Yassin contacts you and you say one word to warn them that we were here I will come back and shoot you all dead. Do you understand that?" he asked.

"Yes I do," he replied.

Ward knew he was telling the truth.

Gilligan finished his call,

"They will be here in ten minutes. Don't worry, I took the liberty of asking for a medic to come with them in case you were concerned," he added.

Ward ignored him.

"I need to make a call. Think you can watch these warriors on your own for ten minutes?" he asked Gilligan as he walked out of the shop.

TWENTY

Outside the shop Ward called Lawson in London.

"Yes?" Lawson answered, clearly out of breath.

"I take it you are with Abbi Beglin right now?"

"Yes. That would be correct," Lawson replied.

Ward heard him moving from one room to another and closing the door.

He momentarily had a vision of Abbi Beglin sprawled naked over Lawson's bed.

"What did you get on Walker?"

"I have literally e-mailed it to you twenty minutes ago."

"You think he is involved in this in any way?" Ward asked.

"It looks likely. Have a look and see what you think."

"And Beglin?"

"She's not involved," Lawson said.

"Actually, she is involved. She just doesn't know it," Ward replied.

"And what do you want me to do with that information?" Lawson asked.

"I want you to sit down with her and run through the Louvre bombing again. Exactly what happened."

"You could do it yourself," Lawson said.

Ward wasn't sure by his tone of voice if Lawson was being serious or defensive.

"How so?"

"She's flying to New York in four hours' time to report on a news awards ceremony there in a few days" Lawson replied.
"And her crew are all coming with her?"
"Yes. They are meeting Walker there," Lawson said, convinced he was telling Ward something he didn't know.
"You know what I am going to say next, don't you?"
"Yes. And I have already booked my ticket. I will ring you when we get there."
Ward hung up the phone.

He walked back into the shop, just as a black van pulled up outside and four guys got out, each one of them nodding at him as they walked in.
"You got that piece of paper with the phone number on?" he asked Gilligan, who then proceeded to check the pockets of his pants before pulling it out of his jacket pocket and handing it to Ward.
"I'll meet you outside," he said.
Outside in the street, he called Nicole-Louise.
"Hello?" she answered.
"I have a phone number. Can you trace it and tell me where it is now?" he asked her.
"If it's on, yes."
He read out the number and heard her tapping on a keyboard.
"Whose number is it?" she asked, obviously waiting for the cell tower she had hacked into to pick up the signal.
"Ali Yassin, one of the names you gave me earlier," Ward replied.
"How convenient."
"What?" he asked.
"I've found the phone."
"Where is it?"
"It's in Hell's Kitchen. At 437, West 46th Street, in a building owned by one of the other names we gave you earlier. The property belongs to Ahmad Saleem. Apartment 24. God we are good!" she exclaimed.
"Yes you are," Ward replied and hung up the phone.

He opened the e-mail from Lawson and read with interest. The excessive money movements, the extreme travel schedules, the history of being sympathetic to the oppressed, it was all there. MI6 had done a good job digging on Walker. But something Nicole-Louise had said earlier niggled away at him.

"*We have been doing this long enough to know when information is hidden not to be found, and when it is put there to be found,*" she had said.

He pulled out his cell and hit redial.

"Forgot something?" she said.

"You know what you were saying earlier about things being put in places so they would be found?" he asked.

"Yes."

"I'm going to send you some information that MI6 found, Can you look at it and give me your take on it, and then maybe dig a little deeper to see how it got there?" he asked.

"I can do anything," she replied.

He hung up the phone and forwarded the e-mail that Lawson had sent him.

Gilligan came out of the shop a couple of minutes later.

"Another mess cleared up," he said and sighed.

It was now 6.30pm, two hours before their scheduled meeting with Martin Walker.

"This all seems like a bit of a mess, doesn't it?" Gilligan asked.

"On the contrary, it is all pretty clear now apart from one thing," Ward replied.

"Which is?" Gilligan asked.

"Who?"

"We know who. It's Fulken or Ismail or whatever you want to call him," Gilligan replied.

"See my friend, that's why I'm in charge. It's always about the bigger picture," Ward replied, realising immediately that he was starting to sound like The Old Man.

Gilligan laughed to himself.

"What?" Ward asked.

"There's a bomb about to go off in New York and you are as calm as anything."

"That's because the bomb will never go off," he replied.

They drove via East 57th Street and Ninth Avenue and parked fifty yards back from Saleem's place.

The building was a white brick, six-storey building with a green yawning over the entrance displaying the numbers '437' in silver. The steps up to the entrance door were painted battleship grey and the entrance door was made of glass with a three inch wooden frame surround.

As they approached the steps a guy was coming out of the building in his running gear and he politely held the door for them as they reached the top of the steps. Ward nodded his gratitude to the guy and they watched him bounce down the steps and set off at a faster than normal pace; clearly trying to impress the people who he assumed shared his apartment building.

They walked in. The hallway was clean and spacious. No clutter anywhere. The carpet was an industrial type, in a light fawn colour. Set against the white walls it gave the entrance a fresh, cared for and probably as intended, expensive feel to it.

"What apartment number?" Gilligan asked.

"Twenty four."

"Great, it had to be on the top floor," he groaned.

Ward drew his weapon and walked slowly up the stairs and this unnerved Gilligan once more. There was nothing to indicate that they were expected or that they were walking into the lion's den. They reached the top floor and number twenty four was right in front of them at the end of the hallway.

"How are we doing this?" Gilligan asked.

"Maybe we should just knock on the door and shout Pizza?"

"Do you think, possibly, that we can go in and ask questions without killing anyone for a change?" Gilligan asked.

"No."

Once again, Gilligan didn't know whether Ward was joking or not.

He walked up to the door and rapped on it three times.

"Pizza!" he shouted.

Gilligan could not believe what he was seeing.

Five seconds later a guy in his early forties opened the door. He looked Syrian, he was athletic but not toned, and he had a look about him that told Ward he had seen enough death and destruction in his life to not be intimidated by anything.

"We haven't ordered Pizza," he said.

Without warning, Ward adjusted his feet and kicked the guy hard between the legs.

The guy doubled over and hit the floor, without making any noise at all, which Ward found strange.

He stepped into the apartment and Gilligan followed, dragging the guy into the hallway and placing his hands behind his back, before cable tying him to the radiator. The guy was unconscious; the sheer pain had made him pass out.

"At least you didn't shoot him," Gilligan said.

Ward ignored him.

The hallway was about twenty five feet long and about ten feet in was a door to the right and another opposite it on the left. Ten feet further down it had two similar doors on either side. They were all a light oak colour. The walls were all painted brilliant white and the carpet was cream with a deep pile to it. It looked like an expensive place. There was a door at the end of the hallway that was ajar.

With his gun to his side, Ward approached it cautiously. He could hear voices coming from inside. He studied the voices for a few seconds and put five fingers up to Gilligan indicating that he could hear five voices inside.

Gilligan had his gun ready but still had no idea what Ward was going to do next.

A voice from inside shouted, "Jamil!" and two seconds later, "Jamil," again, the second time the voice a lot nearer to the door.

Ward took a step back and as the door opened, a Middle Eastern guy in his thirties with a long beard pulled the door back, took one step into the hallway, and then stopped in his tracks when he saw Ward standing there with his Glock pointed at him and as he opened his mouth to speak, Ward shot him straight in the face.

The guys' head exploded and the brilliant white walls and cream carpet were instantly covered with blood and brain matter. He fell backwards into the room and Ward stepped on him as he entered, leaving enough room for Gilligan to come in behind him.

At the table there were four guys.

Their faces froze when they looked at him.

One of the guys was in his late twenties and looked like he was the protector and the only one likely to fight.

He recognised Ali Yassin and Ahmad Saleem immediately from their pictures, but he didn't know who the other guy sitting with them was. He was in his late fifties, sported a long beard and he sat passively and motionless.

He walked took three steps and said, "Put your hands on the table."

They all immediately responded.

"What do you want?" Ahmad Saleem asked.

"Gentlemen," Ward said, "I want to talk."

TWENTY ONE

The four of them sat motionless, staring at Ward and Gilligan but not speaking.

The youngest guy was sitting nearest to Ward, closest to the door, and next to him sat the older guy. Yassin and Saleem sat opposite them.

There was an air of calm about them that said they had been through tough questioning a hundred times and they knew how to play the game.

Say nothing until prompted and show no fear.

These Americans never had the stomach to push beyond the line. They would always go so far, but their liberal rules stopped them from stepping over it.

But there was something different about this British man.

"Couldn't you have just asked to speak to us?" Ali Yassin asked.

Ward ignored him and stood there, studying them all for about thirty seconds. No emotion on his face, just looking at them, one at a time. He knew right then; they would be able to give him all the information he needed if he played it right. There was a dead guy lying on the floor with his face blown apart and they weren't remotely fazed. These were big players and they needed to be handled accordingly.

"Who are you?" Ward asked, pointing to the older guy.

The man looked at the table and said nothing.

Ward turned to Gilligan.

"See," he said, "You try and use manners and be civilised towards people and they just ignore you. Then they ask why we were reluctant to simply just ask to talk to them," he added.

"He is just a friend," Ahmed Saleem said.

"Can he not talk?" Ward asked.

"Not to you infidels he can't," the young protector spat.

"And who are you?"

He said nothing.

"Here's my problem. I know that you have helped Asif Fulken prepare a bomb that he intends to detonate in New York. What I need to do is find him before he sets it off," he said, "In regards to you, I don't care if you live or die, I really don't, but you will help me one way or the other."

The four of them said nothing. He looked at the young protector again.

"Who are you?" he asked, still using a calm and measured tone.

"I am Karrar Qasim," he replied.

"That's better. Now we are getting somewhere."

He looked at Gilligan.

"Have you heard of Karrar Qasim?" he asked him.

"Nope," Gilligan replied, deliberately sounding disinterested.

"What do you do, Karrar Qasim?"

"I don't need to tell you that."

"Actually you do," Ward said, "I need to know where you sit in the grand order of things so I can establish if I need to keep you alive or not," he added.

Qasim looked at the old man next to him for guidance and the old guy slowly nodded his permission for him to speak.

"I look after the affairs of the elders in the community who need my specialist help," he said.

"What are you a specialist in?"

Qasim looked at the old guy once more and again he nodded.

"I punish people for deserting their beliefs and their true callings. I punish people who the elders consider have become weak."

"Like a protector of faith?" Ward asked.

"If you like," Qasim replied.

"And the elders decide who is punished and how?"

"Yes."

"You kill people?"

"No. We are not savages like you. We are brave people, loyal to our faith. What are you? You are a coward. Take away your gun and what do you have left? Nothing! I would crush you," Qasim spat as he clenched his fists.

The old guy next to him put a hand on Qasim's arm and he stopped talking and looked back at the table. Ward turned to Gilligan,

"Well that wasn't very nice," he said.

Qasim snorted.

"So let me get this right. You think that if I put my gun down and stood to fight you like a man that you would crush me?"

Qasim's eyes lit up.

He could sense that a challenge was coming and he believed to the core that he could beat this man to death with his bare hands.

"Are the women, old men and children you punish unarmed?" Ward asked.

Qasim said nothing.

He was mentally psyching himself up for the impending challenge.

"Would you like me to put my gun down and fight you?" Ward asked nonchalantly.

"Yes I would," Qasim replied with a smile.

Ward lifted his gun and shot Qasim in the face from two feet away, the force of the bullet smashed him back into his chair, which immediately rocked onto its back legs and tipped over, Qasim only slid off of the seat when the back of the chair was flat on the floor.

There was blood everywhere. Ward had taken the initial release of blood over his arm and the old guy next to him was covered all over his chest and his beard, the spray even covering Yassin and Saleem. The whole table was a bloody mess.

Gilligan was once again unnerved by the sheer brutality that Ward possessed. He understood that it was fair to take some lives to save thousands and it wasn't that which unsettled him. It was the fact that Ward was by no means psychotic, yet he showed absolutely no remorse for killing bad guys. He was totally indifferent to death. Like a guy who can take pepperoni on his pizza or not.

Ward looked at the other three guys.

Their whole demeanour had changed.

Like they knew that death was inevitable.

The good thing about facing guys in that position is that they will normally take the smallest opportunity to salvage something good out of inevitability.

"You know why I shoot people in the face?" he asked the three of them.

No response.

He asked again.

"You, Yassin. Do you know why I shoot people in the face?"

"No I don't," Yassin replied immediately.

Ward said nothing.

The three of them sat there waiting for an answer to his question but it never came.

Instead he took out his phone and spent a whole minute checking his e-mails just to give them a little more thinking time.

"Who are you?" he asked, turning to the old guy.

"I am a simple grocer who has come for help from these two businessmen," he replied.

"What kind of help?"

"Help in bringing my family over to this country so that they can start a new life."

"Do they help people do that?"

"They have the money and the contacts so yes they do," the old guy replied.

"Are they going to help you?"

"I was waiting for their decision when you came in."

"Apologies," Ward said, "Let them give you their decision now," he added, waving his open palm over the table in a prompt to let Yassin and Saleem speak.

"Yes, we will my friend," Yassin said.

He could see that the old grocer was trying his hardest to look like the weak link.

The one most likely to crack.

The one with the most to lose.

Which meant he was the one with the most to hide.

He turned his attention back to Yassin and Saleem.

"I know that you have both built the device for Fulken," he said, "But that's OK, it won't go off anyway because I have pieced everything together and the people funding him are now in our custody," he lied.

The two men shot each other a nervous glance.

"Now what I need to know is where Al Holami has him holed up, so I can stop wasting any more of my time."

The mention of Al Holami's name visibly shook both of them.

"Tell me," he said looking at Saleem, "Where is he?"

"I do not know. That is the truth," Saleem replied.

"I believe you," Ward said.

He raised his gun and shot Saleem twice in the chest knocking him sideways off of his chair so he landed head first on the floor with a loud crunch.

Yassin shrieked and stood up.

"Sit down!" he demanded.

Yassin sat down.

Gilligan stood behind Ward, rolling his eyes and shaking his head.

"Now, Mr Yassin," he said, "Where is Al Holami hiding Asif Fulken?"

"He, he is down in East 3rd Street. He has him there," Yassin stuttered.

"Now I know you are telling the truth," Ward replied and raised his Glock and shot Yassin twice in the chest,

He fell from the chair in an almost identical fashion to Saleem.

"Jesus," Gilligan said, "Was that necessary?"

"Yes it was," he said. "They had prepared the switches and detonators for a bomb that is intended to kill hundreds of people in my city."

"So why say they were telling the truth?" he asked.

"Because they were," Ward replied, "Saleem didn't know where Al Holami was because he wasn't privy to that information, and Yassin genuinely thought that Fulken was holed up on East 3rd."

"I don't understand."

"Their work was done. Once they had passed over the switches and detonators there was nothing else for them to do, Isn't that right Mr Ayad?" Ward asked, looking at the old guy.

"You have me confused with someone else," the old man said calmly.

"You are Osama Ayad. I had assumed that anyway, but I got an e-mail with your picture on it a few minutes ago," he said.

Ayad said nothing.

"A grocer asking for help coming to a meeting with a bodyguard? Come on, give me a break," he laughed, "You had all you needed from those two," he added pointing towards the bodies of Yassin and Saleem on the floor.

Ayad held eye contact with Ward but didn't speak.

"And you are the one bringing the explosives to the party. The real big stuff," he added.

"You think it is all so simple, don't you?" Ayad said.

"In terms of your part in the overall play, yes I do," he replied, "It's always simple, people complicate it."

"I didn't have a choice. If I fail them or refuse to help them, the brothers can alienate me and I become a pariah," Ayad stated.

"Let's just do this the easy way and I will maybe let you walk out of here," Ward said, "Now, when is Fulken going to get into the country?"

"He is already here."

"That's a good start. I already knew that so we are building trust well."

Ayad smiled.

"Where is Al Holami hiding Fulken?"

"On West 8th Street."

"Next to the recording studio?"

Ayad's eyes widened.

Ward could see his surprise that he knew about the recording studio.

"Yes," he replied, "Number 50, apartment 14."

"How big is the bomb?" Ward asked.

"I got him 300 pounds of explosives," Ayad replied.

"That's a big bomb," he said calmly. "How is he moving it?"

"I don't know. A vehicle I assume."

"When did he collect the explosives and switches?"

"Some men I didn't recognise collected it all three days ago."

"Describe them?" Ward demanded.

"Iraqi's definitely. They said they got lost and so they must have been from out of state. They were all average build, average height and average looks."

"Thank you Mr Ayad. I believe you have told me the truth."

"Are you going to kill me?" Ayad asked.

"Yes I am," Ward replied.

"But I told you the truth."

"But you also planned to kill hundreds of Americans, and if I don't stop the bomb from going off then how do you think it will sit with me if I let you live, knowing that all of those people have died because of you?" Ward asked.

"Please, don't kill me. I can be of use in the future," Ayad pleaded.

"He's not going to kill you," Gilligan interrupted.

Before Ward could respond, Gilligan pumped three bullets into Ayad's chest, knocking him clean off the chair and onto the floor with the others.

"Was that really necessary?" Ward asked with a smile.

"Yes it was. They really see nothing wrong with killing hundreds of our people, do they?"

"No they don't."

"Then we have saved lives in the future."

"We need to get to Greenwich to hunt Fulken. Are you ready?"

"I'm ready," Gilligan replied.

TWENTY TWO

Ward called Centrepoint, as Gilligan sorted out, the by now, over-worked cleaning crew.

"Where are you?" he answered, sounding agitated.

"We have found Fulken," Ward replied.

"Where is he?"

"Holed up with Al Holami."

The Old Man was quiet for a moment,

"Al Holami is a small fish, how come Fulken is relying on him?" he eventually asked.

"Because he is about the only one left that Fulken can turn to," Ward replied.

"Don't be so sure of that," Centrepoint said, "There are almost a hundred willing and resourceful FFW sympathisers throughout New York. There is always someone to turn to."

"There's a lot less than that now."

"Try and be a little bit careful. This whole thing is becoming a real mess and I have just had a call about the number of bodies you are leaving in your wake. People will start asking questions."

"Then it's your job to keep them away from me and to pacify the powers that be."

"Which I will do," he said, "But you have to get a win on this one to justify the trail of destruction you are leaving behind."

"I always win," Ward replied.

"Have you established who Fulken's main sponsor is yet?"

"No," Ward replied, "But I know roughly where to look. The important thing is to eliminate him and ensure that there is no bomb going off. When I have done that, I will focus on who it is."

"Also the why?" Centrepoint asked.

"I know the why. I just can't make it fit yet," he said, thinking back to the one word that Charlie Dunno had written back in London.

"Well, make it fit quickly," Centrepoint demanded.

Ward hung up the phone.

Asif Fulken walked out of the apartment block to make a call. He didn't want anyone to be around when he spoke to the voice.

Al Holami was a bumbling fool but he had done well by ensuring that a safe place was provided and there were a team of four, more than capable looking men, to guard him. But they all had ears and they could all listen.

He headed down the street towards Greenwich Avenue. As he turned into the Avenue he took out his cell and dialled the number.

"Are you ready?" the voice answered.

"Yes I am. Everything is prepared."

"No mistakes?"

"None at all," Fulken replied.

"So you will be ready to finish the job tomorrow?"

"Yes. Have you put the other deposit in?"

"Yes I have."

"Good. I will check shortly."

"It is there. The bonus will be deposited an hour after the event," the voice said.

"Do you know the target?" Fulken demanded.

"It will be the Chrysler building, day after tomorrow at 10.00am exactly. That gives you nearly thirty six-hours to prepare."

"More than enough," Fulken replied.

The line went dead.

Ward and Gilligan arrived on West 8th Street and drove at a slow speed along the road to check out number 50.

They reached it and continued driving past.

Ward did no more than glance at the building.

That was enough.

It was a five storey building and it looked run down. The windows were the old Georgian style, painted white, and the paint was starting to peel off of them. The front brick had been painted red, and on the top floor there were four long wooden windows. Their frames looked rotten, even from just his brief glimpse. The whole building looked as though it wasn't really lived in. The entrance door was light oak coloured, with two big glass panels in it.

The street was relatively quiet.

Ward looked at Gilligan as they drove.

"What do you think?" he asked.

"I'm not sure," Gilligan replied.

"We have to get this right."

"I know, Chief. So far every call you have made has been right and you and your methods have gotten us here quickly. The combined CIA would probably be two days behind so I'll follow," Gilligan said.

"Does that building seem right to you?"

"It looks a bit shitty, but a building is a building, isn't it?" Gilligan snorted.

Ward rolled his eyes.

"You think he will have many guys in there?" Gilligan asked.

"I think they will have a few, no more than that. Al Holami is a small fish. I doubt he has the manpower, and I think the guys we took out earlier were his main people."

"So you think we should go in with guns blazing?"

"I think that when we see Fulken, we take him out immediately, either of us. We aren't going in there to ask questions. We are going in there to stop him from killing innocent people."

"I'm ready," Gilligan said, "Apartment number?" he asked.

"Fourteen."

Gilligan pulled in about thirty yards down the road from the building, there was no crossing the road this time, they walked along the sidewalk and reached the door of the apartment block. Gilligan tried the door and it was open.

He looked at Ward and raised his eyebrows in surprise.

"Think they could be waiting for us?" he asked.

"Maybe, only one way to find out," Ward said as he stepped through the door.

The hallway smelt musty and there was a worn, patchy red carpet running along the hallway and up the stairs. The walls were off-colour beige and there were four doors in the hallway marked one through to four. The paint was peeling off of them too.

"Looks like a shithole," Gilligan said.

Ward drew his Glock and attached the silencer.

Without speaking, Gilligan did the same.

They walked slowly up the stairs, Gilligan taking the position of walking backwards behind Ward, about three feet apart so they had every angle covered.

They walked up the first three flights of stairs and every landing looked the same.

Worn, uncared for, and neglected, and the higher they got the more the damp, musty smell crept into their nostrils.

They reached the fourth floor and saw that number fourteen was the second door on the left of the hallway. Ward put his finger to his lips to tell Gilligan he wanted silence and walked up to the apartment door to listen.

He put his ear to the door.

He could hear some muffled voices but they were inaudible and it was impossible to tell how many people were in there.

Gilligan looked at Ward and mouthed, "How many?" and Ward shrugged his shoulders.

He put his ear back against the door and leant lightly on it to see if he could hear more clearly and as he did so, the door opened, and Al Holami was standing right in front of him.

Before Al Holami could speak, Ward smashed the butt of his Glock into his face with his right hand and, with his left hand, pushed him back into the room with such force that his feet came off of the ground and he fell back, landing on his head while clutching his nose.

Over Al Holami's shoulder, Ward could see there were four men sitting on the sofas in an open plan lounge who were now in the process of urgently getting to their feet.

He scanned them and saw immediately that none of them were Fulken and without pausing, he pumped a bullet into each one of them. Put them down and then talk, he thought. Only this time he had been too thorough, and each shot he had fired was a kill shot.

Gilligan came in behind him, knelt down and put his knee on Al Holami's chest and Ward put his fingers to his lips to indicate he wanted silence.

At the back of the room was a closed door. To the right, two doors that were ajar and on the left, another door closed.

Ward moved to the right and nudged the first door open and then moved back behind the wall for cover.

Nothing happened.

He peered into the room and it was empty apart from a bed and a tatty old sofa. He bent down and checked under the bed, nothing.

He came out of the room and moved to the next door on the right.

He nudged the door again and took cover.

Nothing.

He peered in. Inside there was nothing. It was completely empty.

He came back out into the living area, stepped over two of the guys he had shot dead and moved to the closed door on the left.

He turned the handle slowly and pushed the door wide open. He could see a bath in one corner and a mirror on the wall. He craned his neck so he could use the mirror to see behind the door and all he could see was a toilet and a sink.

He stepped in and confirmed to himself that the room was empty. He came out of the bathroom and looked at the door on the far side of the room that was closed.

He looked at Gilligan, still with his knee on Al Holami's chest.

Al Holami's eyes were following Ward and when he started moving towards the door, his eyes started to show agitation and worry.

He looked scared.

Ward walked up to the door and stood to the right hand side of it.

He looked at Gilligan and nodded towards the door.

Gilligan aimed his gun.

Ward leant on the handle and pushed the door wide open then moved back behind the wall.

No movement.

Nothing.

Gilligan had his gun pointed at the doorway and shrugged in Wards Direction.

Ward put his head around the side and then pulled back to the cover of the wall again. The glimpse he had taken showed him the room had a lot of stuff in it, but no one was in there.

He stepped cautiously through the doorway and scanned the room. The room had clothes, two laptops, an unmade bed and a big leather bag at the foot of the bed.

But there was no Asif Fulken.

He stepped into the room and picked up the bag. There were passports in there, cash and a gun.

He walked out of the room.

"He's not here," he said to Gilligan.

"Where is he?" Gilligan asked Al Holami.

"Who?" Al Holami asked.

Gilligan yanked him to his feet,

"Where is he?" he asked again.

"Who are you looking for?"

Ward walked over to them both and studied Al Holami's face. He was a coward, he could see that.

"I will ask you once. If you don't tell me, I will kill you," he said.

"I don't know. He came here earlier but he went away. I don't know where he has gone."

"Do you know where he has the bomb?"

"No, I know nothing about that."

Ward could see he was lying.

"You know nothing about the bomb or nothing about where it is?"

"I know he said something is going to happen but I don't know what or where," Al Holami said with the genuine fear and anxiety that only a man telling the truth could show.

"There is no one left, you know that?"

Al Holami looked confused, he didn't understand.

"Yassin, Saleem, Ayad. They are all dead. I have killed them all. He has no one else to turn to."

Al Holami looked mortified at this news. He was out of his depth; he was just playing at being important.

"So," Ward continued, "What have you got to give to me that will stop me killing you?" he asked calmly.

"I have a number for him."

"Where?"

"In my cell phone, over there on the table," he said, pointing to a phone on the wooden coffee table, "It is under 'Brother Asif,'" he added.

Gilligan picked up the phone. He touched the screen and a numerical passcode request came up. He threw the phone at Ward who caught it.

"What's the code?" he asked.

Al Holami looked even more frightened than he had earlier. Ward raised his Glock to Al Holami's head.

"What's the code?" Ward asked, looking him right in the eyes.

"Zero, nine, one, one," Al Holami replied.

Ward entered the number '0-9-1-1'. The screen opened up. He clicked on his contact book and found 'Brother Asif'.

"Is this the number?"

Al Holami looked at the phone and said, "Yes."

Ward shot him in the centre of his forehead and Al Holami fell to the floor in a crumpled pile.

"Get the clean-up crew here. It will be their last job. We have obliterated his support network now," he said, "Then get them to get these laptops and the bag over to Nicole-Louise and Tackler immediately; I want to know what we can find."

"Will do," Gilligan replied.

"And get round the clock surveillance on this place in case he comes back. It's unlikely but let's cover all the angles," he instructed.

Gilligan got straight onto his phone.

"Meet me downstairs as soon as you are done. We have one more visit to make," he said as he walked out of the apartment deep in his own thoughts.

He reached the street and exhaled. They had made a lot of progress and now Fulken was alone and that would make his mission a hundred times harder to complete. He was feeling slightly irritated though, that he had come so close to finding him.

He strolled back to the car to wait for Gilligan.

He took out Al Holami's phone and dialled the number for Fulken. There was a message saying it was not possible to connect the call and so he hung up.

He felt frustrated.

His frustration would have been compounded even more if he had turned around and looked fifty yards up the street.

Asif Fulken had turned into West 8th Street and saw a man walking out of Al Holami's building.

This man had an Aura about him that screamed 'Danger' to him.

He watched the man breathe in deeply and then look up to the sky. He watched as he pulled a phone out of his jacket pocket, put it to his ear and then put it back in his pocket.

There was something about the man that Fulken thought was familiar.

Had their path's crossed?

Had he been part of the CIA team that initially brought him to America?

There was something familiar, he just didn't know what.

He kept himself against a shop front, the man's view of him obscured by the trees while he waited to see what would

151

happen next. He pulled out his cell phone, took out the battery and threw it down a drain.

A few moments later a white van pulled up and three men got out in black overalls.

He now knew what had happened.

He turned and walked away down Greenwich Avenue and got lost in the evening crowds.

TWENTY THREE

They arrived at the USBC News offices at twenty past eight so they had ten minutes to spare. Considering the events of the day so far, their punctuality had been impressive throughout.

The offices were almost directly opposite the NBC Experience Store on 6th Avenue. Nice touch, Ward thought to himself, letting the competition know that they were moving closer. USBC News was an expansion of UKBC News and Lord Ashurst-Stevens was now probably the most influential media man on both sides of the Atlantic.

He had slowly been buying up smaller networks and newspapers over the years and before anyone knew it; he had branched into satellite TV, and profits had soared by an unprecedented amount.

His TV companies held the rights to show live NFL games in the States and Soccer in the UK, and these rights had then been sold on to the rest of the world.

This has made the Ashurst-Stevens group of companies crucial to politicians and celebrities alike. If he decided to help them achieve their goals, they would, and on the flip side, he could break anyone just as easily.

Many governments had been elected on the wave of the media support that he decided was most beneficial to his own empire building.

This was now the way of the world, Ward thought to himself, morals, democracy and decency had lost their values a long time ago, he didn't like Ashurst-Stevens.

When they had briefly met back in London, he had the feeling that Ashurst-Stevens thought he was untouchable. He guessed that he was used to being able to make a phone call and get someone, particularly someone asking awkward questions, advised not to ask them again.

The world was in desperate need of change.

The offices had three floors with glass fronts, and the remaining twenty or so floors grew out from the top of the glass like a giant stem from a garden pot.

Not the kind of building that Ward liked. It had no character, not too dissimilar to the majority of the people who worked in there, he thought to himself.

They parked the car and Gilligan said,

"What's this Walker guy like?"

"I don't like him."

"Why?" Gilligan asked.

"See for yourself," he replied.

They walked into the building and were faced by a grand, semi-circle of a reception desk, which looked like it belonged on the Titanic.

There was a security guard in his sixties talking to a pretty, blonde woman in her late twenties. They approached the desk with Ward leading the way.

"We have an eight thirty appointment with Martin Walker," he said.

"Your name, Sir?" she asked.

"Tell him his friend from London is here."

"The appointment has to be by name," she replied apologetically.

"Gilligan," Ward said.

"That's not the name I have sir."

Ward had to pause for a moment and think back to what Lawson had called him in London,

"Chennell."

"That's it," she picked up the phone and dialled a number,

"Mr Walker's eight thirty appointment has arrived," she said, followed by an "OK."

"One of his staff is on his way down to collect you," she said and smiled.

They both moved back from the desk a few feet and looked towards the elevator.

"This guy is too important to come and meet you on his own?" Gilligan asked.

"He wasn't last time."

The elevator doors opened and a guy in his early forties stepped out. He was tall and muscular with a head of cropped hair that was just on the verge of turning from brown to grey. Ward could see he was carrying a gun by the fall of his black suit jacket.

He was sizing Ward and Gilligan up, not with the eye of a personal bodyguard, but with the expertise of someone well trained, with narrowed eyes, calculating his chances, assessing the opposition.

He was around six feet three and had that wiry frame that told Ward that if you put him down in a fist fight, he would get straight back up. He was moving briskly and directly towards them. He was starting to extend his right hand as he got about six feet away. He was starting to smile. He was not, Ward thought to himself, a member of Walker's staff.

"Hello gentlemen," he said.

His voice carried a heavy droll to it, from the Deep South.

"Mr Walker is just finishing a briefing and will be with you shortly. Please follow me up to his offices," he said, appearing oblivious to the fact that both Ward and Gilligan ignored his offer of a handshake, before turning and heading back to the elevator.

They stepped into the elevator and the guy pushed the button with number sixteen on.

Ward stood opposite the guy, looking at him. None of them spoke.

That alone told all three of them what they needed to know. There was an acceptance between them, an unspoken agreement.

They all knew the other was content not to speak and not be unnerved by the situation, which meant that all three guys in the lift were very dangerous indeed. No need for names or introductions. They all knew.

The elevator stopped on the 16th floor and they got out.

"Follow me please," the guy said.

They walked along a corridor that was lined with full length glass acting as office walls.

There were a large number of people on their feet moving around urgently, and it had the same manic feel to it that he had noticed in the London offices.

At the end of the hallway was a partitioned wall, painted magnolia, with a number of certificates in frames hanging proudly, showing the awards that USBC News had received in its young life.

In the middle of the wall was a large, dark oak door with a gold handle.

The guy walked up to the door and knocked. A muffled "Enter," came from inside, and he opened the door and held it open for Ward and Gilligan to walk into the room.

The guy closed the door and crossed his arms, so that his hands were covering his groin.

There was a big table which took up eighty per cent of the room which Ward quickly established had twenty seats around it, nine on each side and one at either end.

At the far end of the table, Martin Walker sat on the left hand side on his own. On the opposite side, three guys all over sixty sat with lots of paper spread out in front of them. The lawyers were in town.

At the head of the table sat someone who Ward was surprised to see.

"We meet again," Lord Ashurst-Stevens said.

Ward looked at the four men and said,

"Is there any particular reason why you are all here?"

"Just wrapping up some business, which is none of yours," One of the lawyers replied, shuffling bits of paper together as he said it.

"Have you made any progress in the pursuit of the bomber?" Lord Ashurst-Stevens asked, looking at Ward, a question that he chose to ignore.

"And you are?" Ashurst-Stevens said looking at Gilligan

"Mr Haggler," he replied, completely serious.

"Please to meet you," Ashurst-Stevens said as he stood up from the table and the four other men stood up a second after him.

He moved around the table and his three lawyers followed him. He got to Ward and stopped two feet away.

"You have powerful friends," he said

"I do?"

"Yes you do. Friends that have told me to pull out all the stops to help you," Ashurst-Stevens replied.

"And have you?"

"Yes we have. Mr Walker will explain. My legal team have briefed him on what he can provide you with."

"Should I be grateful?" he asked, "I would have thought that when it comes to saving hundreds of lives legality does not come into it?"

"The law always comes into it," Ashurst-Stevens said, leaning in towards him.

"Not in my world it doesn't."

Ashurst-Stevens eyed Ward suspiciously.

"Well we have sources and people to protect. Walker will brief you on the assistance that we can give you," he replied, "Keep up the good work," Ashurst-Stevens added and the guy guarding the door opened it, and he watched as they filed out, the legal team scurrying after the boss like children following a gang leader in the playground. The guy by the door shut it again and returned to his crossed arms position.

Ward looked at Walker,

"What do you have for us?" he asked.

"We were told that you believe there was a link to the FFW?" Walker replied.

"So?"

"And that you are hunting people who might be sympathetic to their cause?"

"They are pretty much unable to be sympathetic towards anything anymore," Gilligan interrupted.

Walker looked at him,

"I don't understand," Walker said.

"They have all been visited and what they know taken away by us," Gilligan stated.

"That can't be right," Walker said.

"Why not?" Ward asked.

"Because not thirty seconds before you walked in the room we were talking to our source on the phone."

Ward and Gilligan looked at each other.

"Who is your source?" Ward asked.

"You heard the boss, I can't reveal that. We are journalists after all," Walker replied.

"In the interest of national security we can force you to name him," Gilligan said aggressively.

"No you can't," Walker said, "The bosses lawyers got a signed guarantee from the people way above you that they would respect our journalistic integrity and not request who the source is," he added smugly.

"I could just beat it out of you," Ward said.

The guy guarding the door adjusted his stance and moved his hands to his side, ready for action.

"Easy small fry," Gilligan said to him, "We are a little bit more than newsboys."

Ward ignored what was happening between them.

"And what is your source telling you?" he asked.

"That there is a meeting going to happen tonight," Walker replied.

"Where?"

"Just off of West Street, near Pier 26, Hubert Street."

"What sort of meeting?"

"A meeting where he said someone very important was going to be in attendance," Walker said.

"And who is this person meeting with?"

"The FFW supporters in New York."

Gilligan and Ward looked at each other. This seemed to be never ending.

"Who are the supporters?" Ward asked.

"I can't say."

"You will say."

"Now guys, we are helping you here. Respect what Mr Walker can and cannot say," the guy at the door said in his irritating droll.

Ward was too smart to let anything get in the way of finding Asif Fulken and so he took on board what the guy had said, but he made a note to himself that he would smash the guys face in when this was over.

"OK, fair enough," he said.

Gilligan looked visibly disappointed.

"You think it could be the guy we are chasing?" Ward asked.

"That's what my source said."

"You know his name?"

"No," Walker said, "Don't you?"

Ward ignored him.

"When is this meeting taking place?"

Walker looked at his watch, "In 40 minutes time."

"Where exactly?"

"33 Hubert Street."

"What is there?"

"There are some garages under the apartments that act as a safe place to hide stuff and people meet in the apartment regularly my source informs me. Apartment number seven."

"How many people are there?"

"I don't know."

"Why?"

"I didn't ask," Walker replied.

"Some journalist you are," Ward said.

"He tells rather than answers."

"How reliable is your guy?"

"He's never been wrong yet."

Ward looked at Gilligan,

"Fifteen minutes maximum to get to Hubert from here?" he asked.

Gilligan nodded.

"Let's go," he said. "I'll be back to see you again if it is OK, Mr Walker, there are still a number of things that I need to run through with you. You have been a great help, sorry for our abruptness."

"Of course it is," Walker said in his very rich, well-spoken English accent.

They walked to the door and the guy guarding it opened it. He flashed an arrogant, contemptuous smile at them both as they walked out and down the hallway towards the elevator. They called for the elevator and the doors opened thirty seconds later. They both stepped in.

"I think we should kill that guy," Gilligan said.

"Which one?" Ward asked.

"The goon trying to play tough guy guarding the door."

"Is that necessary?" Ward asked with a smile.

Gilligan never smiled back.

"What's wrong?" he asked.

"I'm pissed," Gilligan replied.

"Because of that guy?"

"No."

"Why then?"

"This was meant to be our last call of the night."

Ward thought back to the conversation they had in the car earlier, about USBC News being their last call and then Gilligan having his son's birthday with him tomorrow morning.

"It will be a quick visit. I'll bust in, you keep lookout outside, and I'll see if Fulken is there. If not, I'll get what I can out of the people inside, and then we can go home," he said.

"And I still get tomorrow morning off?" Gilligan asked.

"Yes you will. Deal?"

"Deal," Gilligan replied.

TWENTY FOUR

Hubert Street was an exclusive and expensive place to live, and not for the first time that day, Ward wondered to himself where all of the money had come from for these people to buy properties in some of the most affluent parts of New York. He also wondered how much CIA money was really involved.

They got out of the car and started to walk down Hubert towards Pier 26.

The street was quiet and nothing seemed out of place.

They slowly walked past the shiny, chrome entrance to 33 Hudson, and noted that there were a number of secure garages, all with green shutter doors and an entrance door built into them.

The door that was marked '7' was locked and there were no obvious indicators from inside the garage or in the street that anything was out of the ordinary.

They walked down to the end of the street and stopped.

"Does this seem right to you?" Gilligan asked.

"It seems as quiet as I would expect it to be," Ward replied.

"Not too quiet?"

 "What are you looking for?" Ward asked, "A sign saying, Bad guys inside, please knock politely?"

Gilligan shrugged his shoulders.

"The door looks pretty secure, let's walk up again and have one last look while we decide how we are going to get inside," Ward said.

They turned and walked back up the street, the whole area looked even less conspicuous the second time. They turned the curved corner again back onto Hudson and stopped.

"You think I should just knock?" Ward asked.

"Pizza again?"

The fact Ward completely ignored this comment panicked Gilligan.

"You can't be serious?" Gilligan asked.

"No I'm not," he replied. "It won't work twice so let's be creative."

"How?"

"We will get into the building, see who is in there and knock on a door. We can say we heard a commotion going on in their garage and maybe they should look at it," Ward replied.

"And if no one answers?" Gilligan enquired.

"You always have to complicate things Marvin," he said to him and smiled.

"One of us has to."

They set off and turned the corner into Hubert for the third time.

They looked just like two friends walking down to the Pier.

They reached the apartment steps of thirty three. There was a long row of apartment buzzers, ten to a panel in three brass rimmed plates.

"Pick a number?" he said,

"Don't want to go high, don't want to go low. Try fifteen," Gilligan said.

Ward pressed the buzzer to number fifteen.

Thirty seconds later they were still waiting for an answer after pressing the buzzer a further two times.

"Not very good with numbers, are you?" he said, before pressing the buzzer for apartment number four. Eight seconds later a tired sounding voice said,

"Is that you Dude?"

Ward looked at Gilligan and smiled.

"Yeah man," he replied.

The buzzer sounded and they stepped into the building. The door to number four opened and a guy in his late twenties, clearly stoned said,

"Who are you man?"

"Sorry?" Ward said.

"You rang my buzzer."

"I live in number twenty four," Ward said. "Was it that guy who just ran out of the door as I came in?" he asked.

"What guy?"

"Your friend, describe him?"

"He has long blonde hair, in a ponytail."

"That guy had blonde hair in a ponytail," he replied, "What else?"

"He always wears a brown jacket," the guy said.

"He had that on, anything else?"

"Yeah, he has a goatee," the guy said, total confusion etched on his face.

"So did that guy," Ward said, "That was definitely him."

The guy looked confused,

"Not sure what happened there but thanks man," the guy said and he turned and shut his door.

The oldest trick in the book Ward thought to himself and the guy fell for it.

They headed towards the stairway.

A quick scan showed that the first floor was numbered one through to six so number seven would be on the floor above. They walked up the stairs, reaching the top, and saw number seven was immediately to their left.

Ward headed past it and knocked on the door of number eight.

A guy in his early thirties with dark hair and a thick beard opened the door slightly but kept the security chain in place, an indication that he trusted Ward and Gilligan enough after looking through his spyhole to see what they wanted, but not trusting enough to leave himself fully exposed to them.

"Can I help?" he asked politely.

"Yes, I live two floors up," Ward said in his clearest accent, "And when I came in tonight there was a lot of noise and what sounded like raised voices coming from the garage of number seven. I have knocked on their door but there is no answer."

"No answer from number seven?" the guy asked.

"No and the noises sounded rather suspicious."

"Have you called the cops?" the guy asked.

"I'm not sure it's that bad," he said, "I don't want to cause any trouble as it might be totally innocent."

"No," the guy said, "Have YOU called the cops?"

"I don't understand?" Ward said.

"Not sure where you were last night but three cops came in and raided number seven. The two women in there had been operating as prostitutes apparently," he said, rolling his eyes in disbelief to emphasise the point.

"Really?" Ward asked, looking equally surprised for effect.

"Yes. The cops were knocking on all of our doors last night, asking if we were aware of anything suspicious and then they carried out four large metal boxes. Evidence I expect, probably toys, whips and God knows what else," the guy said.

"I was out of town," Ward said quickly.

"So maybe the cops are digging around in their garage looking for more stuff, call them and they will probably tell you that it is OK."

"One night away and it turns into a whorehouse," Ward said, smiling at the guy, "I never would have known that looking at them. You just never know do you? They looked so sweet," he added.

The guy looked at Ward quizzically.

"You are thinking about the same two women aren't you?"

"I think so" Ward replied, "One of them blonde?"

The guy laughed.

"You've definitely got those two mixed up with someone else," the guy said pointing at the door of number seven, "I only saw them a few times. You just never know I guess, but I didn't see that coming."

"Why not?"

"Because they were disabled," he replied, "Bit sick if people were buying sex off of them in my opinion, buy hey, who am I

164

to judge, each to their own and all that," he added with a grimace.

"Disabled how?"

"One of them only had one leg and the other only one arm."

"I still can't picture them. What did they look like?" he asked casually.

"Middle Eastern I assume by looking at them. I only caught brief glimpses of them in the foyer previously. Never heard a sound or saw men coming in. I actually thought the apartment was empty," he replied.

Ward and Gilligan looked at each other.

"Well thanks for your help, I'll see you around," Ward said.

"No worries," the guy replied and went to close the door.

"Wait!" Ward said, and the guy stopped closing the door, "Just out of interest, how long did you think the apartment had been empty?" he asked.

"About fourteen months. The couple who used to live there had a kid and moved out of the city."

"Thanks."

The guy shut his door.

They walked back to the stairwell and stopped after descending five steps when they were out of sight of the second floor landing,

"What do you make of that?" Gilligan asked.

"I don't think anyone ever lived there. Whoever those two women were, I think they were just holing up there. I'm pretty sure they are the bomb makers who got unlucky one day. I think this is where they made the bomb."

"Make a quick call and confirm if there was a genuine arrest of two women first," Ward instructed Gilligan.

"OK."

He headed down to the bottom of the stairs. He waited for thirty seconds and Gilligan came down.

"There was no arrest here last night and definitely no one legged or one-armed prostitutes," Gilligan said.

Ward walked across the hall and knocked on the door of number two.

Almost immediately a woman in her forties, with long flowing highlighted brown hair and wearing a smart Armani suit opened the door.

"Yes?" she said abruptly.

"Good evening madam. I'm with the NYPD and was just following up from last night," Ward said,

"I told your colleague last night that I haven't heard or seen anything. The sickos who have been coming in here have not crossed my path or I would have told them to get lost. The noise they were making last night moving everything up and down kept me awake until gone two," she said. "Now if you don't mind I am very busy so if there is nothing else?"

"No, you have been very helpful," he said and the woman shut the door.

"They were moving the bomb," Gilligan said.

"Let's go and check out the apartment."

They walked back up the stairs and got to the door of number seven.

Gilligan took out his gun and screwed his silencer on; Ward took out his Glock and did the same before moving to the right hand side of the door next to the door frame.

"You blow it and I will take the room," Ward said.

Gilligan took aim and fired two shots to the left of the handle. The wood shattered and Gilligan followed up the shots by raising his right foot and ramming the sole of his shoe into the splintered wood. The door swung open and Ward spun around through the doorway and into the room with his Glock aimed straight, in line with his chest.

The apartment was completely empty apart from a workbench on the left which had two spot lamps, one on either side. There were a few short, electrical wires on the floor and nothing else at all.

They walked in.

While Gilligan started checking the rest of the rooms in the apartment Ward stood in front of the workbench and tried to picture the scene in his mind.

The two bomb makers working night and day to create a weapon that would kill hundreds of people. He was now

166

deeply concerned over the size of the bomb. If the people behind this had moved four large metal boxes out then that could mean four smaller bombs or one very big one.

The cover for moving them was obvious. Posing as police to not arouse suspicion, that's why they knocked on the other apartment doors, to justify them being there.

You only see what people want you to see.

"There's nothing here at all. I mean zip, completely empty. Not even a bar of soap," Gilligan said.

"Let's check out the garage," Ward replied, "You had better make a call and get the door sorted and get your people to check and swab for explosives and identify the explosive type so we know for sure what they have."

They walked out of the apartment as Gilligan made yet another call, and headed for the stairs.

Outside, Ward stood looking at the door of the garage marked number seven. He knew there was going to be no meeting, clearly the source that Walker had was right but he was also wrong at the same time.

There were a number of reasons why things could or would have changed. It could be that maybe the bomb makers finished their work quicker than they had anticipated or that Fulken had decided to bring things forward, or even that they had decided to move things to a different location.

He checked along the street and confirmed it was still empty and quiet, and with his Glock in his hand, walked up to the entrance door of the garage and fired one shot which blew the lock out.

He stepped into the garage and saw what he expected to see. Nothing at all. It was completely empty.

He walked back out onto the street just as Gilligan was finishing his call and they stood in front of the door.

"They will be here in fifteen," Gilligan said looking at his watch, "It's meeting time and no one has shown, I think we are twenty four hours too late."

"I know," Ward said, "We are going to have to find out who this source is from Walker."

"You want to go back now?" Gilligan asked dejectedly.

"No, we are done for today," he replied. "There is nothing much we can do now. They have moved the bomb, it will take preparation and planning to get it ready and we will stop it before it goes off anyway so let's call it a day."

"How are you so sure that this bomb won't go off?" Gilligan asked, "You have said from the moment we started that you know who is behind it and we keep getting close, very close to catching Fulken, and yet he always seem one step ahead of us."

"That's how I know."

"Well maybe it is time that you explained to me what is actually happening, because to be honest, the way you are so laid back about finding this bomb is really unsettling me." Ward thought about this. Gilligan was right.

He was so used to keeping people in the dark and operating to his rules, all alone and trusting in his judgement one hundred per cent, that he never shared anything with those he worked closely with until things were finished.

He thought back to earlier and how Gilligan had saved him from being shot on the stairs, and how he had sacrificed family time to stand shoulder to shoulder with him from the moment he had picked him up.

"OK," he said, "There was one thing about the Paris and London bombs that was wrong, and the moment I saw the footage of them both, I knew what was happening. I'm still struggling to fit one last little bit together though."

"What bit?" Gilligan asked.

"Why? A contact in London told me why, and I know he is right, but I can't tie everything together just yet," Ward replied.

"You are still talking in cryptic sentences," Gilligan said, "Just hit me with the basics."

"Right, here's how it all fits in together, ready?" he asked calmly.

His composed expression promptly turned to disbelief because Gilligan wasn't ready.

At the moment that Ward had finished his last sentence, a shot rang out and echoed down the street and Gilligan's whole body jerked to the side, like he had been hit by truck, and he hit the concrete floor, landing hard on the right side of his face.

TWENTY FIVE

Ward hit the ground immediately and rolled forward to take cover behind a silver BMW 'X' series, which was parked on the kerb, just as a second shot rang out, and he heard the bullet whistle past his ear before smashing into a road sign. Whoever was shooting was to his right.

He looked across at Gilligan and he could see a pool of blood seeping from the left side of his chest from his motionless body.

He adjusted himself so that his left foot was flat on the floor and he knelt on his right knee, ready to spring into action. He raised his head slightly and looked to the right and saw nothing. No movement at all. He scanned up down, around and along the street and saw nothing.

The woman who he had spoken to earlier from apartment number two came out and put her hands over her mouth as she saw Gilligan and gasped. She then glanced at Ward with his gun drawn, crouched behind the car and froze.

"Get back inside," he shouted, "And call the paramedics."

The woman turned and ran back inside.

He then looked back in the direction of the shot and still saw nothing.

By now, at least ten people had started to come out from their buildings to see what was happening, and three of them started running towards them to see if they could help.

Even in that frightening and dangerous situation, he thought how remarkable New Yorkers were, and why he felt this was his real home. With no fear of consequence, here were three people with no thought for their own safety, just wanting to help.

Nine-Eleven had strengthened these people, and all they saw was someone who needed help, and they felt an obligation to do something.

He sprinted over to Gilligan just as the first of the three guys reached them.

"My wife is calling the paramedics," the guy said breathlessly. Another man reached them and he heard him say into his cell phone,

"I need the police now, I'm on Hubert Street, and a guy has been shot."

He knelt down, Gilligan's eyes were open and he was semi-conscious.

There was a gargling noise to his breathing, and Ward knew that the bullet had pierced his lungs. He rolled Gilligan over onto his side and supported his head on his knees,

"Hold on buddy," he said to him, "You will be fine, help is coming."

Gilligan looked up at him. He looked petrified.

"Don't you die on me Marvin," Ward said.

He looked down and Gilligan's shirt and jacket were soaked in blood, and as much as he pushed against the wound, he was unable to stem the flow.

"I need a towel," he said to the first guy who had got there, and the he promptly turned and sprinted back in the direction of his apartment.

By now, a group of about fifteen people had gathered, at least ten of them were on their cell phones calling for help.

"Shit this hurts," Gilligan said, wincing as he regained a level of consciousness which allowed him to speak, but also enabled him to feel the pain which was stabbing through his body with a greater intensity with each passing second.

"You just hold on, you will be fine," he lied.

He knew what a dying man looked like better than almost anyone. Gilligan would not be fine.

Someone behind him handed him a towel and he pulled Gilligan's jacket back and lifted his shirt.

There was a hole about two inches in diameter and blood was pulsing out of it each time he took a deep breath.

Gilligan was drowning in his own blood.

He pressed the towel down hard against the bullet hole and Gilligan screamed in pain. It was a high pitched scream which didn't fit with this giant of a man lying on the sidewalk.

"Sorry pal," he said.

"I'm dying."

"You just hold on, you will be OK."

"You look after my boys and my wife," Gilligan pleaded.

There were tears in Gilligan's eyes.

He knew he was dying and Ward felt an emotion he had never felt before.

It was a choking sensation in his throat.

"You look after them yourself when you are better," he replied once he had regained his composure.

"Don't bullshit me man, I'm dying and you know it. You just look me in the eyes and swear you will take care of them," Gilligan begged.

"I swear," he replied, staring deep into Gilligan's eyes.

He knew the towel was not stopping the flow of blood. The guy, who had run to get a towel earlier, came back and handed it to him, and he duly swapped them over.

Gilligan's blood was running down both of his arms and over his trousers.

A slight woman in her forties leant forward holding a medical kit and said,

"I'm a nurse; let me see what I can do."

She softly gripped Ward's hand and slid it away from the towel he was holding.

He supported Gilligan's head while the woman started to unravel bandages from her medical kit.

"You promise me, you owe me," Gilligan said again, his head tilted back on Ward's lap, his sad eyes looking up at him.

"I promise."

Ward didn't know what else to say.

When he usually looked into the eyes of a dying man he knew that they deserved to die and felt nothing, and even enjoyed knowing that they were terrified as he spoke the last words they would ever hear.

But here, looking down into the eyes of a guy he cared about, who he trusted and who he admired, he couldn't think of anything to say.

The sound of sirens started to fill the air and an ambulance rolled into view behind him.

Two paramedics jumped out of the truck and ran over to them. One of them put his hand on his shoulder and said, "We will take him now, Sir," as he placed his hand under Gilligan's head and knelt next to him, shuffling him out of the way as he did so.

Gilligan's head rolled to the left and his eyes fixed onto his, "You promise me," Gilligan said and then his eyes closed.

Ward rose to his feet and looked down at himself. His whole lap and arms, from the elbows down, were soaked in Gilligan's blood and he watched as the paramedics attached a portable defibrillator to Gilligan's chest.

To his right he saw two cop cars speeding down the street, sirens screaming, and he started to step back away from the crowd.

Both cars screeched to a stop about twenty feet back from the ambulance rear doors.

He watched almost in disbelief as the paramedics lifted Gilligan's lifeless body onto a stretcher and started to wheel him towards the ambulance.

Two cops got out of each of the cars, almost in tandem, and he decided to leave.

He did not need to be sitting in a police station for a couple of hours refusing to speak until Centrepoint had sorted things out and got him released.

He walked past the rear doors of the ambulance and as he did so, he heard one of the paramedics say;

"It's no good, we've lost him."

He crossed the street and did not look back. He knew that the crowd watching events unfold would be talking to the cops right then and maybe even pointing at him as he walked down the street towards Pier 26. He called The Old Man.

"About time," he answered in an agitated tone.

"Gilligan's been killed. I need someone to come and get me now and make a call to the cops saying that I am not to be detained urgently," he said.

"Where are you?" Centrepoint asked.

"Just heading towards Pier 26 from Hubert."

"I'm on it, two minutes, but you call me as soon as you get away."

Ward hung up the phone.

As he reached the end of the street he turned and saw two cops jogging down the street towards him.

He crossed over the street towards the water and stopped by a litter bin. He looked urgently for his transport but the road was completely empty apart from a cyclist. As the two cops got to the end of Hubert they stopped and pulled their guns. He kept his palms open and his hands elevated slightly from his sides so that they could both see he was unarmed. They were both in their late forties, short of breath and out of condition.

One was a really short white guy who looked seriously round and the other was a big black guy, around Gilligan's size, but it was probably twenty years since he had a physique remotely similar to his dead friend's.

"Stop where you are and do not move," the white cop shouted, and then took about five deep breaths, trying to reclaim the oxygen that the jog had taken out of him.

Ward stood still and looked at them.

The black cop started talking into his radio almost immediately and then Ward saw a black Range Rover with tinted windows appear on his right from the direction of Pier 25.

"Do not move," the white cop shouted again as he looked up and down the road preparing to cross.

His partner started talking on the radio again and then said something to him and he lowered his gun.

They both looked at him, not in a threatening way, more in curiosity.

The Range Rover stopped by the kerb with the rear passenger door directly in front of him, and he extended his arm to open the door and climbed inside.

There were two guys in the front, neither of them spoke, they knew that if Ward wanted to talk he would.

Their ages were hard to gauge, as he could only see their side profiles, but looking at the muscles in their necks from behind, he guessed they were mid-thirties at most.

"You have to make a call," the guy in the passenger seat said without turning around.

"Tell him I'll call later," he replied.

The guy turned his head towards the driver and looked at him quizzically.

"I think it's really important, so you had maybe best call," the guy in the passenger seat said.

"And I really don't want to talk, so tell him I will call him later," he said firmly, assertion running through his voice.

The guy turned and looked at him, only briefly, and then turned his stare back to the front of the car.

He picked up his cell phone and mumbled something quietly, and then heard a response that clearly surprised him because he put the cell phone back in his pocket.

Ward knew immediately that someone telling Centrepoint what he would and wouldn't do, was unheard of to these guys and more strangely to them, the response of despair but ultimately acceptance on the end of the line, would have thrown this guy completely.

"Where would you like to go?" he asked.

"Take me to Washington Street."

On Hubert Street, the paramedics were frantically trying to resuscitate the giant of a man lying in their ambulance.

"Try one more time," the paramedic who had taken over from Ward said.

175

They slightly increased the voltage on the defibrillator and tried one more time, more in hope than belief, and as the voltage shot through Gilligan's body it jerked violently and then his body went limp once more. The paramedic looked at the monitor and smiled,

"We've got a pulse," he said, "Get us to the hospital now!"

He was outside his apartment within fifteen minutes of being picked up.

"Here will do," he said when they reached the apartment building before his own.

They pulled over and he opened the door.

"Thank you for the ride," he said as he stepped out of the car. He watched the Range Rover pull away and then walked the short distance to his apartment building. Two minutes later, he was in his apartment and closing the door to the outside world.

He stripped all of his clothes off and threw them immediately into the garbage bin in his kitchen, and leant against the sink completely naked, his arms leaning on the taps for support.

He looked down at his arms. They were caked in blood. Gilligan's blood.

He couldn't get the vision of Gilligan begging him to look after his boys out of his mind, and he was struggling to hold back the rage that was building inside of him.

He walked slowly and dejectedly through to the bathroom, opened the door to the enclosed shower unit and turned the handle onto 'Full', and stepped in.

As the spray hit him, for a brief moment, he hoped that it would wash the sadness he felt from his mind, but as the water started to dilute Gilligan's dried blood, the whole of the shower tray started to fill with light red water, and he saw Gilligan looking up at him yet again.

With his eyes closed tight, for the first time since the bullet had hit Gilligan, he started to think about who could have fired it?

He knew for sure that he was going to kill whoever it was, but he couldn't see a clear picture, all he could see was Gilligan's face.

He told himself that he now owed it to Gilligan, and to his boys, to finish this, and that refocused him immediately.

He knew without a doubt that tomorrow this would end and that Gilligan's death would be avenged. He was going to win, this time, not just because it was something that he had to do for himself, but because he now had to win for Gilligan.

By the time he had finished his shower and stepped out, wrapping a towel around his waist, Ryan Ward was back, deadly and focused.

He spent thirty minutes running things through in his head and finally got the list down to one of three people who would have tried to kill them, and why they would want them dead. He dried himself off, put on some jogging bottoms and a tee-shirt and called Centrepoint.

"Are you OK?"

"Yes." he replied.

"Any idea who shot him?" The Old Man asked.

"I think they were trying to shoot us both," he replied, "But the fact that he missed me tells me some things that help me narrow it down."

"What things?"

Ward ignored the question and continued.

"But it made me think that if he wasn't that good a shot then he will make mistakes."

"What progress have you made with the bomb?"

"I know who supplied it, who made it, where it was made and I will know by tomorrow where it is planned to go off."

"Then you need to tell me what you know."

"I'll tell you after, as I always do. Do you trust me?"

"You know I trust you more than any of the others. You know I tolerate your insubordination and lack of feedback simply because I trust you. Why do you ask that?"

"Because when this nears a conclusion I have to know that every decision that I make is done so with your full support, even if you don't know what I am doing," he said.

177

"That sounds ominous," he replied, "Where is this going?"

"I will tell you all about it after. But right now, I'm alone so I need something from you."

"He has been here two days waiting for you, why haven't you called him?" Centrepoint asked.

Ward had an incredible amount of admiration for Centrepoint. He knew that he would need The Optician's help, and he would have been two steps ahead of him in knowing what he would need, in fact it seemed, two days ahead in this case.

"Of course, if you kept in touch and called in regularly then I would have told you this before," Centrepoint added.

"I'll call him later."

"No need," Centrepoint said, "I have already spoken to him. Knowing he never even seems to sleep he is probably outside your apartment right now keeping you safe as usual."

Ward actually believed The Old Man when he said it.

"Mike Lawson is on his way over with the news crew," he said.

"I know. They will be landing in three hours. His bosses have told him to contact you at eight in the morning, so you now have two people by your side."

"OK," Ward said, "One more thing, I need some money."

"Why?"

"Because I need to call in Martin McDermott and his team to help me."

Centrepoint knew Martin McDermott very well. He was an ex-Navy Seal, widely considered the best Navy Seal in a generation.

McDermott had left the service and set up as a mercenary over five years ago, and still helped his country by leading a team of six other incredibly skilled and talented Ex-Seals which included his own son, Paul, among them.

They had helped Ward on numerous occasions in the past and before Ward's time; they had worked with three of the other 'Deniables'.

They were the best.

Centrepoint never had any concerns or worries about his people using McDermott and his team, because he knew they understood how the whole thing worked.

If they got in trouble, they were on their own.

Nothing to do with the CIA whatsoever.

It grated him that McDermott charged half a million dollars a day and Centrepoint thought back to a seventeen day mission in Cuba a few years ago which turned out to be very expensive but amounted to nothing more than recon work.

But he trusted both Ward and McDermott.

"Of course you can," he replied, as if he was agreeing to give Ward a sip of his drink rather than half a million dollars a day, "I'll have it transferred into the account immediately."

"Thank you."

"Just try and keep me informed, OK?" Centrepoint asked.

"I will," Ward said, and hung up the phone.

He felt a little better after speaking to The Old Man and the next call he made was to McDermott.

"Well, well, how have you been?" McDermott said as he answered the phone.

"Are you busy?" he asked.

"All a little quiet at the moment. Why?" McDermott asked.

"Where are you now?"

"In Washington, why?"

"Can you be in New York by 10:00am tomorrow?"

"For how long?"

"I'm hoping for just twenty four hours."

"For what specifically?" McDermott asked.

"Firstly to find and eliminate whoever killed a good friend of mine," he said.

"Who has been killed?"

"Gilligan, my CIA help in New York"

"The guy who looks like Marvin Haggler?"

"Yes."

"I liked him; I met him a couple of times before. What's the other reason?" McDermott asked.

"To help me stop a bomb from being detonated in New York."

There was a pause on the phone for a few seconds and then McDermott said,

"We will be set up and ready for you at 10:00am tomorrow morning; we have a garage that acts as a base by Macomb's Bridge. I will send you the address when you hang up."

"Thank you Martin," he said, "I will send you the information I have and a brief outline of what I want us to do, so you are part briefed by the time you get here, OK?"

"That's fine," McDermott replied.

"See you tomorrow."

"One other thing," McDermott said quickly, "You have our fee arranged?" he asked.

"Yes I do."

"Keep it and give it to Gilligan's wife."

Ward hung up the phone.

His next call was to Nicole Louise and Tackler.

"Hello?" Tackler answered the phone sounding sleepy.

"I need to see you tomorrow morning at eight," he said.

"About?" Tackler asked suspiciously.

"Have you found anything out about Martin Walker?"

"Not yet. What are you hoping to find?"

"Money, travel, phone records; anything that links him to Asif Fulken in any way, or to people who could be linked to him."

"Not a lot to go on," Tackler replied.

"I thought you liked a challenge?" he said, appealing to Tackler's competitive nature.

"OK," Tackler said with an air of urgency, "I'll wake Nicole-Louise and see you here in the morning."

"One more thing, do you have the video footage from the UKBC News teams of the explosions as they happened?"

"You know we do."

"I want you to do something."

"Such as?"

"I want you to edit the footage down to exactly one minute before the bombs go off and one minute after. Just two minutes of footage for each bomb," he said.

180

"OK, we will. But what will that show you that you don't already know?" Tackler asked.

Ward hung up the phone.

He felt a lot calmer and in control again now. He had planned his resources, he was gathering the data he would need to pull every last part of this together, and he was focused and determined to avenge Gilligan's death.

Ryan Ward was once again everything that Asif Fulken should be very, very afraid of.

He turned off the lights in the living area and walked into his bedroom. He set the alarm on his phone for 06:30am and lay down on top of the bed. He closed his eyes and he felt a complete calm and belief that he had everything in order wash all over him.

Tomorrow it would end.

TWENTY SIX

He woke up feeling re-energised, invigorated and strong, and immediately went through his routine of five hundred sit ups, five hundred press ups and five hundred squat thrusts with such ease that he felt that he was cheating himself by the time he had finished.

He felt invincible and alert.

He had a shower and made some fresh coffee. By seven fifteen he was dressed and ready for the day ahead. He felt so ready in fact that he called Lawson.

"Hello?" Lawson answered.

"I'm waiting," he said.

"I was told to call you at eight?" Lawson replied.

"Things have changed. I want you at my place at eight."

"I'm still in bed."

"Alone?" he asked, knowing it was a stupid question as he heard the words echo in his head.

"No."

"Beglin?"

"Yes."

"Well leave her there, get ready and be at mine at eight. I'll send the address."

"What for?" Lawson asked.

"I need a driver," he said and hung up the phone.

He spent the next twenty minutes planning out the day's events in his head.

He knew there was a high degree of searching still to be done, and that he was heavily reliant upon Nicole-Louise and Tackler to point him in the right direction, but he now had a clear plan in his head about how he was going to approach everything. His concentration was only broken when his phone rang.

The Optician's name appeared on his screen.

"Are you watching over me?" he asked, deliberately sounding frightened.

"Yes I am. But you could make it a little easier and tell me where you are going so I don't have to keep getting messages from the Old Man about where you are," he replied, deliberately sounding bored.

"And where would all the fun in that be? The Old Man must employ someone to keep track of my cell every minute of the day so think of it as keeping somebody employed."

"You are all heart."

"It's good to know you have my back, knowing that will make today easier. I need you to do something for me."

"What?" The Optician asked.

He then explained very clearly what he needed him to do and where he needed him to be.

"OK, but don't let The Old Man know I am not watching your back," The Optician replied and hung up the phone.

Ward looked at the clock. It was ten to eight.

He thought that he would walk down to the street and just take in the view of the bridge for a few minutes before Lawson arrived.

He locked his apartment and walked down the stairs rather than take the elevator. He walked out into the street, taking in the view of the bridge, and letting the morning sun wash all over him.

He felt invincible and ready for anything.

He was thinking about Gilligan's kids when a black sedan pulled up right next to him. He looked through the window and saw a beaming Lawson looking out at him. He opened the door and got into the car.

"Good to see you, Mike," he said, "Nice car. Bit of a comedown from what you usually drive."

"You too," Lawson replied, "And the car was provided by our friendly opposites in the CIA who were instructed to push the boat out," Lawson said sarcastically as he looked around the car interior.

"How was your night?"

"Energetic!" Lawson proclaimed.

"Could Beglin be the one after all these years?" he asked in all seriousness.

"Don't be stupid," Lawson said, "I'll be bored of her by the end of the week!"

Ward rolled his eyes. He actually disliked guys who just used women for sex a great deal, but Lawson was just impossible not to like.

He had once told him that he has never slept with a woman and not remained great friends with her. He made a mental note to ask him one day just how many friends he had, but there were more important things to attend to at the moment.

"Where are we going?" Lawson asked.

"Park Avenue."

"What for?"

"There are some very interesting people that I want you to meet. What did you get from Beglin?" Ward asked him.

"Well she doesn't like Martin Walker one bit," Lawson replied, "She finds him creepy."

"He makes passes at her?"

"No, not creepy like that," Lawson said, "More like a control freak."

"In what way?"

"Like when they are on a news report, he dictates how it goes, what it says, how they set up, what they should be looking for and how long it should last."

"Isn't that his job as chief news editor?"

"No. It goes beyond that," Lawson replied. "Like he's obsessed with her and the other female reporters but he doesn't even make it obvious that he finds her attractive."

"Obsessed?"

"He has live links to them when they are out on the field telling them what they can and can't do, and how it looks on the screen and so on."

184

"And he relays this through to her directly?"

"No. To her producer."

"Nigel Reid, the guy we met in London?"

"Not always. They change producer depending on what report they are filming. Her consistent team is the cameraman and the sound man."

"Parker and Lewis?"

"Yes. And they both definitely have the hot's for her." Lawson said with a smile.

They arrived at Nicole-Louise's and Tacklers at twenty past eight.

Nicole-Louise opened the door and she looked at Lawson with curiosity rather than awe. Something he wasn't used to.

"Hello," she said, "Come in please."

Tackler was tapping way on his keyboard as usual and he didn't even turn to acknowledge them.

"This is Mike Lawson," he said to Nicole-Louise and the back of Tacklers head. Tackler raised his left hand above his shoulder to let them know he was pleased to meet Lawson but he was busy, "He's from London and he's here to help us."

"I hope you bring more to the party than just good looks?" Nicole-Louise asked a bemused looking Lawson.

Tackler turned around to check out the new guy on the scene, and as soon as the magnitude of just how handsome Lawson was hit him, he was up on his feet, jockeying for position and importance.

"That stuff you gave us to check out," he said to Ward, "It looks like MI6 are even more useless than we thought they were."

Lawson raised an eyebrow.

"In what way?" Ward asked.

"Like the lazy way that the Brits tend to adopt as a normal approach to things," Tackler replied, looking Lawson up and down with complete contempt as he said it, "The stuff you wanted me to find on this Walker guy, I found it. Lots of it."

"I want you to tell me very clearly and very thoroughly what you have found," Ward said.

"He has had over six million dollars move around a group of hidden accounts that belong to him in the past two months," Tackler said.

"Where did the money originate from?"

"I'm still looking for that and I am hitting a lot of firewalls but I will get there, I'm not a Brit. I don't take the easy option," he replied and for a brief moment, Ward could have sworn that Tackler puffed out his chest and straightened his back to make himself look taller.

By now, Lawson looked totally confused, but quickly realised that there was some serious jealousy going on with Tackler and thought he would use that to their advantage.

"I'm pretty sure our men could get there before you," he said to Tackler, "After all, we invented the internet," he added.

"Yes, but we rule it," Tackler said in a hostile tone before turning around and walking back to his workstation.

Lawson looked at Ward and smiled.

Nicole-Louise studied Tackler, smiled and then said,

"How sweet Tackler, you are jealous!"

Tackler pretended not to hear.

"Tackler is a lucky guy," Lawson said to wind Tackler up even more.

"So, we have what you want on this Martin Walker guy so what else do you need?" she asked, ignoring Lawson's flattery, another thing that he definitely wasn't used to.

"You know about Gilligan?" Ward asked.

Tackler turned back and around and both he and Nicole-Louise nodded and looked at the floor.

"So you also know how important it is that we finish this for him?" he asked.

They both nodded again.

"How much money is in Walker's accounts at the moment?"

"Two million dollars," Tackler replied,

"So four million has been paid out? What do you make that, two million per bomb?" All three people in the room nodded and realised what Ward was saying.

"What would Walker gain from all of this?" Lawson asked.

"That's the bit I'm struggling with," Ward said. He looked at Tackler,

"Did you get that edited footage that I asked for?" he asked.
Tackler nodded.

"Put it on a memory stick for me please."
Tackler turned around and started to prepare the footage for Ward.

"This money trail is so important, how long before you can break it?" he asked Tackler.

"Five hours tops," Tackler replied, waiting for Wards standard reply that would indicate he had half of that amount of time.

"That's fine," he replied, much to Tackler's surprise.

"I need you to do one thing for me Nicole-Louise," Ward said.

"Of course," she replied.

"Find out who the producer was on the footage that we have on the Westminster Abbey bombing and do it quickly please."

"I'm on it now," she replied and walked over to the bank of computers on the opposite side of the room to Tackler.

"We need to go now but as soon as you have anything call me straight away, either of you," Ward said.

"OK," they both replied without turning around.

"I don't think he liked me," Lawson said with a smile as they climbed into the car.

"He's just jealous because you're a threat," Ward replied.

"Well, there was something quite alluring about her so I might have to work my magic on her next time we visit."

"If you do that," he said, "I will kill you myself."
Lawson had no idea if Ward was joking or not so he let the subject drop immediately.

"Where do you want to go now?" Lawson asked.

"We are going to see McDermott."
Lawson knew who McDermott was, he had seen his team at work in London two years ago when Ward called them in.

"Where is he?"

"Harlem River Drive under Macomb's Dam Bridge."

"Why do we need to see him?" Lawson asked.

"Because he is going to kidnap someone for me."

McDermott's garage was set back in a row of six units on a small industrial park.

They parked the car thirty yards away from the garage so that they could be seen approaching clearly. Walking up to a building full of Ex-Navy seals without giving prior warning that you are there, would be the actions of a stupid guy.

The garage was much bigger once you got closer to it. The main roller shutter doors were big enough to fit a bus or large truck through them. They were originally a shiny grey colour, but years of grime had turned them into a lighter shade of black. There was a sign that was fitted above the roller shutter doors that said 'L & B Auto Repairs', with a phone number and website address below.

McDermott was thorough in everything he did and the website was fully functional and the number would be answered by one of his team giving the impression they were an employee of 'L & B Auto Repairs'.

But the callers were always told they were fully booked and unable to take any new customers.

As they got to within ten feet of the building the roller shutter doors started to rise much quicker than they should have; the always thorough McDermott had fitted a bigger motor to the door drive to allow for quicker access and egress.

The door stopped once the opening had reached about five feet, and they ducked under and stepped into the garage.

What they saw once they were inside did not look like a working garage at all. Directly in front of them there were two top of the pile Range Rovers with the window's blacked out. Ward doubted very much that they would have the original engines tucked under the hood, and knew without asking the question that a massive upgrade of power and speed would have taken place.

To the right there was a work bench that stretched at least thirty feet along the side wall and was covered in weapons. There was every conceivable firearm that the Seals liked to use, laid out in a neat line.

At the far wall directly in front of them were countless items of communication equipment. Everything was extremely neat, tidy and organised, and Ward was in no doubt they were already tested and ready for use.

To the left of the interior was a communal area which was simply a kitchen sink with very sparse coffee making materials on a table next to it, a refrigerator to the right of the sink in desperate need of a clean, a TV that wasn't on and a radio that was playing some music that Ward was convinced sounded like the old eighties band Culture Club. There was a small table with six chairs around it and an old beaten armchair which was placed to the far right corner of the table, in a position where the person seated there could hold court.

At the table were six of the most fearsome and individually skilled men that Ward had ever known.

Once all of their individual skills were put together, they became an unstoppable force.

The most startling thing about this group of people was that they all looked the same. They all sported short, cropped brown hair, all stood about six foot tall, and all had the wiry, athletic build about them that all Special Forces operatives throughout the world possessed.

The Special Forces world is no place for the steroid induced muscle men that think their size makes them tough. If they stated they were all brothers, a person would not disbelieve it, and in essence, that is exactly what they were.

At the end of the table nearest the armchair, sat McDermott's son, Paul. He was his father's son without a doubt. He was thorough to the extreme, and always radiated a calm about him. He was the heir apparent and the day when he was going to take over the team was looming ever closer.

Opposite him at the other end was Lloyd Walsh. He was the team's explosive expert and he had detonated and defused more explosive devices than anyone else that Ward had ever known.

The two seats nearest to them seated Danny Wallace and a guy simply known as Wired. Wallace was the telecoms expert of the group and could set up communications systems in any place on earth, no matter how remote.

Wired was the team member who had always interested Ward the most. He was psychotic to the extreme, in relation to his violent manner. Ward had once seen him attack two guys pointing handguns at him while he was unarmed. He beat them to death with unnerving ferocity, and continued to beat them both long after they were dead; until the team had pulled him off and secured him with cable ties to a pole until he had calmed down and regained his composure. Ward always felt that Wired could not cope in the real, every day world, and that being part of the team was the only thing that stopped him from becoming America's biggest mass murderer. He seemed to enjoy killing.

For Ward it was a necessity, a means to an end, but for Wired it was like a drug. But McDermott handled him well, and he always seemed to keep him under control.

But he was definitely not wired correctly, hence the nickname.

In the two seats opposite sat Adam Fuller and The Fringe. Fuller was the complete Seal but he was the quiet one of the team. The Fringe was a guy obsessed with eighties music. He played it at every opportunity and the team seemed to find this a useful tool in their resting periods. That explained the Culture Club music playing Ward thought, and at the same time laughed at the irony of this group of lethal killers listening to a guy sing, "Do you really want to hurt me?"

In the old armchair sat McDermott. He was into his fifties now but still he looked fearsome and incredibly fit. His cropped hair was now completely grey but his eyes were staggeringly alert. His face bore the marks of years of battles and missions, he had a scar running down his left cheek where he had been stabbed in the face a few years ago, and he looked exactly how anyone would imagine a battle-hardened Navy Seal veteran to look.

"Hello Gentlemen," Ward said as he approached the group.

"Hi Stranger," McDermott replied and the team all turned around and nodded.

"Lawson, you OK?" McDermott asked and Lawson nodded back to confirm he was.

"You had a look at what I sent you?" Ward asked McDermott.

"Yes we have. We discussed it this morning," he replied, looking at his whole team as he spoke, "How do you want to play it?"

"We kidnap this guy and get what we want from him and then kill him," Ward said.

"What's his name again?" Danny Wallace asked.

"Martin Walker," Ward replied.

TWENTY SEVEN

Lawson looked at Ward and frowned.

"Walker?"

"Yes."

"I don't understand?"

"I knew when we were back in London when we first visited them there had to be someone from UKBC news involved," Ward said.

"Really? I mean Walker, how?" Lawson asked again.

"How what?"

"How did you know so soon that he was involved?"

"Ergonomics," he replied.

Lawson looked confused.

"It's all a question of the position that you take," he added.

"I'm totally lost now. I mean why anyone from the network would want to kill people doesn't make sense, for what gain?" Lawson asked with a frown.

"I think the best way to get the answer to that is to ask Walker," he replied.

"I will. He was using Beglin all along? I'll beat it out of him," Lawson said aggressively.

"You won't be there."

"What? Why?"

"Because I need you to do something more important."

"What could be more important than that?" Lawson enquired.

"I need you to get back to Nicole-Louise's and Tacklers and help them to dig out everything you can on Walker."

"Seriously, is this for real?"

"Which part?"

"There is a known FFW bomber on the loose who has a vendetta against the West and you think the person behind it is a news editor? It seems completely far-fetched," Lawson said, almost dismissively, "I suppose Dr Death will appear and confess to being the leader of a worldwide criminal gang next?" he asked sarcastically.

Ward ignored his contempt.

"All you need to do is to go back to Park Avenue, work with them to find a financial link between Walker and Fulken, and then ask Beglin exactly how she was told to report on the Louvre bombing by her editor and producer."

Lawson nodded and then shrugged. Clearly feeling disappointed.

"Once you have that, can you let me know?"

"Yes I will but you are barking completely up the wrong tree here, I'm sure of it."

"Why is that?" Ward asked.

"Because Walker is not behind this, I know it," Lawson replied as he turned to leave.

I know it too, Ward thought to himself but he will lead us to the person who is.

With Lawson gone, McDermott looked at Ward,

"Why have you told him we are going to kill this Walker guy?" he asked.

"Because I want him to look at this with urgency," Ward replied, "Lawson is one of the best operatives either side of the Atlantic but he works better under pressure. If he thinks he has a point to prove and that I am wrong, he will prove it. I just need him to prove it quickly."

"So, we take this guy and just get one piece of information out of him and then let him go?" McDermott asked, "Isn't that risky?"

"It's meant to be," he replied, "If he reacts how I think he will react, then he will lead us to the real people we are chasing, and they lead us to Fulken."

"OK. You said in the briefing you sent me that this guy has a bodyguard?"

"What about him?"

"Do we take him out?"

"Try not to. Maybe just set Wired loose on him for a few seconds."

Wired turned around and Ward saw his eyes genuinely light up in anticipation.

"OK. So the next question is where is he now? He could be anywhere," McDermott said.

"We know exactly where he is."

"How so?" McDermott asked.

"Because The Optician is watching him for me and when I call, he will tell me where he is."

As soon as he mentioned The Optician, all six of McDermott's men either turned and looked at Ward, or lifted their heads up to confirm that they had heard his name.

Everyone was afraid of The Optician.

Ward took out his phone and dialled the number. The Optician answered immediately,

"About time," he said.

"Just briefing everyone here," Ward replied, "Where is Walker now?"

"I'm looking at him through my scope. He is on the 14th floor of the offices on 6th Avenue."

"Is he alone?"

"No. There is a guy sitting there with him. He looks reasonably trained but nothing to be worried about."

"OK. I want you to watch him. I am going to call him now and when he finishes the call, I want you to tell me what happens."

"OK," The Optician replied and hung up the phone.

Ward dialled the number from the business card that Walker had given Lawson back in London the first time they had met.

The Optician watched Walker pick up his cell phone and put it to his ear.

"Hello?"

"Is this Martin Walker?" Ward asked, feigning his best American accent.

"Yes," Walker replied.

"I just want to know if you can or you can't find time to have a one on one interview with a budding news editor."

"I can't," Walker replied.

"Can I ask you ten questions about being a news editor in a big corporation?"

"No," Walker responded.

Ward hung up the phone and then called The Optician back.

"Tell me what you see?" he asked.

The Optician watched as the other guy in the room approached Walker's desk and stood in front of him. He could see an exchange of words and then the guy lunged at Walker, grabbed his hair and then slapped him hard around the face. Walker then cowered in his chair before the guy pulled out his cell phone and made a call. The Optician watched as the guy then approached Walker again and handed him the phone. After a one minute conversation Walker handed the phone back to the guy who put it in his pocket and sat down. The Optician relayed all of this to Ward as it happened.

"What do you make of that?" he asked.

"He's being forced to do things he doesn't want to do."

"What did you say to get the guy to slap him like that?"

"It's not what I said; it's what the other guy heard."

"What did he hear?" The Optician queried.

"Yes. I can't. No," Ward replied.

"I don't get it? What did he hear?" he asked again.

"He heard, yes it's me, I can't talk, and no it isn't safe."

"Clever you," The Optician said.

Ward hung up the phone.

"Are we ready to move?" McDermott asked.

"Yes we are. Let's go."

McDermott got up from the old armchair and the six guys at the table immediately stood.

"Paul and Fringe you come with us," he said pointing to Ward, "The rest of you in the other vehicle."

Within ten seconds, everyone was sitting in the Range Rovers watching as McDermott used a remote control to raise the high-speed roller shutter doors and drive speedily out.

They parked fifty yards down from the USBC News building. "How are you going to get him outside so we can take him?" McDermott asked.

"The oldest trick in the book I was thinking," Ward replied.

"Which one, it's a big book?"

"You can get one of your guys inside to activate the fire alarm and then when they are on the street, we take him."

"Whatever happened to being creative?" McDermott asked with a smile.

"I think after this, everything that we are going to do is going to revolve around being creative."

"You two can deal with the alarm activation," McDermott said to Paul and Fringe without turning around.

"We're on it," Paul replied as they both stepped out of the car and headed towards the building. Ward watched Paul carefully.

"He's itching to take over from you," he said to McDermott.

"I know, and in about six months' time he will do," he replied. He then spoke into his microphone,

"Get out in the street and wait for the people to start streaming out," he said, "Once you have eyes on the target grab him and extract him immediately. Wired, you focus on the bodyguard if he comes out; do not let him engage any of our boys. Danny, you have the car in motion and rolling as soon as you see they have him. Are you all clear?" he continued, and then nodded at Ward once he had confirmation that everyone knew their part to play.

A minute later, Fuller, Wired and Walsh walked past the car as Ward and McDermott watched, and two minutes after that, the alarm could be heard ringing out inside the building and the first of the employees began the evacuation out onto the street.

Ward watched as people ran down the steps into the open. Twenty became fifty and then became a hundred and still people flocked out.

He noticed the crowd leaving the building thinning and then he saw Walker walk down the steps with his bodyguard holding his left arm.

Not in support but in detainment.

He watched as the car driven by Wallace rolled slowly past them and then Wired approach Walker and jabbed his right fist hard into the bodyguard's neck. His grip released immediately and he fell to his knees clutching his throat.

Almost as soon as he had let go of Walker, Fuller and Wired stood in front of him. Within seconds, Paul and Fringe were behind them and Walker was boxed in.

They moved forward towards the car and Wallace stopped right in their path, Wired stepped ahead and opened the door and climbed in, and Walker was put in next with Walsh climbing in immediately after. Fuller climbed into the front and the car moved forward and drove off. Paul and Fringe walked back to Ward's car and climbed into the back and McDermott pulled quickly away.

The whole extraction had taken no more than fifteen seconds from the moment Wired had hit the bodyguard and crucially, not one of the evacuees had noticed a single thing.

Ward was suitably impressed yet again by the standard of their work.

"Very impressive," he said.

"Did you expect anything else?" McDermott asked.

"No I didn't," he replied, "Are your boys aware how I want him ready?"

"Yes they are."

"Then you had better slow down," he said, "They need at least five minutes at the garage to prepare him before we get back."

McDermott had slowed down accordingly, and by the time they arrived back at the garage, they were pretty much exactly five minutes behind the first vehicle. He drove in and parked directly opposite the other Range Rover.

They stepped out of the car.

Walker was tied to a chair in the middle of the garage floor and he had a hood over his head. He was twisting his neck side to side, desperately trying to pick up the smallest of sounds, to establish where people were positioned.

He was blind to the fact that after Paul and Fringe had joined them; all six of the team were sitting back at the table in exactly the same positions that Ward had seen them in just over an hour ago.

Ward handed McDermott a piece of paper and leant against the car as he watched him casually stroll up to Walker,

"You are in a lot of trouble Mr Walker," McDermott said.

"Who, who are you?" Walker replied, sounding petrified.

McDermott looked down at the piece of paper in his hand and started to read,

"I am going to ask you a number of questions. If you answer them correctly, we will take you back to work," he said very slowly

"I don't know anything," Walker pleaded.

"Wrong answer," McDermott said, and he slapped Walker hard around the head with his right hand, open palmed, a shot that must have caught Walker full on the left ear, the hood he wore offering very little protection against the blow. Walker rocked on his chair.

"You don't know what I am going to ask yet," McDermott ad-libbed, "I might have asked you the name of the Queen of Britain, in which case I am pretty sure you would know the answer. So you answer my questions and you live, if you lie you die. Understand?" he asked, pulling the hammer on his gun back as he spoke, making as much noise as possible. Walker knew instantly what the sound was.

"I understand," he whimpered.

"It's just three questions," McDermott said, looking down at the piece of paper.

"OK."

"I want to know the name of your source who told you about the arranged meeting on Hubert Street, so give it to me."

"I don't know it," Walker replied.

McDermott looked at Ward for an indication of what do and Ward made a push sign with his hand, and so he used his left hand to slap walker on the right hand side of his head.

Walker screamed a high pitch scream, and started moving his head left to right, bracing himself for the next blow. He was now completely disorientated and did not know when, or on what side, the next blow would come.

"I want to know the name of your source, last time I am going to ask," McDermott said in a calm voice.

"I don't know his name," Walker stuttered, he sounded as though he was crying.

"Wrong answer," McDermott replied and as Walker went rigid and dipped the right hand side of his head into his neck, his natural survival instincts anticipating the next blow being in the same place as the last shot, McDermott raised his right foot and stamped his heel hard down on Walker's left knee. Walker screamed in agony.

"Stop, please, I'm begging you."

"I haven't even started yet," McDermott said calmly.

"I don't know his name," Walker said in a quiet tone, "But I have his cell number."

McDermott looked at Ward and Ward made a rotating motion with his hands that indicated to McDermott to get the number.

"Tell me the number," McDermott demanded.

"I don't know it in my head but I can get it."

"Where is it?"

"Back at the office," Walker replied.

"You know what, I don't have time for this, I'm going to take the hood off and look you in the eyes and then I am going to kill you," McDermott said.

"Wait!" Walker shouted, "I don't want to see you. I've just remembered it's in my wallet in my back pocket," he quickly added.

McDermott nodded to Paul and Fuller and they stood up, walked over to Walker, took an arm each, and leant him forward, lifting the chair off the ground as they did so. McDermott walked around the back of the chair and leant behind Walkers back and pulled his wallet out of his pocket. He threw the wallet to Ward, who caught it and started thumbing through it, while Walker was returned to the position he had been in ten seconds ago, waiting for the next blow to come.

"Next question," McDermott said, "Do you know where the next bomb is going to go off?"

"No I don't, I swear, I don't," Walker said urgently.

McDermott looked at Ward, and Ward raised three fingers instructing McDermott to ask the third and last question.

"One more question to go. You seem to be doing OK so far so don't mess it up now," he said.

Walker stayed completely quiet but continued moving his head from side to side and shrinking it into his neck, hoping to be prepared for the next blow that would come his way.

"The two guys who have been questioning you, the two idiots you sent to Hubert Street," McDermott said, and looked at Ward, who promptly mouthed the word 'Idiots?' to him, "Where can I find them?" he asked.

The question, as anticipated, clearly threw Walker, a fact confirmed by the way his whimpering stopped, and McDermott could sense the frown under the hood.

Ward threw Walker's wallet back to McDermott who caught it in one hand.

"I don't understand," Walker replied.

"It's a really simple question. I want them both dead and the fact you only had one of them killed means I have to take out the other guy," McDermott said aggressively.

"I don't understand," Walker said, "One of them is dead? I just passed over the address," he added.

"I want you to arrange a meeting with whichever one is left," McDermott said, "And in your wallet is now a piece of paper with a number on it, you will ring and tell me when and where, and the rest is up to me. Then I will disappear and as far as you are concerned, I never existed." McDermott added, as he bent forward and put the wallet into Walkers shirt pocket, "Is that clear?" he asked.

"Yes. I promise," Walker replied excitedly.

McDermott looked at Ward.

Ward made a cutting motion to the front of his neck to indicate that the interrogation had ended. McDermott frowned his surprise and said,

"You've been a lot of help. Now we will take you back to your office and you will forget this ever happened. Is that clear?"

"Yes please. I swear I won't say a word. I swear on my children's lives," Walker replied.

McDermott nodded to Paul and Fuller and they immediately stepped forward and cut the cable ties around Walkers ankles and wrists, and then walked him towards the car, opened the back door and bundled him in. Fuller climbed in after Walker and Paul climbed into the driver's seat. He started the engine and using an identical remote control to his father, raised the high-speed roller shutter doors and drove out.

McDermott looked at Ward.

"Why didn't you push to get the names of who was behind it?" he asked, "He was broken, he would have told us anything."

"He would have told us only what he knows, and that is only three things that I already know anyway," Ward replied, "Plus, I don't want him to think we suspect too much. I want him to think we are chasing shadows."

"So, we can catch them unaware when they think we are somewhere else?" McDermott asked.

"No," Ward replied, "So when the people who are behind it torture him, he will not be able to tell them one single thing about what we know."

"Always one step ahead," McDermott said, "So, the number you have, you going to call it?"

"Better than that, I will get Nicole-Louise and Tackler to tell me every word sent or received to this cell," he replied, "Can you take me to their place now, we have a long day ahead."

Thirty minutes later, Paul and Fuller pulled up outside the USBC News headquarters.

"I'm going to take your hood off. You do not turn around and look at us. Then you open the car door, step out and go back to work without looking back. If you look back once I will kill you," Fuller said to Walker.

"I promise I won't," he replied.

And true to his word, as Paul stopped at the kerbside, Walker opened the door and stepped out without looking back. He heard the car pull away and started the climb up the steps into the sanctuary of his workplace. He walked through the doors and into the reception area, and for a few seconds he felt relief and happiness wash all over him. Until his personal protection detail walked towards him in a very intimidating manner and said,

"Get upstairs now you little weasel, we have got a lot to talk about."

TWENTY EIGHT

Ward and McDermott walked into Nicole-Louise's and Tacklers, and saw Lawson sitting next to Nicole-Louise and greeted them both with a smile,
"McDermott," she said and nodded.
"Nicole-Louise," McDermott replied.
"Where are you with your search?" Ward asked Lawson.
"I have to say, she is unbelievable," Lawson replied, "She has found things that were right in front of me, but I couldn't even see them. Amazing," he added and smiled at her.
It was a reply that had Tackler looking towards Lawson and making a grunting noise in complete contempt of him in the process.
Nicole-Louise rolled her eyes,
"Or it could just be that the female race is far superior?" she said.
"It could be," Lawson replied, "But we are cuter."
She glared at him and Ward took this as his cue to speak.
"So tell me where you have got with Walker?"
"We've made progress," she replied, "But we still have stuff to search for."

"He's an interesting one, that's for sure," Tackler interrupted.

"Explain what you mean?" Ward asked.

"Well when you said you were leaving it to us to find what MI6 didn't want to, or weren't capable enough of finding," he said as he gave Lawson another contemptuous look, "I started to think that if he was involved then the money would never have been found so easily."

Ward looked at him and smiled.

Forget the damage to his ego where he felt threatened by the stunningly handsome and masculine Mike Lawson, when it came to digging and seeing what no one else could see, the two of them were quite simply, in a league of their own.

"So then what did you do?"

"I looked at his family and their past expenditure."

"And you found?"

"I found nothing at all. Well nothing out of the ordinary. He makes around three hundred thousand dollars a year; he has two boys, both in private school, and lives in a house worth about a million bucks, so everything is how it should be."

"But you found something else?"

"Yes I did," he replied, "But I am waiting for confirmation," he said looking at his watch.

Ward instinctively looked at his watch too. It was nearly midday.

"How long do you have to wait?"

"By 4pm I will know," Tackler replied, "But I will keep looking until then. Also, something doesn't add up about the money trail. I can see how it got into his account and where it came from, but as of yet, I don't know where it originated from."

"Tackler will piece it together Ryan, he's the smartest man in the room," Nicole-Louise said, clearly aware that the jealousy he was feeling was now uncomfortable for him rather than amusing to her.

Ward looked at Lawson,

"How did you get on with Beglin?" he asked.

"I'm meeting her at two in Central Park. We thought we would take one of those horse drawn carriage rides," he replied.

"Great," interrupted Tackler, "More Tourists!"

"You know exactly what we need to know from her?" Ward asked him.

Lawson nodded confirmation.

"Can I ask something?" Tackler said, looking at Ward.

"Shoot?"

"The footage of the bombs in London and Paris I gave you?"

"What about it?"

"Am I missing something because I can't see whatever or whoever it is that you see, and I have now looked at it at least twenty times, so has he," Tackler said pointing to Lawson.

The whole room went quiet.

Lawson, McDermott, Nicole-Louise and Tackler all knew that Ward had complete conviction that the answer to preventing the bomb from ever going off was evident from the first time he saw the news footage from Paris. The London bombing only served to confirm beyond doubt in his mind that he was right.

"What do you mean?" Ward replied.

Tackler looked awkward.

"Well, you know," he said.

"What if I'm wrong?" Ward asked, "What if I'm having you all run around in circles chasing shadows, and while we are doing that hundreds of innocent people are going to get killed?"

"Well kinda," Tackler replied.

Ward looked around the room. All four of them were waiting for an answer.

He thought how they were all as much a part of this as he was, and how Gilligan had lost his life in fighting to prevent the bomb from going off. They had all supported him and done whatever he had asked without question. Maybe it was time to explain.

"Well?" Lawson asked.

The four of them seemed to be holding their breath, waiting for the revelation that would make everything fall into a nice, neat sequence of events.

"I'm not wrong," he said, "Now, we have something more pressing."

They all looked at each other more in annoyance than disbelief.

"Gilligan is dead. The first thing we have to do is avenge him," Ward said suddenly.

"Agreed," McDermott said at the same time as Nicole-Louise and Tackler nodded.

"We have a phone number of the source who contacted Walker and set up the meeting and I want to know who he is, where he is and what was said," he declared as he passed Nicole-Louise the paper with the number that they had taken from Walker's wallet, "Then we have to know who the bomb makers are, where they are and how the bomb is being hidden and transported."

"And you want all of this done today?" Lawson asked, thinking back to Ward's claim that this would end today.

"It has to be," he replied and added no further comment.

"What have we got to go on with the bomb makers?" Nicole-Louise asked.

"Two women, both amputee's, both Iraqi nationals possibly," Ward replied.

"Specifically what body parts are missing?" she asked.

"One lost a leg, the other an arm."

Nicole-Louise smiled,

"I'll have that within the hour. Address and everything," she said.

"You will find them that quick?"

"Yep. Medical records will give me all I need."

"OK. Tackler will confirm Walker is the bad guy by 4pm today, and in the meantime he will get us the location of the source. Lawson is going to get the information we need from Beglin, and Nicole-Louise is going to get us the two bomb makers and make sure that Tackler finds the source of the money within the hour," Ward said, "Everyone clear?"

The three of them nodded.

"What about us?" McDermott asked.

"We are going to go back to the warehouse and get ready to move on the information that Nicole-Louise and Tackler give us," he replied, "We are going to get ready for war."

Asif Fulken was a worried man. He had a 300 pound bomb built into an exact replica of a UPS van with copied licence plates that were registered to a warehouse in Newark, and he knew the target was now the Chrysler building. But he didn't like waiting for calls from the voice. He was pleased with the quality of work that the two bomb makers had provided, and he was also pleased with the van that the last remaining FFW cell had provided and fitted. But the fact there was only one cell left worried him.

He was now completely alone.

He was aware that all of the other people from Al Holami to Qasim had not only been found, but killed, and he was sure that it was the man he had seen talking into his cell phone when he was on Greenwich Avenue who had done it.

He could not get his face out of his head.

He was sure he recognised him but he did not know where from. The harder Fulken thought about where he could know him from, the more worried he became.

This was an unusual feeling for him, but he decided to use that nervous feeling to become more focused and stay ahead of the people chasing him.

As soon as he knew that the Chrysler building was the target he had instructed the leader of the last cell to find him a lock up about a mile away on Lexington Avenue.

They had provided an empty shop that had garages at the back that were big enough to conceal the van. It had been transported overnight after the cell had moved everything from their bomb making facility in Hubert Street, and he was now sitting in the empty apartment above the shop, looking at his cell phone, almost willing it to ring. His target was only a mile away, he could almost touch it.

Even less than a mile away, over on Park Avenue, at the exact moment he was concentrating on his cell phone, trying to induce it to ring; Nicole-Louise leant back in her chair and said to Tackler, "I've found them."

At the exact same moment in McDermott's garage on Harlem Drive, Ward watched the last of the equipment being loaded into the two Range Rovers. McDermott was more than thorough, he had concluded in the last fifteen minutes. He was obsessive.
The team were equipped with everything from handguns to sniper rifles to machine guns; flares to grenades and switchblades to swords. They literally were ready for a war.
His phone rang. Centrepoint's name appeared on the screen.
"Yes?" Ward answered
"What are you all getting ready for?" he asked.
He knew that the Optician would be outside somewhere, and that Centrepoint had probably had him moving as soon as they had left Nicole-Louise's and Tacklers.
"To talk to the people who made the bomb," he replied.
"Try and take some of them alive," he said, "It's not an easy task cleaning up all of your mess throughout New York. Our people are having to crash all sorts of social media reports of shooting and gun fights, and I've had the headache of coming up with a cover story as to why half of New York's immigrant community have disappeared."
"That's because people like Fulken are hell bent on destruction against us and we think it's a good idea to let them live here. This mess is our doing so it is down to us to clean it up," he replied.
"I want the bomb makers alive," Centrepoint demanded.
Ward was silent.
"I mean it," he said, "I want them alive," he repeated, "They are much more valuable to us alive."
Ward knew he was right but still didn't say anything.
"How far away from finishing this are you?"
He looked at his watch. He did a quick calculation of the forthcoming events in his head and said,

"Three am tomorrow morning is my best guess," he replied.

"You have all you need?"

"Yes."

"I have to insist on one thing. When you have found the bomb and it has been made safe, you tell me immediately. OK?"

"OK," Ward replied and hung up the phone.

He imagined the problems that the last few days would have caused The Old Man. Missing people, dead bodies, politicians no doubt asking questions, and he didn't envy him one bit. He promised himself that the first thing he would do after he killed Asif Fulken was to call him.

His phone rang. It was Nicole-Louise.

"Who is the smartest person in the world?" she asked.

He could hear her laugh as she asked the question.

"You are Nicole-Louise," he replied.

"Correct answer," she said, "I have found them."

"Already?"

"Well, I would like to say that I hacked into the national database for amputee's and using my incredible analytical skills, narrowed it down to two people, you know, like they do in the movies" she said.

"But?"

"The movies lie. That would have taken me at least three days."

He accepted that Nicole-Louise had a habit of building things up but tolerated it because she always delivered.

He played along; "So how did you do it?"

"I hacked into the cameras on the corner of Hubert to the point in time where you said they vacated the building," she replied, before pausing for effect, "And I saw four men, the guys you said were posing as cops loading containers into two vans, and both the women," she added.

"Then?" he enquired in an urgent tone, trying to add to the drama.

"Then they all got in the vans."

He knew the obvious question to ask but decided to ask the opposite.

"And they disappeared?"

"To everyone else, yes. But I then hacked into the traffic system and followed the vans until they reached their destination."

"And then what?" he asked. By now he was getting bored of the build-up but dared not interrupt.

"Then they drove to a house in Fordham Heights and they are still there."

"How do you know?"

"Because they carried the containers in and the vans haven't moved."

"Nothing at all?"

"No," she replied, "The cameras literally face right onto the building."

"No one collected anything or other people turned up?" he asked.

"No. The vans have not moved. All I have seen over the last two days are people going to work, a few delivery vans drive past and the local residents coming and going."

"Go on?"

"So then I checked the address and it came up as registered to a guy called, Younis Ali-Wahim."

"Who's he?" Ward asked.

"He is a former Iraqi national who has been here for twelve years; a local businessman. He owns three modest electrical outlet stores," she replied.

"You have anything on him to go on?"

"No, this guy looks clean. Not even on the radar of the intelligence services. He was granted asylum here after arriving on a boat that docked in Florida."

"So they are definitely all still there now?"

"Yes, I'm looking at the live feed now."

"The women?"

"That was more difficult. That took me at least six minutes to figure out," she said without a hint of arrogance.

Ward was now becoming impatient.

"The short version please Nicole-Louise?" he said softly.

"OK," she said in a disappointed tone, much to his relief, "I hacked into his cell phone records and looked for calls made in the hour prior to them turning up at the apartment on Hubert. There was one number that lit up so I followed that and found it was registered to a woman."

"Go on?"

"Then I hacked into her records and found the most common number called and found that was registered to the other woman."

"The two bomb makers?" Ward asked. She ignored his question.

"So then I checked her medical records and she is an amputee and did the same with the other woman and got the same answer," she said with an air of proclamation, "Then I hacked into the cell towers and the phones are still sitting in the building right now and they definitely haven't left by the front door."

"All six of them are still in there?"

"Yes."

"Tell me about the women?"

"Their names are Sabeen Meram and Sanaa Kasim."

"Which is which?"

"Meram lost her leg, Kasim her arm."

"Send me the address and don't take your eyes off of the camera. If anyone moves you let me know immediately, OK?"

"OK," she replied.

"You really are the best." he said and he hung up the phone. He looked at McDermott.

"We have found them," he said, "And there is a chance the bomb is still with them and that Fulken might be there hiding."

"Shall we go?" McDermott asked.

Before he could answer, his phone vibrated to indicate he had received a message. He opened it up. It simply said 'Apartment 5, 2358 Webster Avenue, Fordham Heights'

"Yes," he replied.

TWENTY NINE

2358 Webster Avenue looked a nice apartment block. It was sandwiched between two other buildings, all five floors high. It was built out of brown brick and had not been ruined by inappropriately coloured fire escapes being fitted down the front of the building. The one escape that was fitted blended in well to the brown brick. It had a smart Glass door as an entrance that was reached by climbing two small steps, and the grey paint used on the masonry surrounding the door and first floor windows made the building look cared for and loved.

There were rows of trash bins neatly stacked at the front of the building to the right.

The vans were still parked directly outside the building.

"Number five will be on the ground floor," Ward said.

"I'll get Paul and the rest to go around the back of the building and we can take the front," McDermott replied.

"We have to take the two women alive," he said, "Direct orders from The Old Man."

McDermott nodded.

He pulled out his phone and called The Optician.

"It would be nice if you gave me a heads up now and again," he said as he answered without offering any greeting.

"Are you here?" Ward asked.

"Just got you in my scope now."

Ward instinctively looked left, right, up and even down for a brief moment but then knew it was pointless even trying to see him and gave up.

"If you see anyone coming out who looks remotely like a bad guy, take them out and ask questions later," he said, "But don't kill the women."

"The Old Man has already briefed me," The Optician replied and hung up the phone.

He looked in his mirror and saw Paul and the others get out of the car and disappear down a side alley.

"Give them a couple of minutes to get into position and then we will move," McDermott said.

Ward nodded.

Fuller and Wired got out of the back of the car without prompting and walked towards the building.

They were casually dressed in jeans, hoodies and jackets, with rucksacks over their shoulders and they looked like two lifelong friends, or work colleagues, heading somewhere non-important. Exactly how they were supposed to look.

He watched as they approached the door, and he was not exactly sure what they did to the locks, but within twenty seconds they were opening the door and stepping into the building.

"Showtime," McDermott said, "You lead the way."

They both got out of the car and walked towards the building, walking within two feet of the vans, but neither of them glancing at them or even acknowledging them just in case there were eyes on them.

They walked straight into the building through the now unlocked door and Fuller was standing to the left of the hall with his silenced handgun hanging casually down by his side. Wired, offering a lot less discretion, was on the right hand side of the hallway with his silenced weapon held firmly in both hands ready to pounce.

213

He had a focus, a deranged look in his eyes, that Ward had noticed every single time that he had seen him in action. This look never ceased to interest him and he made a mental note that one day he would sit down with Wired and try to establish just how his mind really worked.

The door to number five was the third door down on the left. McDermott nodded in the direction of it.

Ward moved forward and the other three followed in single file behind him; Fuller taking the back of the line and walking backwards in case someone tried sneaking up from behind. They reached the door.

"How shall we do it?" McDermott whispered.

"Shoot the lock," Ward said, "I'll go in and take the far right of the room, you take the near right quarter and these two do the same on the left," he added, nudging his silenced Glock which he had now drawn, in the direction of Fuller and Wired.

"You got that?" McDermott whispered to the two of them and they nodded.

"Remember, the women have to be kept alive," Ward said, "Get Paul to move in the back." he added.

"Go in ten," McDermott whispered into his mic.

Ward counted from ten down silently and raised his Glock and pointed it at the door lock, and as he reached zero in his head, he fired a bullet that ripped the door surround clean away, and McDermott used his right foot to kick to the right of the door handle almost as soon as the bullet had splintered the wood, and the door flew open.

Ward took five steps in and moved to the right to take his far quarter of the room and out of the corner of his left eye, he could see Fuller almost exactly in line with him.

All six people they expected to be there were there.

To the right, on a sofa, five feet in front of him, sat one man in his fifties who had a laptop which he was looking at.

Directly in front of him, slightly to the left at a large pine table sat the two women.

To his left, directly in front of Fuller, two men in their thirties were crouched over some small electrical components, both holding screwdrivers, and the fourth guy they expected to see was stood on the left hand side of the room, leaning against the wall drinking out of a mug.

All six, neatly laid out for them.

The six people that they expected to see.

They all looked up in startled shock. At they did so, Paul shouted, "Clear," and came walking through the door at the back of the room.

The two guys who were leaning over the electrical components swooped down and reached out for their weapons, but as soon as their hands had moved, Fuller shot the one nearest to him in the back and the one furthest away in his head. His head exploded and blood and shattered bone sprayed in a three foot semi-circle around him, and his knees buckled as he fell to the floor as if he was an inflatable object having the air suddenly released from him.

The second guy, who had taken the shot in the back, had arched backwards, and as he was falling he caught his head on a stone object laid next to the bench where their electrical components were laid out, and was dead before he hit the floor.

For a few seconds there was an eerie silence in the room and then it was broken by the sound of a silenced shot ringing out. Ward spun his head left to see the guy drinking from the mug fall forward with a hole in his chest and land face first on the floor. Wired was holding his gun directly out in front of him, still retaining the crazed look in his eyes but his face was adorned with a big grin.

Ward ignored this.

The old man sitting on the sofa froze in fear.

The two women sat there calm and looked around the room at the intruders, more in acceptance than anything else.

McDermott moved past Ward and took the laptop from the old man.

"Who are you?" Ward asked him.

The old man sat rigid and said nothing.

Ward raised his gun,

"Last time, who are you?"

"I, I, I am Younis Ali-Wahim," he stuttered.

Ward pulled the trigger and shot the old man straight in the face. His face exploded and he slumped back. He walked over to the table, pulled out a chair and sat down, directly opposite the women.

"Do you know why I shoot people in the face?" he asked them. Neither of them said a word.

Wallace walked in,

"You had better come and see this," he said to McDermott.

Ward followed them out of the main room through the door, and then through another door, into a room directly in front of them.

Inside the room there were four large chrome boxes with the lids off of them. They were all empty.

Ward walked back to the main room and sat back down at the table with the two women.

"Do you know why I shoot people in the face?" he asked again.

It looked as though the one sitting on the left was about to speak when Fringe stepped into the room and said,

"You had better come and see this Ryan."

They followed Fringe out of the room and out of a rear door back into the entrance hallway, about thirty feet down from where they had shot their way into the apartment.

Fringe continued to the far end of the hallway to a door in the right hand corner. He went through the door and down a set of stairs until they were outside, at the rear of the building. He carried on for another fifty feet and arrived at a green coloured, wooden building which at some point would have acted as a garage but was now in a state of complete disrepair.

On the floor was a chain and padlock which looked as though it had just been removed looking at the splinters of the bright wood against the green exterior.

He pulled the door slightly open and walked in. Inside it looked like a very modern workshop. There were neat workbenches, all empty, a hydraulic ram that is found in all garages to lift cars up for inspection, and rows and rows of tools all stored neatly and in descending size, running along all four walls.

But there was nothing else in there at all.

"This is where they put it all together," McDermott said.

"But what did they put together?" Ward asked no one in particular.

"I know the answer to that," Fringe said.

Ward looked at him quizzically.

"Tell us," McDermott demanded.

"I'll show you instead," Fringe replied.

He led them back out of the building and towards a dumpster and lifted the lid up.

Inside were a number of empty paint tins, some spray painting equipment, and some large sheets of paper that would be used to hold advertising stickers that adorn company vehicles.

Fringe leant in and pulled out an empty paint can and handed it to Ward.

He read the tin and it said 'Pullman Brown' on it. He tossed the tin to McDermott.

Fringe looked at him and smiled,

"You get it now?" he asked Ward.

"They have painted a vehicle in Pullman Brown?"

Fringe laughed,

"Maybe this will help?" he said and leant into the dumpster and pulled out a large crumpled piece of paper and then like a magician performing a trick, straightened it out in front of his audience.

They watched as the paper unfolded and then Fringe turned it around and held it up. It was giant sticker in the shape of a police badge, it was coloured gold and brown and there were three letters on it which simply said, UPS.

"Now we know what the bomb looks like. Well done," Ward said to him, before turning and walking back towards the apartment, followed by them both.

When they got back inside, the two women were still at the table looking calmer than they should have looked.

Wired was looking bored as the killing was over, and was leaning against the wall.

Paul was looking at the laptop and the rest of the team were standing with guns at the ready, pointing at the two women.

Ward sat down at the table once again.

He pulled out his cell and called The Old Man.

"Status?" Centrepoint asked as he answered the phone.

"I have the two women," he said.

"Alive?"

"Yes."

"I'll have a crew there in five minutes," Centrepoint said.

He hung up the phone.

The woman to his right was smiling at him. A smug smile that said it was irrelevant that he had found her, they would not stop the impending carnage.

Ward looked back at her with contempt.

"Meram or Kasim?" he asked her.

She didn't reply.

"It doesn't matter anyway," he said, "You are out of business and will probably be beaten daily in Guatemala Bay for the next fifteen years unless I help you."

"How can you help me infidel?" she spat out.

"You can tell me where the bomb is going to?" he calmly asked.

She looked at Ward with pure hatred across the table and then spat in his face, the spit landing just below his eye.

Ward used the cuff of his jacket to wipe the spit away and looked up at her.

He then lifted his Glock and shot her, straight in the face, from two feet away.

The blood from the initial impact of the bullet shot forward and covered his extended hand and the woman next to her screamed out loud. She immediately slumped back and then forward and then rolled down off of the chair in an almost comical manner, and her limp body slid out of view and landed at the feet of her friend. She moved her chair back about three feet from the table by using her feet to push her body back against the chair, the chair legs scraping on the tiled floor as she did so.

"You have no idea where the bomb is or where it is going to go off, do you?" Ward asked her, as she was now probably reconsidering the strength of her faith, "That's why she reacted like that. If you had something to bargain with, you would have approached it from a position of strength not hit out in anger."

"No I don't," she replied.

"Do you know where Fulken is?"

"No I don't."

He raised his gun.

"But he was here?"

"Yes he was. He collected the bomb," she said.

"How is the bomb disguised?"

"In a UPS van."

"How is it detonated?"

"By cell phone."

"Linked to one specific cell or by dialling a number?"

"Linked to the cell number that he gave us."

"Do you have the number?"

"In my head," she replied.

He looked down at her, and knew she was telling the truth. He noticed her right leg was twisted around in an unnatural position, a result of the push away from her dead friends' body.

"You must be Sabeen Meram?" he said.

The woman nodded and then looked down at her twisted leg, aware that her leg would be the only thing people would relate to her.

"I am going to ask you one more question. If you answer it, you live, if you don't answer it you die. Do you understand?" he softly said.

The woman nodded again.

"Good choice," he said, "You might have to tough out a few years in Guatemala Bay but you look like a survivor to me."

"I am," she replied, "I have my faith."

219

"Here's the question," Ward said, "Tell me clearly and slowly the cell number that Fulken will use to detonate the bomb?"

"1-408-255-2109," she said without any hesitation.

Ward looked to his right and McDermott was writing the number down.

He looked at the woman.

He saw someone who would want to survive at any cost, no consideration for Fulken or their mission; she was just looking after herself.

He saw someone who had probably killed hundreds of American and British men, women and children; his people, and thought nothing of it.

He saw someone that held herself in high regard and did not care for anyone else.

He saw a coward who planted bombs to hurt unsuspecting, innocent people in countries far away from her place of birth, and a woman who thought that was an acceptable way to live, because it was under the flag of faith.

He saw someone who at that moment, was lying to him.

He saw someone he was going to kill.

He lifted his gun, pointed it at her head and saw total fear in her eyes for the first time.

She was looking up at him and all she could see before her was a seven foot giant, and as she opened her mouth to beg for mercy, he pulled the trigger and shot her three times in the chest. The force of the bullets knocked her back and the chair flipped over backwards and she landed on the floor, flat on her back. She was dead before she hit the ground.

"That's for all of the innocent people," he said.

"So much for keeping the bomb makers alive," McDermott said in a tone which indicated sarcastic humour.

"She deserved it," he replied.

McDermott nodded his agreement and then Paul, who was still sat on the sofa looking at the laptop they had taken from the old man said,

"You'd better look at this."

They both stepped across to him. What they expected to see was a plan of a building or a written procedure of the detonation. What they expected to see was an 'UPS' van or a picture of Fulken.

What they didn't expect to see on the laptop was a live feed, showing a guy tied to a chair in a dirty looking room with a hood placed over his head.

"Who is that?!" McDermott asked.

"No idea," Ward said, "But don't turn the laptop off," he added as he looked at McDermott, "I need you to get two of the boys to Park Avenue and pick up Nicole-Louise and Tackler now," he demanded.

"Ring ahead and inform them," McDermott replied before heading over to Fuller and Fringe to give them instructions.

Ward looked at Paul and said,

"Put that down very carefully and do not lose the connection." Paul looked around the apartment and saw a charger plugged into the wall and moved over to it and put the lead into the laptop, and then turned and gave Ward the thumbs up to indicate it was charging. He took out his cell and called Nicole-Louise. Tackler answered.

"There are two guys coming to collect you both now I need you over here. There is a live feed being fed to a laptop and I need to know where it is coming from," he said and hung up the phone.

He then dialled The Old Man.

"What do you have?"

"The bomb makers I said were alive, I got it wrong" he replied and hung up the phone.

"Where now?" McDermott asked.

"We need to go over to USBC News. I want to talk to Walker."

THIRTY

It was now just after 2pm and Asif Fulken was becoming more and more irate.

Sitting above the old shop in Lexington Avenue, he started to feel a little vulnerable and exposed.

He could not shake the vision of the man on the cell phone out of his mind.

He was so close to finishing his mission, and even closer to being rich enough to disappear and live in luxury with his family for the rest of their lives.

He was the master of destruction, he was a legend in the FFW, and the CIA were so afraid of him, they had given him money to take up safe haven in their country, along with numerous others from the FFW family.

But he was free of them now. They never appreciated him as they should of.

These stupid people in the West who are governed and influenced by so many liberal people in powerful positions have created so many more problems than they have solved by their actions. They clearly thought more of their enemies than their own people.

His faith had now all but disappeared, and his only motivation was a life of affluence and leisure. His mind started to drift away and became filled with visions of sun, beaches and his family all smiling, when the ring of his cell phone shattered the vision he had created.

"Hello?" the thick, well-spoken English accent said.

"About time," Fulken replied.

"Is everything alright? You sound edgy?"

"I have control of everything, but the longer we leave this, the greater the risk of me being caught, and you not getting whatever you hope to achieve from this," Fulken said.

"What do you think I want to achieve?" the voice asked.

He had thought about this question long and hard over the last four weeks. However he had tried approaching it, whatever angle he put on it, he could never come up with an answer that fitted.

His problem was that he had no idea who the voice on the phone belonged to. His only contact had been by cell phone, and the only people he had seen face to face were the men who took him away from the life he had made for himself in America and threatened his family.

He believed they were CIA men, and he had believed that they were somehow involved in all that was happening, up until he saw the man on the cell phone, whose face kept haunting him.

"You have a grudge against someone and want them disposed of and the first two times were smokescreens, and when I achieve my mission, no doubt whoever you want gone will be gone," Fulken said.

"Very good," the voice replied.

"This is true is it?"

"The bomb is to go off at exactly 9.55am tomorrow, you will stop on the corner of Lexington and East 42nd, right by the crossing on Lexington," the voice said.

Fulken felt a rush of relief flood over him. He now had his final instructions. His initial thoughts were that he would only have about thirty seconds to get himself clear of the bomb, as there was no stopping there, but a 'UPS' delivery van outside a shop would not frighten too many people. He would walk down there later and see for himself the best way to approach it. He would be prepared when 9.55am came, he knew that much.

"I understand," he replied, "And the money?"

"It will be all delivered the moment the job is done."

"And you will walk away from my family and never watch them again as promised?"

"I am a man of my word. Once your work is done the contract will be settled in full, and you will never hear from me again after I end this call. I will take this opportunity to thank you for your work and also take the liberty of thanking you in advance for completing the contract."

The line then went dead.

He looked at his watch and calculated there were just seventeen hours left and then this would be all over. He smiled to himself. He knew he would win, he always did.

He put on his coat and walked out of the shop and along Lexington towards East 42nd Street, to prepare the perfect delivery of the bomb.

In Central Park, Lawson and Abbi Beglin were walking hand in hand towards Strawberry Fields,

"I need to ask you a few more things about Walker," he said.

"Seriously Mike, haven't we exhausted this?"

"Just a few more things."

"OK. But for every question you ask that is a dinner date in London you owe me."

"Deal," he replied, knowing that he would never hold up his end of the agreement.

"Then ask as many as you want," she said with a smile.

He thought about the questions that Ward had instructed him to ask, and even though he thought they were stupid and irrelevant, he had to ask them.

"When you were in Paris, who decided camera angles and what is your best side and what was the best view of the Louvre and so on?"

"I told you, Nigel Reid, my Producer," she replied.

"So he decides every angle?"

"Most of the time."

"What do you mean most of the time?" he asked, "I asked you that before and you told me all of the time."

"Well obviously he will get instructions if it's a big event or if it involves a world famous landmark or building but yes, most of the time he has a free hand," Beglin replied.

"Did he have a free hand in Paris?"

"What did I just tell you, isn't the Louvre famous enough for you?" she asked with a chuckle, "Mike, I am so going to have to educate you in the more refined things in life," she added, before reaching up and kissing his cheek.

"Seriously Abbi," he said, sounding frustrated, "So who was instructing Reid what to do in Paris?"

"Martin Walker obviously," she replied, "He is the chief news editor."

"He always does it, only him?"

"It's only happened once with me in Paris, I don't know about the other reporters. These are odd questions Mike, what are you getting at?" Beglin asked.

"The news alert that you did about the bomber being on the loose," he said, "Did Reid oversee that?"

"Don't be silly," she replied, "Something that big with the ramifications that would probably come with it, would not be left to Nigel."

"So who then?" he asked.

"Walker made the decision and then proof read and agreed the autocue. Why all these questions about Walker? Do you think he is involved?"

Lawson didn't reply. He stood there and without even noticing, he released the grip from her hand and their hands came apart.

"What is it Mike?"

He said nothing. He just stood still, running the questions Ward had instructed him to ask through his mind, and now with her answers, he was starting to piece every part together himself. Ward had been twenty steps ahead of them all this time. He now knew why he had to ask the next question,

"Can you do something for me Abbi?"

"I'd do anything, what is it?" she asked.

"Can you call whoever was producing the Westminster interview and ask them if the instructions were given from the producer or Walker when the bomb went off?" he asked.

"I can, but why?" she enquired, like all reporters do.

"Just do it Abbi, and do it now!" he said urgently.

She took out her cell phone and dialled a number. To Lawson's right the marble circle on the floor seemed to look up at him and the giant word 'IMAGINE' seemed completely ironic.

Not in a million years could he have imagined that Walker would be involved, and yet Ward had known that way back in London.

Now he understood why Ryan Ward was so revered.

Beglin began a conversation which sounded as though she was being switched through to about four different people, and after five minutes she hung up. Lawson was still staring at the word 'IMAGINE'.

"I spoke to a colleague, her name is Sharon Graham," she said, "Obviously she tends to get the smaller stories than I do and that's why she was covering the Abbey, and she says that her producer was getting instructions on the day of the explosion," she said.

"Continue," Lawson said hurriedly. .

"She said her producer, Nathan Hurst was moaning about interference from HQ."

"Who was interfering?"

"Martin Walker," she replied.

Ward and McDermott arrived at USBC News headquarters on 6th Avenue at 2.30pm. They parked directly outside the building.

"You want me to come in with you?" McDermott asked.

"No," Ward replied, "Just in case you speak he will recognise your voice."

"I can pretend I'm mute," McDermott said with a smile. Ward smiled back at him and opened the car door. As he went to climb out McDermott said,

"Wait!"

He stopped moving forward, slid back into the car and closed the door,

"Well, well, well," McDermott said, "Look at that," he added, pointing towards the main entrance doors. Martin Walker was walking towards the steps to the building directly in front of them, his protection in close attendance.

"Well at least I know it won't be a wasted journey," Ward said as he watched Walker go through the glass doors.

"Not him, the guy with him," McDermott said.

"You know him?"

"Know him?" McDermott said, "He used to be one of us."

"He was in your team?" he asked surprised.

"No, not in mine, he passed his training and had a month in Seal Team 6 but got busted out. He wasn't up to scratch. Sometimes the duds get through. I couldn't see him clearly before but now, it's definitely him."

"You know his name?"

"Lucas," McDermott replied, "Can't remember his first name."

Ward stepped out of the car and walked through the glass doors and into the building. The same girl as before was at the reception desk. She smiled when she saw him.

"I've come to see Mr Walker again," he said with a smile.

"Sorry sir, I can't remember your name?" she said apologetically.

"It's Mr Chennell."

She picked up the phone and dialled a number,

"Mr Chennell is here to see you sir," she said in an ultra-professional manner, "OK, thank you," she added as she put the phone down,

"His assistant will be down to collect you in a minute," she said sweetly.

"Thank you," he replied, and went and sat in one of the black leather armchairs that were placed to the left of him.

After five minutes the elevator doors opened and Lucas stepped out. His eyes went to work immediately and when they focussed on him, they were trying to calculate what he knew and what he didn't know.

He had witnessed this guy take a blow to the windpipe and go down like a child. Having found out about him not being up to scratch for the Seal team, he looked a lot less capable than before as he stood to greet him.

"Hello Mr Chennell," he said, shaking Ward by the hand.

"Hello."

"Mr Walker will see you now but would prefer if you could try and call ahead next time. He is busy, but he will fit you in."

He led Ward towards the elevator and pressed the call button. They waited for a few seconds in silence until the doors opened.

"After you," he said, offering Ward into the lift. Ward stepped in.

"Making any progress?" Lucas casually asked.

"Some," he replied.

"Anything interesting?"

Ward couldn't resist the opportunity to lay down a marker, "Just a bit of a fight with some guys playing at being tough," he replied, "I'm sure you've come across plenty of those?"

Lucas smiled, a smug smile and nodded,

"Many indeed, but you escaped unharmed?" he asked in his irritating droll.

"Of course, we came across a few mercenaries who used to be in Seal Team 6, you know the type that stick it out with them for ten years and then sell themselves as tough guys when they are really just overblown boy scouts," he replied, looking straight ahead at the elevator doors.

Lucas was visibly unnerved by this statement. Whether that was because he thought Ward might be on to him, or he knew people from Seal Team 6, wasn't clear. So he pushed harder.

"I mean, how these guys get off on thinking they are tough, I'll never know do you?" he asked innocently.

"Some of them are more than tough. They are natural born killers," Lucas replied in a very hostile manner.

"I'm sorry, I didn't mean to offend you," Ward said, "You weren't a Seal were you?"

Lucas ignored him and didn't speak again until the elevator doors opened,

"Follow me," he barked.

Lucas led him down the hallway that was lined with full length glass acting as office walls, and reached the large oak doors at the end of the hallway. He opened the door and walked in, and once again, Walker was sitting at the large table with Lord Ashurst-Stevens at the head, and the three stooges opposite him.

"Good to see you again," Ashurst-Stevens said to Ward.

"You too," he replied. He looked at the three lawyers, "Are you not allowed out on your own?" he asked him, "Can we talk without those three here?"

"They know all my affairs and there is nothing that you can say in front of them that I wouldn't tell them," Ashurst-Stevens replied.

"I don't like them, so as long as you tell them to keep quiet then we won't have a problem," he said.

Ashurst-Stevens looked taken aback.

"It is a little disrespectful coming in here and speaking to us like that, Mr Chennell," he said, "We are offering you our full support and I have actually had a knighthood bestowed on me by our Queen, so please afford me the appropriate respect."

"I'm not British, so your title doesn't hold any sway with me," he said, "But I will respect you as someone who can help us because we really aren't getting anywhere," he added.

"You aren't British?" Ashurst-Stevens queried.

"No. I'm American, British and Irish for good measure so I guess that makes me everyone's friend," Ward said completely seriously.

"How can we help you?" Ashurst-Stevens asked.

"I want Mr Walker to come with me for a few hours; I need his advice on something," Ward said.

"Advice on what, specifically?" Ashurst-Stevens enquired.

"That I can't share I am afraid. I'm protecting Queen and country and that is classified MI6 information."

"Touché!" Ashurst-Stevens declared.

Walker looked very, very, very uncomfortable sitting at the table.

"Unfortunately," Ashurst-Stevens said, "Mr Walker is needed right now; we have a number of important events to cover in the next twenty four hours and we need his co-ordinating skills here with us."

"You can't spare him for two hours now?" Ward asked, "He doesn't look very busy to me."

"I'm sorry, we really can't. Your colleague Mr Lawson is spending time with our Miss Beglin, so I am sure she can probably tell you as much as Mr Walker can. You are welcome to pick her brains, she doesn't have anything scheduled, I believe until tomorrow morning. Is that correct Martin?"

Martin Walker nodded. He had the look of a man who was completely lost.

"Well if you are sure, Beglin will have to do."

"If it changes, I will let you know, would you like to leave a number where we can reach you?"

"No," Ward said, "Thank you for your time."

He turned and walked towards the door to leave the room.

"Mr Chennell. We will continue to give you all the support you need, but next time you come to see us, please show a little more respect; I have very powerful friends both at home and here who can easily get someone demoted. That is just a friendly warning," Ashurst-Stevens said.

Ward stopped walking and turned around,

"I lost a good friend of mine last night due to information that came from this office, Sorry if that pisses me off and I seem a little abrupt. The truth is, we are getting nowhere and there is a bomb going to go off somewhere in New York in a week or so and we don't know where to even start looking, so if I am agitated, please understand why."

"I had no idea about your friend, the man who was here with you last time?" he asked.

"Yes."

Ashurst-Stevens looked genuinely shocked and saddened by this news,

"I'm sorry to hear that. I understand your anger now. Mr Walker will be available for as long as you need him after the next couple of days. We have an awards ceremony tomorrow night, and after that, he is yours for however long you need him," Ashurst-Stevens said in a much softer tone of voice than Ward had previously heard him use.

"Thank you," he replied and walked out of the room followed by Lucas.

When they got in the elevator, Ward said,

"They just don't understand us these people, do they?"

"No. But they pay well," Lucas replied, and smiled a big grin. 'I'm going to kill you' Ward thought, as he nodded back, 'I'm going to kill you for Gilligan'.

When he got back in the car McDermott said,

"How did it go?"

"Better than I expected."

"Paul called; he has taken Tackler back to his place and wants to know where to go now?" McDermott asked.

Before he could answer his phone vibrated in his pocket and he saw Lawson's number on the screen.

"How's your date in Central Park?" he asked.

"Not too good, I've just told her the date will have to be rearranged for another day," Lawson replied.

"Did you ask exactly what I told you to?"

"Yes I did."

"And?"

"I'm sorry I ever doubted you."

"There are still things that we have to understand and quickly, but we are on the final lap."

"What do you need now?" Lawson asked.

"We are all close to Park Avenue. Meet at Nicole-Louise and Tackler's. I guess it's time to lay everything out."

THIRTY ONE

Aidan Lucas wished he had opted to take out the guy who he
had just escorted out of the building first, instead of the big
guy who looked like Marvin Haggler.
He knew why he had made the choice; it was a question of
size.
He was trained to take out the biggest threat first and his
instincts told him that in an unarmed contest, he would
struggle to overcome the big guy. He made his choice and it
was a good shot after all, he reminded himself. The bullet had
hit him in the stomach and knocked him off his feet like a
paper doll. This Chennell guy had just moved quicker than he
expected and perhaps he had underestimated him.
Sometimes people do underestimate others; he knew that
from his time in Seal Team 6. He didn't fit in with them
because he was too quiet; he had convinced himself of this
over the corresponding years, after they had dared to tell him
he wasn't up to their standard. Sure, there was the mess in

Afghanistan, but that was down to their team commander, not his ability; even though it was him who had taken the fall.

They had been given a straightforward mission to get into an old farmhouse in the Kunar Province to rescue a UN delegate, extract him and then disappear. Intelligence had suggested there would be minimal resistance, but when they approached the building they had come under intense fire. Lucas trailed around the back of the building. He had not ignored his commander's orders to approach from the front as they suggested in his court martial; he was thinking on his feet, like a good Seal would.

Four of the team got killed that day and they put it down to Lucas not taking out the guy at the right front of the building. At his court martial, they even implied that he was a coward and he had frozen, but that was never the truth. The people in command wouldn't know a good Seal if they saw one.

Sure, he didn't mix with the team and that was the problem all along, he told himself one more time.

When he had set up for the kill at Hubert Street, on the 3rd floor of the building opposite the apartment block that he knew they would be visiting, he had visualised two straightforward kills.

The first opportunity that came was the one he took. They were talking and standing about six feet apart. In hindsight, it would have been better to take out the Chennell guy first as the big guy who he had killed was likely to move a lot slower.

On a positive note, he told himself, he can enjoy killing him even more now, after he dared to bad mouth the Seals. Lucas had made a good living as a mercenary and then a bodyguard on the back of being an Ex-Seal, and the payday that he was getting now would set him up for life. He felt strong and he knew that he was a lethal killing machine when it mattered most. The guy who had just left the building, whoever he was, made a very big mistake in bad mouthing the Seals.

He walked into Martin Walker's office and Walker looked up at him in with fear in his eyes.

"Why does he want to see you?" Lucas asked Walker in a menacing tone. A tone that got lost somewhat at the end due to the exaggerated droll he insisted in putting at the end of the last word in each sentence he spoke.

"I don't know," Walker replied.

"Are you lying to me Walker?"

"No. I have not been out of your sight since I was kidnapped," Walker replied nervously.

"About that," Lucas said, "I want to run through that again." Walker looked terrified,

"I have told you all I know and everything that happened," he said, "I told you I will do everything you have told me to do and I have."

Lucas walked around to the side of the desk where Walker was sitting. Walker instinctively hunched his shoulders and his face winced.

"Since when do you tell me anything?"

"I'm sorry," Walker replied.

"Not good enough," Lucas said. He then grabbed Walker's neck in his left hand and slammed his face hard down onto his desk, his forehead smashing hard against the keyboard which sat in front of his computer screen, flipping it up onto its side. He then delivered a solid, quick right hook that smashed into Walkers kidneys which took every last bit of breath out of him. Walker screamed in pain, but was more concerned with trying to breathe and so Lucas loosened his grip. He walked back around to the other side of the desk and sat down in the chair positioned directly opposite and watched in total amusement as Walker slowly regained his breath. Lucas could see the pain that he was in, and he got real gratification from this. Walker started to cry. Light sobs that he tried to disguise, but Lucas could see the tears running down his cheeks. You don't mess with the Seals he thought to himself.

After a few minutes of amusement to Lucas, Walker finally composed himself enough to look up and make eye contact with him.

"Now, tell me what happened again?" Lucas demanded.

"The fire alarm went off, you and me walked out, that guy punched you and put you on the floor, two guys grabbed me from behind, and two other guys sort of boxed me in so I couldn't move, and I felt them shuffling me away from the building, and the next thing I know I'm in pitch black and all I heard was scuffing and big doors and car doors opening and that was it, until the man started asking me questions," Walker replied.

"Tell me again what he said about the British guy?" Lucas asked.

"He said that he wanted them both dead but only one had been killed. He said that I was to arrange a meeting with the British man and I would ring him and tell him when a meeting was arranged."

"Ring him then," Lucas said, leaning back in his chair and cupping his hands behind his head, a gesture that subconsciously told Walker he wasn't listening much to him and he didn't believe him.

"I gave you the piece of paper with the number that they gave me," Walker pointed out.

Lucas dug into his pockets and pulled out the piece of paper that Walker had given him upon his return from his ordeal and threw it across the desk to him.

"Put it on loud speaker," he demanded.

"What do I say, we haven't arranged a meeting," Walker asked.

"Tell him that he should give you a time and you will fit in with him."

Walker looked down at the number and dialled it. It rang five times and then a male voice answered it,

"L & B Auto Repairs, how can I help?"

Walker had no idea what to say. Lucas shot him a threatening look,

"I need to talk to someone about a meeting," Walker stuttered.

"A meeting about your vehicle?"

"No. About a meeting someone at this number wants me to arrange with someone."

"I think you have got the wrong number sir, this is an auto repair shop."

Walker started to panic.

"But I was given this number to ring to let someone know about a meeting I was arranging," he pleaded.

"Then someone gave you the wrong number. If you don't want your vehicle looked at or repaired then you can meet who you want, but I suggest you check your number again."

The line went dead.

Walker looked at Lucas and frowned,

"Dial it again and this time properly, you weasel."

Walker dialled the number again,

"L & B Autos. How can I help?" the voice said.

Walker hung up the phone.

Lucas looked at him and said,

"You are lying to me Martin. You know what happens when you lie to me," and he stood up slowly and walked around to Walkers side of the desk.

Ward and McDermott were walking up the stairs to Nicole-Louise and Tackler's apartment when McDermott's phone vibrated. He listened and then hung up. He looked at Ward,

"Walker made the call," he said.

"That was quicker than I thought," Ward replied.

"Why would he make the call when no meeting has been arranged though?"

"Because he assumes that once he has instruction on when to meet me that he will tell Abbi Beglin, who will tell Lawson, who will tell me, and then I will get in touch with him."

"You could have just given him your number?" McDermott said.

"I needed to see how desperate he was."

Tackler opened the door. He looked at the two of them and then looked over their shoulders to the left, and the right, and then smiled; clearly pleased that Lawson wasn't with them. "On your own I see," he said.

"Lawson will be here in five minutes," Ward said as he walked past Tackler straight into the apartment, catching a glimpse of Tackler's smile visibly dropping as he passed him. Nicole-Louise was at her workstation.

"How far have you got?" he asked Tackler.

"We've both got very far," he replied, "I'll wait for Nicole-Louise to explain."

Ward looked over at the table where Nicole-Louise had her laptops and computers illuminated, and saw the live feed still running of the guy who was tied to the chair with the hood on his head.

"Has anyone been to give him water or feed him?" he asked.

"No idea," Tackler said, "I'm not working on that part."

"What are you working on?" Ward asked, waiting for Nicole-Louise to speak in her own time.

"What you told me to. The money trial, the bank accounts, the history of Walker, and the payment transfers to your bomber," Tackler replied.

Ward had learned over the years that the best way to deal with Nicole-Louise was to let her explain how brilliant and smart she was. He knew that when she got to explaining what she had found that he would have to endure a long explanation, probably switching between them both in doing so, but he also knew that they would have everything he needed. He knew that they still wouldn't have the 'Why?' but he was sure he would know by the end of the day. Nicole-Louise and Tackler would always work it out.

"Hello Ryan, Mac," she eventually said as she turned around. They both nodded.

"So, from the beginning, where are we?" Ward asked the two of them.

There was a knock on the door; Tackler trudged over to answer it.

A beaming Lawson stood there.

"Hello Tackler," he said.

Tackler snorted.

"So, where are we?" Lawson said looking at Ward and McDermott as he walked in.

"We were just about to find out," Ward said.

"If you can be quiet for two minutes," Tackler said sarcastically.

"What did Beglin say?" Ward asked Lawson, ignoring Tackler's animosity towards him.

"She confirmed that Martin Walker was the man who oversaw the productions of both the Louvre and the Westminster bombings, and that he schedules every report and nominates the appropriate team to report," Lawson replied, "She's nearly as smart as Nicole-Louise," he added.

"I feel sick," Tackler said and glared at Lawson.

"OK, let's get to it," Ward said, "Firstly, this guy in this live feed, do we know who he is?" he asked, looking at Nicole-Louise.

"No idea," she said, "But I know where he is," she added. The whole room went quiet and looked at her.

"You didn't think of mentioning that before?" Ward asked, sounding a little disappointed.

"I only found it about thirty seconds before you knocked on the door," she said firmly. Ward smiled back apologetically. "So where is he?"

"I traced the original source of the IP address and..."

"Nicole-Louise, I know you are a genius, you two are the best in the world, but we really need to move on this, we don't have much time left," Ward said sternly.

"OK. He is about ten blocks away on East 70th, building number four; in a basement by the look of it," she replied equally as sternly.

Ward, Lawson and McDermott looked at each other.

"I want you to do one thing when we are gone, Nicole-Louise," Ward said, "Get me the UKBC News schedules for the reporting teams on both bombings, OK?"

"OK."

THIRTY TWO

"Do we need any of the team?" McDermott asked Ward as they were heading towards East 70th Street.

"No," Ward replied, "Unless you are getting scared in your old age?"

"Where do you think this guy in the hood fits in?" Lawson enquired.

"What do you two think?" Ward asked them both.

"It could be someone who knows that a bomb is going to go off or the guy they are going to set up for it," McDermott replied.

"I think you are both part right," Ward said.

"Clever us," Lawson said sarcastically.

"Guessing often leads to the wrong conclusions," Ward replied.

The truth was, Ward had a very, very good idea who was under the hood and why, he just had to be sure. The end game was coming, and it would simply come down to who was the smartest out of three people, one of whom was him.

They reached East 70th Street in just under five minutes and drove slowly past apartment block number four. It was a ten storey building, built out of a mixture of grey cast concrete and brown brick.

To the right hand side there was a drive to a parking lot. They turned at the end of the street and came back for another look. There was nothing that indicated there were spotters outside. They turned again and drove down for the third time,

"Take the drive and park in the lot," Ward said to McDermott.

He carefully inched into the drive and moved down past the side of the building, and pulled into the wide parking lot at the rear.

"Park here," Ward said.

At the back there was a set of steps that descended down, to what they assumed, would be a door at the bottom.

"There's our basement," Lawson said.

"Go and check it out Mike," Ward instructed.

Lawson got out of the car and headed off in the direction of the far right corner of the building with the intention of sweeping around all the way across the front to get a complete overview of what was there.

"He's good, isn't he?" McDermott said.

"Yes he is," Ward replied, "All Ex-SAS are. His only problem is that he doesn't know just how good he is."

"Maybe you should tell him now and again?"

"When he stops thinking with what's in his pants so much, I will," Ward replied.

McDermott smiled.

They watched as he swept the front of the building and then walked up the side and disappeared out of sight.

Ward's phone vibrated, Lawson's name appeared on the screen.

"Problem?" Ward asked as he answered.

"There are two guys down the bottom of the stairs; both middle eastern, it looks like they are having a cigarette break," Lawson said, "I'm going to go inside from the front and check out the access from the inside of the building to see what we have."

"Two so far," Ward said to McDermott, "So whoever it is must be important."

They waited without speaking.

Both of them were playing out the possible scenarios that they might face in their heads. There was an exceptionally high chance that they were both visualising the same thing and the same outcome.

Ward's phone vibrated again.

"What have you got?"

"There are two more outside the internal door; there is a sign saying, do not enter - sewage leak, swinging from a plastic chain at the top of the stairs. The two guys are wearing white overalls, posing as workmen," Lawson said.

"Can you take them out alone?" Ward asked.

"Of course," Lawson replied.

"OK. You take the internal door and we will come in through the back. If anyone comes through your door you shoot, OK?"

"OK. I'll give you exactly two minutes to get into position," Lawson said, "And then I will deal with my two," he added before hanging up the phone.

"Let's go," Ward said to McDermott as he screwed the silencer onto his Glock.

They stepped out of the car and walked towards the stairwell. As they reached the top, one of the two guys standing outside the door looked at Ward and said,

"You can't go in there Sir, there is a sewage leak, and with the escape of gasses, there is the potential for an explosion."

"I'll be two minutes," he said, "I have some papers down there in storage and I need them urgently for work."

"I'm sorry sir, city rules. Tell me where they are and give me your number and I will call you if I can get to them," the guy said.

"OK. Fair enough," Ward replied.

He moved his right hand behind his back as if he was removing his wallet from his back pocket to get out a business card, but instead wrapped his hand around his

Glock, and in one continuous, sweeping motion, he swung his arm around and shot the guy two times in the head. His head exploded and blood, bone and matter sprayed his smoking colleague, and his white overalls became red in an instant. He went to reach into his pocket,

"Stop!" he shouted, and the guy froze, "If you move your hand one inch more you will be dead in one second," he added, as he started to descend the stairs with McDermott stepping down with him but facing backwards, monitoring the rear. The guy stood still but Ward noticed that he didn't look afraid.

His eyes weren't afraid.

"I know why you aren't afraid," Ward said, "So no matter what you think your friends inside can do, that isn't going to help you now because they don't know we are coming."

The guy smiled.

He knows something, Ward thought to himself.

Then he looked above his head to the right and knew why the guy wasn't afraid. There was a CCTV camera, clearly very recently fitted, facing straight onto him. So much for Lawson's reconnaissance skills.

"If you want to live, tell me how many guys are in there?"

"You can't shoot me with witnesses," the guy said.

"How many guys?" he repeated.

He said something in Arabic that made no sense, and started to move his hand, so Ward shot him twice in the chest. He dropped to the floor like the complete dead weight he now was. They moved to the bottom of the stairs and McDermott had to pull the guy out of the way so that they could open the door.

"So much for not needing the team," McDermott said, "Should I call them now?"

"No time; the guy in the hood probably has a minute left to live, we have to move now."

They slowly pulled the door half open. Inside it was poorly lit, and there was a hallway that had all manner of pipes and cables fixed to the walls running alongside.

They stepped in.

242

Ward facing forward, McDermott facing the rear.

They moved slowly along the hallway. It seemed to go in a straight line the whole length of the building, and there were no doors or other hallways that led off of it. Eventually, after walking almost the entire length of the building, they came to a set of stairs that led down to another level, and into another hallway that took them back the way they had come. This hallway was as dimly lit as the one they had just walked along. When they reached the end of the hallway, they came to a large square open room which was at least seventy feet square, with rows of racking set up, and divided into bays. All had number plates fitted to the front which indicated apartment numbers Ward concluded. They had a variety of objects placed on them which ranged from sets of dumbbells, to cardboard boxes. He even saw a giant teddy bear which stood at least three feet high and was wearing a jumper which was emblazoned with the words, 'Augusta 2nd'. There were four doors in the centre of the four walls that made up the room.

"Take your pick time," McDermott said.

Ward stood still and thought for a second.

If they came in through the back door, they would have gone to the nearest door which was the one slightly behind him to the right. They wouldn't have risked dragging the hooded guy through the front of the building, too many residents and passers-by, so he had to be in there.

He took out his phone and called Lawson,

"Status?"

"Mine are down," Lawson replied, "You?"

"Down too but they have CCTV cameras so whoever is guarding him in here knows we are here."

"Shall I come in?" Lawson asked.

"Yes. We are in an open plan storage area two floors down, come and join us," he replied and hung up the phone.

McDermott looked at Ward,

"This doesn't feel right. If they knew we were coming because of the CCTV, why didn't they jump us on the way in?" he whispered.

243

Ward thought about this and immediately knew the answer. "Because there is no one else here," he said in a loud voice.

Lawson appeared a moment later,

"Where is he?" he whispered.

"No need to whisper Mike."

"The guy with the hood isn't here?" McDermott said to Ward.

"Yes. He's here," he replied, "Try that door first."

"How do you know there are no more guys here?" McDermott asked.

"Because the CCTV cameras weren't for the guys in here, they were for the person who has him held here; probably another angle on the live feed."

McDermott opened the door that Ward had directed him to and the open area filled with light, "He's here," McDermott said.

Ward and Lawson walked over to the door and looked in.

On a steel chair sat the guy, his arms and ankles tied tight with cable ties, and a hood fitted over his head.

McDermott and Lawson raised their guns and then watched Ward tuck his back into the back of his waistband,

"You won't need them," he said to them both.

"Better to be safe than sorry," Lawson said.

"I don't think this person will hurt you."

He stepped up to the guy and put a hand on his right shoulder. The guy's head shot up and he went rigid with fear.

"It's OK," Ward said, "I'm a friend of your dad's. He has sent me to get you. You are safe now," he added, and then he slowly lifted the hood off of the guy's head.

As he moved it, Lawson and McDermott saw the face of a fifteen year old boy appear. His eyes were red where he had been crying so much, and his nose was running.

Joseph Walker, Martin Walker's fifteen year old son, looked into Ryan Ward's eyes and saw safety, someone who would comfort him and someone who would protect him. He then promptly burst into tears and sobbed loud and hard, like the child that he was, would be entitled to.

McDermott leant down and carefully cut the cable ties holding Joseph Walker to the chair. When they had all been cut off he stood up, a little uneasy on his feet, and he opened his arms and wrapped them around Ward and sobbed a little harder.

Ward wrapped his arms around the boy and held him tight.

"We are going to take you back to a safe place where our people will protect you," he said.

"What about my dad, what have they done to him?" Joseph asked, fear ringing through his voice.

"He's fine, I spoke to him this morning," Ward replied.

He pulled away and looked at Ward with his big blue, tear-filled eyes.

"Have they hurt him?" he asked.

"No," he replied, "They have just tried setting him up for mass murder and terrorist offences."

Ward put his arm around the young boy's shoulder and slowly led him out of the room; Joseph winced when he stepped over the bodies of the two guys dead on the floor, before climbing up the stairs and back into the sunlight.

Ward stopped in front of the CCTV camera on the outside of the building and still with his left arm supporting Joseph Walker, protecting him, making him feel safe, looked straight into the camera, raised his right hand and made a cutting motion across his throat. Then he turned and walked away, out of site of the camera.

The watching Aidan Lucas slammed down the lid on the laptop in front of him.

They got into the car and McDermott tossed a bottle of energy drink to Joseph and said,

"Drink that, it will stop you becoming dehydrated."

"Ring Nicole-Louise and tell her what's happened," Ward said to Lawson.

Ward took out his phone and dialled Centrepoint.

"About time."

"I need a clean-up crew on East 70th Street."

"I know, The Optician has already told me."

Ward hung up the phone.

"Let's get back to Nicole-Louise's," he said to McDermott, "Then I need to see his dad."

They drove without speaking; the silence only occasionally broken by Joseph Walker's whimpering; although Ward knew that the whimpers were now of relief rather than fear.

They arrived back at Nicole-Louise and Tackler's and as soon as the door was opened, she put her arms around Joseph and took him through to the bedroom. It was the first time that Ward had ever seen the strong and always in control Nicole-Louise act in a gentle way.

"Did you find out the schedules?" he asked Tackler.

"There were no schedules," Tackler replied.

"Nothing at all?"

"For everything but the two reports you asked for," he replied.

Ward smiled to himself and nodded.

"I need to go to USBC News now. Lawson, you can come with me," he said.

He looked at McDermott,

"Can you get the team on standby to go at a moment's notice?"

"They already are," McDermott replied.

"I think you need to move them closer to us," he said, "Have you got room for six more guys for a few hours?" he asked Tackler.

"Of course we have," he replied, turning his nose up at Lawson in the process.

"Let's go," he said to Lawson.

They both walked out of the apartment and headed down to where Lawson's car was parked.

Ward took out his phone and called Centrepoint.

"I find it increasingly irritating when you hang up on me," Centrepoint said as he answered, "So explain to me what exactly is happening."

"We have a problem that you are going to have to somehow put right when I've dealt with it."

"What is it?"

"I can stop this bomb, in fact, I will stop this bomb from going off, so I need you to use all of your influence with all your powerful friends to accommodate my actions," Ward said.

"What are you going to do?" The Old Man asked; concern in his voice.

"I'm going to beat a knight of the realm until he tells me where the next bomb is going to go off. Then, I am going to kill him," Ward replied.

"Hold on, you can't..........." Ward hung up the phone.

THIRTY THREE

"You seriously think that Ashurst-Stevens is behind this?" Lawson asked, "That's a bit way out there!"

"I know," Ward replied, "The one piece I can't figure out is why?"

"I mean, seriously, the guy must be a billionaire, and he is a Knight for God's sake, there would be nothing to gain from this for him," Lawson added.

"Charlie Dunno told me in London why, I just can't see it yet."

"Can you explain how you knew right from the beginning that they were behind it?"

Ward's phone vibrated, it was Eloisa.

"Hello?" he answered.

"Hey. How are you? Keeping us safe?" she softly asked.

"Yes we are."

"I know you are busy but I have something that we want you to look into," she said, "But I can wait until you have time to talk to me," she added.

Ward found her voice so soothing. He felt a calm wash completely over him, and whenever he heard her voice, he missed her so much more. He would happily listen to her talking about the ingredients required to make the perfect omelette.

"It's fine, I have ten minutes," he said, "Give me an overview, I could do with the distraction."

"There is a guy in Ireland. A gypsy leader who is getting girls sent over to Ireland from desolate countries, with the promise of a better life. He has a contact in both countries who takes money from the parents and he transports them for him," she said.

"Why can't the locals deal with it?" Ward asked.

"This is massive Ryan. He is moving them from all over Europe after he has primed them and he has a high number of local and international police in his pocket," she continued.

"His name?"

"Michael O'Leary."

"Put everything together as usual, all the information, and as soon as this is done we will deal with it."

"OK."

"Eloisa?"

"Yes?"

"I miss you, so tomorrow night how about we order takeout and sit in and watch some old movies?"

"I am smiling so much right now," she said excitedly, "I can't wait! Keep safe and ring me when you have saved New York."

"I will"

"Promise?" she asked.

"Promise," he replied. The line went dead.

Lawson looked at Ward and was going to ask about Eloisa and then decided against it.

They arrived at the offices of USBC News and parked right outside.

They walked into the reception area, the pretty young receptionist was still there and the old security guard had reappeared.

Ward walked straight past without acknowledging them and called the elevator.

"Have you got an appointment?" the girl shouted across the reception area to Ward,

"Yes, he told me to come straight up."

She smiled at him and he noticed she didn't pick up the phone to call through and check.

The elevator doors opened and they stepped in.

"Remember you work for MI6, Mike, so leave this to me. They can't touch you if you are just watching, you are on American soil, and The Old Man will keep you protected, providing you do nothing but observe," he said.

"I'll try my best."

The elevator doors opened and they stepped out.

As they walked along the glass panel walled corridor towards the boardroom, Aidan Lucas came out and closed the door. He stood there with his arms by his side.

"Can I help you gentlemen?" he asked as they got to within six feet of him. Neither of them said anything.

"You'd better stop right there," he said, adjusting his weight on his feet and slightly turning his body. Ward kept moving forward.

"I mean it........"

When Ward got two feet away he launched a lightning fast jab with his right hand that caught Lucas full in the throat, and by the time his hands had come up in self-defence, he was jabbing him in his bulging eyes with the fingertips of his left hand. He crumpled to the floor.

He bent down over him, yanked his head up by his hair so he was looking in his eyes and said,

"Don't play at being a Seal Lucas, you are not worthy of even saying the name."

He pushed him to one side and opened the door.

The people inside were in exactly the same seating positions that they had been the previous two times that he had entered the room.

Walker looked startled sitting alone on the left hand side of the table, Ashurst-Stevens sat at the head, retaining his calm, and the three lawyers sat at the left of the table looking at Ward with contempt.

"You three, out," he said to the three lawyers.

"I beg your pardon?" the one nearest Ashurst-Stevens said.

"Out now or I will throw you out!"

"You are very much out of your depth here," the lawyer said. Ward walked around the table, and when he got level with him, he unleashed a half strength right hook full into the old guys face. He felt his nose break as his knuckles connected with his bone.

The other two jumped.

"You are in so much trouble!" the lawyer furthest away from Ashurst-Stevens shouted.

Ward then took three steps back, and with the back of his hand, slapped the guy hard in his face and knocked him off of his chair.

"The only people in so much trouble are you," he said to the table, as opposed to one individual.

"You think that I will follow protocol and keep in line with your absurd laws, and not step outside of the parameters that you as lawyers have decided are acceptable, until it suits you for them not to be?" Ward asked.

"What do you want?" Ashurst-Stevens demanded.

"Your old lawyers can't help you," he said to him. "This is my playground, my rules and I'm untouchable because I don't exist, so you will tell me all I need to know now, or I will kill you," he said calmly to Ashurst-Stevens, who by now, kept looking at the door waiting for Lucas to appear.

"He won't come, he's crying like a girl on the floor," Ward said, "You are so far out of your depth in my playground you fool. Who would employ an idiot like him and think he could protect them?" he asked, maintaining his calm manner.

"Tell your three stooges to leave. If they stay, after I have killed them, I will kill their families and everyone who has lived on the proceeds of their immoral, pathetic existences."

"Leave, now. All of you," Ashurst-Stevens shouted.

Walker stood up to leave.

"You can sit down Mr Walker," Ward said.

The three lawyers left the room without turning back once. Lawson accompanied them outside.

"We are going to have a talk," Ward said "But first things first," he added and then paused.

He looked at Walker, who looked terrified.

"Mr Walker, I have your son. He is safe and being well looked after, so the threat against you has now gone. No harm will come to him at all. I promise. He has a whole team of the best killers on the planet protecting him right now, so you need to help me out, OK?"

Walker's eyes filled with tears and Ward could see the complete relief and joy flood across his face.

Walker nodded.

"Thank God!" Ashurst-Stevens exclaimed.

Ward looked at him.

"We've been worried sick," he continued, "When we first knew that Joseph had been taken we employed Mr Lucas to make sure that Martin would be safe. We knew that there were people who were setting Martin up; that is why my lawyers have been so heavily involved."

"But you knowingly went along with the deaths of innocent people," Ward reminded him.

"No, that is not what happened," Walker said.

"You knew about this, both of you, when we met in London, yet you kept everything from me."

"We didn't know until the Westminster incident and by then, our only concern was to keep Joseph safe," Ashurst-Stevens said.

"You had better tell me everything from the start," Ward said to Walker, as he started to wonder if he had gotten everything so dramatically wrong.

"He can't," Ashurst-Stevens said.

"I wasn't talking to you," Ward said.

"No, I meant he can't because he knows only as much as I do."

"What do you mean?"

"The instructions were coming from the lawyer whose nose you have just broken."

"Instructions from whom?"

"We don't know."

"What were the instructions?"

"That we would have a film crew at a set location at a set time and if we didn't, Martin's son would be killed."

Ward thought back to when they were in London reviewing the footage of the Paris bombing and how Walker had brought them into the room, and then gone out immediately ten minutes before the bomb exploded in Westminster Abbey. He had gone out to give instructions.

"There is money washing through his accounts," Ward said pointing at Walker, "Where did that come from?" he asked.

"We don't know, but if it's money he needs to pay back I will provide it. Martin has been with me from the beginning and we have built this empire together. I am not going to desert him in his hour of need," Ashurst-Stevens said.

"It's not about the money. So, neither of you know who is behind it?"

"Obviously if we did, we would point you in the right direction," Ashurst-Stevens said.

Ward stood up and opened the door. Lucas was now on his feet looking uneasy,

"Where is the lawyer?" he said to Lawson.

"Cleaning his nose in the bathroom."

Ward walked halfway down the hall to the toilet and walked in, it was empty.

"The lawyer has gone," he said to Lawson when he walked back from the toilet and into the boardroom, before stopping at the head of the table,

"I want you to call the lawyer back now," he demanded of Ashurst-Stevens.

"I can't."

"Why not?"

"Because he doesn't work for me."

"You said he was part of your inner circle."

"What was I meant to say? They have my dear friends son held hostage; I was hardly going to tell you anything with him here until I knew Joseph was safe. I'm his Godfather for God's sake."

"So who does he work for?"

"I don't know. He appeared two weeks ago with a video of Joseph tied to a chair and said we had to follow three simple instructions and he would be unharmed."

253

"What was the third instruction?" Ward asked.

"We don't know yet," Ashurst-Stevens replied.

"The other two lawyers?"

"They work for me," he said, "Their role was to try and make sure that I wasn't compromised in any way."

Ward was almost convinced that Ashurst-Stevens was telling the truth, Walker was for sure,

"When can I see my son?" Walker asked.

Ward thought back to Gilligan's dying words and about how important his boys were to him. He thought about McDermott and how proud he was of his son Paul. He thought about his own hidden desire to be a father and have a son of his own, and he saw how desperate Walker was to hold his son and hug him and tell him he loved him.

"You can come with me right now to see him," Ward said, "He hasn't stopped asking for you since we found him. His only concern was that you were OK. You should be very proud of him Mr Walker, he stayed strong for you," Ward exaggerated.

Walker's eyes filled with tears and they slowly started to run down his cheeks.

Even Ashurst-Stevens had to swallow hard to regain his composure.

"You contact me as soon as they get back in touch with you," he demanded to Ashurst-Stevens.

"Yes I will."

"Let's go," Ward said to Walker.

He walked out of the room and Walker followed.

"We are going back to Nicole-Louise's," he said to Lawson.

"Just like that? We are further back from where we started," Lawson replied.

"You are wrong Mike. I now know the one answer I couldn't fathom out."

THIRTY FOUR

Back at Nicole-Louise and Tackler's apartment, McDermott and his team were waiting. Ward watched as Walker hugged his young son and would not let him go. It was a warming sight that brought a human element to the events that they were faced with, and Ward gave a quick thought to the mothers, fathers and loved ones who would have lost someone close to them in the Paris and London bombings. The warmth he felt was quickly replaced by a wave of anger as a picture of Gilligan's wife trying to console her two sons, who would by now be aware that their giant of a father was never coming home again, washed through his mind. Nicole-Louise put her hand in Tackler's, and in a room full of nine lethal killers, no one spoke.

Until Lawson unintentionally pulled Ward back into focus when he whispered,

"I still can't believe it."

Ward ignored the comment.

"OK everyone, we still have a bomb to find," he said.

"How did you know that his son would be there?" McDermott asked.

Ward thought about how he knew and how it was probably time to explain everything clearly to the others who had risked their lives. With Walker in attendance, Ward was hoping he could fill in the parts that didn't add up.

"OK. From the beginning," he said and watched as every person in the room adjusted into a position of comfort, like they were a class full of junior kids waiting for a story to be read out to them.

"I need a laptop," he said to Tackler, who promptly stood up and picked up a grey laptop that was already running. Ward took out the memory stick that Tackler had prepared for him and plugged it in. They watched as the file directory opened up and saw two headings, 'Paris' and 'London'. He moved the cursor onto 'Paris', and double clicked it, opening a media window, and he pressed the pause button.

"The moment I saw this footage I knew it was completely wrong," he said.

"That was in London when you said you knew who was behind it," Lawson said, "I've watched that twenty times and I still can't see a link between the footage of the two bombs or any people who were in both places."

Ward ignored him.

He pressed the play button and they watched as for five seconds, Abbi Beglin was talking with the Louvre behind her and then it switched to her talking for a further fifty five seconds before the explosion ripped out through the Metro station.

He then pressed pause at the point that the smoke was starting to bellow out of the station.

He then looked around the room. Walker looked at the floor; he was the only other person there who knew what Ward was looking at, because he had instructed it to happen.

He closed the media window and then clicked on 'London', and opened it up and pressed play. The footage showed a politician talking with the Abbey behind him, and then there was a close up of the Abbey, and then back to the politician

256

talking, and they all watched as a black cab pulled up behind him and thirty seconds later, exploded. Ward pressed the pause button again.

"Now do you see it?" he asked everyone in the room.

Walker continued to look at the floor.

"No," Lawson said.

McDermott shook his head.

"They should never have caught those incidents on film," Ward said to the room. They all looked at him blankly.

"Let's try it this way," he said, "Mr Walker, what is one of the golden rules of news production?"

"To keep the camera rolling at all times," he said quietly.

"On what?"

"On the subject matter," he replied.

Ward looked at everyone else in the room and he immediately saw the realisation of what they were looking at hit hard; so hard with Lawson that it almost made a noise.

"How can I have been so stupid?" Lawson said.

"I still don't get it," McDermott stated.

"I do," Tackler said, "I looked at that twenty times with him," he said in a hostile tone pointing to Lawson, "I can't believe I was that stupid not to see it," he added.

"Help me out someone?" McDermott pleaded.

"If you were filming an interview in front of The Louvre or Westminster Abbey, where would you point the camera?" Ward asked him.

"At the buildings," he replied.

"Not at the Metro station or the road behind?" Ward asked him.

"Oh my God!" McDermott exclaimed, "They knew it was coming."

"No they didn't," Ward replied.

The room went quiet again.

"But Mr Walker did," he said, still conscious of the fact his son was in the room, and referring to him formally in response to this.

Walker was still looking at the floor.

"He instructed the on-site producers to change camera angle so the blasts could be caught going off on film because that is what the people behind this wanted," Ward said.

"And if he didn't do it, then he would never see his son again, because they would kill him live on webcam?" McDermott asked, actually sounding pleased with himself.

Walker visibly shook at the thought.

"Very subtle," Ward said, giving McDermott a heavy stare as he said it.

"So why go through all of this to get it caught on camera?" Tackler asked, "I mean the whole world carries a cell phone with a camera built in that has equally as good quality and someone would have filmed it, they always do."

"That was the 'Why?' part that I couldn't put together, no matter how I looked at it. In any event that takes place, anywhere in the world, there is always something to gain for someone; but on this, even though I had the 'Why?' given to me in London, even now, I can't make it fit," Ward replied.

"Charlie Dunno?" Lawson asked, "He wrote a word on a piece of paper for you, to a question you wrote down, what was the word?"

"Money."

"What was the question?"

"Why would a news corporation sponsor a terrorist to detonate bombs?"

"So he was wrong," Lawson said, "It was about saving this kids life?"

"No, he was right," Ward said, "We still have to find out why?"

Ward looked at Walker; he was still looking at the floor in shame.

"The lawyer," Lawson said, "If we find him, we find who was behind it and we beat them until they tell us the why."

"No. We know who was behind it already," Ward replied.

"Who?"

"Ashurst-Stevens."

Walker still looked at the floor. Joseph looked at Ward,

"That can't be right, he is my Godfather and my dad's friend," he said.

"It is right. I almost believed him an hour ago but he was lying. So we need to confirm three things to prove it," Ward said to the room.

"What three things are they?" asked Tackler.

"First the origin of the money that went through Mr Walker's account. You said you still can't find the source of it, correct?"

"I haven't found it yet, but I will," Tackler replied.

"We know it ended up with Fulken and where it came from, but we have to find who put it there. Mr Walker knew nothing about it, I know that," Ward said.

Walker still looked at the floor.

"Secondly, what has Ashurst-Stevens gained from this?" Ward asked, "Nicole-Louise, I want you to tear the accounts of his whole empire, including subsidiaries, apart until you find something," he demanded.

Walker still looked at the floor.

Tackler turned his back on the room and started tapping on his keyboard immediately.

Nicole-Louise got up from the armchair and moved to her side of the room and did the same thing.

"And the third thing?" Lawson asked.

"We need to find out where the third bomb is due to go off?"

"So we need to pay Ashurst-Stevens a visit?" McDermott asked.

"We need to find Fulken first."

"How?" Lawson asked, "We've been chasing him for nine days yet still got nowhere."

"The UPS van," Ward said, "We find it."

"How?" Lawson asked.

"We know where the bomb was made. Nicole-Louise told me that there had only been a few residents and delivery vans pass the building, so one of them will be our bomb. If Tackler concentrates on the money trail, Nicole-Louise can hack into the traffic system and follow any U.P.S vans that were in the area, between the two vans from Hubert Street arriving and us turning up."

"I'm on it," Nicole-Louise said.

"Then you can send two of your team to each possibility to check it out," he added, looking at McDermott who nodded back immediately.

"What about me?" Lawson asked.

"We have something personal to do," Ward replied.

"I have to ask, how do you know that Ashurst-Stevens is lying?" Lawson asked, "There are still a number of unproven and unquantified suggestions that you have given us."

The whole room went quiet. Nicole-Louise and Tackler stopped tapping on their keyboards and turned to see Ward's reaction.

"Mr Walker still has something very important to tell us, don't you?" Ward said, looking down at him.

Walker raised his head for the first time and looked sullenly at him.

"Yes I do, I'm sorry," he said, "I know who killed your friend."

"Gilligan?" McDermott asked.

"Yes," Ward replied, "That's how I knew Ashurst-Stevens was lying. He told me that they had employed Lucas for protection, but Mr Walker has been held as a virtual hostage. Ashurst-Stevens put him in place to stop him telling us anything he shouldn't. Even though they had Joseph there as collateral, they needed to keep an eye on him at all times. Right back in London, when I was told Mr Walker was unavailable when we went to the UKBC News offices and then he suddenly reappeared, I knew this."

Everyone looked at Walker.

Walker's eyes stayed fixed on the floor as Ward continued, "I made a call to Mr Walker and led him into giving short replies to arouse Lucas' suspicion, to see what the reaction would be, and he struck Mr Walker, so it was clear that he was never there to protect him, he was there to guard him. Only Ashurst-Stevens would have needed that. The lawyers were simply there to protect Ashurst-Stevens. He will be covered legally no matter what."

"That's why he gave us enough truth about what he knew so that if Walker did talk, he can claim he was supporting him?" Lawson asked.

"Exactly. He has set Mr Walker up perfectly to be the fall guy if anything goes wrong," he replied, "Even when we kidnapped him, it was obvious that apart from protecting his son, he had no idea what was happening," he added.

Walker looked up from the floor,

"That was you?" he asked, looking at Ward.

"Yes it was," Ward replied, "For your own protection."

"I was petrified," he said, looking back at the floor.

"When we told you that one of the men asking questions was dead you were genuinely surprised, you couldn't fake that. Tell me what happened when you got back to the USBC offices?"

"Mr Lucas punched me until he was convinced that I hadn't told you anything," Walker replied.

He then stood up and lifted up his shirt. His whole body was covered in bright purple and blue bruises.

"He then demanded to know every single word you had said to me and I recited it almost word perfect," he added.

"And he was happy with that?" Ward asked.

"Eventually, yes. Then when I told him about you wanting me to call a number because you said that you wanted to kill the Brit, he told me that he would take care of you and that he had already killed the big guy, and that you got lucky by darting behind a car. He told me that he enjoyed it and that after he had killed you, he might kill Joseph just for fun because he liked killing."

"We should pay him a visit," Lawson said.

"Yes we should," he replied, "And maybe we can invite The Optician too," he added.

"Is everyone clear on what they have to do?" Ward asked.

The room echoed with a united 'Yes', and Ward looked at Walker,

"Stay here with your son Mr Walker. This will all work out OK, and the mess left behind will get cleared up, it always does. In a couple of days you will be able to go back to your

261

normal life, and in time, you will forget this ever happened, or that we existed."

"I doubt I'll ever forget you people," he replied, smiling for the first time since he got to the apartment.

"You had better forget us." Ward said menacingly.

THIRTY FIVE

Ward looked at his watch. It was now 4.25pm.

He was sure that Lucas would still be at the USBC News offices, no doubt offering a long excuse to Ashurst-Stevens as to why he got put on the floor.

"It's really important that we don't let Ashurst-Stevens think we know anything," he said to Lawson.

"No worries, I'll be nothing but courteous."

"Lucas is our concern here. We need to get him out of the building and take him somewhere quiet, and then he can tell us everything he knows, although I doubt he knows too much about the intricacies of this whole show."

"Even if we stop the bomb…." Lawson said.

"When!" Ward interrupted.

"Even *when* we stop the bomb, and take Ashurst-Stevens to task, I get the feeling there is more to this than we think."

"I've had that feeling from day one, but all we can do is what we are tasked to do, and that is to stop it from ever happening."

They arrived at the offices and walked into the reception area. The same girl was there but the old security guard was nowhere to be seen. Ward approached the reception desk, "Can you tell Mr Ashurst-Stevens we are here to see him?" he asked politely.

"Lord Ashurst-Stevens is not here," she corrected him, "He has an appointment at the NYPD police fundraising event in Brooklyn."

"Any other appointments?" he asked.

She looked down a list on a piece of paper, "Only the awards ceremony tomorrow night."

"I have an invite to that, Abbi invited me," Lawson interrupted, looking rather pleased with himself.

Both Ward and the girl ignored him.

"Is Mr Walker's assistant still here?" he asked.

"I think so," she replied, "Shall I check?" she asked, as she reached to pick up the phone.

"It's OK, we'll walk up. It is a personal item of Mr Walker's that I have to give him, and if he's not there we will come straight back."

"OK," she replied without a hint of suspicion, she had clearly got used to him coming and going by now.

They walked over to the elevator and pressed the call button.

"Are we going to kill him?" Lawson asked.

Ward pondered the question for a moment and then said, "Wait here, I have a better idea," and he stepped away from the elevator and took out his cell phone. He thumbed through the contacts on his phone and dialled The Optician.

"You know where I am?" he asked as soon as it was answered.

"Yes, I've just got here. The Old Man is in a panic about this. He's worried that you might upset this Lord and he will go running to his powerful friends," he said.

"Tell him not to, he's down the list of priorities at the moment," Ward replied.

"So what do you want?"

"You know Gilligan was killed?"

"Yes, I heard. I liked him," The Optician replied.

"We are here now to collect the guy who killed him."

264

The line went quiet, a cue to continue.

"We intend to extract him, take him somewhere quiet, close to here and question him."

"And after that?" The Optician asked.

"How much did you like Gilligan?"

"Let him go and I will do the rest. I will give him exactly five minutes to live when you release him," The Optician replied and then hung up the phone.

He walked back to Lawson who was holding the elevator door open with his foot. They both stepped in and Lawson pressed the button for floor sixteen.

"Who was that you called?" Lawson asked as the elevator began its journey up to the sixteenth floor.

"The Optician."

"Oh dear, poor Lucas," he said with a smile.

The elevator reached their floor in ten seconds. They stepped out; walked down the familiar route to the boardroom, opened the door and walked in.

Lucas was directly in front of them, sitting at the head of the table where Ashurst-Stevens would normally sit.

He stood up and assumed a defensive position immediately.

"Sit down idiot," Ward said, as he pulled out the chair where he had seen Walker sitting every other time he had been in the room, and sat down.

Lawson walked around the table and sat in the chair next to Lucas where the Lawyer who had his nose broken by Ward had sat. He looked at them and reluctantly sat down.

"Against our better judgement we have to put Walker back into your care," Ward said, "But before you come with us and collect him, I thought we could have a chat," he added.

"You caught me with a sucker punch, I wasn't ready," Lucas said quickly, totally not comprehending the seriousness of his predicament.

The guy really was an idiot Ward thought to himself.

"What was your brief in regards to Walker?" he asked.

"To protect him, that was all," he replied in his irritating droll.

"You didn't make a very good job of that," Lawson said.

265

Lucas looked at him and then looked back at Ward.

"There was a team of people, they caught me when I wasn't ready," Lucas said defensively.

"Isn't your job to be ready at all times, idiot?" he asked him.

Lucas didn't say anything, but a confused look appeared on his face.

"Anyway, how do we know that if we let you come back with us and collect him, that you will keep him safe?" Ward asked.

"Because this time I will be ready at all times?" Lucas replied, like a child answering a teacher in class.

Ward felt a rage wash over him. He was struggling to control it. How could a great man like Gilligan, a man who had risked his life a hundred times and saved his own life, fall to a guy like this? It made his loss even more insulting.

"OK. But we will give you our number and you call if you get in any trouble. Deal?" he said softly.

"Deal."

Ward stood up and walked towards the door, Lawson joined him.

Lucas still sat there.

"Well come on," he said, "We still have a bomber to catch so the sooner Walker is out of our hair the better."

Lucas stood up and walked over to them. He pulled his handgun out of his pocket and took the safety off.

"OK, let's go," he said to them both and walked past them, heading towards the elevator with great purpose.

Lawson looked at Ward in bemusement.

Ward shrugged his shoulders.

Lucas called the elevator and stood directly in front of the doors waiting for them to open. Ward studied him. He was capable, that much was obvious, and he thought back to the first time that he saw him and how he had the impression that in a fist fight; Lucas would not stay down unless he was unconscious or dead. He also thought about how his demeanour had changed dramatically since the kidnap of Walker and the punch to the throat Ward had delivered the last time that he saw him. It's all about perceptions Ward concluded.

Once McDermott had told him that Lucas could not cut it as a Seal, he became a totally different person. The truth was; he was probably more than adequate ten years ago when he was going through Seal training, and not only would his body have ben finely tuned, his senses would have been too.

But ten years on, and living a civilian life; that edge had disappeared. He was competent as a sniper, the kill shot on Gilligan proved that; but the fact he missed Ward demonstrated that he was no more than average.

The elevator doors opened and they stepped in.

"How long were you a Seal?" Ward asked him.

"Five years," Lucas lied.

"See much action?" Lawson asked.

"I can't discuss that."

Lawson had to stop himself from bursting out in laughter. The elevator reached the ground floor and they stepped out. They walked through the reception area and out through the big glass entrance doors.

Lawson climbed into the black Sudan to drive and Lucas leant to open the back door,

"You take the front," Ward said, "I'm being dropped off on the way to you collecting Walker," he added in a casual tone.

Lucas moved forward and opened the door to the passenger seat and stepped in. Ward climbed in behind him. Lawson pulled away and they drove up 6th Avenue to West 54th and turned down the street. Lawson saw a side road adjacent to an Italian restaurant and drove down it.

It was a secluded area, made up of a few parking spaces for the employees of the restaurants which made up the block, and a number of dumpsters, which probably got raided on a daily basis by the homeless people. But at 5pm, there was no one about. It was way before the evening rush.

Ward took out his phone and hit redial,

"Can you see where we are?" he asked The Optician.

"I'm just coming onto 54th now," he said, "I'll be ready in one minute."

Ward stepped out of the car and Lawson followed.

Ward opened the passenger door,

"Out!" he demanded to Lucas.

Lucas reluctantly stepped out, his eyes darting left, right, up and down, but Ward could see that they were moving too quickly to allow his surroundings to register properly and there was no point in even trying to see The Optician.

Lucas' hand started to move towards the side of his jacket where his handgun was placed and as he did so, Lawson unleashed a thunderous right hook that caught him full in the stomach, and he doubled over and fell to his knees, exhaling the air in his lungs in sync with a very loud groan. Lawson pulled his head back with his right hand and removed the gun with his left. The whole move took no more than three seconds.

"You are in a lot of trouble," Ward said calmly, as Lawson pulled Lucas to his feet with one strong hand and leant him against the car.

Lucas looked terrified.

"I'm going to ask you some questions and the first time I think you lie to me, I am going to kill you. Is that clear?" he asked.

"Yes," Lucas replied without hesitation.

He knew the situation.

He either defended someone who signed his pay checks or lost his life. He knew that Ward was not bluffing.

He would tell the truth.

"What was your real brief regarding Walker?"

"To keep him away from you or any other member of the secret service," Lucas replied.

"You think I'm secret service?"

"No I don't."

"What do you think I am?"

"I think you are MI6 and you work closely with the CIA."

"And the lawyers believed that they could control me because of their powerful friends?" Ward asked.

"They did at first, but then it became clear that people had no influence on what you did, whoever you are," Lucas replied.

"You beat on Walker, why?"

"Because Ashurst-Stevens said I had to know what he was doing and who he was talking to all the time."

"You killed my friend, why?"

"Because the Lawyers said that you were a threat and that you couldn't be controlled. They contacted MI6 and the CIA to find out about you."

"And?"

"No one knew anything, other than the people at the CIA were instructed to grant you access to all areas."

"That's because I don't exist," Ward replied.

"That's what they said," Lucas replied.

"So, you killed my friend and then tried to kill me. What would you do in my position?"

"I would try and find out where the bomb is due to go off."

A response that Ward felt moved him up from idiot status to just stupid.

"Do you know where it is going to go off?" he asked.

"No. But I could find out. If they think I killed you they might trust me and tell me."

Lucas was trying his hardest to offer a solution that he thought might tempt Ward.

"Or I could just go and see them and torture them until they tell me. Everyone breaks in the end, you should know that," Ward replied.

The look on Lucas' face showed he understood he was all out of options.

"Were you a good sniper?" Ward asked.

"I was above average. I would have taken you out too if you hadn't of moved so quickly."

"And now you wish more than anything you had because you know you are going to die?"

"But I have told you the truth!" Lucas protested.

"I know you have. But you haven't told me anything I don't already know and you killed my friend, so you know I can't let you live."

Lucas stood upright, put his hands behind his back, closed his eyes and said, "Do it quick," and braced himself for the bullet. He could hear the sound of a car door opening and opened his eyes to see Lawson stepping into the Sudan. Ward was opening the passenger door.

"You have five minutes to live," Ward said.

"I don't understand?"

"You were a Seal. Ever heard of The Optician?" Ward said as he climbed into the car.

Lucas' face went white.

The whole of the Special Forces world had heard of The Optician.

Lawson turned the car around, and they drove back past Lucas who was rooted to the spot. Ward lowered the window and as Lawson drove slowly past him, he looked at Lucas and said,

"You won't see him."

With that, they drove up the side road out of sight.

As they did so, a 7.62mm bullet smashed into the dumpster directly behind Lucas; whistling past him, deliberately close enough so that he would almost feel it.

The Optician was here.

Lucas sprinted to his left and crouched down behind a dumpster. He had heard stories of The Optician when he was halfway through his Seal training. They were stories of a man who was originally a Seal, but was so good at what he did that the U.S. government actually loaned him out to their allies. At the end of one particularly hard days training when the trainees were in their billet, 'Shooting the shit', as they called it, exchanging stories about Seal legends, he had heard about the time The Optician was dropped into Afghanistan completely alone, with the aim of taking out one of Bin Laden's chief lieutenants. He had enough supplies to last three days and no communications equipment.

The legend went that a team was sent to find him after five days and an extensive search by a Seal team found no trace of him and he was declared dead.

Four days after that, The Optician turned up back at base, strolling through the gates and confirming his mission was completed. The story went that he had not only achieved his objective and wiped out the target, but when he was unpacking his kit; he still had three days' worth of supplies left. No one during Lucas' time with the Seals had ever seen him, but during sniper training, the instructors referred to him as being very real.

Lucas told himself to breathe slowly. The worst thing for him was the eerie silence that seemed to have descended, almost as though the whole world was holding its breath waiting to see what would happen.

He listened as hard as he could, tilting his head to the left and pointing his right ear to the top of the dumpster, in the direction of where the shot had come from, to see if he could hear anything.

He looked down at his watch.

Thirty seconds had gone.

He considered his options. Stay still for five minutes and then hope The Optician would let him go because he beat the clock, before immediately realising how lame that was and dismissing it, or to make a run the ten feet to the next dumpster outside the adjoining building, and then continue for three more dumpsters until he could take shelter behind a brick outhouse that had an alley running alongside it?

He looked at his watch.

One minute had gone.

He decided to go for the next dumpster. He crouched into a start position, exactly like an athlete at the beginning of a race, and pushed with all his strength off of his left leg and burst forward towards the next dumpster. As soon as he got five feet out into the open, he felt a sharp pain in the top of his right arm, a pain that could only be described as a red hot poker being pushed slowly into, and then through, his flesh, and he fell forward, his momentum carrying him to the safety of the next dumpster. He had never felt such a pain in his life, but the adrenalin and his survival instincts kicked in.

Two more dumpsters to go.

He looked at his watch.

One minute thirty seconds had gone.

Without hesitation and with a desperate need to reach the alleyway; he assumed the starting block position again and exploded out towards the next dumpster as quickly as his legs would carry him. As he burst out into the open and was into his third stride, he felt a similar sensation as before in his right thigh and his leg completely gave way. He started to fall to the floor, but fortunately for him, there was enough speed in his forward momentum, that even as he fell, he managed to hit the floor in exactly the same position where the dumpster started. By the time he had come to a stop, he was behind it. He looked down at his leg. He got lucky. The bullet had only just caught his thigh at the top and gone in and out, about half an inch below the skin. Painful but not life-threatening, he thought to himself. He was an Ex-Seal; he could block the pain out of his head easily. Sure, he was restricted in his movement but one more dumpster to go and then he would be free.

He looked at his watch.

Two minutes fifteen seconds had gone.

Without hesitation and feeling re-energised by the fact he could almost touch the alleyway, he assumed his starting block position again and pushed hard off of his left leg. He sprinted out from behind the dumpster and reached the other side. No pain, no bullet, nothing. He reached the dumpster and crouched down. There was a wooden fence between the alleyway and the dumpster that stood three feet high. On his hands and knees he crawled forward until he felt the daylight replaced by the dark shadows of the sanctuary of the high brick walls on either side of him. In the alleyway there were piles of trash bags and sporadic trash cans but they were not blocking his route to safety. At the end of the alleyway, he could see the main street; cars and people were passing with reassuring regularity, all on their way home from work.

He looked at his watch.

Three minutes had gone.

He pulled himself to his feet and started to move towards the street. He took three steps and felt a sharp, searing pain in his left arm. It knocked him to one side and he stumbled against one of the alleyway walls. He had never known a pain like it in his life.

He panicked.

The Optician must be coming behind him he thought to himself and so he started to jog forward as well as he could, and took no more than five strides when he felt a searing pain rip through his left leg and he collapsed to the floor.

He now understood.

The Optician wasn't trying to kill him, he was toying with him, making the last moments of his life a nightmare of fear, desperation and loneliness. Alone, frightened and dying in an alleyway. His life was not meant to be like this.

He looked at his watch.

Four minutes thirty seconds had gone.

The pain was swimming through his body, the predominant pain changing from his left thigh, to right arm, and then back again. He started to lose consciousness. As everything was starting to blur, he saw a figure come into view in front of him from behind a large pile of trash bags. It was a figure that looked like a giant who was holding a rifle in his right hand. He could see the figure clearly but everything started to blur and he could not make out a face.

He looked down at his watch.

He knew he had only ten seconds to live.

"Please, don't," he begged.

"You killed Gilligan. I liked Gilligan," the figure said, and raised his rifle.

He lowered his head so all he could see was his watch.

Three more seconds and the five minutes was up.

He felt he tip of the rifle barrel under his chin and it forced his head up. As he looked up towards the figure, he felt the barrel push against the exact centre of his forehead.

Everything went dark.

And The Optician vanished into thin air once again.

THIRTY SIX

Asif Fulken was becoming more and more anxious. It was now almost 5pm. He had control over his own actions. He had the bomb, he had the time and the place, and he had the plan to get his family to safety and to live in luxury all neatly set out. He should have been able to enjoy these moments.

When he planted the bomb on the train in Paris he was enjoying the moments before it went off looking at a pretty waitress. For the London bomb, he was drinking coffee outside a café, savouring the noise of the sirens, and watching the fear on people's faces, close enough to almost feel the panic.

But this was different.

He felt anxious for a number of reasons.

He was by now aware that virtually every contact he had in New York had disappeared. He had built up an efficient and reliable support network, and it seemed to have been obliterated in the space of a few days. He felt no personal sorrow for their loss; after all, they laid themselves down in the name of their faith, so it was their choice. It was more the destruction of what he had built that agitated him. He had come to America just over two years ago. He was, at the time, the FFW's most trusted bomber, and he was rapidly climbing the ranks. His faith and commitment to the cause was rocked

when he discovered that some of the funds that his brothers raised throughout the Middle East were being syphoned off by the elders allowing them all to live in relative luxury. Virtually all of their family members were living in the West, under the guise of infiltrators, but everyone knew they were placed there to keep them safe and to build new lives.
Only the stupid West would allow this to happen. The CIA had confirmed how stupid they were when they brought him to America. It had all happened so quickly and before he knew it, they were throwing money at him.

When the CIA found him, he was preparing to detonate a 500lb bomb in a U.S. army base in Kabul. He had been working on the plan for three long weeks. The idea was to allow the CIA to infiltrate a minor cell, made up of people who had no real knowledge of the inner workings of the FFW, in case of capture, and to feed the CIA information on a bomber considered less valuable than himself by the elders, so that they would concentrate their efforts on finding him and lose focus elsewhere. It was not unusual for the elders to sacrifice someone for the greater good. Fulken never had any sympathy for these people, they should have been better at their craft.
Unfortunately, the elders had underestimated just how much the sacrificial cell knew, and his name had soon been passed over to the CIA. He was holed up in a filthy apartment, five miles outside of Kabul, when in the middle of the night, the doors crashed open and before he knew it, everything had gone dark and his body had been punched, kicked and thrown around, while being transported to a secret holding place. The next time he saw daylight was when his hood had been removed and he was cable tied to a chair sitting at a table opposite three people, two men and one woman whose names were never revealed. He had braced himself for the standard torture techniques that the CIA uses, such as waterboarding, sleep deprivation, shackling and beating. What he had not been prepared for during his training on CIA techniques in

the FFW training camp, was simple good old-fashioned bribery.

They offered him a life of wealth, free of hiding and death, in return for the names and whereabouts of three specific elders. To tempt him, they provided him the opportunity to taste the wares of three western women for a night and after the pleasure they had bestowed upon him, he was ready to negotiate.

He laid down his own conditions on where in the States he lived, and the degree of freedom that they were going to afford him. They agreed to this on condition that he would operate under a handler who would ask him to identify people of interest who entered The States, and to keep them constantly updated on what he knew.

After that, everything happened so quickly. He was living in New York two weeks later. They had helped him set up spotter cells in and around Times Square, and they gave him a whole apartment building to generate a legal income, as well as depositing $300,000 in a bank account.

They changed his name to Sameh Ismail and gave him a handler called Gill Whymark, who would ask for information twice a week, information that Fulken had delivered. He knew that the FFW had put a death sentence on him, but by then, he had built up such a close network in The States that he knew they would all willingly die for him. And it seems that they all had. Fourteen months ago, he had been walking to his favourite restaurant, when a van pulled alongside him and three armed men bundled him into it. He knew it couldn't be the CIA, and he was initially convinced that the FFW had hired a team of mercenaries to eliminate him. Once again, a hood was put on his head, but this was different. There were no beatings and no threats, his captors even telling him to watch his head as they walked him out of the van.

When the hood was removed he was sat on a sofa in a plush room, he assumed in a private house, and the three men were standing behind him, no weapons drawn. Opposite him in a chair was an old man, he was definitely a lawyer, Fulken knew without a doubt. The old man laid out a number of photographs of his sisters, brother and their children going about their everyday life, and in each photograph there was the same man in the background. The old lawyer had gone on to explain that he had a proposition for him.

 In return for his family being allowed to carry on with everyday life he was required to do something for them; something that would make him very rich in the process. He was to detonate three bombs in three different places to a set time, and in return, he would be paid two million dollars for each bomb successfully detonated. Fulken had bartered and was proud of the fact that the old lawyer even considered his demand of four million dollars on completion of the mission; and even more surprised when the old lawyer agreed to his demands.

He was given a cell phone and four separate numbered sim cards, and told that the person who would contact him was the person who would decide when and where the bombs would go off, but he was told from the offset that they would be somewhere in Paris, London and New York.

He was provided with the resources he needed to get out of The States, a fake passport and money, but after that, the rest was down to him.

He was warned that if he failed in any part of the mission, or if he did not achieve his objectives, his family would face the consequences.

He agreed unconditionally and he was told that he had twelve months to prepare and that he should leave the country and get everything in place.

He was in Sweden thirty six hours later and he spent twelve solid months preparing plans and resources, just waiting for the call.

The first call came exactly thirteen months later. The voice on the end of the line was English, very well spoken and firm. He had followed the instructions that the voice had given him to the letter and now he was almost finished. They had kept their word and so far, had deposited four million dollars into the bank account he had allocated for use. Everything had gone perfectly.

This morning he had contacted his family and they were ready to move tomorrow afternoon after the mission had been completed.

What he didn't have control of, and what made him the most anxious, was the silence and the constant nagging at the back of his mind that the man with the cell phone fitted into this as much as he did. No man had ever made him feel anxious before, this was a new feeling to him, and the more he told himself to forget about him, the more his mind went into overdrive trying to establish how he recognised him. He gave up yet again after a few minutes and let his mind drift back to the future he had created for himself and his family. He looked at his watch again. 9:55am was only fifteen hours away.

This is going to be a long fifteen hours, he thought to himself.

Ward and Lawson arrived back at Nicole-Louise and Tackler's. They knocked on the door and Tackler let them in. McDermott was still there with Fuller,

"The rest are out and mobile but are staying within a two mile radius," McDermott said.

Ward nodded his approval.

Walker and his son were still sat on the sofa,

"Do we need to still be here?" Walker asked looking at Ward.

"It's probably the safest place for you right now. Don't worry; it will all be over soon," he replied

"We have something that I am pretty sure you want to see," Nicole-Louise said.

Ward walked over to her workstation and Tackler got up to join them, brushing past Lawson as he did so.

Ward looked at the screen.

Looking back at him was a picture of the lawyer whose nose Ward had broken.

"Who is he?" Ward asked.

"His name is Thomas Barnard Q.C.," she replied, "He is one of the most prestigious lawyers in the U.K. Charges around four thousand bucks an hour," she added.

Ward looked at Lawson,

"Ever heard of him?"

Lawson shook his head.

"Come over here," Ward said to Walker, beckoning him with his hand.

Walker came over to join them huddled around Nicole-Louise's screen.

"What do you know about him?" he asked Walker.

"I know that he is ruthless and strikes fear into most people within the legal profession back home," Walker replied, "I know that anyone with money hires him, and no matter how guilty they are, he will invariably get them off of the charges."

"How many times had you seen him before the sequence of events that you were involved in?" he asked.

"In the flesh? Never. In footage of him on the steps of the Old Bailey, several times, in celebration of another high profile court case he has won," Walker replied.

"No doubt he has gone running back to London," Lawson said, "I'll make a call, get some of my people to pay him a visit," he added, taking his cell phone out of his pocket as he said it.

"No need," Nicole-Louise said.

"Where is he now?" Ward asked.

Nicole-Louise rotated her head to a screen on her right. It had a map of New York on it, and in the middle there was a little red dot, pulsing.

"He's just got back to USBC News," she said.

"Back from where?" Ward asked.

"The Chrysler Building."

Ward walked into the kitchen and pulled out his cell phone.

"I hope you have finished with killing people for the day?"

Centrepoint answered, "I've just had to send the clean-up crew to an alleyway."

279

"No I haven't," Ward replied, "There are three more to go."

"Listen, you have to be very careful about what direction you take. There is only so much even I can cover up."

Ward ignored him.

"Where are we with this whole mess?"

"The short version?" Ward replied.

"Yes."

"Ashurst-Stevens wanted three bombs to go off. I can't link him to Fulken yet, but he is the one behind it. The intention was to set up a guy called Martin Walker, by letting us find money flowing through his account to a Swiss account, which within the hour we will have linked to Fulken," he said, "He then made enough evidence available to link him indirectly, in that he was supporting a colleague and his Godson, so that if he is associated with it, he can admit it and say it was for the good of his employee and the lawyers will walk him out of court in the full glare of the public."

"But you haven't done it yet?" Centrepoint asked.

"No, but Tackler is on it and I know he will find it."

"Continue."

"They kidnapped Walker's son so that he would have to dictate to the on-site crews where the cameras should be at the exact moment that the bombs went off, so that they could catch it all on camera."

"For what purpose?"

"I asked Charlie Dunno in London the same question."

"What did he say?"

"Money," Ward replied, "Although it looks like Fulken is getting a payment of two million dollars a bomb so there must be a huge of amount of money to be made somewhere else."

"Where?"

"That's what I don't get," Ward replied, "So I think the target isn't New York, I think it is someone whose demise would lead to a new and very profitable investment for Ashurst-Stevens."

"And how are you going to establish who this person is?" he asked.

"I'm going to pay his lawyer a visit."

"You need to tread carefully," Centrepoint said, "Wiping out terrorist cells will probably get you an audience and a medal from the President. Setting your sights on a lawyer and a Knight of the British Empire is unchartered territory and there will be huge repercussions."

"Not for me," Ward said, and hung up the phone.

He put his head around the door and said to Tackler, "Can I see you a moment?"

Tackler walked through the door a few seconds later.

"We have a problem that I want you to sort out and quickly."

"What is it?" Tackler asked.

"You are the second best at what you do, we both know that, almost as good as Nicole-Louise, but I would never say it in front of her," Ward replied with a smile, laying down the challenge to him.

Tackler took the bait immediately and said, "Tell me what you want?"

"This bomb is for someone, not some place," he said, "I'm sure of it."

"But you don't know who?"

"No I don't. But I need you to find someone from a business point of view, whose death might weaken a company and leave a window of opportunity for Ashurst-Stevens to take advantage of and add them to his company portfolio."

"A media company?" Tackler asked.

"I think so. But you need to cross reference it with an owner who is in New York today, tomorrow or both," Ward said.

"And when I find him?"

"You will have found the target," he replied, "Don't mention it to the others; I want your full focus on this."

"OK. I didn't have time to tell you," Tackler said, "I've found the money into Fulken's account and where it came from."

Ward raised an eyebrow,

"And you didn't think of mentioning that as soon as I walked in?"

"You didn't give me time. You went straight over to Nicole-Louise," he replied.

"I'm sorry. You are right," he said softly, "Where from and where to?"

"From a subsidiary of UKBC Sport into a Swiss account that Fulken has set up under the name of Shah Daud Sultanzoy."

"What about the USBC News schedules?" Ward asked.

"There are none listed."

"Not one?"

"Well one. The National News awards ceremony tomorrow night, but I doubt very much that Ashurst-Stevens is intending to blow himself up as he is due to present five of the awards," Tackler replied.

"And all the world's media big hitters will be there too?"

"I assume so."

"So you somehow have to narrow the playing field. Look for hostile takeover attempts from Ashurst-Stevens, and when you find possibilities, find their schedules for the next few days. That should give us a good starting point."

"I'm on it now." Tackler replied, and he walked out of the kitchen.

Ward leant against the sink feeling tired. He closed his eyes and rolled his neck. He then lifted his arms up and stretched them as far as they would go and let out a big sigh as they reached their limit.

He was focussed again.

He walked back into the living area and over to where Nicole-Louise was seated, by now scrolling through some company accounts, presumably linked to Ashurst-Stevens.

"Has Barnard moved at all?"

"No," she replied, "He isn't even moving around the building, he is probably sitting at a desk, but I don't know what desk or what floor yet."

"I do," Ward replied and he turned towards Lawson,

"Let's pay another visit to USBC News," he said.

THIRTY SEVEN

"What did you ask Tackler to do in the kitchen?" Lawson asked Ward as they were driving back to the USBC News offices.

Ward ignored the question and looked at his watch.

Almost 5:20pm. He was starting to think that his estimation that this would all be finished by 2:00am might have been a little too optimistic.

"Ignore the question then," Lawson said to himself, before adding a longer than required sigh at the end for effect.

"I should have thought of this before," Ward said, "Charlie was right. With people like that it is always about money."

"Thought of what?" Lawson asked.

"That there had to be a mammoth gain to be made. I was thinking that increased sales and advertising was the motivation here. I remember asking in London what was on the second floor and they told me it was the advertising and marketing department, and when we were there, it was busier than the news rooms."

"That's how they become obscenely rich; even more money than they ever need isn't enough for people like that," Lawson said.

"It's more than that," Ward added, "This is about ego and empire building. These people genuinely believe that they are untouchable."

"They normally are," Lawson replied.

They arrived at the offices of USBC News and parked in the exact same spot that they had parked in twice before. A government registered black Sudan was not going to get towed away.

"Maybe you need to keep your hands clean on this one?" Ward said.

"Not this time. I doubt very much you are going to keep him alive to tell the tale anyway, so thanks for the offer, but I'm coming with you," Lawson replied.

They walked through the glass doors again and into the reception area. Once again the same girl was behind the desk, and this time, she completely ignored Ward and offered up the biggest, most flirtatious smile she had in her armoury in Lawson's direction. She was so fixated on his good looks that she didn't even ask where they were going as Ward walked up to the elevator and pushed the call button. Lawson leant with his back against the elevator wall, smiling towards the latest addition to his fan club. The elevator doors opened and they stepped in.

"I might get her number on the way down," he said.

"Seriously, what is it with you?" Ward asked, "You do realise that if you spent less time thinking with your loins, you would probably be running MI6 by now."

"Was that a compliment?"

"You are wasting what you have. You are exceptional at what you do and I trust you with my life. In a fight, you would be the first person I would want beside me, but seriously Mike, it's time to grow up and utilise the superb skill set you have to full effect."

"Is that another compliment?"

"Take it as you wish."

The elevator doors opened.

They stepped out and started the walk along the glass-wall lined hallway to the boardroom door, and without knocking Ward turned the gold handle and walked in. Barnard was sitting in his usual seat, surrounded by papers and three big, red, thick legal books. No one else was in the room.

Barnard's nose was swollen and he had bruises starting to appear under both eyes. He looked up at Ward and completely ignored Lawson.

Ward sat down.

"Have you any idea of the trouble I am going to make for you?" he spat at Ward. "I will tear you apart and then your despicable house will come down on top of you."

"How so?"

"I will haul you before the courts for assault, trespassing and illegal data collection, and then I will prove that the British security forces had prior knowledge to your actions, and I will humiliate them too."

"I'm not British dipshit," Ward replied.

"Nowhere is safe for you to hide from me. I will hunt you to the ends of the earth," Barnard said, his voice relaying a dramatic tone that had no doubt served him very well in court over the years, but wasn't helping him much now.

"You don't understand, do you?" Ward said.

The response seemed to confuse Barnard.

Barnard was used to always getting his own way. Members of the British parliament, senior police officers and even members of the clergy, all backed off when he made personal threats to them. The man sitting opposite him made no attempt to either pacify him or confront him.

He just sat there.

"Don't understand what?" Barnard demanded, trying to maintain the assertive tone to his voice.

"You don't understand that the next five minutes will decide if I just kill you, or if I kill you and destroy your reputation. How you die is your choice," Ward calmly said.

"You think you can threaten me?" Barnard asked aggressively.

"Let me explain something. You might look in the mirror and see a man who knows a legal system inside out, and can find a loophole in every situation, but I just see a man with no morals and someone, that in my world, doesn't count for anything," Ward said.

"Your world?" Barnard asked.

"In my world, I do what I see fit. Think of me as a bit of a Judge Dread. I am judge, jury and executioner, and right now I'm inclined to kill you just for the sake of it."

"You can't do that, there are laws and rules that we have to live by. You have no choice. It is how everything works."

Ward took out his Glock and started to screw the silencer on very slowly and deliberately.

"I have to be honest, I want to kill you and forget about you because to me, you are completely insignificant, but I will probably just have as much fun with the alternative that I can offer you. Providing you give me the information I want of course."

"Alternative?" Barnard asked.

"The best computer graphic artists in the world are, right now, applying the finishing touches to videos and photos that show you engaged in sexual activity with a fourteen year old boy. They are good, very good. Their work is without equal, and there is not a graphics expert anywhere on earth who could analyse their work and not declare it to be authentic," Ward said, before looking at Lawson who was leaning on the wall by the door.

Lawson nodded his agreement and smiled.

"You can't do that; I will defend myself in court," Barnard replied.

"You still don't get it."

"What don't I get?" Barnard asked.

"I'm going to kill you anyway. It's just a question on whether you were the victim of a mugging and your obituary in The Times says great things about you; or I kill you and release the evidence and the police chase a fictitious boy that you abused. He doesn't exist, but nonetheless, you and your family will be destroyed."

The colour drained out of Barnard's cheeks.

"That's absurd," Barnard said, "What sort of barbaric world do you think we are living in?"

Ward ignored him and made an overly dramatic point of tightening the silencer on his Glock one more time.

"There are people who saw you come in here, there are people who will be trying to contact me on an hourly basis. If you even hurt one hair on my head, there will be the full weight of the British justice system coming down on you," Barnard declared. His voice had a quiver to it, he was frightened.

Ward knew he was going to tell him all he knew.

"You still don't understand," Ward said, "You have knowingly contributed to the deaths of nearly two hundred people in London and Paris, and judging by the size of the next bomb due to go off here, there will be at least another two hundred. Does that sit OK with you in terms of justice?" he asked.

"You have no proof of anything" Barnard declared.

"That's the beauty of what I do," Ward said, "I don't need proof."

"You will never get away with it," Barnard replied, visibly shaking now.

"No one likes Lawyers in general, you know that right?" Ward asked.

Barnard ignored the question

"You think that the smallest written technicality, no matter how much evidence is against the people you defend, is justification for setting them free."

"Everyone has a right to a fair defence," Barnard replied.

"But it's not fair, is it?" Ward said, "It's all about who can afford to pay for people like you to swim into your world of books, precedents and loopholes until you find a way."

"My crime is I'm good at my job?"

"Look at you," Ward said, "You are a physically weak man who is on the verge of bursting into tears. How is the fact you are good at your job helping you now?"

Barnard looked down at the table. He knew Ward was right. No amount of legal wrangling was going to help this situation. He looked across the table and all he could see was this monster, this frightening man who looked about seven feet tall, sitting opposite him, holding a gun and giving off an air that said he had done this a hundred times. A different approach was required.

"I was training to be a barrister once," Ward said, "I was good at it. I'm smart, very smart actually. My IQ is probably way above yours, but do you want to know why I got out of it?" he asked.

Barnard just sat there.

"I couldn't stand the dishonesty of it. I couldn't stand to know that because I am smarter than the average man; that no matter how guilty someone might be, I had the ability to get them cleared of any crime they may have committed," he continued, "It didn't sit properly with me. Who defends the man in the street, the guy who gets up at 5am every morning to go to work in a factory?"

"If you don't harm me, I will tell you all I know and then you can go after the people who have all the information that you need," Barnard said.

His tone was that of someone who was bargaining from a position of strength; clearly refined over many years in courtrooms, and in dealing with plea bargains.

"For someone who claims to be very good at their job, you are extremely dumb," Ward replied, "You've just told me that you personally don't have any information, but you can point me in the direction of someone who does," Ward shook his head in dismay, "I almost feel disappointed in you. On my way over here I had visions of us standing toe to toe and having an intellectual battle."

Barnard was visibly starting to panic now. The pressure of his predicament had made him lose focus. He knew that he had just given away his whole game. He briefly thought of the witness's he had destroyed in courtrooms using the same technique over the years, and for the first time since he left law school, he felt like a physically weak man who was on the verge of bursting into tears. He started to cry.

Ward looked at Lawson,

"Not so terrifying is he?" he asked.

"He reminds me of that man we killed last week who soiled himself before we finished him off," Lawson said, holding a serious expression on his face.

"Now, I ask the questions, you answer them and depending on what you tell me, I'll decide if you get destroyed in death, which will totally devastate your family, or if your obituary celebrates you," Ward said.

Barnard nodded slowly.

"What is your role in this?"

"I had to protect Lord Ashurst-Stevens legally. It was down to me to show that he acted under duress and he had no choice with his Godson's life in danger."

"So you created the paper trail that would hold up in a court of law?"

"Yes. That was all I did," Barnard replied.

"Did you know who had kidnapped Joseph Walker?"

"No."

"Why didn't you know?"

"I didn't want to know. It was arranged through his contact who knew the man who detonates the bombs."

"Who is this contact?" Ward asked.

"I don't know. I did ask that question and was simply told that it was a place that I didn't want to go. Whoever it is, he is extremely powerful," Barnard replied.

"So someone is assisting Ashurst-Stevens?"

"I don't know. Initially in terms of making contact then yes. I did not ask the question again after my initial enquiry."

Ward thought back to the rescue of Joseph Walker. The four men they took out were all Middle Eastern and all likely to be related to the FFW.

"Who is Ashurst-Stevens planning to kill with the bomb?" Ward asked.

"I don't know. I looked after the paper trail of the money involved because we knew that eventually it would be traced back," Barnard said, "Lord Ashurst-Stevens told me very little."

"Where is the bomb going to go off?"

"I don't know." Barnard replied.

Ward raised his gun,

"But I know when!" Barnard quickly said.

"When?"

"10am tomorrow morning."

"How do you know that?"

"Because Lord Ashurst-Stevens rarely gives live interviews, but he has arranged one for tomorrow morning at 10am in the boardroom," Barnard eagerly said.

It made sense, Ward thought to himself. Ashurst-Stevens being broadcast to the world on live TV when the bomb went off, particularly if one of the people who died had a link to him. It was the perfect alibi.

"OK. You've been very helpful," Ward said.

Barnard took this as an opening, a starting point for negotiation,

"I can testify for you. If you want Lord Ashurst-Stevens, I can help you," he said. Ward could almost hear the cogs in his brain ticking over, trying to find a new angle. Self-preservation, a typical lawyer he thought to himself.

"No need for that," he replied.

"Think about it," Barnard said, "With me as a witness there would be no way out for him."

"I have no need for that" he repeated.

"Why not?"

"Because I'm going to kill him too."

"You are going to kill Lord Ashurst-Stevens?" Barnard asked in disbelief. These people really did think they were untouchable.

"Why do you still refer to him as Lord all the time?" he asked.

"Because that is what he is."

Ward looked at Barnard across the table. He could see that he was starting to feel that he might have a way out of this. He was thinking he could negotiate somehow. He was so used to people holding everything he said in such high regard that he believed Ward was going to hang on every word he said. Ward stood up and looked down on him,

"People don't trust or respect the legal system anymore and it is all because people like you that have diminished its value," he said, "No one stands up for the little man anymore because they are governed by your rules and the immoral and deceitful people who implement them. You are as bad as Asif Fulken, yet you convince yourself that you only deal in paper. I lost a friend of mine yesterday who was trying to stand up for the little man, to protect him and keep him safe, and you were one of the people who sent him to his execution. He had a wife and two boys who were his world. Do you think they would find comfort in the fact that you only filled in the paperwork?" Ward asked.

"Please, don't," Barnard begged, and started crying again.

"I'm going to kill you and then before I kill Ashurst-Stevens I am going to make sure that pictures of you in disgusting acts with a young boy are broadcast to the world."

Ward lifted his Glock and pulled the trigger. The bullet smashed into Barnard's chest and the impact pushed him back against the back of the chair and he rolled off of the right side onto the floor. Ward walked around the table. His eyes were open and he was still breathing. He pointed the gun again and fired one more shot into the same area where the blood was pumping out of him. Barnard stopped moving. Ward paused for a few seconds and then fired two more into the same place. Barnard's body jerked and then went limp again.

Ward stood over him, staring at his lifeless body.

"I think he's dead," Lawson said.

He didn't say anything. He leant forward and went through Barnard's pocket and pulled out his cell phone and put it in his own pocket.

"Four bullets was probably overkill, which puts you into the psychotic category," Lawson said casually, trying to lighten the mood.

Ward still didn't speak. He just stood there looking at the body.

"Did you really have those pictures and videos generated?" Lawson asked.

"No."

"Seriously, four was a bit too much," Lawson said.

"It was the right amount."

"Why?"

"One for Gilligan, one for Gilligan's wife and one each for his two boys."

Lawson chose not to speak this time. He understood.

Ward took out his phone and called Centrepoint.

"What is happening?" he demanded.

"I need a clean-up crew urgently to the offices of USBC News, sixteenth floor, the boardroom," Ward replied.

"Oh my God, tell me you haven't killed Ashurst-Stevens?"

"Not yet," Ward replied and hung up the phone.

He looked at his watch. It was now 5.45pm.

"Stay here until the clean-up crew arrive and then meet me back at Nicole-Louise's," he said, and he walked out of the boardroom.

He thought he would feel a sense of gratification in avenging Gilligan's death but he didn't. He felt nothing. He knew immediately that only by killing Ashurst-Stevens, would he achieve that feeling, as he started the short walk back to Park Avenue.

He now knew three things; who, how and when. He only needed to find the where.

As he walked, one thing kept nagging at him. There were higher powers at play Barnard had said, but who?

THIRTY EIGHT

Now things were pretty straightforward. He had two more people to take out: Fulken and Ashurst-Stevens. It was a task he was sure he would complete.

He looked at his watch and it was now 6:05pm. Just under sixteen hours of his estimated finish time left. He felt he would not need all sixteen hours. His phone vibrated in his pocket. He pulled it out and Eloisa's name flashed on the screen.

"Hello you," he answered.

"How is it going, has my knight in shining armour made the streets safe yet?" she asked.

Ward smiled to himself; just the sound of her voice always brought him to life,

"Almost," he replied, "How was your day?"

"I'm still here, it will be a late one for me."

"How late?"

"About eight thirty."

"How about we meet for a coffee when you are done?" he asked, "Give me a break from saving the world."

Eloisa's giggle seemed to shoot down the line like electricity. It always had that effect on him. This was the woman that he loved and wanted to be with, and he had yet to find one little fault in her, in the four years he had known her.

"I'd love that," she replied, "Where are you now?"

"Park Avenue."

"Good, we can meet in Leno's on Lexington, say eight forty-five?"

"Perfect," he replied "I'm literally only five minutes away."

"I can't wait to see you," she said excitedly.

"Snap," Ward replied and he hung up the phone.

He knocked on the door and Tackler opened it,

"I've never seen you so much in one day," he said with a welcoming smile, still buoyed by the fact that Ward had held a private audience with him in the kitchen; building his ego and confidence up to unchartered levels.

"What can I say?" he replied, "I missed you."

He walked into the room.

Walker and his son were still sitting on the sofa, but they looked much more relaxed now. McDermott's presence alone being all the comfort they needed.

Nicole-Louise was sitting at her desk and spun her chair around,

"Where's Lawson?" she asked.

"Shot hopefully," Tackler mumbled, loud enough only for Ward to hear.

"He'll be here shortly, he's just cleaning something up."

"Well, would you like to see all that I have found?" she asked.

"Only if you tell me you have found something worthwhile," he replied.

Nicole-Louise shot him a stern look,

"I've found everything," she said, "Have a seat," she added, pointing at the armchair nearest to her on her right.

Ward sat down,

"Can you give me the short and simple version please Nicole-Louise, we are pushed for time," he asked in the nicest possible tone that he could produce.

She looked offended but said,

"OK."

"Thank you."

"Firstly, the money flow," she said, "Short version. I told you it came from a subsidiary of Ashurst-Stevens and there were four million dollars transferred and two million pending, correct?"

"Correct." Ward replied.

"Well there is actually six million dollars pending."

"Six?"

"One impending transfer of two million dollars one of four."

"Another bomb?"

"No," she replied, "This is linked to be released by notification tomorrow, so it will be a bonus payment, or a pre-agreed figure upon completion."

"So, in simple terms, what can you prove?"

"That Ashurst-Stevens will have paid the bomber a total of ten million dollars to blow people up," she replied, "Simple enough for you?"

Ward then felt bad for offending her earlier,

"How clear is it?"

"It would stand up in any court of law in the world."

"It won't get to court," he replied.

Nicole-Louise knew what he meant and so dropped the point immediately,

"The lawyer you spoke to has gone, I also know that," she said,

"How do you know?"

She turned around and looked at the screen to her right,

"Because if he isn't, he is standing in this room now and I can't see him."

He remembered the phone he had taken from Barnard and dug it out of his pocket. He handed it to Nicole-Louise and she put it down on the side.

"Now," she continued, "The advertising revenue and increase in paper sales, and other commercial arms of the Ashurst-Stevens Media Empire has increased by 1700% across the world for him."

"How?"

"People love reading about death and destruction unfortunately."

"This is common?"

"No, it's unusual," she replied.

"Why?"

"Easy. He leaks that the security services are chasing a bomber but they don't know where he is, and that New York could be his next target, and people want to know what's happening so they buy newspapers, log onto websites and the conspiracy theorists go into overdrive."

"So how does that make money?" Ward asked, fascinated to learn the answer.

"Supply and demand," she said, "If I am advertising a product on one of his news websites, on a normal day with two million visitors, I might pay fifty thousand dollars. But the more viewers, the bigger the target audience and then the cost of advertising goes up?"

"By that much?" Ward enquired.

"It rockets when you jump from two million visitors to fifteen million visitors a day. And most people click back on three or four times a day and so that fifteen becomes sixty million."

"And the price goes up to what?"

"Around two hundred and fifty thousand dollars and the companies are desperate for an audience that big, so they line up to pay it," Nicole-Louise replied.

Ward remembered the activity on the advertising floor in London. Bad news was good news for Ashurst-Stevens.

"That seems too simple," he said.

"Not really," she replied, "People love watching a drama unfold. Think back to the OJ Simpson car chase. It's the same here. Most people are willing the bomb to go off so that they can say they watched the drama unfold right before their eyes. Nine eleven was another example. People became addicted to it," she added.

"So, how much cash would 1700% convert to?" Ward asked.

"I looked at that," she said, "And I've calculated it to be around thirty million dollars worldwide."

All the money that Ashurst-Stevens has and he still wanted this all done for nothing, and makes a hefty profit on top of it; Ward thought to himself. It was clever. Fulken takes the risks and it doesn't cost Ashurst-Stevens a penny, yet he is at least twenty million dollars up.

"I'm in the wrong line of work." he said to Nicole-Louise.

"No," she replied, "You are in the right line of work because we can steal whatever we want and they will never catch us," she added with a smile.

Ward looked at her; she had something on her mind, he could see it.

"Suggestions?"

"I'm sure that Mrs Gilligan could use some money to make sure her family is secure?"

"I agree," he replied, "A figure in mind?"

"Oh, I'd say about four million should cover it."

Ward gave her a satisfied nod.

"College can be so expensive now," she added with a grin.

"Take Fulken's money?"

"That's exactly what I was going to do, it's money already paid, so it will take no more than five minutes to move."

"Nicole-Louise, you are a genius," Ward said, as he beamed at her.

"I know," she replied, "And that was the short version!"

"Two more things I need you to do first," he said.

"Name them?"

"I want you to go through that phone," he said pointing to Barnard's phone next to her.

"What do you want from it?"

"I want Ashurst-Stevens' number and then I want to know where he is."

"Secondly?"

"I want you to find me Fulken's number from Ashurst-Stevens' call records and let me have it immediately," he said.
"I'll have that in ten minutes," she replied and turned around, and began to tap on her keyboard once more.
Tackler nodded towards the kitchen and then stood up and walked through the door.
Ward followed him.
"What have you got?" he asked him as he closed the door.
"All the big hitting media players from around the world are in New York for this awards ceremony tomorrow night," Tackler said, "So there is an element of guesswork in what I have concluded."
"Go on?"
"It's not easy because Ashurst-Stevens has tried taking over pretty much every competitor out there," Tackler replied.
"But you have a name?"
"The best I can do is narrow it down to three."
"Who are?" Ward asked.
"Theodore Chambers the third. Ashurst-Stevens tried taking over his media company two years ago. He covers the U.S and South America. He almost succeeded but the deal fell through at the last minute."
Ward had heard of Chambers before. He assumed that he had caught a glimpse of his name on the news.
"Next?"
"Gerrard Herrera, a Spanish based tycoon who owns the networks and newspapers that cover most of mainland Europe."
"Relation to Ashurst-Stevens?"
"The same," Tackler replied, "He's pretty much tried a hostile takeover of everyone in the media world. Ashurst-Stevens is huge."
"The third?"
"Sir Andrew Higgins." Tackler replied.
"Another regal name?" Ward said.
"They used to be partners thirty years ago, in a number of joint ventures. There was a falling out and Ashurst-Stevens

has been chipping away at Higgins' Empire for the last twenty years."

"So why him?" Ward asked.

"Because the jewel in the Higgins crown is Millennium Media and it is building up a network to compete against the monopoly that Ashurst-Stevens has on sports both sides of the Atlantic," Tackler replied.

"And your best guess is that it is one of them?"

"Yes. But it is just that, a guess."

"I knew you could find them," Ward said.

Tackler smiled and Ward could see the pride that Tackler felt. He could also see the reassurance wash over him that the one they were looking for was among those three names.

"There is one last thing I need you to do," Ward said,

"Anything," Tackler replied.

"I want to know where all three of them will be at 10.00am tomorrow morning."

"I'm on it."

Ward patted him on the shoulder and they both walked back into the living area.

Nicole-Louise turned around from her workstation as Ward walked in.

"OK," she said, "What do you want first?"

"The phone, what did you get from it?" Ward asked.

"Lots," she replied, "I have Ashurst-Stevens cell locked in and he is currently having dinner at Masa, at West 60th and Broadway."

"And a number I might be interested in?"

"I've got it," she said, "They were different numbers, probably swapped sim cards, but I looked at who he called in Paris, London and New York over the last two weeks. No other calls were made to the numbers so it has to be him," she added, handing him a piece of paper with the number written on it.

"Where is it now?" he asked.

"It's about twenty blocks away, on Lexington Avenue by East 35th Street, but the signal keeps dropping in and out."

"Turning it off and on?"

"Probably, at the moment it is off."

"Nicole-Louise, you are the best at what you do in the world," he said, and then watched as Tackler raised both eyebrows.
The apartment buzzer made everyone startle. Tackler pressed the intercom,
"Yes?"
"It's me," Lawson's voice echoed around the room.
Tackler hit the button to release the building door.
Nicole-Louise continued,
"So, I have four million dollars here ready to spend on college fees," she said with a smile, "Would you like to do the honours?"
Ward walked up to the desk and Nicole-Louise gestured for him to hit the return button on the keyboard to send the money.
"Won't she phone the bank to ask them about it?" he asked.
"Already taken care of," she replied, "The bank can only say it is authentic and not a mistake and the money is hers," she added.
"Definitely?"
"Guaranteed."
Ward hit the return button. At least the Gilligan's were financially secure now, even if their giant of a husband and father wasn't there to hold them.
Lawson knocked on the door; McDermott opened it and he walked in,
"Where are we now?" he seemed to ask the whole room.
"You will stay here with Nicole-Louise, Tackler and these two," Ward said, pointing at the Walkers, "As soon as Tackler tells you where the three people we are looking for are going to be at 10am tomorrow, you call me and let me know. Mac, as soon as you know the three places, can you roll your team to each location and do the recon work?"
McDermott nodded.
"Where are you going?" Lawson asked.
"I have a few calls to make and then a coffee date," Ward replied.

He understood everything completely now. It wasn't so much about money; it was about worldwide control of the news. If Ashurst-Stevens took over even one of his main competitors, he would have total control over what people read and therefore in essence, what people thought. He wasn't just an egomaniac or a man trying to build a mountain of wealth beyond the comprehension of a normal person. He wanted to be something else. He wanted to be the most powerful man on earth. He wanted to be The Newsmaker.

THIRTY NINE

"Have you finished killing people for the day?" Centrepoint asked as he answered, "I'm getting calls from all sorts of departments, and I have spent virtually the whole day cleaning up your mess."

"Almost," Ward replied.

"I'm being serious. Have you any idea of the body count you have amassed since you got on this in London?"

Ward paused for a moment and started to mentally add up those who had been killed but soon gave up.

"Two more, that's all."

"They are?"

"Fulken and Ashurst-Stevens," he replied.

"Again, I'm serious, Ashurst-Stevens is off limits."

"Are you for real?" Ward asked, "The guy is behind all of this, I have complete proof of that, and you want him left alone?"

"It's the bigger picture; he's worth more to us alive."

"How can that be?"

"Think about it. We can use him to control the news, cover our work up, and misinform people to assist our work."

Ward was a realist. He could see that there would be huge benefit in having that kind of control, and how it would probably save a lot more lives than Ashurst-Stevens had cost, but he kept thinking about Gilligan, and at how this moment in time, avenging his death, which was firmly at the feet of Ashurst-Stevens, was his priority,

"I'll see how it plays out," he replied.

"Where are you with Fulken?" Centrepoint asked.

"I know where he is but I still don't know where the bomb is due to go off. Ashurst-Stevens is having an expensive meal right now, and they are the only two who know where it is due to go off. I don't think Fulken will break due to his training, so we are trying to find the bomb ourselves."

"Can't you just go to where he is?"

"No. We don't know if he has the bomb there or if he has people helping him. What if he has support and the bomb is miles away, and we take him out, and we then have no lead at all if Ashurst-Stevens won't talk."

"You are going to stop that bomb from ever going off, aren't you?" The Old Man asked, "I need some justification for the trail of destruction you have left in your wake."

"Yes I am," Ward replied and hung up the phone.

He walked a little further down the street and took out the piece of paper that Nicole-Louise had given him with Fulken's number on it. He dialled the number and got a network carrier message that said they were sorry but they were unable to connect the call right now, and so he hung up.

He walked down Park Avenue and cut across on East 61st Street, onto Lexington Avenue. He got a cab down to East 32nd Street and got out. He knew Fulken was here somewhere and he strolled along looking for a potentially vacant building that could hide a 'UPS' van.

In total, he spent thirty minutes walking up and down the Avenue. Come out, come out, wherever you are, he thought to himself.

He took his phone out of his pocket and dialled the number again. This time it rang.

"Hello?" the voice said.

It was Fulken without a doubt.

"I've been looking for you," he said.

The voice on the end of the line went quiet.

"Don't be shy," he continued, "I've put a lot of effort into finding you."

Continued silence.

Ward could sense the fear.

"You have nothing to say?" he asked, "That's a disappointment."

"You? You are the man I saw on the cell phone?" Fulken eventually replied.

Ward had no idea what Fulken was on about, but he wasn't going to let that get in the way of the dialogue they were about to engage in,

"No," he replied, "I'm the guy who wanted you to see him on his cell phone."

"I recognised you, how do I know you?" Fulken asked.

Ward was confused at this. He knew for sure that he had never met Fulken, or even been in the same room as him, but he continued to play along,

"You forget, how hurtful," he replied.

Fulken went quiet.

Ward could almost hear him trying to put his voice to whoever he had seen on their phone, and he wasn't sure if it was computing with him or not, but he continued,

"We took you in, gave you a chance of a good life and you turned on us," he said.

"There was no choice," Fulken replied.

He calculated immediately that the only thing that would make a man like Fulken not have a choice would be a threat to those people close to him.

So he took a gamble,

"You think after this your family will be safe?" he asked.

No reply, just heavier breathing than Ward had initially heard.

"Well they won't. No matter where you think you will take them to be safe, we will find you and them."

"We?" Fulken asked.

"I'm the guy who has taken out your American network and who is going to stop you from ever detonating that bomb. And after that, Ashurst-Stevens is next on my list."

"Who?"

Ward knew immediately that Fulken had no idea who was behind this plot, because he had never met him face to face.

"The guy giving you instructions, the English guy, the money man. His name is Ashurst-Stevens."

Silence on the line again.

He could hear the light tapping of keys on a keyboard and knew that Fulken would be searching for information on Ashurst-Stevens online right then.

He left a ten second gap in the conversation so that Fulken could digest the information that he was no doubt looking at.

"That surprised you didn't it?" he asked.

"Indeed it did."

"So how about you tell me where and when the bomb is due to go off and it can save us a load of time and energy?"

He heard Fulken laugh,

"And let me guess my friend, then you let me live?"

"No," he replied, "I'm going to kill you regardless."

No reply.

"You are afraid of me, I can hear it in your silence," Ward said.

"I would be stupid not to be afraid of you," Fulken replied, "You seem to have single handily wiped out all of the FFW sympathisers in New York."

"You can add London to that too, but you had already run off before you could find that out."

"I still can't put your face to a place, how about you help me out?" Fulken asked.

Ward thought about this for two brief seconds before deciding that another gamble was in order,

"You really don't remember me, do you?"

No reply.

"Nothing?" he asked, in the process buying a few more seconds to think.

No reply.

"Think back to the FFW," he said, "You aren't remembering properly."

Ward could almost hear the wheels in Fulken's brain turning.

"You want some help?"

"Yes please my friend, humour me." Fulken replied.

"I'm the one who way back set you up to be caught by us."

"I don't understand."

"I'm the one who is behind all of this."

No reply.

"Think about it," Ward said, "You have led me to every single FFW cell in both London and here, and now they are all gone."

No reply.

"You've single handily done more damage to the FFW than the CIA have managed in the past five years."

"You overestimate the value of my faith to me my friend," Fulken replied.

"No," Ward said, "We evaluated it perfectly."

"Explain?"

"We knew you would jump at the money we have paid you to set off those bombs. Your faith means nothing to you, we knew that when we brought you over here."

Silence on the line again.

"But the faith of the members of the FFW cells is unquestionable," he continued.

"You used me to get to them?" Fulken said, thinking out loud and not asking a direct question.

Ward thought this was a good point to move the conversation back to another point. Leaving Fulken with a lot of things to chew over when the call had ended,

"What I don't understand is how you can't remember me," he said, "It's not like we have never met."

Silence on the line again.

"So I will ask you one more time, walk away now, tell me where the bomb is, and your family might just live." Ward said.

"I'll take my chances my friend," Fulken replied and the line went dead.

He smiled to himself. He had given Fulken enough information to confuse him and he knew right now, that Fulken would be analysing every part of their conversation, playing it over and over in his head for the next few hours. That would mean that he would be distracted, and when distraction entered the equation, mistakes always got made.

He hailed a cab and made his way back to Park Avenue. Tackler opened the door to the apartment when he arrived and he looked confused.

"Everything OK?" he asked.

"Yes and no," Tackler replied as he moved out of the way for Ward to enter the apartment.

Inside, Walker and his son were still sitting on the sofa. Ward looked at McDermott who was still standing to the side of the sofa like a sentry, focussed, alert and ready for action if required.

Lawson was texting on his phone.

"Why don't you take those two out to stretch their legs and to get some air for an hour?" Ward said to McDermott.

McDermott nodded. Walker looked terrified again.

"Don't worry," he said to them, "He is probably the one man in the whole world that all of the bad guys are afraid of. You will be completely safe."

Walker looked instantly re-assured.

The two Walker's stood up, and in identical rhythm, and with the same hands, scooped up their jackets and put them on.

"How long and how far?" McDermott asked.

"A couple of hours and not too far," Ward said, "I might need you to move at a moment's notice."

McDermott nodded his head and led the way out of the apartment with the Walkers two steps behind him.

"What's wrong?" Ward asked Tackler.

"I've found out where the three competitors that I identified will be tomorrow at 10:00am," Tackler replied.

"Tell me?"

"Well, Herrera will be in the Chrysler building attending a charity event that his organisation sponsors for homeless children."

"The likelihood of it being him?"

"In terms of financial gain, high," Tackler replied.

"Next?"

"Theodore Chambers has a meeting arranged at the United Nations with an ambassador from Argentina."

"Chances?"

"In terms of financial gain, probable."

"The British guy?" Ward asked.

"Sir Andrew Higgins has an appointment with a host of different network producers," Tackler replied.

"Where?"

"Believe it or not, It's at the USBC News headquarters." Ward looked confused.

"How does that work?" he asked.

"Most companies do it. They have steering groups who regularly meet and discuss new technology, methods and shared satellites. It was the turn of the Swan Media Group to host it, but it was changed to USBC News last week," Tackler replied.

"Will Ashurst-Stevens be there?" Ward asked.

"Yes. He has an interview planned."

"Likelihood?"

"Extremely high I would say, wouldn't you?"

"Maybe," Ward said.

"Only maybe?"

"Yes."

"Surely by blowing up his own building it would look like an attack on him also so he has a double alibi?" Tackler asked.

Ward ignored him and looked across at Nicole-Louise.

"Where is Ashurst-Stevens now?" he asked.

"He's still at the Masa restaurant. If he's having one of their five hundred buck, fifteen course meals, he will be there a while yet," she replied with clear disdain in her voice.

Ward looked at his watch. It was eight fifteen. He took out his cell phone and dialled McDermott's number.

"Hey," McDermott answered.

"I need you back here immediately," he said.

"Three minutes, I can see the building from here."

He hung up the phone.

"Fulken's cell has lost signal I take it?" he asked Nicole-Louise. She nodded her response.

"The money for Gilligan's wife?"

"Already done. The payment transfer was made from an account I set up, which has now been wiped and never existed. She's stuck with it." she said. The warm smile that accompanied it, for a brief moment, made Ward appreciate the values of the human race again.

"Thank you, Nicole-Louise."

The buzzer rang and Tackler got up to buzz down for the front door to open. Thirty seconds later, McDermott was walking in with the Walkers no more than two paces behind him.

"What's up?" he asked.

"I need you to move the team," Ward replied.

"Where to?"

"This van will be parked somewhere ready to move. Somewhere close to one of three places."

"The three places?" McDermott asked.

"The United Nations, the Chrysler Building and USBC News Headquarters."

"How close?"

"Well Ashurst-Stevens knows that we have pretty much pieced all this together and so does Fulken."

"How would he know?" McDermott asked.

309

"Because I've just told him."

Everyone in the room stopped what they were doing and looked at him.

"You told him?" Tackler asked.

"Yes. And his silent responses to what I told him, told me I was right," Ward replied.

"You spoke to him?" Nicole-Louise asked.

Ward nodded.

"OK," McDermott said, "How close do you think?"

"No more than a mile," he replied, "He will know we are all looking for the UPS van, and there would be no point in increasing the travel time. It just increases the chance of getting caught before he reaches his target."

McDermott nodded,

"I'll get them rolling now," he said, "But they will need me out in the field to co-ordinate this with them."

Ward nodded.

"You two will have to stay here until I am done," he said to Walker and his son. They both nodded but the increase in anxiety visibly spread across their faces.

"It will be fine," Ward said, "These two will protect you."

Nicole-Louise smiled.

Tackler looked like he was about to protest but changed his mind when Ward glared at him.

FORTY

Ward made his way to Leno's coffee shop on Lexington and walked in at eight forty. Eloisa was already in a booth with two steaming mugs opposite each other on the table. He walked up to her, leant down and kissed her gently on the lips, and then slid into the opposite side of the booth.

"I've missed you," she said.

"Likewise."

"Have you nearly sorted this thing out?"

"It's a lot clearer than it was."

"When can we spend time together?" she asked.

"As soon as this is over, I'm yours," he replied with a smile.

Eloisa looked awkward for a moment.

"What's wrong?"

"This thing I spoke to you about on the phone earlier, it really can't wait," she said.

Ward thought back to their conversation about the next problem that Eloisa wanted solved.

"Then if it can't wait, you had best tell me all about it."

"God, I love you so much," she said, "You really are the most selfless man in the world."

Eloisa reached into her bag and pulled out a large brown envelope.

"Everything is in there."

He put the envelope on his lap without looking at it.

"His name is Michael O'Leary and he needs stopping," she said.

Ward nodded.

"We should go away soon," Eloisa said, "I need a break and I know for sure that you do."

"Still on for the old movies tomorrow night?"

"I have to fly to Michigan first thing tomorrow for a conference," she said, "But we will go somewhere hot like the Bahamas and sit in the sun all day drinking cocktails when I'm back."

They finished their coffees and spoke about the Bahamas and laughed at how they would have the waiters' running back and forward to their sun loungers all day long. After thirty minutes, they stood up and walked out of Leno's and hugged in the street. Ward hailed a cab and he opened the door for her to step in. He kissed her on the lips and closed the door and watched the cab drive up Lexington and out of sight. He hailed a cab and said to the driver,

"Masa at West 60th and Broadway."

He arrived at Masa and stepped out of the cab, leaving a hefty tip to the driver who had a very accurate view on how the New York Mets had been performing.

The entrance to Masa was bright and shiny; lots of chrome, with a big sign that simply said 'Bar Masa' hanging down, and a declaration that it served modern Japanese cuisine to the bottom left.

He walked into the restaurant. To the right there was a long bar with every stool taken. There was an open area where you could watch the chef's preparing the food, and the main dining room had a large group of individual tables that covered most of the floor and to the left; there were more spacious and secluded tables. Where the real money ate or rather just ordered the most expensive food on the menu, regardless if they liked it or not.

As he walked in, the floor manager looked up at him, "Good evening Sir" he said, looking Ward up and down.

He suddenly realised that he was most definitely not dressed for a night out at one of New York's most expensive eateries.

"Good evening," he replied, "Sorry about my attire, I've just stepped off of a plane."

The floor manager smiled. A practiced smile designed to cause no offence whatsoever.

"Do you have a reservation?"

"I'm part of the Ashurst-Stevens party," he replied, "Can you tell him that Mr Chennell is here."

The floor manager smiled and said,

"Please wait here."

He turned and walked towards the money tables. He disappeared from sight and Ward stood there waiting for a good three minutes. He started to wonder if Ashurst-Stevens would try escaping out of a rear door, when the floor manager returned.

"Follow me please Sir," he said and turned, leading Ward into the main restaurant. They walked past all the other diners, a number of them taking a second glance at him in his inappropriate clothing, and they came to a large, pine table with eight chairs around it. The guests that Ashurst-Stevens had been eating with were all walking towards him as he got to the table.

"Hello again Mr Chennell," Ashurst-Stevens said, offering his hand as Ward reached the table.

Ward ignored the offer.

"Lawyers and bankers, so incredibly boring," he said, "Now, what can I help you with?"

"You can tell me where the next bomb is planned to go off?" Ward said, in a very matter of fact tone.

Ashurst-Stevens studied him for a few seconds.

"I'm not sure what you mean. I thought that we had given you our full co-operation and use of our extensive resources?"

313

"I've got everything worked out. I've got it down to three places; you could just save me a lot of time if you told me which one it is, so we can find Fulken and the bomb prior to any distress being caused."

"Distress?" Ashurst-Stevens asked.

He knew at that exact moment, that Ashurst-Stevens was going to see this through to the end, regardless of the consequences, because he had no choice. Backing down now would definitely prove that he was behind it all. So Ward considered a different approach.

"I get that we have nothing specific on you in relation to the bombings, and that you want to see this through, but there is no way you will get to either Herrera, Chambers or Higgins," he said.

"I have no idea what you are talking about."

"Yes you do," Ward said, "I can see it in your eyes. The whole plan relied upon everyone being focussed on Fulken and the FFW, but it was always about you and your empire."

Ashurst-Stevens looked both surprised and impressed at the same time; Ward saw this as encouragement to continue his approach of antagonising him.

"It wasn't that difficult really," he said, "Once I had met you, your character flaws were obvious. That's how I knew."

Ashurst-Stevens laughed out loud,

"My character flaws?" he said, "I wasn't aware that a billionaire could have character flaws. Let's measure my success in life against yours shall we?"

Ward ignored the response and carried on.

"Hiring Lucas was a mistake. That's a flaw right there. You go for the cheapest option all the time. That didn't work out very well for him."

As he finished his sentence, his phone vibrated. He took it out of his pocket, willing it to be a message from McDermott that they had found the van, but it was just a text from Lawson saying that he was getting bored.

Ward continued.

"Everyone who died was an innocent person with family and loved ones. There's a flaw there."

314

"I have no idea what you are on about, but I will amuse you," he replied, "So, hypothetically, why would that be a flaw?"

"Because that made me an enemy."

"I have more powerful enemies than you, that's for sure," he replied in an arrogant tone.

Ward ignored the baiting.

"So, the person you want will not be where you want him tomorrow morning, and you have no way of getting hold of Fulken now, that I am sure of, so playing this out to the end all now seems a little pointless," he said, "And as Barnard said, his testimony in a court of law will carry an awful lot of weighting. He's writing it up right now as we speak."

Ashurst-Stevens smiled,

"You think with my friends, even if I was involved in this ludicrous plot you speak of, that I would ever get to a court of law?" he asked smugly.

Ward knew that nothing would be resolved through simple communication so he gave up.

"Maybe I have you all wrong?"

"I think you do," Ashurst-Stevens replied.

Ward stood up without saying another word and walked out of the restaurant.

When he got outside, he called Lawson.

"Hello?"

"I want you to come and meet me, I'm at Masa. Nicole-Louise will tell you where," he said.

"I know it," Lawson replied, "Me and Abbi have booked a table there."

Ward hung up and dialled McDermott.

"I need something done quickly."

"What is it?" McDermott asked.

"I need you to kidnap Ashurst-Stevens for me. And I need it done now."

"The team are out hunting for the van."

"Lawson is available; he's at Nicole-Louise's. Call him and co-ordinate with him," he said

"OK."

"Hurry up," Ward said and hung up.

He moved across the street and stood in an apartment doorway. He had no way of knowing how Ashurst-Stevens intended to leave the building, but he doubted whatever arrangements he had made would be sufficient to stop the three of them from taking him.

He prepared himself to wait for however long it took.

Asif Fulken was becoming more and more agitated. It was now 10:45pm, less than twelve hours to go and this would all be over, but he could not place the man on the phone anywhere. He had a British accent but spoke about Americans as 'Us'. His only contact had been with the CIA and so he had to be a part of that.

The man sounded so calm and in control when he was speaking to him that he must know a number of things that he didn't. He knew about his family and he said they would never be safe. He had discarded the phone immediately after their conversation had ended but he regretted doing so now. He wanted to call him back, he had so many questions. He felt that the answer to where he had seen him before was almost on the tip of his tongue, but he couldn't put the final piece together.

A normal man would run, protect himself and disappear but he was a warrior, a protector of faith and family and he would not let fear beat him.

Everything had been so simple at the start until this man got involved.

But everything will be so simple in the end. He told himself over and over, but he kept going back to the same question, the more he tried convincing himself that he was in control. Why was the man on the phone the one in control of everything? He had said that he was the person behind everything, but no matter what he did, he couldn't piece it together. He had seen all about the man called Lord Ashurst-Stevens and understood that he was the money man, but where did the man on the phone fit in.

He was confused and distracted because of the man, and he sat on the sofa with his eyes shut, trying to work out who this man was. Very confused and distracted.

So confused and distracted in fact, that he did not notice the two men outside the building creep through the shadows and head towards the wooden garage where the UPS van was stored.

Twenty minutes after he had called them, Ward was standing with Lawson and McDermott.

Ashurst-Stevens had still not left the building. McDermott had parked the Range Rover as close to the restaurant as possible, which was about forty feet away from the entrance, "Nicole-Louise could not find any limousine's booked or payment to any security company, so we are going to have to take this as it comes," Lawson said.

"He knows both of us so if you take the restaurant side of the street near the door, and Lawson and me will rush in from this side then we can box him in that way," Ward said to McDermott.

They watched as McDermott crossed the street.

"What do we do if we don't find the van?" Lawson asked.

"We are covering that now," Ward replied.

"So we get Ashurst-Stevens to tell us where the target is and that narrows our search down?"

"Yes Mike," he said, "That is why when you use what is in your head rather than your trousers, you are exceptional at your job."

Lawson smiled.

"So," Lawson said, "I have a question?"

"What?"

"Were there many attractive women in the restaurant?" he said with a smile.

They waited for a further five minutes and only a handful of diners left the restaurant.

McDermott stayed as alert and focussed as ever, checking the road and the entrance, and then all three of them watched as a black Mercedes with tinted windows pulled up, and two

317

thick set guys stepped out and walked towards the restaurant entrance.

"This could be the transport," Lawson said.

Ward looked across to McDermott who nodded at them both. They saw the two guys enter and talk to the floor manager, then watched as the floor manager walked off and disappeared out of sight, as he had when he led Ward to Ashurst-Stevens table.

"This is it," Ward said, "Take the driver out," he said to Lawson.

He watched as Lawson walked up to the Mercedes and knocked on the driver's window. The driver lowered the window about eight inches and Lawson said something, and then the driver lowered the window all the way down and Lawson unleashed a thunderous right hook that caught the guy square in the face and he slumped sideways, his seatbelt holding him upright. Lawson opened the door, undid the seatbelt and pulled the driver out. He was completely unconscious. He lifted him to his feet and yanked him onto his shoulder. Lawson had incredible strength that matched his physical size.

He watched as he walked towards an alleyway, with the guy over his shoulder like a sack of potatoes.

He entered the alleyway and thirty seconds later; returned alone and sat in the driver's seat in the Mercedes, raising the window back up completely.

A minute later, Ward saw Ashurst-Stevens walking behind the two men as they walked out of the restaurant.

McDermott stepped out in front of them as Ward started to cross the road.

The guy at the front assessed McDermott as a threat and stepped towards him immediately. He reached McDermott and put his hand on McDermott's chest in a forceful stop action. This guy has no idea how dumb he had just been, Ward thought to himself.

McDermott rammed his elbow down onto the guys arm and Ward could hear the arm snap from twenty feet away. The other guy turned his head and it took a few seconds to compute what was happening. By the time it had registered, McDermott was standing right next to him and he jabbed him with lightning speed in the throat. The guy fell straight to the floor.

It had taken no more than five seconds to wipe out Ashurst-Stevens' protection. Ward continued his walk across to the sidewalk without changing pace and stopped next to Ashurst-Stevens.

There was a look of fear on his face that Ward had not seen in the previous times that they had met. This would be easy, he thought to himself.

He grabbed his arm and forcibly pulled him over to the Mercedes and opened the door.

"What is the meaning of this?" Ashurst-Stevens demanded, "Have you any idea what a mistake you have just made? You will face the full wrath of the British government," he added.

"I'm not British dipshit," Ward said, "So, get in the car; I want to talk to you."

FORTY ONE

Ward climbed into the back of the car with Ashurst-Stevens, while McDermott got in the front next to Lawson and they pulled slowly away.

"Whatever you think I do or don't know, or what you think I may or may not have done, I can't help you," Ashurst-Stevens said.

Ward ignored him.

"Where are you taking me?" he demanded.

Ward ignored him.

"Have you any idea how powerful the people I know are?" he shouted, "You have no idea what you have just done. People way above your pay grade and that of your bosses will destroy you!"

Ward still said nothing.

It was a technique used to unsettle people. A non-response eventually led them to thinking that you had a plan, and that caused panic. Once you interrogate someone who is panicking, you can find out whatever you want to find out.

"I told you, I know nothing about that bomb," Ashurst-Stevens protested.

Ward still ignored him.

They drove for a few more minutes and then Ashurst-Stevens started protesting again but this time in a quieter voice. The few minutes thinking time had panicked him.

"What do you think will happen to you if anything happens to me?" he asked.

Ward ignored him.

"There are people very, very powerful at play here, way out of the league of the security services, so what do you think will happen?"

Still Ward ignored him, but he thought back to Barnard and how he said that there were people above Ashurst-Stevens who were involved; but he had dismissed that as the words of a desperate man. But here it was again from Ashurst-Stevens. Maybe another desperate man, or perhaps there was an element of truth to it.

"You will be crushed," he spat, "All three of you."

Ward ignored him.

They drove another few miles and reached McDermott's warehouse.

They stopped outside the roller shutter doors, while McDermott opened them with a remote key, and then quickly closed them after they had bundled Ashurst-Stevens inside.

"I'll get the kit ready," McDermott said as he moved a chair into the same position where Martin Walker sat.

Ward pulled Ashurst-Stevens over to the chair and pushed him down by leaning on his right shoulder. He kept his weight fully applied while he waited.

McDermott came back carrying a large bag, the type that a contractor carries onto a construction site, and put it on the table. He went into the bag and tossed Lawson a plastic bag full of large cable ties.

Lawson took three out and tied Ashurst-Stevens ankles to the chair first, and then pulled his arms behind the chair, ran the cable tie through the back supports and tightened them around his wrists. He was completely trussed up and unable to move.

Ward nodded at Lawson and walked out of the room to the reception area with McDermott following them, closing the

321

door so that Ashurst-Stevens was left with nothing but the eerie silence of the empty warehouse.

All alone.

Ten minutes to sit there looking at the tool bag, playing the most hideous scenarios over and over in his head, should be enough to unsettle him and get him to talk, Ward thought to himself.

"Do you have a kettle and coffee here?" Lawson asked McDermott.

"Only inside, but there is a coffee shop five minutes down the road, if you want to make him wait for fifteen minutes and really put the frighteners on him?" McDermott replied.

"I fancy a coffee, you two?" Lawson asked.

They both nodded. This could take some time, so refreshments would be a good idea. Lawson left the reception area, and twenty seconds later they heard the car start and pull away.

"Have you heard anything from your teams?" Ward asked

"Nothing," McDermott replied, "As soon as they find anything, we will know."

Ward felt his phone vibrate in his pocket, he pulled it out and saw Centrepoint's name. He put it back in his pocket.

"There is only one part of this that doesn't make sense to me," McDermott said to Ward

"There's two parts that don't make sense to me," Ward replied.

McDermott raised an eyebrow.

"Why a rich guy like him," McDermott said, pointing towards the door that led into the main warehouse, "Would go to those extremes to make more money is the obvious one."

Ward nodded.

"I thought initially that he was just greedy, but then the lawyer told me that there were higher powers than Ashurst-Stevens at play. I dismissed that at first, but now he has said it again, and he sounded so confident in telling me that, I think he might be telling the truth," Ward replied.

"More powerful than him would mean someone very, very, very rich," McDermott replied.

"Or rich in another way"?

"Like?"

"Influence. We now know how this is meant to be played out, Agreed?" Ward asked.

"Agreed."

"So I am starting to think that Ashurst-Stevens could not have dreamed this up himself."

"He seems pretty capable to me," McDermott replied.

"No. I think the extra revenue that his media group made and the death of one of his competitors could be his payment from someone else."

"For effectively assuming control of the operation?"

Ward's phone vibrated again. Centrepoint's name appeared on the screen. He looked at it and put the phone back in his pocket.

"Yes. But the word of a lawyer just before he was going to die, doesn't hold much weight," Ward said, "You know better than me that a man with a gun pointing at him will say anything." McDermott nodded.

"It was the confidence of Ashurst-Stevens that makes me think that there is someone else involved," Ward continued. "I could see it in his eyes. He genuinely thinks he is untouchable."

"He isn't looking untouchable right now," McDermott replied with a smile.

Ward laughed.

"Even ignoring the claims that two desperate men make, there is one last thing that is nagging at me, which no matter how I try and piece it together, I can't," Ward said.

His phone vibrated again and he looked at the screen, it was Centrepoint yet again.

"I think The Old Man is desperate to talk to you," McDermott said.

"I know. I don't want to talk to him, I know what he will say."

"So what is the other thing that you can't piece together?" McDermott asked.

Ward looked at him. The fact that McDermott had not given a thought to one small thing, momentarily made him think to himself that he was looking for problems that weren't there. The fact that neither he nor Lawson had ever mentioned the point that niggled away at him bothered him a great deal. He looked at McDermott.

"How on earth do you think Ashurst-Stevens knew that Fulken existed and where to find him?" Ward asked.

"I assumed that news corporations have investigative journalists, and that one of them has a source, who has a contact in the CIA, and they found him that way," McDermott replied, "You think we were meant to think that?"

"I'm not sure what to think either way but I am sure that Ashurst-Stevens will tell us."

They heard a car pull up outside and McDermott glanced at the CCTV screen.

"It's Lawson," he said.

Lawson walked in and handed a coffee each to Ward and McDermott. Ward's phone vibrated again. He looked at the screen. It was Centrepoint again. Ward put it back in his pocket.

Again.

Lawson looked at his watch; it was now 11:00.

"We'll drink these and then start?" he asked, "Let's give him 20 minutes to panic."

Ward nodded.

"How do you think they knew who Fulken was and where we were hiding him?" he asked Lawson.

"They are journalists, they always pay someone, who pays someone else, who tells them things they want to know," he replied.

Maybe they were right after all.

"The Old Man has tried calling me three times," Lawson said as they all sipped their coffee, "I didn't answer but I think he knows about Ashurst-Stevens now and he isn't very happy."

"He told me not to kill him; he said that he is worth more to us alive, that in the bigger picture, he will be of great use to us in the future," Ward said wearily.

"I think he is more worried about the fact that he is a high profile man. The government in the U.K. kiss his arse all the time, simply because he can decide who gets elected, and who stays elected," Lawson added.

"Are you going to kill him?" McDermott asked.

"Probably," Ward replied, as he tilted his cup and swallowed the last remaining mouthful of coffee.

"Good," Lawson said.

Ward put his cup down and they walked into the main area. Ashurst-Stevens was sitting on the chair, rocking his upper body backwards and forwards trying to loosen the cable ties.

"It's a waste of time," Ward said, "They won't break. You need to save your energy for what is about to happen," he added as he approached him.

He stopped two feet in front of Ashurst-Stevens and looked down at him. He looked straight back at him. He noticed that there was a resilience in his eyes that wasn't there twenty minutes ago.

He knelt down so that he was now eye level with him,

"OK. Here is how this will go," he said, "I will ask you questions, you will answer them, and if I decide that you are telling the truth, then I may let you live."

"May?" Ashurst-Stevens replied, "You need to work on your negotiation skills son, you aren't giving me much encouragement."

"I'm not your son," he replied and he raised his right arm and smashed his elbow down hard onto the top of Ashurst-Stevens' left knee. He felt the whole kneecap jerk down as his elbow connected.

Ashurst-Stevens let out a high-pitched scream, which for a split second reminded Ward of a child reacting to seeing a big spider.

He got to his feet and walked over to the table where the tool bag was placed. He pulled the two sides apart to reveal the contents. There were pliers, knives and two small vice type devices. He knew what they were for, but still picked them out and held them up for McDermott to see.

"The one in your left hand is for the fingers and toes," McDermott said, as Ward tried his best to look innocent as to what they were.

"And this one?" he asked, waving the device in his right hand.

"That's for the testicles," McDermott replied, as he looked down at his watch to look as disinterested as he possibly could.

"Interesting, I've never used one of these," Ward lied.

"They are great," McDermott said, "You can hear the bones crushing in the fingers and toes as you tighten them, and the other one is amusing," he added.

"Why amusing?" Lawson asked, lying equally as well as Ward.

"Because the testicles are really resilient up to a point but when they go they let out this really loud popping noise," McDermott replied.

As Ashurst-Stevens eyes darted from one man to another, Lawson deliberately looked suitably impressed.

Ward walked back over to Ashurst-Stevens carrying the vices and knelt back down to the position that he had previously taken up, one foot away from him at eye-level.

"Let's try again," he said, "This is how it will work. I will ask you questions and if I think you are telling the truth, I may let you live. Do you understand?"

Ashurst-Stevens nodded but never spoke.

"That's better."

He felt his phone vibrate in his pocket but he ignored it. He let the vibration stop before he spoke again,

"You need to tell me now where the bomb is going to go off?" he eventually asked.

Ashurst-Stevens sat still, tight-lipped. There was no declaration of innocence, or arrogant statements this time, just a determined silence.

The silence was broken by the sound of a loud vibration coming from Lawson's pocket. He pulled out his cell phone and hit the ignore button before turning the phone off. Ward glared at him and he shrugged back.

"It's really simple," he said, "I want to know where the bomb is meant to go off at 10:00am tomorrow morning."

Ashurst-Stevens did not respond, so he raised his left elbow and rammed it down onto the top of Ashurst-Stevens right knee.

The same impact, the same movement in his kneecap, and the same scream echoed around the room.

Ward held the miniature vice level with Ashurst-Stevens' eyes, and made a big gesture of studying it. He started to unscrew it and as he did, he lowered it so that his own eyes were looking straight into Ashurst-Stevens.

"There is no way that you will last ten minutes with the pain that I am going to inflict upon you," he said, "Let alone last through until 10:00am tomorrow morning."

Ashurst-Stevens was only about fifteen minutes from breaking, Ward calculated, and that would still leave plenty of time, so he wasn't going to rush this and look too desperate. That would give Ashurst-Stevens a position of strength, and it was crucial that right now, he fully understood the gravity of the situation, and that he had no choice but to tell Ward everything he wanted to know.

"The higher powers you spoke about. Where are they now?" he asked.

Ashurst-Stevens said nothing; he just bit his lip to indicate he wasn't ready to talk.

"That's the thing when you dip your toes into the world that we live in," he continued, "Lies and promises all the time and the only person that you can really trust is yourself."

Ashurst-Stevens finally spoke,

"If I knew where the bomb was going to go off, I would tell you but I told you before, I don't know anything," he said.

"You only made one mistake." Ward said.

Ashurst-Stevens had a look in his eyes of curiosity so Ward just continued staring into his eyes. After thirty seconds, Ashurst-Stevens said,

"What was the mistake?"

"You killed my friend," Ward replied, and unleashed a lightning fast jab onto the bridge of Ashurst-Stevens nose.

The crack of the bone breaking echoed around the room and Ashurst-Stevens squealed again, and his head shot back, a movement that sent shockwaves through his neck and down his spine.

"That was a soft one. I want you conscious to feel the pain I have in store for you," Ward said.

He felt his phone vibrate in his pocket again. The Old Man would be furious, he thought to himself, but he would deal with that later. Stopping Fulken and the bomb took priority over everything.

"Who is the target and where is the bomb going to go off?" Ashurst-Stevens looked down at the floor and still said nothing. He was fully aware that the moment he told Ward where and who, that he would be dead. It would be a declaration of guilt and with the guilt would come a confession that he had sent Ward and his friend to their deaths. In his mind he was cursing Lucas for not killing them both. He also cursed the people who had fed him lies and guarantees that he would remain untouchable, because right now, every touch that was being laid on him was excruciating.

"Fancy another coffee?" McDermott said to Ward.

Ward nodded, stood up and walked out of the warehouse into the reception area with Lawson following.

"What's wrong?" Ward asked McDermott.

"He seems tough for an old man," McDermott said, "So maybe you want me to have a go as time is moving on?"

Ward felt his phone vibrate in his pocket. He ignored it. Yet again.

"Good idea but let's give him five minutes first to think about what he is going to say," Ward said. "He's fully aware that the moment he tells us where the bomb is and who the target is, that I am going to kill him because of Gilligan, so let's see if he can think of something else that he can give us to save his sorry ass."

FORTY TWO

Wired and Danny Wallace were the two man team who had to assume the Chrysler Building was the target. They had started from East 43rd Street, and driven around each block for potential places to hide a UPS van. They had followed three dead ends before they had moved onto Lexington Avenue. They found two underground multi-parking bays and neither of them had drawn any luck. They continued along Lexington and found a row of shops that had an old, gravelled alleyway next to the end of the building.

"We may as well check this place out, so let's park thirty yards up there and walk back," Wired said, pointing to the end of the road.

They got out of the car and walked back, with Wired on the alleyway side, and Wallace on the other side of the road. As they casually walked, they discreetly looked up towards the apartments above the shops, to check for lighting, movement or any spotters. As they reached the alleyway, Wallace crossed over to Wired and when they were twenty feet down the alleyway, they both pulled out their silenced handguns. "OK, stay in the shadows," Wallace said, "You take the left hand side of the alley and I will take the right."

Wired nodded and they both backed up hard against the buildings that towered over either side of the alley, and slowly started moving forward.

They stayed in the shadows and even the people who walked past the end of the alley would not have noticed them even if they had looked. Their ability to become invisible was outstanding.

They continued forward and reached the end of the alley. There was a large open area that had loading bays backing into loading ports on the right hand side and goods bays where the endless restaurants on Lexington unloaded their daily deliveries. To the left, there were a row of old wooden garages that served as secure, or rather not very secure, parking spaces for the residents above the shops.

The garages were set back from the open area and they were all clearly visible from the windows in the apartments. Between each garage was an alleyway which led to doors into the apartment building. Wallace crossed over to Wired, "Got to be worth a look in those," he said, and Wired nodded. They stayed in the dark and slowly moved towards the garages.

They approached the first one and there was no padlock on it, just a sliding latch. Wired nodded at Wallace, and turned to cover the rear, as Wallace carefully pulled the latch back without making a sound. He then gently pulled on the latch to open the door and it started to creak instantly, indicating that it rarely got used. He stopped as soon as the first creaking sound echoed out, the noise compounded by the general silence of the night.

They both scanned the area, Wallace looking at the building, while Wired looked for any movement in the open area. There was no movement anywhere, No lights coming on, no curtains moving and no one looking out from the back of the restaurants to their right.

Wired nodded at Wallace to continue.

A creaking door tends to creak louder the slower it is opened, so Wallace gave it a short pull. A pull that opened the garage doors eighteen inches but also alerted someone in the apartments behind the garages and a curtain moved.

They stepped into the shadows again and saw a young woman looking out into the dark. She looked left, then right before cupping her hands against the window and pushing her forehead against the glass, shielding the light from inside her apartment so that she could see outside. After thirty seconds, she looked left and right again and then her curtains fell back into place.

They waited for a whole minute, not moving, pressed back into the dark and then Wired nodded at Wallace.

Wallace peered into the garage and saw that it was empty. "Nothing at all, it must have belonged to one of the empty shops," he whispered.

One garage had taken them six minutes, they would need to move quicker Wallace thought.

They moved across the pathway to the second garage, maintaining the same positions, Wired watching the rear, Wallace the buildings and they melted into the shadows once more.

The second garage had a lock on it, it was a newish lock, already stained with rust due to exposure to the elements, and Wallace's first instinct was to ignore this as it looked like it had been there a long time, but had been used regularly. However, McDermott had always emphasised how important it was to be thorough, and so Wallace pulled out his knife and pulled away at the hasp. It gave way pretty easily as the garage doors were full of rot and the hasp swung around effortlessly. Wallace pulled on the hasp to open the door and it swung back without any noise at all. He looked inside.

He saw a large vehicle.

He turned around and looked at Wired and nodded his head four times. Wired walked backwards to the garage, still covering the rear,

"Use your flashlight to identify what vehicle it is," Wired whispered.

Wallace pulled out his small LED light, stepped into the garage and pulled the door shut. When he was inside, in absolute darkness, he turned on the flashlight. The vehicle was a black Volkswagen van, with roller shutter doors on the back. He shone the light on the side and a sign read, 'Howards Laundry Services.' He walked to the back and shone the flashlight on the roller shutter doors. They were about eighteen inches open and so he shone the flashlight in the back and saw it was completely empty. He slowly pushed the doors up and climbed inside. He checked the walls of the van, and then the floor to ensure that there was nothing concealed, and after three minutes of very thorough checks, he knew that this was not the van. He climbed out and stepped back out of the garage.

"This is going to take forever," Wired said.

"I know. Suggestions?" Wallace asked.

"Apart from shooting all the locks off, and waking up the whole neighbourhood, nothing, you?" Wired asked.

Wallace shook his head,

"Then let's continue," he said.

They crossed the next pathway to the third garage; holding the same positions. When Wallace reached the garage door he stopped, looked down and then whispered to Wired,

"What do you make of this?"

Wired looked down at the door. There was a brand new four-number combination lock, which ran through a brand new hasp, fitted to a brand new stainless steel strip of metal that ran all the way across each door and joined in the middle.

"It looks like either someone has been robbed lately and the insurance company are insisting that this is done to keep the premiums down, or someone wants to keep something locked up securely," Wired replied.

"I hate combination locks," Wallace said, "It could be any number."

"Then just rip it off like the other one," Wired said.

"This will make way too much noise if I do that."

"Try a few numbers then."

Wallace tried the obvious one first. Zero, nine, one, one. It didn't work. He looked at Wired.

"Any ideas?" he asked.

"Try one, four, one, and two."

Wallace tried it but it didn't work either.

"Why that number?"

"It's my birthday," Wired replied with a smile.

"We will be here all night at this rate," Wallace said.

Wired stepped forward and without warning, raised his gun and shot the combination lock. The loop shattered and it dropped to the floor. The sound of metal striking metal echoed around the open area. They moved back into the shadows,

"That was smart," Wallace whispered.

Wired just shrugged.

The young woman looked out of her window again. She was focussing on the far left side of where they were standing, clearly only worried about her own garage. She looked out for only ten seconds this time and then the curtains fell back into place once more.

"That was stupid," Wallace said.

Wired shrugged again.

Wallace moved forward and lifted the hasp of the two adjoining stainless steel strips of metal. He pulled the left hand door ajar and looked inside.

He saw a large vehicle.

"I'll check this out," he whispered and stepped inside.

He walked in, closed the door and turned on the flashlight.

And instantly saw a large van, in Pullman Brown with a giant UPS sign on the side.

He moved around the back and saw there were two doors at the rear of the vehicle with a silver handle in the middle. He tried the handle. It was unlocked. He opened the door as quietly as he could and shone the flashlight inside.

And immediately saw three hundred pounds of explosives linked to a complex array of wires, surrounded by open tubs of four inch nails, bolts and two inch tubes of solid metal. He stepped out of the garage and closed the door.

"We had better call the boss," he said to Wired, "We've found it."

Ward's phone vibrated in his pocket yet again. He ignored it.

"He will be going nuts," Lawson said with a smile.

McDermott's phone vibrated and he put it to his ear. With Ward and Lawson both studying him, he replied,

"When? Where? Get Walsh there immediately. Get the whole team to within one hundred yards and now!" he said urgently.

He looked at Ward,

"Herrera at the Chrysler was the target. We have just found the van on Lexington Avenue."

"Fulken?" Ward asked.

"They have literally just found it; the team are on their way. Walsh will make it safe," he replied.

"Fulken will still be close," Ward said, "Let's go," and they walked straight out of the building into the night air and towards the Mercedes, without a thought for Ashurst-Stevens, who was alone and tied to a chair in a dirty warehouse. The Lord of the realm started to sob.

Asif Fulken heard a faint noise which sounded like someone striking a barrier with a metal baseball bat, from the back of the apartment, and crouched down and looked through the hole that he had torn in the curtains, out onto the open area beyond the garages. Probably just one of the restaurants emptying the food waste into their dumpsters and slamming the lid down he thought, but it was always best to be alert.

If he hadn't been so distracted thinking about the man on the phone, then he would have been focussed and looking out of the window, and not having to guess what the noise he had heard was, he would have known.

He would give the man on the phone no more thought whatsoever. He would never find him; he could change his plans when this was all over. He knelt down and adjusted his position, so that he was comfortable. Then, to his horror, he saw a flicker of light break out from the back wall of the garage.

He stared down at the wall and then he saw it again.

And five seconds later, again.

He stood up in panic and moved closer to the window. He had the lights off and this enabled his eyes to adjust immediately. He froze. "This cannot be!" he said out loud to himself. Not now he thought, not after all he had done, and not with the wealth he now had at his disposal, and not for the safety of his family.

He strained his eyes and he saw a figure move to the edge of the shadows. He saw the light from the screen of a cell phone illuminate the darkness, and he caught the glimpse of a man as he lifted the cell phone to his ear. He then caught a quick glimpse of another man on the edge of the shadows, and at the same time, a glistening of light on a handgun.

It was over.

All he could do now was save himself; get as far away from this country as possible and make do with the money that he already had. He stepped back from the window and picked up his rucksack. He had weapons, a passport, money and fake credit cards, all packed and ready to go in the eventuality of something like this happening. Distraught as he felt right now, he would remain focussed on his escape. He put on his jacket and walked out of the apartment, closing the door without looking back.

Lawson drove like a mad man and they were on Lexington Avenue in just under twenty minutes. They drove along the Avenue until McDermott leant over Ward's shoulder from the rear seat and saw one of his Range Rovers, then said to Lawson,

"Pull in there, behind the Range Rover."

They screeched to a stop and jumped out of the car.

Another Range Rover came rolling down the Avenue and stopped behind the Mercedes. Walsh jumped out of the Range Rover and Paul followed him.

Fuller and Fringe arrived thirty seconds later in the last Range Rover.

"It's around the back," Walsh said and jogged off in the direction of the alleyway.

The rest of them ran after Walsh.

As they turned the corner they saw Wired and Wallace standing outside the garage.

Ward approached them,

"Brilliant job guys," he said to them as he walked quickly past them and into the garage which now had its doors fully open. They both nodded.

Fuller and Fringe took up the position of watching over the open area, both holding assault rifles and crouching down on one knee, Wallace and Wired stood with weapons drawn either side of the garage doors, and within five seconds the area was as secure as Fort Knox.

Walsh was already in the back of the van when Ward walked in. McDermott and Paul came in immediately behind him.

"Is it armed?" Ward asked.

"Yes," Walsh replied as he contorted his body into different angles to work out the complexities of the bomb.

"You can disarm it?"

"Yep. No problem," Walsh replied.

Ward knew instantly that Walsh wasn't trying to display calm or an arrogance to reassure anyone, least of all himself, he knew that Lloyd Walsh was the best explosives expert he had ever known and that if he said it would be no problem to disarm, then it really would be no problem to disarm.

He walked out of the garage and Lawson and the two McDermott's followed.

Above the garage there was a gold plate with the number eighteen etched into it in black italic engraving. Lawson noticed it at the same time as Ward.

"You two take the front of the building, Lawson and I will take the back," Ward said to McDermott and he watched as father and son sprinted out of the garage towards the alleyway.

Ward ran down the pathway next to the garage and followed it to a door which was locked.

Lawson said,

"I've got it," and Ward moved to the side as Lawson lifted his right foot and smashed it into the door frame just below the lock, and the wood splintered and the door flew open.

As Ward ran in, he saw three doors numbered one to four on the ground floor and a flight of stairs to his right. He headed for the stairs and sprinted up them, pulling his Glock out without breaking stride, with Lawson right behind him.

They sprinted up four flights of stairs and reached the landing of number eighteen. They slowly walked towards the door and took up a position either side of it. Ward put his ear to the door.

It was all quiet.

"The door could well be rigged with explosives," Lawson said.

Ward nodded.

"How are we going to do this?" Lawson asked.

"Knock I suppose," Ward replied and he knocked on the door three times.

Lawson smiled and rolled his eyes.

No answer.

Ward knocked again three times.

There was still no answer.

Ward tried the handle and it moved all the way down and the latch disengaged.

He looked at Lawson,

"Feeling brave, lucky or stupid?" Ward asked.

Lawson smiled at him and said,

"All three," and he pushed past Ward and walked straight through the door and into an empty room. All that was there was a few pieces of sparse and worn furniture.

Lawson walked through the living area and checked all the other rooms,

"Nothing," he said to Ward as he came back into the living area.

Ward sat down on the sofa and closed his eyes.

'Where would you run to Fulken?' he asked himself.

"He could be anywhere by now," Lawson said, "He will disappear."

"Not if he is being followed."

"By who?" Lawson asked.

"By us," Ward said as he pulled out his cell phone and called Nicole-Louise.

"Hello?" she answered.

"We've found the bomb and McDermott's team are taking care of it now," he said, just as the two McDermott's stepped into the room, "But now we need to find Fulken."

"Thank God," she said, "What do you want me to do?" she asked.

"Hack into the city's CCTV and find out when he left the building which is almost on the corner of Lexington Avenue and East 51st Street, follow him and then bring it up to real time so that we know where he is. I will need a running commentary as he moves," Ward replied.

"I can do that."

"You have to Nicole-Louise," he said.

"I will."

FORTY THREE

Nicole-Louise had hacked into the CCTV cameras by the time Ward had pulled himself up from the sofa in Fulken's apartment. She had a perfect view of the building, and could see three Range Rovers and a Mercedes, all black, parked behind each other in a neat line. She began rewinding the footage at eight times its normal speed.

She saw the two Range Rovers reverse back out of sight, then the Mercedes, leaving the Range Rover that Wired and Wallace had arrived in.

As she looked at the last remaining vehicle, she noticed someone walking out of the building and she paused the footage. She looked at the time in the right hand corner of the screen. It was 11:35pm.

Just fifteen minutes ago.

Walker and his son both stood up and walked over to her workstation,

"Is that him?" Walker softly asked.

Nicole-Louise adjusted a few buttons on a control toolbar on the bottom of the screen and zoomed in.

He was wearing a brown jacket and a baseball cap. While the quality was not perfect, it was clear enough to give her a definitive identification,

"Yes, that's him," she said to Walker.

Tackler came out of the bathroom and said,

"What's happening?"

"They've got the bomb, now we have found Fulken, and he is fifteen minutes ahead of them. We have to find him."

Tackler went over to his workstation and pressed his screen into life,

"What area are you looking at?" he asked, as he tapped furiously on his keyboard.

"I'm looking at the apartment building on the corner of Lexington and East 51st."

"OK, I will get into the camera on Lexington and East 52nd and see what I can see."

Nicole-Louise dialled Ward's number and put it on loudspeaker,

"What have you got?" he answered.

"He left the building fifteen minutes ago," she said, "He headed north."

Ward looked at Lawson and said,

"We need to move now," and headed towards the door.

McDermott and Paul walked into the apartment just as Ward and Lawson reached the door,

"It's done," McDermott said, "Walsh has disassembled the bomb completely, and they are packing it into one of the Range Rovers now."

"Different class," Ward replied, and Lawson nodded his agreement.

"You need to assemble everyone downstairs, we are fifteen minutes behind him, your three teams and us," Ward said, as he paused and pointed at Lawson, "Means four separate units hunting one man in a three mile radius."

"He hasn't got a chance," McDermott said.

"Are you still there Nicole-Louise?" Ward asked.

"Yes, I can hear everything."

"McDermott has three teams that need to be kept in the loop on where Fulken is when you find him," Ward said, "Can you do that so that you keep us all open?"

"I can do anything," she replied, "Get them to all dial into my cell number and I will do the rest," she added.

Nicole-Louise looked at Walker and his son; they still looked petrified,

"What about Mr Walker?" she asked.

Ward had actually forgotten about the two of them.

"Can he hear me?"

"Yes," Walker senior replied loudly.

"You can go now Mr Walker," Ward said, "Nothing can hurt you now," he added in a calm voice, more to reassure the son than the father.

"If you don't mind," Walker replied, "Can we stay here until you have the bomber?"

Ward could picture the fear on both of their faces, and for the first time, he gave a thought to the trauma that they had both been through, and how jumping into his world would be completely intimidating to the strongest of men.

"Any objections Nicole-Louise?"

"None."

"Nicole-Louise?" Ward said, "Find him."

Asif Fulken could not believe what had happened.

This was all down to the man on the phone, he knew it.

Damn that man he cursed to himself.

He had nowhere to go; all of his allies and support networks had been wiped out by this man, and even as he crossed 3rd Avenue and continued down East 51st Street, he could not stop thinking about where he recognised him from.

He had to find a safe haven, a place where he could blend in and not be recognised.

He knew that by now, they would be checking CCTV footage and they would be following him. He could spend time finding a shop and changing clothes, but that would be time he did not have.

All that mattered now was survival.

He knew that if he got far enough away, he could easily get lost in the crowds, as he did in Paris and London, and so he continued to walk, briskly but not fast enough to attract attention.

Where did he know the man on the phone from? He asked himself over and over. He has ruined everything.

When he reached 2nd Avenue he turned north.

There were still a large number of people milling around, enjoying the nightlife, and he felt safer in their company.

Finding a man alone in a secluded street was easy, in a busy street he could easily hide.

Most of the revellers were students, drinking way too much, and no doubt the future politicians and liberals, who will continue with their open door policy to people with his beliefs.

That's why this will never end, he told himself.

Unless the CIA have another fifty of the man on the phone, that could possibly finish it.

But who was he, he asked himself again.

Where do I recognise him from?

Ward and Lawson were sitting in the Mercedes and while Lawson was trying to connect his cell phone to the car charger deck, Ward closed his eyes and leant his head back against the head rest.

Where would I go if I was Fulken he thought to himself? I would want to be near crowds, more chance of getting lost.

He would want to escape New York and get as far away as possible, but he wouldn't be thinking of leaving the country too soon.

He was sure that Fulken would have planned an escape route for after the bomb had gone off, but that would have been heavily reliant upon the police and the security services being pre-occupied with the aftermath of the explosion, making it easier.

No, Fulken was panicking, and he was probably trying to piece his escape plan together as he moved. Ward's thoughts were broken by Lawson,

"It's me, can you hear me?"

"Loud and clear," Nicole-Louise replied

"Have you found him yet?" Ward asked.

"We are on it now. We have him crossing 3rd Avenue and continuing on East 51st. We are now only four minutes behind him."

"We are just pulling onto East 51st now," Ward heard Wired say through the speakers.

"When you find him, injure and detain him first, there are still things I need to ask him," Ward interrupted.

"East 51st Street here we come," Lawson said.

Asif Fulken was still walking, but unable to establish a clear plan in his head of where he was going.

The face of the man on the phone kept coming back into his thoughts all the time. He had never been so distracted in his life.

He continued up 2nd Avenue and was grateful for the fact that the student nightlife seemed to be in full flow.

He scanned them all as he walked the Avenue and thought how ungrateful they are to live the life they live, with no suppression, and their excessive comfort and wealth. And then he resented them because that was the life that he had planned and craved so much.

The man on the phone would have lived a life like that.

His British accent, and affiliation to the Americans, how he said he was one of them, told him that he had probably spent a life being raised in sickening wealth in America, and then sent to one of those expensive boarding schools on the outskirts of London, for an education that only the wealthiest can buy.

He would have lived a life like that, while his own people lived in poverty and destruction, with no basics, such as decent schooling or hospitals.

He hated the man on the phone for the first time.

He admitted to himself that he admired him for his skills in their field, but now he hated him for his privileged life.

But who was he and where did he remember him from?

He consumed his thoughts as he turned off of 2nd Avenue and headed east along East 57th Street.

As Ward and Lawson reached East 23rd Street Nicole-Louise's voice echoed around the interior of the car,
"He has left East 51^{st,} and has now headed onto 2nd Avenue," she said, "We are trying to find him now."
"Wired, you take the end of East 51st, Fringe, you take the top of 2nd Avenue, and we will come up from the bottom of 2nd," McDermott's voice said.
"We will take the middle of 2nd Avenue off of East 51^{st,}" Ward said.
They drove along East 51st and came to 2nd Avenue.
He looked out of the window as Lawson slowly moved the car along.
He saw people outside bars, smiling and laughing, and thought that they would never know how close they came to witnessing death and destruction on their own doorstep.
He watched how groups of students came out of bars, arms linked, their faces adorning smiles that only those who have not joined the real world yet possess.
They drove past one café and he noticed someone standing up at the end of a large table, holding a leather bound book, and reading to the captivated audience that were packed around the table.
He saw groups of people deep in discussion, probably discussing politics he thought, and he wondered if this would be the next generation of CIA analysts.
He saw couples walking the street hand in hand, looking happy and content, and genuinely believing that they had found their one love, even though in six months' time, they would be feeling the same thing about someone completely different.
The young minds, the future.
The young Americans.
He closed his eyes again and leant his head back into the head rest.

He could still picture the people outside and then, for the first time since he started chasing Fulken, he exhaled a long, content sigh and his face broke out a smile.

Lawson looked at him when he exhaled and noticed the smile. "What's wrong with you?" he asked.

"I know where he is going," Ward replied.

Asif Fulken reached 1st Avenue and turned into it heading north.

There were more and more people walking around and it seemed to be getting busier, so he was starting to feel a little more in control.

He had walked past six officers of the NYPD and none of them had given him a second glance.

He was now starting to blend into the background and soon he would melt away.

The man on the phone was probably chasing him right now and he wondered how close he was.

His face, he knew that he had seen it before but where was it? He thought yet again to himself.

In another life they may well have been good friends he thought. A thought that made him smile.

He had always believed that he had no equal in the world, but the man on the phone had changed that perception.

He would disappear and never see him again, but he had a feeling that it would take a long time for him to forget him.

He was now feeling positive.

He had enough money to live well, four million dollars, which would enable him to get his family together and set up in a new country, maybe in South America. As long as there was a beach, he would be happy.

He wondered if the man on the phone had similar dreams; dreams that one day he would stop running around in the mad world that they lived in and lead a normal life. He concluded he did. Everyone did.

He continued along 1st Avenue, milling through the crowds of young people laughing and smiling, and then he smiled to himself. He knew where he would go to disappear and the man on the phone would never find him.

But who was he?

How did he recognise him and why couldn't he remember him?

Ward had told Lawson where to drive to and Lawson said, "Are you sure about this?"

"Yes," Ward replied.

"OK, but shouldn't you tell the others?"

"No, let them carry on, if I am wrong, they are still closing the net so we find him either way."

"Are you going to be wrong?"

"Have I been wrong yet?"

"Can I ask you something?" Lawson said.

"If you must," Ward replied.

"Why do you shoot some people in the face and others you don't?"

The question took Ward by surprise.

"You were in the SAS, you tell me?"

"How do you know I was in the SAS?"

"I know everything about you. You think I am going to let someone cover my ass who I know nothing about?" Ward replied.

Lawson smiled,

"I guess not, so why the shooting in the face? They remind you of someone?"

"It's a psychological thing. I only do it when I want to know something," Ward replied.

Lawson looked blank.

"Think about it? You have two people in front of you that both have the information that you want. What do you do? What were you trained to do?" he asked.

"You identify the weakest link," Lawson replied.

"Exactly, so you shoot the one that is less likely to talk in the face, obliterate the person they know, let them see the blood and the brains, and it's much more effective than a hole in the chest," Ward replied.

"I must tell my brother to get that written into the SAS training manual," Lawson said, rolling his eyes, "Sometimes I think there are things very, very wrong with you."

"So, have I answered your question?"

"You have. But considering you weren't after information from half of the people you have shot in the face, I shall draw my own conclusions," Lawson replied.

Ward ignored him.

They arrived at their destination and parked the car.

"Let's go," Ward said and climbed out of the car, "We will take either side of the entrance and wait, we shouldn't have to wait too long."

Asif Fulken walked up 1st Avenue and was now one hundred per cent confident that he would be free and out of New York within the next twenty-four hours. After that it would be easy.

The man on the phone was good but not good enough. He continued along 1st Avenue until he came to East 63rd Street turning onto it and heading east. One more block and he would be in the sanctuary of where he was heading. He could see the entrance at the end of the road and he felt an excitement that he had not felt since he was a raw recruit back in his early days of the FFW. He had come a long way since then.

He wondered if the man on the phone had taken a similar journey.

Rising up through the ranks of the organisation at rapid speed and being held in the same high regard as he used to be. At least that was until he was sold out, and he lost his faith and then he became the enemy.

No doubt the man on the phone had lots of enemies within the CIA; the best always had resentment aimed towards them eventually.

Jealousy was one of the curses of the Western way of life.

He finally consoled himself with the fact that he may have lost this particular battle but he had won the war.

He had beaten the man on the phone.

As he reached the end of East 63rd Street and crossed over York Avenue, he saw the grey wrought iron fence that ran all the way along the front of The Rockefeller University, with the two brick pillars directly ahead, with two grey iron gates hanging on either side.

The man on the phone would never find him now.

The man on the phone will tell stories in the future of how the only person to beat him, to evade him, was the great Asif Fulken.

He would always be the nemesis of the man on the phone.

He walked through the gates casually, looking like he was meant to be there, and as he stepped no more than three steps through them, he froze.

The man on the phone was standing right in front of him. Holding a handgun, with a silencer attached, no more than twelve inches from his face.

FORTY FOUR

As Fulken stood rooted to the spot, Lawson moved in and took the rucksack that he was carrying off his shoulder. He then pulled out a cable tie from his jacket pocket, and pulled Fulken's hands behind his back and yanked the cable tie tight around his wrists.

Ward then took Fulken's arm and led him to the Mercedes, and bundled him into the rear seat.

Ward then climbed in the back and sat next to him.

"You still there Nicole-Louise?" he said out loud.

There was a look of total confusion on Fulken's face.

"We have him," he said, "Ask McDermott to meet me and Lawson back at the warehouse."

"You want me to make arrangements for our new guest?" McDermott's voice filled the car through the speaker.

"He won't be coming," Ward replied, "I have something else in mind for him."

"You ready?" Lawson asked.

Ward nodded and Lawson pulled the car away.

"I told you I would find you," Ward said, "Bummer eh?" he added with a smile.

Fulken looked at Ward.

He finally remembered, he knew where he had seen him before,

"It's you!" was all he could think of to say.

"Not giving too much for me to confirm, are you?" Ward replied, before unleashing a short, sharp jab to Fulken's throat. His head shot back and then rocked forward, and he struggled frantically to get his breath back.

"Don't talk to me again unless I ask you a question."

Fulken looked down at his lap.

He knew that the end of his life was inevitable, and he felt more vulnerable, alone and scared than he had ever felt before. He was still struggling to regain his breath, and this was compounded by the fact that he could not use his hands to rub his throat.

"Now, tell me where you have seen me before?" Ward asked calmly.

"My handler had a photo of you on the wall in the apartment where we used to have our meetings," Fulken replied.

He thought back to the name of Fulken's CIA handler. Gilligan or Centrepoint had mentioned it but Ward could not remember it.

"What was his name?" he demanded.

"Gill Whymark."

"Why would he have a picture of me on his wall?"

"I don't know," Fulken replied, "But it wasn't only you."

"How many pictures were there?"

"There were ten in total; I used to see them every time I was there."

"Describe the people in the pictures to me?"

Fulken was still struggling to breathe, he could see that clearly, but Ward could also see that he was trying to think of the best way to describe the people in the photos, but he couldn't.

"They were all like you," Fulken eventually replied.

"What do you mean?"

"They were all people who had that look about them. The look that says danger and all but one of them were people you could remember but not recognise."

"What was different about the other one?"

"She was a woman," Fulken replied.

Ward knew that the ten pictures were probably the team that Centrepoint had assembled, he thought he knew who they all were, but there was not a woman among them. He decided to warn Centrepoint of this at a later date.

"You know that your four million dollars has gone I presume?" he asked.

Fulken's reaction told Ward that he didn't, "So all of this was for nothing," he quickly added.

He then unleashed another sharp, quick jab, this time it caught Fulken on the left cheek, just below the eye.

"I took it. I gave it to the wife of a friend of mine. A friend who is now dead because of you," Ward continued, "And right now, your family are being tortured in a cell, on an isolated boat, all because of you," Ward lied.

"If you hurt my family, I will search for you in hell and burn you," Fulken screamed.

"Of course, one call from me and I can stop it," he said.

Fulken took a deep breath and visibly tried to control himself.

"What can I do to get you to make that call?"

"How many people contacted you and gave you instructions once the ball was rolling on this?" Ward asked.

"Just the one, The British Lord."

"Ashurst-Stevens?"

"Yes."

"How do you know it was him?"

"Because after you had told me who he was, I searched the web for him and found videos, and listened to his voice and I am good enough at this to recognise the right voice."

"You don't look so good at it now."

Fulken looked down at his lap again.

"You understand that I am going to kill you, yes?" Ward asked.

"Unless I can be of some use to you?"

Ward looked at him.

There wasn't the fear in his eyes that people who were going to die normally had. It made him reflect for a moment how he would react if the day came when he was faced with imminent death. He assumed he would probably react exactly as Fulken was, more in resignation than fear.

"How can you be of use to me?" he asked.

"In my bag there is an external hard drive. On it are the names and contact details for the European network of FFW cells. I can give you that in return for my life, and the pledge that I will never return to these shores."

Lawson leant over to the front passenger seat and tossed the rucksack back to Ward. He opened it and pulled out a nearly new Smith & Wesson handgun. He dropped the magazine out and checked the chamber for a bullet, it was empty, and he tossed it back onto the front seat next to Lawson. He then pulled out a thick wad of dollar bills.

"How much is here?"

"Thirty-five thousand dollars," Fulken replied.

He tossed the money on the seat next to Lawson,

"Here," he said to Lawson, "Buy some humility and modesty with that."

Lawson laughed out loudly.

Next he pulled out three different passports.

"You won't be needing these," he said and tossed them onto the front seat.

At the bottom of the bag was a black external hard drive, not much bigger than a cigarette packet, with a small lead attached to it, for connecting to a USB port.

"Is this it?"

Fulken nodded.

"Password protected?"

"Yes."

"What is the password?"

"If I tell you that I am dead," Fulken replied.

"You are dead anyway."

"I think the CIA would rather that I was kept alive."

"I don't work for the CIA."

He had no doubt that Nicole-Louise and Tackler could break into the hard drive, and so he tossed it onto the front seat too. "It seems your bag is all empty," he said, "You have nothing left to give."

"I have names, knowledge, whatever you need. I can tell you who is who in America, New York is not the only State. I can be the most valuable asset that you have ever had," Fulken said, looking desperate for the first time.

"That's what you told the CIA when they caught you last time was it?" he asked, "And they took you up on your offer, and then they set you up over here, and you turned around and abused that."

"It wasn't like that. No one got hurt in New York did they?"

"But lots of people got hurt in Paris and London," Ward said, "And worst of all, my friend died as a direct result of your actions, and for that, above all else, you are going to die."

Fulken smiled at Ward.

"Your friend was doing his job I take it?"

"There are only two people left to deal with. You and a guy I have trussed up waiting for me in a garage. You will both die tonight."

"You think that by killing me in revenge for your friend's death that it will make you feel better about losing him?" Fulken asked.

Ward thought about the two bomb makers, Lucas and the lawyer, and how it had felt when he killed them, and how he did it for Gilligan.

"Yes, it will," he replied.

"Agreed on that," Lawson said.

Asif Fulken looked down at his lap. He knew that this was the end, and he knew that there was nothing left that he could do.

He knew that the man with the phone had won.

And he had won comprehensively.

He stayed looking down towards his lap and his eyes filled with tears.

Lawson drove for another ten minutes and then said,

"Will here do?" as they passed a business park full of warehouses and office buildings.

"Perfect," Ward replied.

Lawson drove into the business park and continued around the one-way system until he saw a side road that ran behind a warehouse and stopped in front of four big industrial sized open containers, full of metal. He pulled alongside the biggest and least full one at the end, and turned the engine off.

He stepped out of the car and walked around to the side of the door where Fulken was sitting. He opened the door and said,

"Out!"

Fulken stepped out.

Ward walked around to the front of the car.

Fulken was trying to look defiant and strong but Ward could see the fear starting to rush through him with each passing second. He thought of Gilligan and how he wished that he was alive to see the conclusion of everything coming together. The bomb had been found, Ashurst-Stevens was the chief architect behind it, and he was going to meet his maker very soon, and Fulken was standing here, alone and scared.

He missed Gilligan for the first time right then.

But he would make Fulken's last few minutes on earth miserable. Mentally miserable, just as he had with the lawyer, he told himself, as he shoved Fulken hard, forcing him to fall back against the car and then slide down onto his backside.

"Now is probably the time to tell you something," he said.

Fulken did not speak but started muttering a prayer to himself.

"You think that God will forgive you for your sins?" he asked.

"He forgives everyone," Fulken replied.

"Do you think your family will forgive you?"

"My family stand by me. That is what a family does."

"There is no family anymore. They were eliminated four hours ago under my instruction," Ward lied.

Fulken looked up at Ward and yanked at the cable tie behind his back and screamed. It was a long, high pitched scream, full of devastation.

Lawson moved forward and kicked him hard in the ribs, stopping the scream immediately.

"How does it feel to know that I have killed them and didn't give it a second thought?" Ward asked.

"You will burn in hell. You are an animal," Fulken screamed. He was crying now and there was residue running from his nose down to his mouth. He looked a pathetic sight. He looked just how Ward wanted him to look.

"That is exactly what the families of the people in Paris and London think of you," Ward said.

"That was different," Fulken said, "They were strangers, you deliberately took everything away from me," he sobbed," You will burn in hell."

"You stepped over a line. You came into my country and made a choice to kill innocent people. You should have accounted for the fact that we have got wise to you and your way of thinking," Ward said.

Fulken looked up at Ward slightly confused. So Ward continued.

"We decided to fight back. Like for like. So they got people like me to lead the fight. No rules, a level playing field and no accountability," he said, "And you know what?" he asked.

Fulken said nothing.

He just sat on the dirty gravel, leaning against the car, crying like a child who had just endured his first beating at school.

"You know what?" Ward asked again.

Lawson moved in and kicked him on the arm.

"What?" Fulken reluctantly asked.

"We are much, much better at this than you are," he said.

"You will burn in hell, you will burn to a cinder," he replied, "You have already won so why not use me to help you keep winning?" Fulken begged.

Ward looked down at the pathetic figure on the floor below him.

A figure he had chased across the Atlantic and around New York and he felt anything but victorious.

He felt duty.

He felt duty to the people of Britain and America every day of his life and now, at this moment, he felt a duty to the people of France too.

He felt that he was the one who was allowed to stand up for them in any way that he saw fit and that sat very, very well with him.

"No one has won," Ward said, "All that happens here is that I live to chase down the next bad guy."

He looked at Lawson and Lawson nodded at him.

He slowly and calmly pulled out his Glock and pointed it at Fulken.

Fulken started sobbing louder.

He looked up at Ward and all he could see was a seven foot giant peering down at him.

He could see the calm in Ward's eyes.

A calm that unsettled him even more.

He saw no hatred, no anger or any sense of victory.

He didn't see good and he didn't see evil.

He saw the end.

He saw all of the people that his bombs had destroyed over the years, swimming in Ward's deep dark eyes, staring at him. He felt as scared, vulnerable, weak, insignificant and frightened as it was possible for a human being to feel.

"Please, don't," he begged.

Ward ignored him and raised the Glock,

"You will burn in hell!" he screamed and Ward pulled the trigger four times. One second apart.

The first bullet hit Fulken in the centre of the chest and his body slammed back against the car.

That was for Mrs Gilligan.

The second bullet hit Fulken in the heart.

That was for the youngest Gilligan.

The third bullet went straight into his heart too.

That was for the eldest of Gilligan son's.

The last bullet hit Fulken in the centre of his face and literally blew it apart.

That was for Gilligan.

Lawson stood over the dead body and pulled out his own gun. He pointed it down at Fulken's limp, lifeless body and pulled the trigger.

The force of the bullet made the body jump slightly and Ward noticed the satisfaction spread across Lawson's face.

"That one was for you," he said.

Ward nodded back his appreciation.

"I have a feeling he wants you to burn in hell," Lawson said, trying to lighten the mood.

Ward laughed softly.

"So now back to his Lordship?" Lawson asked.

"Yes, the last man standing. Or tied up and sitting, to be more precise," Ward replied.

"You want me to call the clean-up crew?" Lawson asked, reaching for his phone to make the call.

"No."

Lawson frowned.

"Why not?"

"I want him left there. Like a dead animal. That's all he is. It can be smoothed over with the NYPD when he is found. He doesn't deserve the dignity of being removed," Ward replied.

Lawson understood.

He started the car, put it in reverse and moved back down the driveway slowly. The beam of the lights focussed on Fulken's crumpled body, and they both watched as it became smaller and smaller, until Lawson turned the car out of the driveway. Ward took one last look at the body as Lawson put the car in drive and moved forward. And then the view of Fulken was gone forever, replaced by warehouses and office blocks.

Ward looked at his watch.

It was 00:15.

By the time he had finished with Ashurst-Stevens and laid down the appropriate punishment, it would be 01:00am. An hour earlier than he had originally projected.

For the first time over the past few days he offered himself some self-congratulation. Perhaps I am better than I think I am, he thought to himself.

FORTY FIVE

They drove back to the warehouse in complete silence.
Ward was thinking about Gilligan all of the way. He had
considered going to see Gilligan's wife, but thought that
would do more harm than good. His last words were to make
him promise to look after his boys, but he figured that they
already knew how much they were loved by him, and he
concluded that giving them the vision of their giant of a
father dying by the side of the road, begging for someone else
to protect his children, would not be something they needed
to know. He knew the four million dollars that Nicole-Louise
had put into Mrs Gilligan's account would help in the future,
but it would not dull the pain she was feeling right now.
He took his phone out of his pocket and saw that there were
seven missed calls from Centrepoint.
He decided not to call him back until Ashurst-Stevens was
dead, and he would deal with the fallout then.
Instead, he called Nicole-Louise.
"Hello," she answered.
"It's over," he said, "Tell Walker and his son they are free to
go."
"I'll put it on loudspeaker."
He heard a click and then Nicole-Louise said,

"You're open."

"Mr Walker," he said, "You are free to go and you will be safe."

"The bomber is dead?" Walker asked in a worried tone.

"Yes he is."

"Lord Ashurst-Stevens?" Walker asked.

"He will be soon. I'm sure that you will be covering his death when you go back to work, and so it will be a busy few days for you, but the distraction is exactly what you need to get your life back to normal," he replied.

"Thank you," Walker said, "For everything you have done. And that's from both of us. You saved my son's life; I will never be able to repay you," he added.

Ward felt a sudden rush of emotion surge through his body. Walker did what he felt he had to do, for the sake of his son. He would have to live with the consequence of his actions and the blood on his hands through the Paris and London bombs, but he was a father first. A father's love is limitless. Ward had seen that with Gilligan and now with Walker. And he felt envious.

"You will be able to repay me if you get on with your life and make sure that your son becomes the best he can," he said.

"I will," a muffled, younger voice said in the background. Ward smiled to himself.

"Nicole-Louise, can you turn the loudspeaker off," he asked. Another click could be heard and then he continued.

"Thank you so much you two. You and Tackler have contributed more to this than anyone. You have saved a great number of lives yet again, and you are the most important two people I know," he said.

"We all played an equal part Ryan," she replied.

Ward suddenly remembered the target that Eloisa had set in Ireland and so he said.

"Tomorrow, I might need some help on some freelance work, are you two available, this one is a choice?" he asked.

He heard her speaking to Tackler and then came back on the line,

"He said he will on one condition," she said.

360

Ward knew immediately what that condition would be.

"Tell him that I will have Lawson back in the U.K. by tomorrow night, and I won't mention his name in his presence," he said with a smile.

"Then we are in," she replied with a soft giggle, and hung up the phone.

Lawson looked at him mystified.

"No more flirting with Nicole-Louise to piss Tackler off," he said to Lawson.

"I think she wants me."

"If you go near her, I will kill you myself," he said.

"That's the second time you have said that, you wouldn't really, would you?" he asked.

"Hurry up and get to the warehouse," he replied, and he closed his eyes and leant back into the soft, leather headrest of the Mercedes.

Ten minutes later they were pulling up outside the garage. Ward knew something was wrong immediately.

McDermott and Paul were standing outside waiting. The three Range Rovers were parked neatly inside, and Ward could see Fringe and Wired loading equipment into the back of them. They were clearing out.

"What's wrong?" he asked.

Paul looked at the floor while his father said,

"You had better come and take a look inside."

The chair where Ashurst-Stevens had been sitting was back around the table.

"We got back from searching for Fulken and he was gone. All that was here were these," McDermott said, holding up three cable ties which had clearly been cut.

"Well he didn't cut them himself," Ward said.

"We literally got back and he was gone," McDermott repeated.

"We should have kept one person here. We made a mistake," Paul said.

"No. You focussed on catching Fulken. That was exactly the right thing to do. And we caught him so don't worry about this," Ward replied.

"We are done here then?" McDermott asked.

"Yes we are. The money has already been paid into your account," he said, "You saved a lot of lives."

"I told you; give it to Gilligan's wife."

"And I told you, that was covered," Ward replied, "Keep it, pay for some psychiatric help for Wired," he added with a smile.

"I think I need more than half a million dollars!" McDermott replied.

The rest of McDermott's team came in. Ward walked around to each of them and hugged them all.

Brothers in arms in every sense of the word.

Ward and Lawson walked out of the garage and got back into the car.

"Where do we find him?" Lawson asked.

Ward didn't reply but took out his phone and dialled The Optician.

"Hey," The Optician answered.

"Did you take Ashurst-Stevens?" he asked.

"I was just doing what The Old Man ordered me to do."

"I know. What do you think about that?" he asked him.

"I never question the reasons why, you know that. I just do."

Ward respected The Optician more than anyone else in the world. He displayed loyalty and a sense of duty that most men could not comprehend. Ward changed the subject.

"I will want your help in Ireland over the next few days," he said.

"I'll be there for you when you call. As always," The Optician replied, "Someone has to look after you," he added, and he hung up the phone.

Ward looked at Lawson,

"Take me back to Brooklyn, we are finished," he said.

"What about Ashurst-Stevens?"

"I'll deal with him when you are safely back in England."

They drove back in silence.

He felt deflated and carried an overwhelming feeling that he had unfinished business to attend to.

Thirty-five minutes later, Lawson was bringing the car to a stop outside Ward's apartment in DUMBO.

"Thanks for everything Mike," he said and extended his hand for Lawson to shake.

"I have this awards ceremony to attend to with Abbi and I will be flying straight back tomorrow morning," he said. "If you need me until then, I'm yours"

"I think our hands are tied on this," Ward replied, and went to step out of the car.

"Wait!" Lawson said.

Ward turned and looked at him.

"One question?" Lawson asked.

"Shoot?"

"Are you the great Ryan Ward?"

"I'm the great Ryan Ward, only if you are the great Mike Lawson," Ward replied with a smile and got out of the car.

He didn't turn to watch Lawson drive off as he walked into his apartment building.

Thirty minutes later he was showered and relaxed.

The last few days had been adrenalin-fuelled, and this was the first moment that he had to relax. He looked at his watch. It was 02:00am. He picked up his phone. There were no missed calls from Centrepoint. He dialled his number.

"One of us knows how to answer a phone."

"Why did you take Ashurst-Stevens?" he asked.

"There is no way on earth that we can eliminate a worldwide prominent figure and get away with it," Centrepoint replied.

"Regardless of what he has done?"

"It's not that simple. I keep telling you. It's about the bigger picture."

"And what is the bigger picture?"

"We now have him where we want him, and we can use him in the future to control the news for our benefit."

"So you want to be the newsmaker now?" he asked with a tone of disgust in his voice.

"Look," Centrepoint said, "I feel as bad as you do for all the lives that have been lost because of this, but I know without a doubt that in the future we will need him, and we will save a great deal more than we have lost."

"Do you want to go around and tell that to Mrs Gilligan?"

Silence on the end of the phone.

"What provisions have you made for her?"

"The standard insurance pay-out I assume."

"You think that will be enough to raise two kids?" he asked sarcastically.

"Added to the four million dollars that Nicole-Louise stole and put in her account, yes I do."

Ward decided to leave that issue there.

"I want to kill him, for Gilligan," he said.

"When we have no more use for him, if that day ever comes, then I will not authorise it but I won't get in your way either," The Old Man replied.

Under the circumstances, Ward would take that for now.

"Both the lawyer and Ashurst-Stevens said that there were higher powers at play, really powerful people. What do you make of that?"

"I'm pretty sure that I would say the same thing if you were pointing a gun at me too."

That had been his initial feeling in both instances and he decided to let that matter go too.

"Don't underestimate what you have done and how fast you did it," Centrepoint said, "You've earned a rest."

"I need to do something quickly over in Ireland," he replied.

"I know, The Optician has already told me that he might be unavailable for a few days."

Ward decided to leave that point too.

"Gill Whymark, Fulken's handler. Where is he?"

"He's gone, disappeared. Why?"

"What do you mean? Disappeared?"

"He has literally disappeared. No one can find him. They aren't looking too hard mind; this whole thing with Fulken was a mess that could have rocked the government to the core, so he has probably disappeared in shame, why the interest in him?" Centrepoint asked.

"Because Fulken said that he had my picture on the wall in their safe house, along with nine other people. I assume that means he knows who all ten of your Deniables are, including me?"

There was a long silence on the phone until Centrepoint said, "What else did Fulken say about that?"

"Nothing," he replied, "Apart from the fact one of them was a woman."

"Leave that to me, I'll find out what that means," Centrepoint replied.

"I'm not happy about this Ashurst-Stevens business."

"I know. But I am sure that when we need him and use him to our advantage you will be glad that you kept him alive."

Ward hung up the phone.

Later, he sat down on his sofa and prepared to draw a mental line under the whole sequence of events of the past ten days. It was a customary mental exercise that he carried out. It was counterproductive to carry issues, regrets or resentment from a previous mission into a new one. He had learnt that very quickly. It caused distraction. And as Asif Fulken had found out, distraction invariably led to downfall.

He leant back, closed his eyes, exhaled loudly and started to wash his mind of the past. He was taking back control.

What he had no control over was the future.

A future that would take him to the darkest and most dangerous parts of the world.

A future where his ability to trust would be called into question daily.

A future where his belief in love would be destroyed.

A future where the hunter became the hunted.

A future where friendship would crush him but also prevail.

A future where his faith in everything he did would be destroyed and then born again out of the ashes.

A future that was going to unravel, bit by bit and piece by piece over the next six traumatic months.

To be Continued.....

If you enjoyed The Newsmaker, visit the authors' website, Twitter or Facebook and leave a comment;

Website;

www.therealtomfield.com

Twitter;

@therealtomfield

Facebook;

The Real Tom Field

Volume One – Part Two

Traffic

She was dragged into the room by her hair. She was no taller than five two and she was painfully thin. She had been stripped and violated by her transporters en route to the sprawling mansion which was situated in an exclusive part of Beverly Hills. She had entered through the obscenely grand gates, which were painted a rich gold colour, and driven slowly up the immaculately laid tarmac drive which led directly to the mansion doors. No mistakes had been made in completing the drive to the exact specification. The King would not tolerate mistakes; any deviation from specific instructions would result in punishment and the full wrath of his anger. He would view incompetence as a crime against him, and any crime against him would be punishable with the most sickening and unimaginable pain being inflicted. He enjoyed this part of being The King.

She had been pulled out of her room by three men just five and a half hours ago. It was a room that contained only five beds and one chest of drawers. She had begged for another chance as soon as they had burst through the door, her pleas met with a sharp slap to her face before the men laughed as they stripped her. All she could smell was vodka and cigarettes. It was a smell that reminded her of her uncle back home in Albania. She was afraid of him too.

She was shaking, not through cold, but through a fear that ran through every inch of her body. She felt sick and her voice had deserted her. Her tears were clouding her vision and she felt disorientated. The pain of her hair being pulled had long since subsided, and was now replaced by a pain in the pit of her stomach that was restricting her breathing.

The King was sat on his throne waiting.

Literally, it was a throne. He believed it impressed all who saw it. But it didn't impress the girl, as her tears thinned and her vision returned. It terrified her.

She saw the devil.

The eyes of twelve equally frightened and thin girls looked at the floor, refusing to look at her, as she was thrown down like a bag of garbage that had hung around for too long.

Her crime?

She had tried to escape.

Her name was Tatiana.

She was fourteen years old